THE MIRROR OF BEASTS

NOVELS BY ALEXANDRA BRACKEN

Lore

Silver in the Bone series

Silver in the Bone

The Mirror of Beasts

The Darkest Minds series

The Darkest Minds

Never Fade

In the Afterlight

Through the Dark

The Darkest Legacy

Passenger series

Passenger

Wayfarer

Prosper Redding series

The Dreadful Tale of Prosper Redding

The Last Life of Prince Alastor

THE MIRROR OF BEASTS

Silver in the Bone
BOOK 2

ALEXANDRA BRACKEN

Alfred A. Knopf
New York

THIS IS A BORZOI BOOK PUBLISHED BY ALFRED A. KNOPF

This is a work of fiction. Names, characters, places, and incidents either
are the product of the author's imagination or are used fictitiously. Any resemblance
to actual persons, living or dead, events, or locales is entirely coincidental.

Text copyright © 2024 by Alexandra Bracken
Jacket art copyright © 2024 by Tomasz Majewski
Frame art copyright © 2024 by Virginia Allyn
Interior art used under license from Shutterstock.com

All rights reserved. Published in the United States by Alfred A. Knopf,
an imprint of Random House Children's Books,
a division of Penguin Random House LLC, New York.

Knopf, Borzoi Books, and the colophon are registered trademarks
of Penguin Random House LLC.

Visit us on the Web! GetUnderlined.com

Educators and librarians, for a variety of teaching tools, visit us at RHTeachersLibrarians.com

Library of Congress Cataloging-in-Publication Data
Names: Bracken, Alexandra, author.
Title: The mirror of beasts / Alexandra Bracken.
Description: First edition. | New York : Alfred A. Knopf, 2024. |
Series: Silver in the bone ; book 2 | Audience: Ages 14 and up. | Summary: "Tamsin and her friends
look for a magical object strong enough to trap Lord Death"—Provided by publisher.
Identifiers: LCCN 2024003958 (print) | LCCN 2024003959 (ebook) | ISBN 978-0-593-48169-1
(hardcover) | ISBN 978-0-593-48170-7 (library binding) | ISBN 978-0-593-48171-4 (ebook)
Subjects: CYAC: Fantasy. | Magic—Fiction. | LCGFT: Fantasy fiction. | Novels.
Classification: LCC PZ7.B6988 Mi 2024 (print) | LCC PZ7.B6988 (ebook) | DDC [Fic]—dc23

ISBN 978-0-593-89658-7 (int'l. ed.)

The text of this book is set in 11.75-point Adobe Garamond Pro.

Editor: Katherine Harrison
Cover Designer: Liz Dresner
Interior Designer: Jen Valero and Jinna Shin
Copy Editors: Artie Bennett and Melinda Ackell
Managing Editor: Jake Eldred
Production Manager: Tim Terhune

Printed in the United States of America
10 9 8 7 6 5 4 3 2 1
First Edition

Random House Children's Books supports the First Amendment and celebrates the right to read.

Penguin Random House LLC supports copyright. Copyright fuels creativity, encourages diverse
voices, promotes free speech, and creates a vibrant culture. Thank you for buying an authorized
edition of this book and for complying with copyright laws by not reproducing, scanning,
or distributing any part in any form without permission. You are supporting writers and allowing
Penguin Random House to publish books for every reader.

Or, in the words of the Sistren:

May worms feast upon the mind
of any thief so wicked and unkind
to take this book from off its rightful shelf
and from its rightful owner: you, yourself.
And should they crack the spine or tear a page,
then by my curse, they'll know your seething rage.

For LD—

May your life be full of magic and wonder.

DRAMATIS PERSONAE

THE UNMAKERS

CAITRIONA—Once chosen to be the new High Priestess, Caitriona was the de facto leader of Avalon until it was destroyed. She now struggles to adapt to the modern world.

NEVE GOODE—A cheerful, caring self-taught sorceress who searches for information about her parentage and mysterious powers.

TAMSIN LARK—Thrust into the world of Hollowers as a child, Tamsin possesses no innate magical ability, but does have a photographic memory and a keen business sense. She's determined to save her brother from Lord Death's influence.

OLWEN—The half-naiad former healer of Avalon, who fights to hold her friends together as darkness descends.

HOLLOWERS

EMRYS DYE—The scion of the Dye dynasty, founders of the North American guild. Unimaginably wealthy, annoyingly charming, and a Cunningfolk Greenworker, he is Tamsin's main rival within the guild and enjoys provoking and flirting with her.

NASHBURY LARK—Tamsin and Cabell's guardian. A notorious figure among Hollowers and sorceresses alike, known for his roguish ways and elaborate storytelling.

HECTOR LEER—A crony of Septimus and Endymion.

EDWARD WYRM—The leader of the London guild at Rivenoak Manor.

SEPTIMUS YARROW—An infamous Hollower who was killed in Avalon, he is best known for recovering Herakles's club.

SORCERESSES & MAGES

ACACIA—Cruel in nature, she is one of the sorceresses who takes Tamsin, Neve, Caitriona, and Olwen captive.

HEMLOCK—A sorceress Tamsin meets at the Dead Man's Rest.

HESTIA—One of the sorceresses, along with Acacia, who takes Tamsin and the others captive.

ISOLDE—A skittish sorceress who attends High Sorceress Kasumi.

KASUMI—The High Sorceress of the Council of Sistren.

MADRIGAL—A mysterious crone sorceress known for her deadly dinner parties. Hires Emrys and Tamsin to find the Ring of Dispel.

MORGAN—Leader of the priestesses who rose against the Druids and were later exiled. Half sister to King Arthur, and lover to Viviane.

ROBIN—Going by the gender-neutral title of Mage, Robin is a recordkeeper for the Council of Sistren.

THE WILD HUNT

LORD DEATH—Having posed as the knight Bedivere and now King Arthur, Lord Death has crossed into the mortal world and is intent on revenge against the sorceresses.

ENDYMION DYE—Emrys's cold and imperious father, who once ruled the guild with an iron fist.

CABELL LARK—Tamsin's brother, who seems to be suffering a curse that turns him into a monstrous hound. He now serves Lord Death as his seneschal.

PHINEAS PRIMM—Formerly a member of Tamsin's Hollower guild.

OTHERS

THE BONECUTTER—An enigmatic figure who procures skeleton keys to open Veins, as well as other oddities, such as basilisk venom.

BRAN—The pooka bartender at the Dead Man's Rest.

DEARIE—The sorceress Madrigal's pooka companion, who acts as both her butler and enforcer.

ELAINE, THE LADY OF SHALOTT—An unfortunate love rival to a sorceress, she was temporarily trapped in the Mirror of Shalott.

FRANKLIN—Tamsin's lovesick tarot customer, who would really benefit from actual therapy.

GRIFLET—A kitten given to Mari.

THE HAG OF THE MIST (OR GWRACH-Y-RHIBYN)—A primordial deity who occupies liminal spaces and has the ability to pass between the boundaries of worlds unimpeded.

THE HAG OF THE MOORS (OR ROSYDD)—Like her sister, the Hag of the Mist, she is a primordial deity able to open the boundaries of worlds and who has a penchant for eating mortals.

IGNATIUS—The hand of glory Tamsin carries to tap into the One Vision, also capable of opening any locked door.

LIBRARIAN—An automaton that tends to the library and protects its many treasures. Has a passion for soft, fluffy things and vacuuming.

MERLIN—Once a Druid and mentor to King Arthur, he attached himself to the Mother tree to survive a duel and now babbles nonsensical prophecy to the few who will listen.

THE NINE OF AVALON—Arianwen, Betrys, Caitriona, Fayne (Flea), Lowri, Mari, Olwen, Rhona, and Seren.

VIVIANE—The last High Priestess of the Arthurian age, who lived for centuries as she waited for the new Nine to be chosen.

Greenwich, Connecticut

Summer storms had a way of waking the house's slumbering ghosts, drawing them out of the shadows and through locked doors forgotten decades ago. They peeled away from the walls, wilting with the faded silk coverings. They fell like dust from the sheets that covered once-sparkling chandeliers and the ornate furniture. If you closed your eyes, you could feel them gliding like ribbons around you, greeting you in every dark hall.

The trouble with these old houses, Emrys decided, was that the longer they stood, the more magic and energy and darkness they absorbed, until they became living things themselves.

They allowed their families to repaint their faces, to break the bones of their walls and reset them. They watched as children left and never returned, suffered the silent indignation of being sold to wealthy strangers. And all the while, as years turned to centuries and the houses remained, they patiently collected the dead of their families, swallowing the magic woven into their souls before their bodies had the chance to cool in their beds.

Once, when Emrys was five, maybe six, barely old enough to understand that death was the only certain promise of life, his mother had told him to talk to their house. To greet it as he came and went, and treat it like a friend, so that it might treat him like one in kind.

So he had. *Hello, house; goodbye, house; you look exceedingly lovely today, house . . . Good morning, house. Sleep well, house . . .*

And sometimes, in the haze of exhausted delirium, or after polishing off one of the lustrous bottles in his father's liquor cabinet, he could have sworn Summerland House recognized him. Answered back.

Hello, boy.

And each time it happened, all he could think was *I can't die here.*

Not like the generations of ancestors who'd come before him. The ones who'd laid the house's first stones. The ones who'd expanded it into an estate. The ones who'd found the first relics now lavishly displayed in its halls. Both sides of his bloodline were brimming with Cunningfolk, and he knew the house had greedily sipped at their magic as they performed their talents, the way he could sometimes feel it doing to him when he worked in the gardens.

Named for the Otherland of the mysterious, and perhaps mythical, beings known as the Gentry, Summerland House wasn't so much a member of Emrys's family tree as the tree itself. All their lives had been carved into it, or maybe from it.

Emrys cleared his throat as he made his way down the shadowed hallway, listening to the rain battering the roof. With the invading damp came the musty smell of age. It clung to the carpets and velvet drapes, revived the moment the storm clouds appeared in the distance. The wind tore at the side of the house, as if trying to rip it out from its rotten roots. His garden would be a mess by morning, the flower beds flattened and the vegetables drowned.

"Evenin', Grandmother," he said as he passed the portrait of a stiff-backed, glowering woman. Emrys stooped slightly, using the clouded antique mirror beside the painting to tame the waves of his rain-slick hair. "How's the view from down in hell?"

He almost laughed when a crack of thunder answered.

"That's what I thought," he murmured. He could practically feel her long fingernails digging into his earlobes to silence him. "Stay toasty, you old bag."

The note crinkled in his jacket pocket as he tucked his shirt back into his jeans. He'd found it on his bed after crawling up the trellis to get back into his room. His father's precise handwriting had sent a chill through him. *See me in the study once you've returned from your tantrum.*

Tantrum. His top lip curled.

After a dinner that saw his mother's face cut by his father's wineglass, and the struggle to get her safely to her room, which had left him hoarse and burning with rage, Emrys had gone for a drive. Through town. Through the next. Through the empty, winding roads until the sky was cloaked with midnight and the car's gas gauge was begging him for mercy.

He'd had to get out of the house before he added one more ghost to its collection of Dyes.

Not for the first time, Emrys had been frightened by his own fury. Suffocated by knowing he'd inherited that darkness and it lived inside him like a seed, only waiting for the first drop of claimed blood to bloom.

I'm not like him, Emrys told himself, the words sounding as hollow to his ears as they felt in his heart. He could never keep that icy veneer of control that came so naturally to his father. *I'm not a monster.*

His lungs gave a painful squeeze as he checked his appearance again, swiping the back of his hand over his mouth.

The note hadn't been a surprise. This was their routine, and Emrys knew what to expect next: his father would be brooding in his study with a glass of Scotch. Emrys would apologize. His father would not. They would agree never to speak of it again.

On and on, turning like the Wheel of the Year.

His feet slowed as he passed his parents' wing of the house, but if his mother was still barricaded inside her bedroom, he couldn't hear even a whisper of evidence. Rain thrashed against the windows, as desperate to get in as his mother was to escape. Neither ever succeeded.

On sunny days, Emrys could make a case for Summerland House

feeling like a museum dedicated to the accomplishments of his great-something-or-others. The sword of Beowulf, its ferociousness dulled by age and the glass case that imprisoned it. Herakles's bow. On and on; countless relics, stolen and traded and bought.

But on nights like this, when a chill crept through cracks in the window frames, when there wasn't another soul around and the ornate sconces cast even the most brilliant treasures in ghoulish light, Summerland House felt more like a mausoleum.

The long hallway brought Emrys to the marble staircase in the foyer. Then, just to the right of the entrance hall, the ancient black oak doors that guarded his father's study. The spiraling patterns of crystals and iron hammered into the wood had their own dark beauty, but also told the story of his father's poisonous paranoia. The sigils carved around them created a protective ward, impenetrable to anyone—mortal or otherwise—without an invitation.

Emrys, however, had the misfortune of being invited.

Ordered, more like, he thought, reaching for one of the silvered door handles. The shape of it, like a gnarled branch, reminded him instantly of the ridiculous pin his father and his cronies from the various Hollower guilds had taken to wearing. They fancied themselves a secret society, but their collective brainpower seemed to be somewhat lacking. As far as Emrys could tell, they mostly just met to complain about the sorceresses hoarding the best relics.

The door swung open at Emrys's touch. He caught an unusual green scent—fresh and sweet and so unlike his father's tobacco and sandalwood cologne, which usually clung to this room. With one last deep breath and a swipe at his unruly hair, Emrys stepped inside.

The shadows of Summerland House seemed to love this room best, stroking the books on the shelves and lounging on the old, velvet-tufted chairs gathered before a cold marble fireplace.

But tonight, the room was draped in crimson silk curtains that concealed all but what lay at its center.

A ring of candles glowed around him, making the fabric shimmer.

With the storm's thunder muffled by the static growing in his ears, and the pounding dread that seized his body, it felt, for a moment, like Emrys was trapped inside a chamber of a throbbing heart.

On the floor, a garland of holly and a garland of oak leaves had been knotted together in a strange pattern. One that seemed vaguely familiar.

"What in the hell . . . ?" he breathed out, taking a step back toward the door. But when he felt for it, the handle was gone.

There were a rustling of fabric and a shift in the air behind him. Emrys's pulse jumped violently as a hooded figure parted the silk curtains and stepped out, a long silver ceremonial knife clutched in his hands. An eerie wooden mask, utterly expressionless, covered his face, but Emrys recognized the man's rigid gait, the signet ring on the left little finger, the familiar scent of his tobacco and sandalwood cologne.

"No . . . ," Emrys began, his shock burning like bile in his throat. "Dad—"

It was the house that answered, triumphant and ravenous from the shadows.

Goodbye, boy.

PART ONE

THE WINTER HOST

1

"No, Tamsin. To break yours."

As Nash's words faded in the air, other sounds rushed in to fill the void of silence they left behind. Distant cars and voices moving endlessly through Boston's old streets. Music from a nearby bar whispering through the walls. My upstairs neighbor pacing, his feet beating out a muted rhythm through the ceiling. The rasp of Nash's fingers torturing his hat's brim. All vying to fill the long silence that stretched between us.

And still, I couldn't bring myself to speak.

"It's been a long time, I know," Nash continued, his voice gruff. "A long time past too long . . ."

Whatever he said next vanished beneath the roar of blood rushing in my ears. The throb of my heartbeat that seemed to make my whole body shake with the force of it. My hand closed into a fist, and before I could stop myself, before I could tame that surge of pure, unadulterated fury, I punched him.

Nash staggered back, swearing beneath his breath.

"Tamsin!" Neve gasped.

I shook out my stinging hand, watching with grim satisfaction as he pressed his own against his face to stanch the flow of blood from his nose. He reached up, resetting the bone with a terrible *snap* that made even Caitriona wince.

"All right," he said, his voice muffled by his hand. He pulled a handkerchief from the pocket of his leather jacket, holding it to his face. "I suppose I deserved that. Good form, by the way."

I forced myself to take several deep breaths. As quickly as the anger had come, it abandoned me, and the emotion that welled up in its place was as useless as it was unwelcome.

When I was a little girl, I used to spend hours in our Hollower guild's library, tucked between the lesser-used shelves of Baltic legends and incomplete Immortalities, staring at a glass display case it seemed everyone else had forgotten about, or didn't care to remember.

The light above the polished chunk of amber inside sent a warm glow rippling over the dark shelves, beckoning. Inside its crystalline depths, a spider and a scorpion were knotted around one another, still locked in their battle for supremacy. Perfectly preserved by the same pit of resin that had killed them.

The amber might as well have been a window in which past could see present, and present past. It was frightening and beautiful all at once—it told a story, but it was more than that. It was a sliver of time itself.

I used to think that my memory was like amber, capturing each moment that passed, preserving it in excruciatingly perfect detail. But looking at the man who had once been my guardian, the same one I'd been so sure had abandoned my brother and me seven years ago as children, I began to question that.

I began to question everything.

Nash looked twenty years younger than the final memory I'd captured of him. Before I'd punched him, my mind had registered that the bridge of his nose was straight again, as if it had never been broken in a pub brawl, let alone three others. And his expression, so grave . . . there was none of the reckless adventurer, no sly grins or lying eyes.

Or maybe I was guilty of what I'd always accused him of: mythologizing the man just to tell a better story.

"Tamsy?" he prompted, brow furrowing. "Did you hear what I said about the curse?"

Exhaustion dug its claws into me. My lips parted, but the only words spinning through my mind were the ones he had spoken. *No, Tamsin, to break yours.*

"You don't believe me, I see it in your eyes." He glanced toward the door, momentarily distracted by the way it seemed to rattle as the wind picked up. "But I need you to listen to me carefully—to truly *hear* me—and do what I say for once in your stubborn life, because like spring, you are cursed to die young."

"So?" The word was out before I could stop it.

The others turned to me, horrified. I almost wished that I felt the same way—that I felt anything at all. Instead, an almost comforting numbness settled over me, as if I'd known all along. Maybe I had. People like me . . . we weren't meant for long lives or happy endings.

"What in the Blessed Mother's name are you talking about?" Olwen demanded. "Who would have cursed her, and in such a way?"

"Was it the White Lady?" Neve asked softly.

The bruiselike stain on my chest, just above my heart, turned icy, prickling the warm skin around it. My pulse started a drumming beat, off-tempo from the throbbing of the mark. As if a call, and an answer. Every hair on my body rose as the seconds stretched with the agonizing silence.

Nash took a step toward me, bringing with him the smell of damp soil and grass and leather. "No, Tamsy was born with it. But the magic of the curse did draw the spirit—"

The dark air of the apartment shifted violently, forcing me back as another blur of movement raced forward. A flash of silver hair—of a silver blade.

Caitriona launched herself at Nash, using the force of her momentum to slam him back against the front door. The hat and handkerchief fell from his hands, both slipping along the threadbare rug to land at my feet. Olwen gasped, hands pressed to her mouth as Caitriona brought one of my kitchen knives up to Nash's bare throat. Her other arm rose to pin him in place.

"Who are you?" Caitriona demanded. The edge of the blade drew a faint line of blood to the surface of his clean-shaven skin.

A bolt of panic shot through me as her words sank in, electrifying my mind.

It's not him.

We'd found his body in Avalon. As much as I wanted the last few hours to be one long, unending nightmare, it wasn't. I could lie to myself about any number of things, but that wasn't one of them. Nash was dead.

"Who are you?" Caitriona repeated. "There are many creatures that can wear the face of another, all tricksters, most wicked."

The man stared at me with a familiar look of indignation, exasperation, and amusement. The air burned in my lungs, begging for release.

"Who?" Caitriona repeated.

His answer was to shift his stance, hooking his leg through the inside of hers as his open palm shot out and slammed against her solar plexus. Breath burst from her in an explosion of shock and anger, but his foot had hooked her knee and she was falling before any of the rest of us could lunge to catch her.

"Cait!" Olwen moved to kneel beside her, but I caught her arm, holding her in place.

The being reached down to claim the knife, the corners of his mouth quirking with a suppressed smile.

"All this blade's good for is picking teeth and buttering toast, dove," he said.

"Put down the knife and step away from her." I'd never heard Neve's voice as cold as it was then, her face hardening with anger. "Touch her again and you'll have hands for feet and feet for hands."

Her wand, through magic or some strange stroke of luck, had survived the destruction of Avalon—I had completely forgotten about it until I saw her reach into the bag at her waist and pull its long body free. Nash—or Not-Nash—stared down at the razored tip pointed toward him, then looked at me, a bushy brow arching.

"Never thought I'd see the day you'd be cavorting with a sorceress, Tamsy."

"Keep going," Neve said. "Your face can only be improved by swapping your mouth with your nose."

The man tilted his head to the side for a moment, as if pausing to picture this. But he did as asked, setting the knife down on the floor and kicking it out of Caitriona's reach.

"Are you of Avalon?" he asked Caitriona. "Are you the reason it's merged again with our world?"

The words were like hands around my throat. The others flinched, retreating from the accusation—but we were guilty of it, all of us. We had performed the ritual thinking it would heal the Otherland and free it from a cursed existence, but it had only restored it to our own world. The collision of the isle and modern Glastonbury had wrought death and destruction I couldn't begin to think about without wanting to claw at my own face.

You didn't mean for it to happen, I told myself. *None of us did.*

It was a mistake. It was a terrible, terrible mistake. I could rationalize that all I wanted, but it didn't stop the waves of nausea from spreading through me, or the gripping horror at knowing what we'd done.

"Tamsy—" he began again.

"Don't," I got out around the knot in my throat, "call me that."

"That's what I've always called you," he said. "From the time you were nothing but a wee imp. The first time I used it, you kicked me in the shins and called me a dingus. That was your favorite insult for a while."

My stomach clenched. The others looked to me, searching for the truth of it in my face.

Caitriona finally rose from the floor, backing toward us, eyes scanning the room for another weapon.

"How . . . ?" I whispered. *How are you alive?*

A low grumble of thunder moved through the city, bringing him up short. Nash returned to his perch by the door, his body tensed as he looked through its peephole. Whatever storm had blown in was only building in ferocity. When he turned to me again, it was with that same look he'd had when I'd opened the door.

"Were you able to find the ring in Avalon?" Nash asked, as if I hadn't spoken at all.

"Yes, but—" Olwen began.

"Cabell needed the ring, not me," I whispered. That was the most unforgivable part of all this. If I had been able to use the ring on Cabell . . .

The thought of my brother just then, the only other person who'd understand the chaos of my thoughts, who'd be able to help me untangle them, was a knife to the gut.

"Cabell is beyond its help," Nash said. The dismissiveness of his tone made bile rise in my throat.

"How would you know?" I snarled. "You haven't even cared enough to ask where he is!"

"Do you really think I don't know why he's not here? Do you truly believe I don't know what you unleashed into this world?" Nash shook his head, blowing out a hard breath. "Where's the Ring of Dispel now?"

"It's—" Neve glanced at me, as if not sure she should say. "Emrys Dye took it."

"You let a Dye have the ring?" Nash exploded. "For the love of hellfire, Tamsy!"

"Call me that again and I'll make sure you stay dead this time," I warned him.

"Tamsin didn't have a choice in it," Neve continued. "He was hired by a sorceress."

"Which one?" Nash pressed, reaching down to swipe his hat off the floor.

I got the name out through gritted teeth. "Madrigal—"

Her name vanished beneath an explosion of thunder. It seemed to erupt from above us and below us all at once; the force of it made the dishes in the kitchen chatter like teeth and sent books falling from the nearby shelves. At the sound of a flat-toned blare, deeper and more wrenching than any ship I'd heard before in the harbor, a chill walked its bony fingers down my spine.

A stream of furious words burst from Nash as he jammed his hat back onto his head and gripped the doorknob, struggling to open it against the taunting of the wind.

"You're *leaving*?" Caitriona asked, aghast.

"Of course," I said bitterly. "It's what he's best at."

Nash finally wrenched the door open and whirled around. His right hand pressed to his heart in a mockery of a vow. "All I've ever wanted—all I've ever tried to do—is protect you."

"Since when?" I spat.

Neve's hand curled tighter around my arm as she drew me closer to her. I'd never seen her like this, all but trembling with anger. It radiated from her until it became indistinguishable from my own.

The December air billowed in around Nash, exhaling delicate flakes of snow. Thunder boomed once more, loud enough to rattle the town-house-turned-apartments down to its foundations. A sharp, acrid scent like ozone filled the apartment, making my toes curl in my boots.

Behind Nash, far above the festive garlands and twinkling Christmas lights, the sky had turned an eerie shade of green. The furious wind tugged at his clothes, drawing him toward the waiting night. Behind him, the trees bowed to the storm, groaning.

"I'm going to get that bloody ring to break your curse," he snapped. "If you hear that sound again, closer than it is now, run as fast as you can—but until then, stay here, or so help me, I will wring your scrawny little necks myself!"

He pointed a finger at the four of us in turn. "You haven't the faintest idea what's coming—what hides within winter's icy depths. Listen to me and you may yet survive this horror you've brought upon us."

The door slammed shut behind him.

"Wow," Neve said after a moment. "I *hate* that guy."

My knees turned soft, and I was grateful that Neve still had such a grip on me, that she didn't seem inclined to let me go. My heart sped furiously as I stared at the closed door, my breath shallow.

Was that really him? I wondered.

The apartment had taken on an unreal quality, hazy and uncertain. The storm seemed to have spread to my mind, swirling those same questions around until I felt suffocated by them. *Was that really him? How?*

And the only one who could have understood—really understood—the way I trembled with confusion and adrenaline and anger wasn't here.

"Are we . . . going to go after him?" Olwen asked faintly.

It felt like being torn in two. The logical part of my mind demanded I stay in the apartment, but the ache in my chest urged me to follow him, to demand the answers I needed.

All of it could be a trick, my mind whispered. *Even if it is Nash, you know better than to trust him.*

"No," Caitriona said sharply. "That's not our plan."

"From everything Tamsin has told us, we have no reason to believe him," Neve added, echoing my thoughts. ". . . Right, Tamsin?"

"Right," I said, when I found my voice again.

"Is our plan still what we agreed upon earlier?" Olwen asked, looking between us. "We'll seek out the person Tamsin believes can repair the High Priestess's vessel?"

She gestured toward the small basket at the foot of the couch, a blanket hiding the shattered bone sculpture that had contained Viviane's memories.

All of which would be lost to us, including the memory in the shard that Lord Death had stolen and hidden away, if we didn't repair it.

With each moment that passed, my thoughts darkened, until that frail hope began to fade.

It was absurd, wasn't it? All of it. Even if we found the Bonecutter, what were the chances they'd know the ancient druidic art of vessel-making? Some of the bone fragments were no bigger than needles, while others had been ground down to dust—what if there was no fixing it?

Nausea burned in my stomach, rising in my throat. I don't know how I managed to say, "Yes. We should start searching for the Bonecutter as soon as possible."

"About that," Neve said. "I know we need to find the Bonecutter, but maybe we should go to the sorceresses first. What if they don't have the full story of what happened when Morgan broke the bargain with Lord Death? If they don't know he's still alive, they might not realize he's back and coming for them to get his revenge."

"But Cabell said the sorceresses sealed off the pathways to Avalon from *this* side, to keep Lord Death from being able to follow them into the mortal world," I said. "To me, that says they know some part of him survived."

Merging Avalon back into our world was the only way to circumvent the barriers, which was why Lord Death had gone to all that trouble to manipulate us into performing the ritual.

Caitriona released a harsh breath through her nose. "Indeed."

"Have you changed your mind, then?" Olwen asked Neve. "Do you want us to find the sorceresses—the Council of Sistren, as you called them? To warn them?"

"Yes. I think we should do that before anything else." Neve chewed on her lip, wearing her indecision plainly. "I know we need to repair the vessel, but . . . the more I think about it, the more I believe we need to work alongside them to stop whatever Lord Death's greater plans are."

"Then send word to them, but we owe them nothing more than that," Caitriona said sharply. "Because the more *I* think about it, the more I believe they're the ones that brought this pain and blood upon themselves. The only thing that should matter to us is righting that mistake and finishing what they couldn't by killing Lord Death. Our hunt should begin now."

"And if he kills sorceresses in the meantime?" Neve pressed.

Caitriona lifted a shoulder in a shrug. "So be it."

Even I startled at that. A slow thread of anxiety began to wind through me as the air took on a different, angrier charge.

Neve inhaled sharply, squaring up to Caitriona as if the other girl didn't have almost six inches on her. "You don't mean that. I know you care about innocent people dying."

"That would require the sorceresses to be innocent, which they are not," Caitriona shot back.

"But we don't even have a way of stopping Lord Death. Rushing out to find him is only going to get *us* killed," I said. "What if the vessel can give us that information? Shouldn't we be prioritizing that?"

Neve whirled toward me, betrayal flashing in her eyes. "So you don't care if they die either?"

"I didn't say that," I told her.

"You all but did," Neve pointed out.

I bit the inside of my mouth, anxiety churning my stomach. We couldn't fight—we had to stay together. In the face of Avalon's death, we'd chosen one another. And if we were to break apart . . .

I shook my head against the thought, my heart crimping painfully in my chest. *I will have no one left.*

"You *know* my main concern is Cabell," I said. "All I want is to get him away from Lord Death before whatever hold that monster has on him deepens. You're the one who suggested it—that the real Cabell is still in there, trapped inside the servant Lord Death created."

Death magic, born of Annwn, the Otherworld of the monstrous dead, had corrupted Avalon, poisoning its land with shadows, rendering it unrecognizable as the paradise of legend. If it could happen to a place of such power and purity, there was no way Cabell's mind would have been strong enough to resist whatever enchantment Lord Death had cast over him.

Neve blew out a hard breath, but I knew she understood that much. Whatever she might have said was interrupted by a faint *meow,* as Griflet, the scraggly kitten who'd journeyed with us from Avalon, edged out from where he'd been hiding beneath the couch.

"Oh, there you are," Olwen said softly, stooping to retrieve him. The gray tabby purred as she held him to her chest, finally content. But the priestess's own gaze was anything but. She sent a helpless look my way as Caitriona and Neve turned their backs on one another, both silently fuming.

"Listen, you're both right," I said, trying again. "We owe the Council of Sistren a warning, but I don't think we should hold out hope they'll do anything other than retreat into their vaults and try to wait him out."

What I didn't say was that while Neve might have been a sorceress herself, I had far more experience dealing with them as a Hollower. And when the sorceresses weren't fighting among themselves over relics and centuries-old grudges, they were nurturing their deeply held instinct for self-preservation.

"Sorceresses aren't cowards," Neve said, her voice streaked with anger. "They'll fight."

"But this is *our* fight," Caitriona countered. "Lord Death deserves to be punished for what he did to Avalon, for killing—" She stopped herself, steadying her breathing before whispering, "For destroying everything, and everyone."

I tamped down my memory before it could punish me with images of vacant eyes, bodies, blood snaking between the tower's stones.

"Careful, Caitriona," Neve said. "You're sounding an awful lot like a sorceress with all that talk of revenge."

Caitriona let out a cold laugh. Her earlier words, as we'd stood together illuminated by the funeral pyre of everyone she had loved, echoed back, terrible and hollow. *I am the priestess of nothing. That is all I shall ever be.*

"Avalon is gone," Caitriona said, "and so are my obligations to it and its Goddess. If I do not call upon her magic, I am not beholden to her laws."

A surge of helplessness rose in me as I exchanged another look with Olwen, too afraid to say anything in case it made the situation worse. Her lips parted, the blood draining from her face.

"What?" Neve gasped out. "You—you won't even use your magic? After everything, you'd turn your back on her?"

"She abandoned us first," Caitriona said. "Will you be next?"

"*Stop it!*"

Olwen inserted herself between them, whorls of ink-blue hair rising around her shoulders, as if caught in drifting water. Her face was so stricken, my whole chest ached with the sight of it.

"Stop it," she repeated, softer this time. "We cannot do this—we cannot fight one another and fight the darkness, too. It's all toward the same end, isn't it? No one, not the sorceresses, not us, will be safe while he walks in this world."

She gestured toward the small basket at the foot of the couch, the blanket hiding Viviane's shattered vessel.

"All of the memories this vessel contained will be lost to us if we cannot find a way to remake it," Olwen continued.

My hands curled into fists at my sides.

"We stay with our original plan," Olwen told us, her chest heaving with the force of her breath, her body vibrating with exhaustion and desperation. "The one we *all* agreed upon not more than an hour ago. We will find the sorceresses and tell them what's happened, and then we will seek out the person Tamsin believes can repair the vessel. Yes?"

"Yes," I said quickly. A painful knot constricting my chest released as the tension in the apartment eased. After a moment, Neve nodded. Caitriona crossed her arms over her chest and looked down, her jaw sawing back and forth.

Thunder split the sky above us like a hammer's fall, devouring every other sound as it shook the walls. And then, like the deep bellow of some primordial beast, came the unearthly blare we'd heard before.

"Okay, what in all the hells *is* that?" I said, stalking over to the door. By the time I had the cold knob in my hand, Caitriona was right behind me.

"Didn't Nash *explicitly* say we should run if we heard that sound again?" Neve asked.

We were seven years past the point of him being able to tell me what to do.

If that was even him...

The wind shoved the door open against me. I threw up an arm, trying to shield my face from the biting cold and the sharp flecks of ice that swirled through the dark air as the storm fell upon the city. I slipped down the icy stoop.

The neighbor in the unit to my right had stuck her head out of the door, only to retreat inside once the sleet turned to outright hail. A gasping "Holy sh—!" from the side of the converted town houses told me my upstairs neighbor had made a similar decision and bolted back up their private stairwell.

"This storm is—!" I could barely hear Caitriona over the whipping winds. Olwen covered her head with her arms, protecting it as she made her way back into the apartment on unsteady, sliding feet. Come morning, I thought, the city would be frozen solid.

"Do you see anything?" Caitriona shouted to me.

I turned my gaze up, cupping my hands around my stinging eyes. The sky still bore that sickly shade, glowing with a hideous fluorescence as lightning snaked across it, splintering the mirror-like surface of the gray clouds.

"Come on," Caitriona said, tugging at my arm. Ice crusted in my hair, only flinging itself loose when I shook my head. Neither of us was wearing a coat, and the chill had turned unbearable. A stop sign tore loose from its post, hurtling through the air until it smashed into a nearby car window.

"Go in!" I told her. "I just need—!"

I couldn't bring myself to say it, but she understood. Her freckled hand gripped my shoulder as she passed me, carefully making her way back to the stairs. Snow collected on my lashes, in the folds of my clothes. The longer I stood, the easier it became to convince myself that it wasn't the wind that was howling.

I strained my ears, searching for the thread of it again, the monstrous chorus of baying voices.

A crash sounded from inside the apartment. I spun, sliding back toward the stoop. The lamp near the window flickered, then went out.

The wind pushed the door open for me, nearly sending me sprawling to the floor with the force of it. The dark living room greeted me, silent as I struggled to shut the door again.

"Guys?" I called, venturing toward the bedrooms. My heart rose into my throat. "Hello?"

I turned the corner at the kitchenette and stopped dead.

Caitriona lay prone on the floor, her eyes shut, a broken flowerpot from the kitchen in pieces around her. A figure in a dark hooded robe bent over her and wrapped something around her hands.

"Don't touch her—!" I surged forward, wild desperation exploding in my chest. I drew my arm back to shove the intruder away, but my joints locked and I slammed onto the floor.

"Don't!" I gasped, trying to crawl toward Cait. Where were the others? Where was—

Pain exploded across the back of my skull as something cracked against it. The stench of warm blood flooded my senses as it dripped through my hair into the puddle of melting ice and snow beneath me. A low, scornful laugh curdled my blood.

The floor pushed against my cheek, rattling with approaching footsteps. Somewhere, Griflet yowled. The shadows of the hall grew long, spreading across the floor like a spill of tar, devouring Caitriona, devouring all.

And hard as I fought, when the darkness reached me, I was gone.

2

A drip of icy water struck my cheek.

I woke slowly, my skull pounding in time with every other ache in my body. Another drip, this one against my brow, made me crack an eye open, but it was an echoing voice nearby that finally pierced the black veil of unconsciousness.

"—haven't had word yet, they want us to keep them here until the Council's voted—"

My mind sparked, sputtering back to life as it seized that single word. *Council.*

There was only one council I knew of.

"Can't they just make a bloody decision for once?" another woman complained. "They'll have to drag the elder crones out of those crypts they call homes."

"By whatever stringy wisps of hair they have left, hopefully," the first answered. "I'd pay my last gold coin to see it, the old goblins."

My heart lurched in my chest as realization conquered my disbelief. *Sorceresses.*

It had been sorceresses in the apartment. *Sorceresses* had attacked and abducted us, finding us before we could even formulate a plan to find them. Unbelievable.

If my head hadn't felt like it was on the verge of splitting open like a melon, I might have laughed at the sheer irony.

But there was nothing funny about this. Not when I couldn't see the others.

"Hello?" I whispered. "Is anyone there?"

I strained my ears, but the only answer was the faint sound of breathing nearby.

The air hung like a black curtain around me, heavy with damp and an almost mineral smell. Each endless second it took for my eyes to adjust to the low light was agonizing.

Bit by bit, my mind was coming alive to the situation, collecting vital details: I was flat on my back, my wrists pinned down against the flat stone ground with what felt like solid stone manacles. I tugged at them, but there was no chain, no give. My legs were free, but a hell of a lot of good that was going to do me when I could barely sit up.

We were surrounded by rough-hewn walls of ancient stone on three sides. To my left, thick stone bars jutted up from the ground like stalagmites, sealing off the small alcove that served as our prison.

Another drip of water slapped my face and I scowled up at the darkness. I lifted my head, straining my neck until I could just make out the silhouette of someone sitting against the wall forming one side of our cell. *Olwen.* To my right, I caught a hint of the reflective fabric on the old sneakers I'd lent Neve. I heard a third person breathing from somewhere behind me. That would be Caitriona, hopefully.

I released a shaky breath. Blood returned to my muscles with the force of a thousand scalding pins, but I barely registered it as a short-lived wave of relief passed over me.

The sorceresses might have saved us the hassle of tracking them down, but the fact that they'd been searching for us at all, that we were now being treated no better than crooks, spoke to some kind of misunderstanding. Or worse.

Whatever these sorceresses wanted with us, it wasn't a chat and a cup of tea. We needed to get out of here and regroup.

Based on what I could see, which admittedly wasn't much, we

seemed to be deep underground—in a cavern of some sort. The air had that certain, musty stillness as it all but wept with moisture. And a tomb would have smelled worse, frankly.

"So we can expect a vote at some point in the next century," came a new voice from somewhere deeper in the cavern. "After they waste a lifetime deciding how to conduct said vote, of course."

Great. I stifled a groan. There were three of them, and this one, while more soft-spoken, sounded just as surly as the other two.

"Don't let any of the others hear you speaking in such a way, Acacia," warned the first voice. "They're all desperate to get in Her Serene Smugness's good graces, thinking that'll save them."

Finally, new details carved themselves from the darkness—and none of them good.

There was a hallway beyond the bars of our cell, its floor adorned with swirling patterns of mosaic tiles, visible only because of the contrast of the white tiles against the darker ones. The longer I stared at them, the colder my blood ran. Here and there, curse sigils were disguised in the repeating pattern.

I closed my eyes again and sighed, beyond irritated at myself. It should have been my first guess. I'd been in far too many of them to not recognize a sorceress's vault at first glance.

Now the exit, I thought, craning my head around to try to peer down the hallway. There'd be one entrance, which would open to a Vein. I scoured my memory for a sorceress named Acacia, but there were no useful tidbits tucked away there.

I pulled on the manacles around my wrists, testing them again. Biting my lip, I hunched and contorted my shoulders in turn, twisting my wrists around in the restraints to feel for sigils carved into the ground or the metal itself.

My fingers skimmed over a swirling shape on the left cuff, just above where it attached to the ground.

"Yes," I breathed out shakily. The quick exploration had left the

delicate skin of my wrists scraped raw and bleeding. I pushed my left arm down through the restraint as far as I could, freeing up more of that hand's mobility. With another steadying breath, I drew my right leg up and crossed it over my body, turning my foot until the sole of the boot brushed against my fingertips.

Cabell and I had hammered metal spikes into the bottoms of our work boots for better traction on jobs. You tango with an acid pit and you'll do just about anything to avoid a second dance.

I felt along the ridges of my shoe's tread until I found a loose spike, twisting it until it pulled free.

Swallowing a little noise of triumph, I bent my wrist at a painful angle, pressing the sharpened tip of the spike against the stone cuff. It took more than a few tries, but finally, I got a good enough grip on the spike to start scratching against what I hoped was the sigil. Distorting the symbol might not be enough to break the spell locking me in place, but at least it would weaken it.

A soft pressure glanced against the top of my head and I jerked in surprise, the spike nearly slipping from my fingers. I craned my head back farther than before, twisting my neck painfully to look over my left shoulder.

Relief soared in me at the sight of Caitriona, her silvery hair bright even in the dark. Her hands were chained above her head to the stone bars. Even with her impressive height, she'd only just managed to stretch the toe of her tennis shoe out to reach me.

Her eyes flashed in the dark, as sharp as any nocturnal predator's.

Where? she mouthed.

Before I could speak, one of the sorceresses—the younger one, if my ears hadn't betrayed me—raised her voice enough for it to carry clearly down the hall.

"The terror we've feared for centuries is upon us and the High Sorceress can't be arsed to even look for the bloody thing he's demanding we return?"

Caitriona's eyes met mine again, widening.

My body tensed. What *thing* did Lord Death want them to return?

At least we won't have to warn them about anything, I thought miserably.

"What's going on?" Olwen's voice was groggy as she came to. "Where are we?"

"Shh," Caitriona whispered. "We're all right."

"How is *any* of this all right?" I whispered back.

"Does . . . ," Neve rasped out from my right. "Does anyone know where we are?"

"A vault," I told her, scraping the spike against the metal restraint as hard as I could.

"Oh. Well . . . that's not the worst thing, is it?" Olwen said. "Didn't you say you have experience with sorceress vaults with your job as a . . . what did you call it?"

"A Hollower." A glorified treasure hunter of legendary relics. "And my experience is with breaking *in,* not out."

"We're with sorceresses?" Neve said.

I realized, a split second too late, what was coming. "Wait—!"

"Hey!" she shouted. "This is a mistake! *Hello?* Did you hear me?"

I let my head fall back against the stone ground with a sigh. So much for the element of surprise, never mind the distant dream of escaping.

Footsteps echoed down the hall. Three cloaked figures strode toward us, emerging from somewhere deeper in the vault. An antique-style lantern floated beside them, as if carried by an unseen spirit.

"Marvelous," one said, and I recognized the voice belonging to Acacia. "You're finally awake."

Her face was like white velvet beneath the braided crown of her pale hair, and the flawlessness of her beauty set her apart as something *other,* something to fear, because it could only be a lure. And her eyes . . . they were spiteful as they assessed us, before turning to her companion. "I told you it wouldn't be much longer, Hestia."

Hestia revealed herself to be the wiry one with tan skin and a slightly pinched expression as she declared, "Best to start with the one that doesn't have magic."

The cuffs around my wrists fell away, and in a rare moment of composure, I scrambled back on clumsy limbs, colliding with a soft form behind me—Neve.

"How quickly courage flees when their master is not there to protect them," the nameless one said. Her pale blue eyes were rimmed with heavy plum liner the same shade as her knotted hair.

"M-Master?" I croaked. "Hang on, what are you talking about?"

"Listen," Neve began, sounding entirely too reasonable for the situation we were in. "There's clearly been some sort of misunderstanding—"

A hot band of pressure locked around my waist and yanked me back toward the stone bars of our cell. I bit my tongue painfully, blood exploding in my mouth as Acacia spun her hands in a mocking show of reeling me in. The small spike slipped from my fingers as I tried in vain to drive my heels down to fight the pull of magic.

"Stop this!" Olwen pulled against her manacles. "We're not your enemies!"

"Is that so?" Acacia flicked her wrist, and I was flung like a doll up against the bars. Stars burst behind my eyes as my temple collided with the rock. Magic shoved at me from behind, and my ribs screamed in protest.

"Release her!" Caitriona roared.

"Please!" Olwen begged. "We were coming to find the Council of Sistren, to warn you about Lord Death!"

"*Warn us?*" Plum Hair grated out. "Warn us of what, precisely? That resisting his demand was futile? As if slaughtering five of our sistren weren't message enough!"

"We were—we—" Each word I spoke only increased the pressure from behind. I wondered, fleetingly, how much force my body could withstand before it was crushed against the stone bars.

Caitriona let out a noise of pure rage, trying to rip her hands from the restraints.

"You led him directly to Stellamaris last night—*admit it!*" Acacia snarled.

Despite the pain ratcheting through my body, my mind latched onto that name. The Sorceress Stellamaris lived on the outskirts of Boston. Cabell and I had done a recovery job for her, retrieving her mother's ring from another sorceress's tomb. She had been—*pleasant* wasn't the right word, and neither was *harmless*. She had been . . . uncomplicated to deal with.

The storm. It couldn't have been a coincidence that the city experienced a freak blizzard the same night she was killed.

"We ought to rip every last detail about their master from their minds," Plum Hair said. "Surely the Council won't punish us if we get what they're after?"

"What are you talking about?" Neve asked, beyond agitated.

"Unmakers of worlds," Hestia sneered. "The four servants of Death, maidens of winter—the others may dress you up in pretty names, but we know what you are. We know the rot in your hearts."

"We do not serve Death!" Caitriona raged. "We are his sworn enemies!"

At that, all three women laughed riotously. And through the pain, through terror, all I could imagine was kicking them into the nearest curse sigil.

"I'm one of you!" Neve cried. "I'm a sorceress! They're—they're priestesses of Avalon! We tried to stop Lord Death, not help him!"

The last of the air left my lungs as the force of Acacia's magic drove harder against my back, threatening to snap my ribs, my spine. My vision darkened at the edges as I struggled to draw in even a shallow breath.

"Your fork-tongued lies mean nothing to us," Hestia said. "There wasn't a soul alive in Avalon when your master compelled you to destroy it."

"We were trying to save the isle," Olwen said, pleading. "We thought the ritual would purify it—it was a mistake!"

She began to hum, a shaky, desperate sound, to summon a spell. Neve joined her, her voice breaking with her sobbing breath.

The sorceresses only laughed, the flickering lantern light deepening the harsh lines of their faces.

"Singing spells? How *quaint*," Acacia said. "Your cell is warded against the use of magic. Try it again and you'll certainly be carrying your friend home in pieces."

"It was a mistake! All of it!" Neve swore in desperation.

"More lies," Plum Hair sang. She glanced toward Acacia, enjoying the show.

"Tell us what your master is after," Acacia demanded. "And why he wants it by the winter solstice."

"We don't know what you're talking about!" Caitriona thundered.

"They must truly hate their friend to wish her dead," Hestia said. "I don't know about you, sistren, but I would be all too glad to avenge the mortals who perished at Glastonbury. The ones *slaughtered* as you unmade the boundary and brought hell raining down upon this world."

The agony finally overcame me like a tide, ripping through the last bit of strength I had. I cried out, hot tears streaking my face. My limbs, my skin, strained against the stone, stretching painfully, threatening to tear.

"*Stop!*"

Blue-white light erupted through the cell with Neve's shattering cry, incinerating the darkness with its unbridled intensity.

The sorceresses stumbled back, flinging their arms over their faces to shield their eyes. The light produced no heat, but it radiated a dizzying pressure with each shuddering breath Neve took.

"You said you blocked their magic!" Hestia shrieked.

"*I did!*" Acacia shrieked back.

The pressure crushing me against the bars released and I hit the ground hard, gasping. My fingers clawed at the rough stone as I tried to steady my galloping heart.

"Tamsin?" Olwen called out. "Are you all right?"

I couldn't answer. Couldn't speak just yet. As the light retreated, it cast the cell back into a deeper darkness. I blinked against the spots floating in my vision, and even then, I wondered if I was imagining it—the way the magic seemed to linger on Neve's skin like a dusting of stars before it winked out entirely.

My breath was stilted, burning in my aching chest. At the sound of the sorceresses' steps shuffling forward, I curled down into myself, my entire body bracing for more pain.

"What . . . are you?" Acacia ground out. The three sorceresses were unharmed, but their hair was flying loose, their long robes and gowns askew, as if they'd barely come through a windstorm.

"I told you," Neve said, the pleading note back in her voice. She pulled against her restraints, trying to sit up. "I'm one of you."

"That was not the Mother's magic," Hestia said, breathless. "That was not *our* magic."

"It must be *his*," came the third. "Death magic. The power of Annwn."

"No!" Neve said, pleading. "It's not! I—it's—"

Hestia turned her back to us, lowering her voice to a mere whisper. For the first time, she sounded uncertain as she spoke to the others. "Do we kill her?"

I rolled onto my stomach, fear roiling in my gut. Caitriona slammed her back against the stone bars, as if she could break them with sheer will.

"Try it," she warned, the words brimming with lethal promise.

"What is that dull old saying? It's better to beg forgiveness than seek permission?" Ice shot through my veins as Acacia's gaze fixed on Neve. "I think it best we kill them all."

Then, through the veil of terror descending over the vault, came the knock.

It wasn't a timid sound so much as polite. I thought I'd imagined it until it came again, louder and more insistent.

The sorceresses looked to one another.

"Were you expecting someone?" Acacia asked the others.

"If it's one of the Council—" the nameless one began.

"Well, go and see to it, then," Acacia said, waving a dismissive hand in her sistren's direction.

"Me?" Hestia complained. "Why do I have to do everything?"

There was a third knock.

"Fine, I'll do it myself," Acacia groused, the skirt of her sapphire-blue dress whirling with her. "If any of them so much as whimper, break every bone in their bodies."

My pulse thundered in my ears as I forced myself to sit up.

"Ah-ah," Hestia tutted. "Stay where you are."

"We didn't mean to hurt anyone," Neve whispered.

"Then you're worse than traitors to the Goddess," Hestia said. "You're fools."

Moments later, Acacia's shuffling steps returned, her black cloak flaring out behind her with the force of her fury.

Hestia arched a thin brow. "Who was it?"

Acacia shoved a rumpled piece of parchment against her chest, then turned to glare at us, indecision passing over her face. Hestia's eyes widened as she read it. Plum Hair ripped it out of her hands to read it herself, then turned to someone I couldn't see.

"This cannot be real," Plum Hair murmured. "This is a trick."

"Are you willing to bet on that? Because I'm always up for a friendly wager," said a voice from behind Acacia.

Every inch of my skin prickled with sudden awareness.

The shadowed figure stepped out from behind her into the floating lantern's light.

"I wouldn't stake your life on it, though," Emrys said.

3

I hated that I wanted to look at him.

Hated that I noticed how his chestnut hair had been trimmed and tamed, that he was back to wearing perfectly tailored clothing with his usual disregard, sleeves rolled up to reveal the thick bands of scars across his skin. Hated the warm jacket he'd slung over one shoulder while the rest of us tried not to shiver in the damp cold. I hated that tilt of his head, that smirk, as if his wealth and name might protect him from these sorceresses, too.

But more than anything, I hated that the only mark the last days of Avalon had left on him was a hollowing of his cheeks, when the horror of those last hours had carved our pain down deep to the bone.

The betrayal stung anew, revived in an instant. Any soft relief I might have felt at seeing him alive dissolved, until only the humiliation and smoldering anger remained. He hadn't just taken the Ring of Dispel, he'd . . .

What the hell was he even doing here?

"I don't believe this for a moment," Hestia declared, ripping the letter back out of the nameless one's hands.

"Which part, that Madrigal has come slithering up out of her viper's nest, or that the High Sorceress believed her?" Acacia muttered. Her brows rose suddenly, the bitterness there replaced by some new, no doubt horrible, revelation. "It says we're to release them, but it does not specify that they have to be alive."

Look at me, I thought, staring at the perfect lines of his profile. *Look at what you did.*

He wouldn't. It began to feel like a challenge. I was baiting him, *daring* him to look. To see the venomous fury that was coursing through my veins and risk my gaze turning him to stone.

But then, that was one of the privileges of wealth, wasn't it? Never needing to face the consequences of your actions.

"Actually," Emrys said smoothly, leaning over Hestia's shoulder to point at something on the paper, "it does riiiiight there—bottom of the third paragraph? Put in the request for that one myself."

"Wow," Neve deadpanned. "What a hero."

I gritted my teeth, resentment billowing up inside me. I didn't want his help. Didn't need it. The mere fact that he thought we might welcome it . . . I'd rather have been torn apart by the sorceresses.

"And just *there*," Emrys continued, pointing farther down, "you'll notice the High Sorceress makes a special request for you to return to the Council for a new assignment. But look, she also sends some praise for a job well done, so bravo."

Acacia looked as though she'd love to stamp him out like a roach beneath her bootheel, and I would have loved nothing better than to watch.

"Why would Madrigal vouch for them, after what they've done?" Plum Hair scowled. "She never sticks her neck out unless it's in the hope someone will clasp a diamond necklace around it."

"Working every angle, as always. Her standing has suffered since . . . well, you know," Hestia said.

The others did know, apparently. My infernal curiosity perked up its ears, but no further details came.

"Can we be done, then?" Hestia continued. "Your vault *is* rather lacking in creature comforts, Acacia."

"Though, truly, it has wonderfully evocative atmosphere," Plum Hair said, gesturing to the bleak stone walls around us.

Acacia sniffed, allowing the compliment. "Then let us go before the Council agrees to waste yet more of our time."

"A wise idea," Emrys said pleasantly. "We never know how many days we'll be given."

Acacia turned on her heel with a noise of disgust, making for the vault's entrance. The others scurried after her, exchanging pleased looks behind her back.

Emrys cleared his throat, and they stopped.

"What is it now, you pestilence?" Acacia demanded.

He gestured helpfully to the stone bars, and to our restraints.

Acacia stamped her foot, letting out a little noise of annoyance. She retrieved her wand from what must have been an enchanted pocket of her cloak and used the knife end to scratch out a sigil on the nearby wall.

The stone bars snapped back down into grooves in the ground, the thunderous impact rattling my already hurting body. The manacles fell away from our wrists, dissolving to dust as they hit the earth.

Neve sprang to her feet with a relieved sigh. Caitriona ran on unsteady legs into the pathway, but the sorceresses were already gone. She muttered something darkly beneath her breath that was likely better left unheard.

I wasn't sure I could have moved even if I'd wanted to. Olwen rushed over to me, kneeling at my side, worry etched into her grime-streaked face.

"Are you all right?" she asked, beginning her examination. I gasped as she prodded a sharp ache on the right side of my ribs.

"Well, I *was*," I squeezed out.

"Just bruised," she noted. "I don't have any healing salve with me. Can you tolerate it a bit longer?"

"Do I have a choice?"

"What happened?" Emrys asked.

That persuasive smile was gone now, the aura of swagger extinguished with two soft words. If it had been anyone else, I would have called his expression concern.

He was looking now. He studied each of us in quick succession, with the fleetingness of light glancing off glass. In the end, Emrys Dye really was a coward; he couldn't even summon the nerve to lift his eyes to our faces. And damn him, because those eyes . . . they had the audacity to still be so beautiful. One gray as a storm cloud, one green as the earth—trickster's jewels, meant to tempt the unsuspecting thief.

Caitriona edged closer, until she'd partially blocked me from view.

"Not even a hello?" he said lightly.

My top lip curled as the bitterness churning in me fermented to a deeper hate.

The silence from the others bolstered me from all sides. I rose slowly, with Caitriona's and Olwen's help.

A flicker of something crossed his expression, breaking through the pleasant veneer he wore. I knew better than to believe it was anything like regret.

I'd known him for too long not to see through this act. I knew what he wanted now. *Information.*

Time had moved differently between our world and the Otherland . . . until, of course, we'd shifted them back into alignment with the ritual. For us, it had only been a little over a day since he slipped away with the Ring of Dispel, taking it back to Madrigal for all the gold and freedom she'd promised. For him, it would have been days, maybe more than a week.

But he deserved nothing. Not the truth of what had happened. Not kindness.

Not *us.*

The professional in me had understood, even if I hadn't wanted to, why he'd done it. Maybe, with the distance of decades, or lifetimes, I would have found a sliver of acceptance. Let the wound scar over. But the wound he'd left was still bloody and gaping, and I'd be dead and damned before I let him drive another blade in.

In the end, Olwen broke first. She charged forward, forcing him back a step as she jabbed her finger at his heart like a dagger.

"*You!*" The word dripped with shocking vehemence. "I liked you and—and trusted you! We all did, every one of my sisters and friends! How dare you? How dare you take the ring and leave us—!"

Her voice choked with emotion. "Goddess forgive me, but a part of me wishes you had died, because at least I could go on believing that you were good, and kind. That you were *our friend*. But now you are nothing but a stranger and a thief."

Olwen, I thought, an ache opening deep in my chest.

Emrys's face turned wan. He held his hands out, the palms turned up as if in supplication. "Please, just listen—"

"And allow you to lie to all of us again?" Caitriona said coldly. She held a hand back toward me, not to reach for mine, but to bring me closer to her.

"How did . . . ," Emrys began, each word he chose more uncertain than the last. "How did it happen? Did anyone else make it?"

"We are the only ones who survived," Caitriona said.

I looked down as Emrys recoiled, absorbing her words like a blow to the gut. "Even Cabell?"

I wondered when that awareness of him would finally leave, if it could be burned out of my soul like a fever. Even now, I felt him watching me, sensed the way he angled his body toward mine.

He might have been a coward, but I wasn't.

I looked up, forcing him to meet my gaze, to *see* me, as I said, "Are we supposed to believe that you care?"

He fisted a hand in his hair, his breathing turning shallow as the silence swelled between us. "Will you let me explain? Or are you too damn stubborn to even listen?"

My broken fingernails curled into the cuts on my palms, and I focused on that sharp bite of pain to steady me.

"Oh, now we get a choice?" I snapped. "You haven't shut up the entire time you've been here."

His jaw clenched, but I'd given him the opening, and he took it.

"I had to bring the ring to Madrigal," he said. "It wasn't a choice—not a real one. Madrigal didn't just promise me what I needed to get my mom away from my father. She kept my mom captive to ensure I saw the job through."

I stared back, the muscles in my stomach quivering as they tightened.

"We all had people we were trying to protect," I said coldly. "You were the only one who had to betray everyone to do it."

All that imploring softness fell away as his expression hardened to match mine. A part of me was relieved to see it. This was the real Emrys, the one I'd always known. The prince of the guild, the unwelcome rival. Him, I could handle.

"That's rich coming from you, Lark," he said. "Didn't you lie to Neve about how the ring had to be taken?"

Lark. My mind snagged on the name.

"Do *not*," Neve warned, finally stepping forward, "compare omitting details to leaving your supposed friends to die in a dark wasteland overrun by monsters."

He had the decency to look chastened by that, at least. "You're right. And I'm sorry it had to be that way." His gaze slid back toward me. "But you saw her—my mother. You saw what Madrigal had already done to keep her in line. You *saw* her, Tamsin."

"I have no idea what you're talking about—" But even as I said it, my mind was already painting the fading opulence of the Sorceress Madrigal's home.

In that short visit, I'd observed only a handful of people: the sorceress herself, Emrys, her pooka companion Dearie, the dinner guests and their horrible animal masks. And the elderly maid near the door.

The maid.

She'd looked as fragile as the etched-glass drinkware that had tumbled from her tray, shattering against the floor. Age had stooped her shoulders, but that was the only normal thing about her appearance, the rest of which had been startling. Her one visible eye had been pure white, with no iris or pupil. Her skin hung from the bones of her face like clay melting off its form. In a word, she'd looked ancient.

But when I lingered on her face, trying to layer it over the few images I'd seen of Cerys Dye, I could almost see it. The fine bone structure. The shape of her eyes. Emrys's mother had been famed for her beauty—it couldn't be her.

But Emrys's grave eyes told a different story.

"Is that true?" Neve asked, glancing between us.

"I think . . ." My words trailed off. I'd thought a lot of things about him. Believed far more than I should have. "Maybe."

"It *is* true," Emrys protested. "And once I returned with the ring, Madrigal let us both go."

"Where is your mother now?" Olwen asked, seemingly despite herself.

"She's safe . . . she's . . . recovering with a friend," Emrys said. "And when Madrigal heard the Council had ordered that the four of you be taken and imprisoned, she even sent the High Sorceress a letter vouching for you, as a peace offering. The Sistren are calling you the Unmakers. They think you're working with Lord Death."

"Yeah, we worked that one out ourselves, thanks," I said. My exhaustion caught up to me again, and this time, I didn't try to fight it. "What's the real reason you're here? Why would Madrigal feel she owes us anything? I know she's not doing it out of the goodness of her heart—she'd need to actually possess one for that to be true."

"She doesn't want you to reveal that she has the ring to the other sorceresses," Emrys said. "So no one shows up trying to kill her for it."

"What did she need it for?" Olwen asked.

"She didn't say, and I didn't see her use it," Emrys said. "And before you ask, I have no idea where it's hidden now."

I blew out a hard breath, rolling my eyes. Of course. How convenient for them both. It hardly mattered; as long as it was in the sorceress's possession, it was beyond our reach. Madrigal would put every ounce of her power into ensuring it would stay that way.

"What else?" I said. "That can't be the only reason she petitioned the Council for us."

Emrys folded his arms over his chest again, drawing my eyes to the crosshatch of scars covering his skin. Whatever reason he'd had to hide them before, it had no hold on him now. "Madrigal wants a heads-up if we think Lord Death is going to target her."

That, at least, was honest. She'd always struck me as a creature who prioritized her own survival over all others, even her own kind.

"I just heard an unwelcome *we* in that explanation," Neve said sharply.

"I want to help," he said quietly. "I want to make amends."

"Oh yes, because you're *known* for your virtuous, valiant nature," I scoffed.

It might have been the darkness, but I could have sworn he flinched. "Believe me or don't. I'm still going to try."

A freezing drip of condensation struck my neck and slid down the ridge of my spine. "You seem to be laboring under the delusion that your 'help' is something we'd want, when it's not even something we need."

"You did just now," he pointed out.

"That was Madrigal, not you," Neve said. "And we would have gotten ourselves out of this, somehow."

"Please . . . ," he said again, a hand rising to press against his chest. After a moment, he added quietly, "I don't even know what happened."

"And who do you have to thank for that?" Caitriona said.

He flinched, as if her words had been a knife to the heart. But it wasn't enough for me. I wanted to twist it and twist it until he felt the same pain we did.

So I told him. Everything. In the smallest, bloodiest detail, sharpening the truth's claws to tear at him until there was no color left in his face and he looked like he might be sick.

Good, I thought. Our eyes met and some twisted part of me was glad to see him gutted. *You get to feel it too.*

What I realized too late, however, was that I couldn't mortally wound him without cutting the others. In the long silence that followed, tears dripped down Olwen's anguished face. Caitriona reached for her, only to be waved away.

"I'm . . . it's fine," Olwen said, pulling away, turning back in toward the cell. Neve reached out and punched my arm with a look that promised another lesson in how to behave like a considerate human being.

"That's . . . ," Emrys began softly. But there wasn't a word for it. Nothing could encompass the magnitude of what had been lost.

"You said you want to help?" Neve said, rounding on him. "Lord Death sent a message to the Council of Sistren asking for something to be returned by the winter solstice. What is it?"

He balked. "I don't know. None of the sorceresses do."

"Is this you demonstrating your usefulness?" I asked.

"You said you brought Viviane's vessel from Avalon to find what memory Lord Death stole, right?" Emrys said. "Are you taking it to the Bonecutter to see if she can fix it?"

I opened my mouth. Shut it.

She. He'd said *she.*

The Bonecutter had been little more than green ink words on paper for as long as I'd been a Hollower. Green ink didn't have a face, or a gender, and no one else in the guild, not even Librarian, had seemed to know who or what they were.

"Is that who you wanted to find, Tamsin?" Caitriona asked, her dark eyes shifting between us.

"Yes," I grumbled.

"Then I'm at your service," he said. "Because I know where her workshop is."

The words struck me like a strangling curse. "You do *not* know that. No one knows that."

"Then I look forward to proving you wrong yet again."

I gritted my teeth.

"If he knows where it is . . . ," Neve began.

"We can find it ourselves," I groused.

"Not before Lord Death kills another sorceress," she finished. "If he's wrong, or lying, then we'll just . . . kick him off a cliff."

"Conveniently enough, there's one close to her establishment," Emrys said.

"You guys can't be serious . . . ," I began in disbelief.

But clearly, they were. And as Caitriona made her way toward Emrys, I knew I was outvoted.

"Let's go," she said. When Emrys started after her, she spun with all the vicious elegance of a viper, pinning him against the rough wall with her forearm. Emrys's eyes widened, but unlike Nash, he made no move to escape. He simply took it.

"Betray us again," she growled, "and I will gut you like the swine you are."

"Noted," he gasped out.

She released him, following along the pathway to what I sincerely hoped was the entrance, stepping over the swirling curse sigils embedded in the tile work beneath her feet. Emrys followed.

Olwen lingered a moment more, taking my hand to give it a gentle squeeze.

"Not you too," I said.

"I know," she told me. "But what other motive would he have now?"

"Let's see," I began. "Stealing Viviane's vessel once it's repaired? Spying on us for Madrigal? Using us to find whatever Lord Death wants first? Give me a few minutes, I'm sure I'll come up with more."

"Your mind, I swear," Neve said, shaking her head. "Here's the thing—if it's a choice between working with him and spinning ourselves in circles searching for the Bonecutter, I'd rather use him and lose him. Deep down, I know you would too."

I grunted, refusing to agree.

"The winter solstice is, what, ten days from now? And we have no idea what Lord Death is looking for, and why he needs whatever it is by then," Neve said. "What we need is time. He can give us that."

I blew out a long sigh. Right.

Olwen gave my hand one last squeeze. "It doesn't change what matters. We're still with you, no matter what."

My feet remained rooted to the ground as she followed Caitriona and Emrys out. I started after her, only to realize Neve had hung back.

The sorceress stood at the edge of what had been our cell, her brows lowered, her lips pressed in a tight line.

"Neve?"

Lost to her thoughts, Neve startled as I touched her shoulder.

"Sorry, I . . . ," she began, shaking her head. "Let's just get out of here."

"Is this about the sorceresses?" I asked, absently rubbing at my sore chest.

"No. Maybe." Neve's shoulders slumped. "Yes."

My anger, still so close to the surface, stirred again as I remembered what the sorceresses had said. The way they'd laughed. Neve had been rejected by the Council of Sistren when she'd sought out training. To see them rebuff her again, to not even accept that she was one of them, was more than I could bear.

"Don't you *dare* take anything they said to heart," I told her sternly. "They're all probably four centuries past the point of experiencing anything resembling empathy, and they have no idea who we are, or what we went through."

Her fingers worried the pendant hidden beneath her T-shirt. The rare, pale stone was a Goddess Eye, said to amplify magic, and had been left to her by a mother she'd never known.

"But she didn't ask who I was," Neve said quietly, hugging her arms to her center. "She asked *what* I was."

The air around us took on a deeper chill. I fought the urge to rub some warmth back into my arms.

"*You*," I said firmly, "are a powerful sorceress. Not to mention you're wearing an amplifier they were stupid enough not to take off you. Of course you could overcome their measly little wards."

She bit her lip. "It's . . . that light spell . . . I didn't think anything of it while we were in Avalon. Sometimes magic can well up in an uncontrolled way, especially in moments of great danger or emotion. But the way those sorceresses reacted . . ."

"Doesn't matter," I told her firmly. "We know what death magic feels like—it's cold, and remote. The Children were born from it and your light destroyed them, remember? It's never hurt any of us."

"You're right," she said. "I shouldn't have let them get into my head like that." Her lips twitched with a satisfied smirk. "They were totally freaking out, weren't they?"

"Like cats caught by the tail," I confirmed, letting her loop her arm through mine. "And I haven't forgotten my promise. We're going to find your mom, and you'll have whatever answers you need."

Neve let out a soft hum of acknowledgment. That pensive look was back as she said meaningfully, "Maybe you'll get a few of those yourself."

I couldn't think about that now. Any of it. For once, I was grateful for the dark chaos swirling around us, and I gladly surrendered to its all-consuming horror. Nothing else could matter right now.

Nothing, and no one.

I swept my gaze around the shadows, guiding us over the curse sigils disguised in the mosaic floors, making sure neither of us brushed up against the walls, where a thick layer of moss could hide more markings. Step by step, the darkness of the vault bled away, and soon an arched doorway appeared in the craggy wall ahead of us, framed with light.

Caitriona and Olwen passed through the Vein first. Emrys approached the doorway, and for a moment, I forgot—I forgot he wouldn't stop or look back over his shoulder, waiting for me to catch up the way he had a hundred times in Avalon.

But even that had been a lie. Embarrassment rang in my chest like a bell, deep and endless as it echoed against my bones.

"I can get rid of him, you know," Neve said as he stepped through the door. "Stick his body in some forest where the fungi can happily eat his rotting flesh and regenerate into something that's not a lying worm."

I was genuinely touched. "I'll keep that in mind."

"I've been working up some interesting curse options, too," she added.

"Interesting in what way?" I asked, stopping at the edge of the Vein. The sight of the spiraling threads of magic never got old.

"Stuff like, every pair of socks you own will always feel wet when you put them on . . . finding a maggot in every meal . . . having a bad itch you can never reach . . . burping every time someone says your name . . . always getting the squeakiest shopping carts . . ."

I laughed for the first time in what had to be days. "Can you really do all that?"

Neve lifted a shoulder in a shrug. "Give me a few more days, I'll figure it out."

I shook my head, trying to run a hand back through my tangled hair as I faced the Vein, and what waited on the other side. I'd made some terrible mistakes in my life; I just had to hope we wouldn't live to regret this one before we found out what memories had been stolen from the High Priestess's vessel.

Greenwich, Connecticut

In all the time he'd been a member of the Hollower guild, Cabell had never been invited to the Dyes' Summerland estate.

Curiosity might once have been enough to tempt him, especially if it came with the assurance of a big job—an expedition he'd never be able to fund himself for a relic he might otherwise never set eyes on. But on the whole, it had been easy to live without knowing what the inside of the palatial home looked like. He hadn't even tormented himself with wondering what treasures or resources the Dyes were jealously guarding from the rest of the guild behind their tony walls.

Nothing good came of coveting things that were never going to be yours. It only made you feel bad, knowing what you lacked. Better to focus on what was meant for you, and to hell with the rest of it.

The gravel driveway crunched under his feet as he stalked forward, matching the powerful strides of the dark figure a step ahead of him. They'd arrived in an icy whirlwind of shadows that had bit at his senses. It wasn't necessary to travel by Veins now. His lord could transport them between locations in the blink of an eye.

Cabell had never been a stranger to magic, but this—Lord Death's magic held the vastness of a night sky. It was no misty, sweet song. It thundered, triumphant and unrelenting. It was inescapable, like death itself.

The elaborate iron gate at the base of the driveway had been left open, anticipating their arrival. Cabell shook his head. That was the way of it with the Dyes. They assumed everything would always go to plan, that others would come when they called, that nothing was beyond their reach, not even a god.

Their house reflected that confidence with its grim-faced determination to take up as much space as possible. He wasn't sure he'd ever seen such a grand structure, accented by turrets and sweeping stone arches, outside of actual castles.

The sharpness of the air promised snow. A chill rolled down his back, not from cold but from the green scent of holly adorning the impressive marble steps. Two stone hounds guarded the landing. He sneered at the sight of them.

Black candles shuddered in their sconces on either side of the iron door, then went out, extinguished by some unseen wind.

The cold seemed to coil around his stomach as he neared; that same feeling of receding, of shrinking, came over him. His steps slowed.

"Whatever is the matter, my boy?" His master's voice was silk in the air, soothing even his most shattered edges.

"I should wait out here," Cabell said. He was a stain that would only tarnish his master in the eyes of the men inside. "I can stay with the Children."

Their chittering always set his teeth on edge, and something about the way they moved, that essence of human still left in their spidery bodies, unsettled him. He felt their glowing eyes on his back, watching from the line of trees at the edge of the estate, but didn't look, even as his instincts screamed for it. He wasn't a coward, but sometimes, at dusk, he thought he could see an echo of the human faces they'd once possessed.

"Hmm," Lord Death hummed, wearing another's face himself. A king's. "Have these men treated you poorly?"

Cabell ducked his head. "No, my lord. They didn't care enough to."

"Then shall we show them their mistake?" his master said. "Being underestimated has its advantages. Or do you think I wouldn't pick a worthy knight to stand at my side? Do you believe I would choose a fool to be my seneschal?"

Cabell straightened as the tension in his gut eased. He stared at his master, not daring to hope. "Your seneschal?"

"I shall need someone to run the household, here and in Annwn," Lord Death said. "To be my most faithful and loyal companion. Will you accept such a role?"

"Yes," Cabell breathed out. He couldn't let himself forget that again. Of all the apprentices his lord had trained, it was Cabell who had been chosen.

"Remember who you are," his master said. "You are where you belong."

Cabell had thought he'd understood what it was to belong before, but there'd always been a part of him, some feeling, that he was at the edge of this world and not part of it. He'd spent years staring down through the cracks of the library's attic floor as a child, watching as the members of the guild left to seek relics, returning with the most priceless treasure of all: pride.

All from having dared to try.

After he claimed his membership, it hadn't mattered how hard he'd worked, the curses he broke, or the miles he traveled. To his sister and the man who had raised them, he was worse than different—he was *wrong*. The others seemed to sense that about him too. Most days, he was barely tolerated. A source of amusement, maybe, but little better than dirt tracked in on Endymion Dye's boots.

Now he knew his worth, and there was no greater power than that.

His lord had supplied him with a heavy coat of the deepest black, the sort that absorbed all light. The silken quality of his new clothes and the soft leather of his boots were unlike anything he had ever worn, far too fine to be the product of mortal hands. He straightened the coat one last time, smoothing his hands down over wrinkles that weren't there.

"It is time you know your true name," Lord Death said. "Bledig."

The word resonated in his chest as his soul recognized the truth of it. That was his first name. Cabell belonged to a life he needed to shed like a hound's summer coat.

Lord Death lifted his hand, signaling to the Children of the Night. Several broke away from their pack, moving around the house to scale its rose trellises and walls, settling along the rooflines, where they would remain, guarding Summerland House against all enemies.

The door opened. Endymion Dye's pale face hovered in that slit of darkness. Lord Death stepped forward and lowered his hood. His face—the face of the man who had once been Arthur Pendragon—was cold as he took stock of the mortal man.

Cabell smirked at Endymion's groveling look of veneration and pride to find the King of Annwn standing on his threshold. The pleasure he took from it, however, was nothing compared to the satisfaction that purred in his chest when Endymion's eyes shifted over to him.

A flicker of shock passed over Endymion's sharp features as he recognized Cabell—a no one, a nothing in the hierarchy of his world—standing beside the god.

"You have summoned me here through ritual and smoke," Lord Death's baritone voice began. "And yet you do not invite me in. Tell me, Endymion Dye, are you so ungracious to all your guests?"

Endymion bowed, opening the door wider and backing into the shadows of the house with a nervous flourish.

Cabell almost laughed. The rush that pitiful display gave him was intoxicating, spreading an almost dizzying warmth through his whole body. How snakes turned to worms when a bigger predator arrived. Lord Death glanced over, arching a knowing brow.

"I've never seen him so . . . agreeable," Cabell said. "Allow me, my lord."

He stepped through the door first, knocking his shoulder into Endymion to push past him. In life, you were either the person who charged forward or the one who stepped aside. Cabell refused to step aside ever again. He would never need to.

Once inside, he surveyed the grand foyer, letting his gaze skim over the handsome oak staircase curving up either side in perfect symmetry. A dazzling chandelier sent candlelight sparkling down upon the cold marble floor.

He drew in a deep breath. The hair on his arms rose and stung, as if threatening a shift into his other form. There was something off about this place. Cold, yes, but that he'd expected. A kind of . . . stillness, then. The smell of must and something else lingered—decay.

He tilted his head toward another door to the left of him, this one looking like it had been ripped off an ancient fortress. The wood was inlaid with swirling patterns and symbols made from iron. Strange. He didn't recognize them, but he did recognize the scent that escaped from the room behind them.

Blood. Old blood.

Cabell turned sharply on his heel. He nodded to Lord Death, feeling again that prickling of pride that he had been entrusted with such a powerful god's safety.

Lord Death entered Summerland House as if he had done it thousands of times before. He stopped beside Cabell, assessing its fine offerings for himself.

"I hope it is to your liking, my lord," Endymion said, with yet another bow.

Lord Death cast a cold eye on him. "It will suffice. For now."

"The others are eager to meet you," Endymion said. "I cannot tell you how long we have awaited your return. To bring you forth into this world."

To his credit, he knew not to show his back to Lord Death. That, as Cabell had witnessed, was an insult the god wouldn't tolerate.

Instead, Endymion Dye—the great, proud Endymion Dye—walked backward, his eyes lowered like the servant he was. Cabell was unsurprised to discover that their destination was the imposing door with its strange symbols. He studied them again as they drew closer. Some looked vaguely like the sigils the sorceresses used for protective wards, but he couldn't be sure. Of the two of them, Tamsin—

His throat tightened. Cabell rested a hand on the sword hanging from his side, gripping the hilt until his fingers ached with it. At the edge of his vision, pale blond hair flashed. He spun, searching for the source of it, but found only shadows.

The massive door swung open with a sound like a dying beast. Cabell felt his feet slowing as he entered, almost against his will. Sheets of silk had been draped to block off the rest of the room, dividing the ordinary from the sacred. Before them, a dozen men, some he recognized from the Hollower guild, stood in the shape of a crescent, wearing crowns of holly. The table, or what might have been a desk, had been transformed into an altar. Beneath the stench of incense, greens, and nervous sweat was the faintest hint of old books.

Cabell's gaze drifted down. At his feet, a dark stain was just visible on the carpet. The muscles of his stomach tightened, and for the first time, he wondered what ritual had been powerful enough for Lord Death to feel the summons.

"Lord Death," Endymion began, taking his place in the assembly of men. All of them wore simple robes, and a silver pin that Cabell recognized from his old life. A hand holding a silver branch. "We welcome you once more to the mortal world, and offer you our service, to whatever end."

"You offer more than what I ask," Lord Death said, enjoying the way some of the men quailed under his scrutiny. Cabell took more than a little pleasure from walking in slow, searching loops around them. It felt good, so good, to give in to that need. It was in his blood to herd.

"My lord?" Endymion prompted.

"No one summons death, unless they seek its power," the god continued. "Tell me, then, what you desire of me in exchange for your service. Will you be like the ancients, who merely wanted to smite their enemies? Will you walk in the steps of the druids, grasping at knowledge and power forbidden to mortal men?"

Endymion seemed to regain some of his composure, though he still didn't dare look into Lord Death's pale eyes. "We seek to hunt those you hunt yourself. To serve as your sworn blades, your disciples in magic, and end the tyranny of those who hold power they do not deserve."

Of course, a voice whispered in Cabell's mind. *This has always been their objective.*

It was only a wonder he hadn't guessed it before. Some men hunted relics for the glory. These men, to steal power from the sorceresses.

Cabell sat at the edge of their pathetic altar, arms crossed over his chest, his pulse quickening. His breath came in light pants. He watched the god eagerly. No one would ever replace him. Lord Death had sworn it.

He would have a different role for these fools to play.

Lord Death paced in front of them, a king inspecting his soldiers. When he came to Endymion again, he stopped. A small smile slanted over his face as the man struggled to hold his head high. His bowels had probably turned to water by now.

"You wish to serve in my retinue?" Lord Death asked. "To join the Wild Hunt?"

"Yes," Endymion said, scarcely above a whisper. "More than anything, my lord. Grant us your power, and we will not fail you."

Lord Death placed a gloved hand on the man's shoulder, leaning in closer, as if to embrace him. "I accept."

Endymion let out a shuddering breath, his eyes closing behind his thin-framed glasses.

"But, my dear child," Lord Death continued, his voice low and tender, like a true father. The room's shadows gathered to the hand hanging at his side, wrapping it in writhing ribbons unseen to the others. "Do you not know my retinue is not comprised of the living?"

Endymion's eyes flashed wide, his breath choking off as Lord Death plunged his fist straight into his chest. Passing through skin and muscle and bone to reach the soul—and tear it out at the root.

Cabell closed his eyes and breathed in deeply, releasing the weakness that had held him captive for so long, welcoming in the darkness, and the terror, and the screams.

4

Winter had settled over the little seaside village like a curse from an old fairy tale, imprisoning it, and all those who lived within its reach, under a low, dreary sky.

It was the sort of bone-deep cold that invariably slowed the pulse of life and left behind a heavy stillness that wouldn't be broken until morning. Here and there, frosted windows were aglow with unseen life, but no one dared to venture outside now.

No one but us.

A soul-chilling wind blew in from the coast, lashing the age-worn stone buildings until snow misted off the low garden walls and thornlike icicles broke from the thatched roofs to shatter on the ground. It became a bitter companion, following us through the narrow cobblestone streets, moaning like a restless ghost determined to put us off our search.

It was appropriate, in a way, I supposed—the village's Welsh name, with its intriguing combination of consonants, had been helpfully translated by the One Vision to Spirit Point.

While it was not on any map, I recognized it from a particularly infamous entry in Nash's journal, in which he'd described getting so blisteringly drunk he lost his boots, gave himself frostbite on both big toes, and stole someone's Sunday roast right off their table. He'd been so preoccupied with eating his turkey leg, he'd ended his night by nearly walking off the nearby cliffs.

Cabell would have been beside himself to finally see this place. I'd have to bring him here, once it was all over. Preferably in the summer. Because right now, having wandered the dark streets of the village for over an hour, searching for a place that *clearly* did not exist, I was beginning to worry about my own fingers and toes.

I glared at Emrys as he circled the narrow street, baffled.

"Just admit that you lied," I sneered at him, too proud to let my teeth chatter. "You have no earthly idea where the Bonecutter is, and you never did. Is this all one big game to you?"

I'd sent Emrys to retrieve whatever gear and coats he could find in the library's lost and found—our polite name for the box of freebies left behind by dead Hollowers—but the pickings had been fairly slim. Avalon had destroyed my one good winter coat, and the green utility jacket I was wearing wasn't up to a Welsh winter. Worse, it still smelled like the tuna sandwiches Amos Martinus had eaten every day until his last.

At least Olwen had been able to apply salve to my aching ribs, and the worst of my cuts. Small movements no longer felt like a hot knife through my chest, though I was beginning to suspect my whole body had just gone numb from the cold.

Emrys stopped circling, his hands on his hips. He, of course, was well bundled in a scarf and a stupid tweed jacket. His brow creased as he shot me a look of irritation. "I didn't lie. I said I knew *where* she was, not that I'd been there."

"And where did that information come from?"

He shoved his hands in his pockets, looking down at the road. "Maybe one day you'll have enough money to find out."

God's teeth, I hated him.

My breath blew out in a cloud of white as that old, potent blend of shame and indignation rose like bile in my throat. If he was going to use what I'd told him to hit me, then I'd gladly return each blow.

"If only Daddy's money could buy you a brain," I crooned back at him, hands curling into fists, "then maybe next time you'd think to buy some actual directions instead of being taken for a fool."

The hit had landed, but there was none of the satisfaction I'd craved, only more of that gnawing anger, that revulsion. Emrys turned his back to me, stalking past where the others had stopped to rest against the wall of a sweet shop.

"Have you even s-seen the B-Bonecutter?" Neve asked, bouncing on her heels as she tried to rub some warmth back into her arms.

"No," he grunted out. "No one has ever met her."

Caitriona pushed away from the icy stone wall, shucking off her own black wool coat. Without a word, she wrapped it around Neve's shoulders, then went back to her post, keeping watch on the empty street.

Neve tried to take it off, protesting, "You're going to freeze—"

"I'm used to the cold," Caitriona said with a dismissive wave. Remembering the oppressive gloom of Avalon, I didn't doubt that, but I also didn't like it.

It was strange to see Caitriona dressed like any other mortal; her jeans, a smidge short, and the button-down flannel shirt were strangely discordant with the very essence of her—it was like watching a king playing peasant. Her unusual, silvery hair was tucked up into a knit cap to avoid attracting unwanted attention. The black coat had highlighted the unhealthy pallor of her skin, matching the heavy smears of shadows beneath her flinty eyes.

She cut her gaze around at the cheery Christmas decorations on the nearby shops and flats, her top lip curling at battery-powered candles flickering in the windows above us.

Night had come early, as it always did when the Wheel of the Year turned to winter. It looked like everything had been closed for hours. In these farther-flung places, villagers had been set in their routines for centuries, and had a well-earned suspicion of outsiders.

Salted ice crunched under my feet as I stepped forward, gesturing to one of the buildings with lights on. "That's a hotel of some kind—maybe someone there will know where to find the Dead Man's Rest, or tell us what happened to it."

"It's here," Emrys insisted, more to himself than to the rest of us, as he continued down the street. "It's around here somewhere."

"The maggot suddenly seems too kind to curse him with," Neve muttered as she followed him, wrapping Caitriona's oversized coat around her like a blanket.

Caitriona trailed two steps behind, her gaze still sweeping the street for some unseen danger. I spun on my heel, realizing we were missing someone.

"Olwen?" I called.

She was on the other side of a bright red postbox, greeting an inflatable snowman. With all the gravity of a formal introduction, Olwen took one of its twig arms and gave it a courteous little shake.

She leapt back as the decoration lit with a flashing whirl of lights and began to scream-sing a cloying rendition of "We Wish You a Merry Christmas." While she marveled at it, stooping to poke it again with her finger, I saw the word *extraordinary* form on her lips.

I sighed, then went to retrieve her.

"Tamsin, what *is* that thing?" she asked. "What purpose does it serve? Is it a talisman to frighten away malevolent spirits or mischievous fae?"

I considered the singing snowman. "I think it's just supposed to be . . . merry."

"Cait, look!" Olwen called over my shoulder, gesturing to the warbling nightmare. "Isn't he jolly? Air passes through him, yet he is unbreathing—"

The others had doubled back for us, but at the sight of the decorations and Olwen's tentative smile, a hard mask slid over Cait's features. Her words were harder still. "Enough of this. We haven't the time to waste."

Olwen, to my surprise, had quickly shed her shock at being in a new world and had taken to investigating it with both fascination and alarm, but mostly fascination. She pushed every single button she encountered no matter what it did, poked at car tires and intriguing machines, and stopped to inspect each new, peculiar plant. The holiday decorations with their colorful lights, the trees laden with glittering ornaments, the ribbon-kissed wreaths, had only deepened her wonder.

"You're right, Cait, of course," she said, quickly picking up the basket she'd set down. Griflet let out a soft *meow* from inside.

Caitriona inclined her head toward the hotel. "The liar has received instructions on how to find what we're looking for."

She marched on ahead of us, her long strides eating up the distance far faster than Olwen's and my shorter legs could. I caught a glimpse of downcast Olwen's face out of the corner of my eye.

"He *was* very jolly," I told her.

Olwen let out a soft laugh. "I know I'm being silly, but I want to understand this world. Every now and then I'll see something, and it'll remind me of home—like the garlands? They're so similar to the ones we would make for the Yule celebrations. The sap would stick to my fingers, and I could smell the sweetness of it and the pine needles for days, even after washing."

My breath painted the air white, the cold stinging my eyes. I wished Neve were walking with us, because she would have known the right thing to say.

"But then I remember that all of that's gone, that I have no home but this place now, and I'm not sure how I fit here," Olwen said. "I'm not sure I ever can."

My chest squeezed at how matter-of-factly she said it. "We celebrate the Yule here, too. When all of this is over, you can teach me how to make the garlands. I can't promise mine won't look like a child made it, but I'll try."

She smiled, glancing up as Neve rushed toward us.

"We've been looking in the wrong place," she announced, exasperated. "The pub's just outside the village's limits."

Rather than head back up the winding road, we walked down the main road as it curved around the buildings and continued past the edge of town, toward the cliffs. As we passed by the last house, the paved road turned to well-worn dirt, its grooves carved by centuries of wandering. The moon cast down silvery light, guiding our way. It made Emrys's solitary figure at the front of the pack look almost ghostly, a figment of a lost dream.

The pub soon came into view, its thatched roof spotted with snow. Its white stone face had been whipped raw by the wind, and the whole structure slanted ever so slightly to the right. Below, the winter sea roared as it churned against the ragged coastline.

We hurried up the path. There were a few cottages scattered around, breaking up the stretches of dead grass and what was left of the last snow. A wooden sign hung from the low-slung line of the roof, depicting a skeleton sitting at a table, his hand resting against his chin and a full pint in front of him. THE DEAD MAN'S REST, it said.

"See?" Emrys said, gesturing toward it. "Told you it was here."

"And to think, it only took you three hours to find it," I said. "Hope you're not expecting a ticker-tape parade."

"No, but you're welcome to lead the toast in my honor, Lark," he said smugly. "Don't worry, I'll buy the first round."

He had to be doing it on purpose—pulling and pulling on that thread. And for what? To entertain himself by watching me unravel?

Out of the corner of my eye I saw Olwen and Neve exchange a wary glance, but I wouldn't give him the satisfaction of taking the bait.

I turned back toward the door to the pub, relieved to see the lights were still on. Better yet, the sound of laughter and voices met us at the door. I reached for the quaint old handle, but the door swung open first, and with a faint tinkle of bells, a monster spilled out.

My pulse leapt and my ribs screamed in protest as someone grabbed me from behind, yanking me back. I gasped in pain and surprise.

A pale, ghoulish figure materialized in front of me, riding on a draft of heat and chatter. Towering in height, it seemed to float above the ground, the white fabric that covered its body streaming around it like a swirling draft of snow.

There was no flesh on its long snout—it was pure ivory bone. The set of its long teeth gave it a jeering appearance. Red glass ornaments had been placed in its empty eye sockets. Three young men trailed behind it like devoted acolytes, spilling out into the night.

I looked back just as Emrys released his hold on me, letting his hand fall back to his side.

"Bloody *hell*," one of the drunk strangers yelped. "Sorry—sorry, didn't see you there!"

My mind caught up to my fear, releasing with a shaky breath as I held up a hand in acknowledgment. The same, however, could not be said of Caitriona, who reached into her sleeve for the kitchen knife she'd strapped to her forearm. She turned, preparing to follow them back toward the village.

"—too cold for it now, no drink's worth losing bits to frostnip—" one of the young men was saying, tugging his wool cap down over his red ears.

"No, no!" I caught Caitriona's hand before she could retrieve the blade, and drew her back to the door of the pub. "No need for stabbing."

She shot me an incredulous look, her dark eyes hardening as she assessed the retreating threat. "What infernal darkness has descended on this night?"

"I don't know," Neve said, a bit starry-eyed. I grabbed the collar of Caitriona's borrowed coat before she could follow the revelers. "But I *love it*."

"Was that a horse skull?" Olwen said, cocking her head to the side.

"It's what's called a Mari Lwyd," Emrys said. "They're over three weeks early with it, though."

I'd seen the tradition performed years ago, at the highly impressionable age of six, to be exact. Nash had brought us to a Welsh village not unlike this one, and a group with their Mari Lwyd had barged into the pub where we were eating. They'd made sure to torment the tiny blond child trapped in the corner booth, making the Mari Lwyd clack horribly until I'd tried to slip under the table to get away.

Truly a Twelfth Night I would barter with a demon to forget.

I shoved the pub door open, letting the smell of ale, woodsmoke, and leather wash over me. My skin prickled painfully as it came alive to the warmth emanating from the glowing fireplace. On first glance, not a single soul in the pub fit the mental image I had of a purveyor of bone and poison.

"Okay, so they bring the horse thing around to houses, and it's like a rap battle between the wassailers and the people who live there," Neve said when Emrys finished his quick explanation of the Mari Lwyd tradition. "Except when you inevitably lose because you can't think of another verse about why they can't come in, they enter your home and terrorize your children by chasing them around with a skull attached to a stick. And then, to get them to leave, you have to give them free food and drinks?"

"Supposedly they help clear out the evil spirits in your house and bring luck, but yes," he said, leading us to one of the booths in the far corner. Thankfully, there were only a few patrons left in the pub this close to last call, but all of them looked up from their drinks as we entered.

I was coming to realize that, much like the Cunningfolk and sorceresses, Caitriona and Olwen had an otherworldly quality to them that invariably caught the human eye. No amount of drab mortal clothing could smother the effect. Considering we needed to lie low, my very mortal plainness suddenly felt like a gift.

Like a beetle blending into bark, I thought. *Or a toad in the mud.*

My gaze slid around the room, assessing. Thick white plaster covered the uneven walls, but here and there it had broken off, revealing the rough stonework beneath it. The low beams and bracings made the space feel far smaller and darker than it was. Old, rusted armor helmets lined the walls on either side of the massive carved stone fireplace, as if someone had gone out and trophy-hunted the Knights of the Round Table. And honestly, I didn't hate it.

On the whole, it was a humble space, completely at odds with the magnificence of the bar.

It had been carved to look like a sleeping dragon, its body curved around the veritable hoard of glasses and bottles of booze gleaming on the wall behind it like the most princely of baubles. The bartender was as tall and narrow as a cattail, with feathery black hair. He didn't look up from where he was polishing the silver taps.

The hair on the back of my neck prickled with the weight of some unseen gaze, but when I turned, Emrys was already looking away, and I couldn't be sure it had been him at all.

A portrait of a mysterious woman hung above the mantel, but she was largely hidden by some of the gaudiest Christmas decorations I'd ever had the misfortune to lay eyes on.

Tinsel garlands had been strewn from one end of the pub to the other. A fake tree was decorated with furry pom-poms and plastic fairies painted with alarmingly murderous expressions.

Caitriona let out an impatient huff as she slid to the center of the banquette. She cast a cutting gaze at our table's sole decorations: a battery-powered candle flickering in a fake holly wreath.

"Where is this . . . *cutter*?" she demanded in a raspy voice. "We've wasted hours we could have spent hunting our enemy."

One of the younger men at a nearby booth caught sight of her and rose, coming toward us with a dreamy smile before I could warn him away.

"Hello there—" he began.

Whatever Caitriona said to him in the language of Avalon was helpfully translated by the One Vision into: "Kiss iron and return to the bosom of the wicked fiend that bore you."

Her accent, melodic but unplaceable to the average ear, added another layer of fire to the words. I choked.

He blinked and turned on his heel, sailing back toward his table of friends, all of whom were now howling with laughter.

"Kiss iron?" I managed to ask.

She looked down, running a finger along the grain of the table. "Iron is poisonous to the Fair Folk."

"It's something Betrys used to say," Olwen added quietly, taking the basket from me and joining her sister in the booth. Neve slid in on the opposite side from Caitriona, shooting her an anxious glance. I took my own seat beside Olwen at the booth's edge.

"Have no fear," Neve told Caitriona, passing her coat back to her with a grateful smile. "I'll protect you from any other scoundrels who dare approach, fair maiden."

Caitriona ducked her head in acknowledgment, hugging the heavy fabric in her lap. Even in the low light, I could see that the tips of her ears had gone pink. "That will not be necessary."

Griflet stuck his little fuzzy head out from beneath the blankets as Olwen started rummaging around in the old satchel I'd given her to store her things. Drawing out the Ziploc bag of jerky I'd packed, she fussed with the opening until it finally parted with a *snap*. Eyes wide, she closed it and opened it again several more times, gaping at it.

"Wait until you see Velcro," Neve told her.

Emrys lingered at the edge of the booth, but I didn't move in, and neither did Neve. Correctly sensing he wasn't wanted, he claimed a chair at a nearby table.

"Should you be feeding a kitten that?" he asked.

Griflet gave him a look that asked, *Is it any of your business?*

I'd tried to get the kitten situated with the other library cats before we set out. I knew they were prone to theatrics and moodiness, but even so, their aggression toward Griflet had shocked me. I was lucky to get the two of us out of there with our eyes intact.

"Griflet has to eat *something,* and this is the best we can do at the moment," Olwen said, smoothing the stubborn curls escaping her braid. With her naiad ancestry, she was the least human of the four of us, and it showed in her inky-blue hair and the luminous ring of cerulean around her dark irises.

I'd given her the bright yellow down jacket from the guild's lost and found bin in the hope that an old thieving strategy of Nash's would still prove effective. The best distraction from anything unusual was something even more eye-catching.

Neve had been delighted by my assortment of thrift store finds at home and had been all too happy to change out of the clothes ruined by the vault. She picked at the beads on her sweater's embroidered flowers, watching as the patrons began to pay their tabs and leave. I had to admit it looked better on her than it ever had on me, the soft blue complementing her brown skin.

"All right," Neve began, her voice low as she scanned the few remaining patrons in the pub. "Anyone see any candidates for this Bonecutter person?"

We'd be sitting here all night if we were going to rely on gut intuition.

"I'll make some discreet inquiries," I told them, then added in a hushed tone, "No one stab, steal, or touch anything, please."

I stood and moved slowly through the nearby tables. A chair screeched back behind me, and I knew without looking that it was Emrys. The smell of pine and sweet greens followed me through the pub's cluttered array of tables. A fly would have been less annoying.

"Go back to the table, Trust Fund," I ordered.

"No," he said flatly. "Because you're right about the need for discretion, and you're about as discreet as a hobgoblin when you get frustrated."

Don't do it, I told myself. *Don't look at him.*

"Wow," I muttered. "This sure doesn't look like a workshop."

"You really think she'd make it that obvious?" he answered.

No, I didn't. Like him, the Bonecutter was always working the shadows to her benefit.

"Feel free to leave at any time now that you've fulfilled your self-serving desire for redemption," I said coldly.

"Nah," he said, stopping just behind me. He leaned forward over my shoulder, using his height to his advantage as he brought his mouth close to my ear. The back of my neck prickled with the warmth of his nearness. "I think I'll stay. Night's still young."

I wouldn't step away. I wouldn't flinch. As angry as the taunting made me, the confusion his nearness brought was worse. My mind recognized that I was being played with, but my body didn't care.

I gritted my teeth, focusing on the last few patrons at the bar. I wasn't going to rule out the men, no matter what Emrys believed, but none of them seemed to fit the profile of the Bonecutter. Finally, at the far end where the carved dragon's head rested on its legs, my gaze settled on something I hadn't expected.

A little girl, no more than ten, maybe eleven years old, sat next to her grandfather at the bar. A sinking feeling grew in my chest as I watched her.

Her ringlets were as black as a crow's wing and danced around her shoulders as she wrote something in a notebook—homework? Her stocking-clad legs swung freely above the footrest. She wore a red crushed-velvet dress, the kind you might choose for a fancy recital. It was immaculately neat, even with the basket of crisps in front of her.

How many times had I sat at a bar beside Nash, waiting for him to find answers to his existential angst at the bottom of a glass, or meet a potential partner for a job?

"Closing now!" the bartender called. I startled, momentarily unnerved by the squawking quality of his voice.

I moved away again, leaning over the bar. The bartender's gray eyes stared down his long nose at me, waiting. His fingernails, filed to careful points, tapped an impatient tempo on the counter.

"Is there a . . . ," I began, trying to figure out how to ask this. "Ah . . . a collector, or trader, or . . ." *Grave robber. Bone snatcher. Gossip procurer.* Finally, I settled on, "Are you the owner of this fine establishment?"

"No." The bartender turned back to his work, ignoring my look of irritation.

The white-haired man with a pockmarked face was the last customer to leave, sliding off his stool with only a grunt of acknowledgment to the bartender. He left behind an empty pint and a few crumpled pound notes.

And his granddaughter.

I watched in disbelief as he pulled his coat off the rack and walked out the door, letting it swing shut again behind him.

"What the hell?" Emrys said beneath his breath, starting after him. "Hey—!"

"Afraid to use my name?" came a cranky little voice beside me.

Emrys and I turned slowly.

The little girl tossed her hair back over her shoulders, shutting the thick leather notebook. Her ledger. In her hand wasn't a pen at all, but a quill carved out of joined fingerbones.

"It's just as well," the little girl said, propping her chin against her fist, "that I'm not afraid to use yours, Tamsin Lark."

5

"You?"

The child was almost doll-like in appearance, her features unbearably soft save for her green eyes. There was no innocence to them; they were shards of glass capable of cutting someone open to see what was hiding beneath their skin. It was the gaze of someone who'd seen history unspool itself over centuries—of a soul too old to be wearing that face.

"I've an ointment that'll help you with your locked jaw," the girl said. "It'll only cost you three gold pieces, or a favor."

Her tone was formal, carrying some unidentifiable accent that made every word sound like a line of ancient poetry.

I promptly shut my mouth. "I'm . . . how?"

The Bonecutter looked to Emrys. "I suppose I have you to thank for this unpleasant surprise. I'd heard your father was stirring up old ghosts and throwing money around to see what ex-clients would bite."

"He did indeed," Emrys said, struggling to contain his own shock.

"That's the way of it with you Dyes," the Bonecutter groused, rolling her quill against the counter. "There's not a job you won't pay someone else to do for you, if you can."

"Oh my goodness!" I heard Neve sing as she came up behind us. I turned with slow horror, but it was already too late to stop her. "Aren't you adorable? I *love* your dress!"

The girl's eyes narrowed, hardening like flint. The air around us darkened, as if the light itself had shrunk away in horror. The temperature plunged.

The glasses on the shelves rattled, threatening to dance off into shattered oblivion. The bartender merely steadied the wineglasses with one hand while wiping down the back counter with the other.

All at once, the pressure released, and the glow of the fire returned to the pub.

"But I really do like her dress," Neve murmured from somewhere behind me. Olwen hushed her.

The Bonecutter glanced past my shoulder.

"No need for blades, Caitriona of Avalon. I'm certain you wouldn't enjoy an introduction to my own collection."

Caitriona lowered her knife, but only to her side. "You know who I am."

"I know all of you," the Bonecutter said. "The four who shattered the bonds of ancient magic to rejoin the worlds, at deadly cost. The Unmakers. And the tragic Dye heir, of course."

I thought Emrys might offer up one of his usual quips, but he only looked down at where his hand gripped the back of the stool beside him. There was something in his expression, the way his eyes hadn't quite focused, that sent an unwelcome ripple of dread through my thoughts.

"You don't understand," Olwen began.

"Oh, but I do," the Bonecutter said. "I understand far more than what you might wish to believe. About the unpredictable nature of magic. About the monsters that have appeared on this very isle. Whispers reach me from far and wide, from the living and the dead."

The Bonecutter slid off her stool. Not being tall myself, I was still shocked to see her diminutive stature. "That is why Nashbury Lark sought advice about his cursed child all those years ago, and why, out of great curiosity, I have allowed you to stay. I suspect you're about to show me something quite interesting."

Cursed child. With everything that had happened, I'd been able to push Nash's words from my mind. His warning. The Bonecutter couldn't possibly have guessed he'd only just spoken of it, but . . . the knowing quirk of her brow was unsettling, to say the least.

"We need your help," I told her. "Though this may be beyond even your skill set."

The Bonecutter smirked. Holding up her left hand, she snapped her fingers, and all the lights—natural and false—extinguished around us. The locks on the windows and doors turned with a harsh *snap*.

"The night's come, Bran," she told the bartender. "Be off with you."

He nodded, ducking to retrieve something from under the register—a stone tablet with a sigil for warding off unwelcome guests. Neve leaned over my shoulder to get a better look at it. She caught my eye as the bartender hung it around the doorknob.

"There are far more protections you cannot see," the Bonecutter said, retrieving her large ledger and pressing it to her chest. "Nothing and no one shall enter the pub unless I will it. You'll only need to worry about your own foolish impulses and sticky fingers."

She was looking at me as she said the last part. My temper prickled. "I'm not Nash."

"You'll answer for his sins all the same."

She gave a dismissive wave to the bartender. The air heated around us, then ruptured with a torrent of spiraling light. The transformation couldn't have taken more than a scant sliver of a moment, but every detail of it seared into my mind with stunning clarity—the way the man's bones shrank, how his form twisted and knotted around itself until nothing human remained and a large raven soared out from the sparks of magic still drifting in the air.

The bird tore through the haze of smoke in the fireplace, then up through the chimney. I reached out a hand, catching a long black feather in my palm.

Pooka. A shapeshifter. One of the last races of the Fair Folk in our mortal world. They often allied themselves to sorceresses and became companions to the women, offering their services in exchange for protection.

Which meant . . .

There had been countless rumors about who the Bonecutter was over the years. Most assumed it was a sorceress, or one of the Cunningfolk—you needed a certain magical skill set and vast stores of obscure knowledge to run this kind of outfit, after all. I'd always believed that if she was a sorceress, the Council of Sistren would have put a stop to one of their own profiting off the bones of their dead.

Not so, apparently.

Neve made a pained noise, all but shaking with the effort to keep her questions to herself.

"If you'll be so good as to join me in my workshop," the Bonecutter said. She ran a small pale hand along the carved spikes of the wooden dragon's spine as she rounded the bar. There must have been a small stool tucked behind the counter, because she was suddenly able to reach up and press a hand to one of the dragon's glass eyes. I took a step forward, squinting—and there it was, hidden in the painted lines of the iris. A small sigil.

Just behind her, the weathered planks of the floor pried free, stacking themselves neatly on either side of the staircase hidden below.

"The kitten is not allowed to join us," the Bonecutter said, starting down the steps. "In fact, I'd rid yourselves of it immediately."

"Not much of an animal person, are you?" I asked.

"Not unless they have rare fangs, claws, or skin to offer," the Bonecutter said.

Griflet hissed.

Olwen hesitated, but I gave her a nod. Gently, she set the basket down and pulled the protesting kitten out of the blanket.

"Now, don't be like this," Olwen told him, giving his head a gentle stroke. She removed her jacket and set the kitten down on it, so it had a soft surface to lie on. With one last irate yowl, Griflet extracted his teeth from her oversized sweater and curled up in a sullen circle on the makeshift bed.

"Come along, then, and watch your head for webs—I leave the spiders to catch any unwanted pests," the Bonecutter said, continuing down the steps into the darkness below. "Though, sadly, you lot are far too big to be snared."

No one moved.

"Fine," I grumbled, taking the basket. I went first, carefully descending each narrow step. True to her word, an alarmingly thick layer of pale webbing covered the slanted roof of the enclosed staircase. Here and there, delicate wisps had fallen, drifting down into our path.

A shudder rippled through me as I held out a hand, trying to protect my hair from any spiders looking for a new home. When I risked a glance back, Neve was searching the webs with hopeful eyes.

"No," I whispered. "No arachnids, and no picking up random bones."

"Not while you're watching, at least," she whispered, ignoring the look I sent her.

Emrys came next, followed by a clearly unhappy Caitriona, both bending at the waist to avoid knocking their heads.

As the Bonecutter reached the bottom step, the basement lights fluttered on, revealing the space in all its mundane glory.

The basement wasn't exactly the vast, creepy warehouse I had imagined. It was cramped, carefully packed with kegs and shelves of liquor bottles and cleaning supplies. The air was dank, but perfumed by warm wax and something vaguely earthy.

At the very center of it all, directly ahead, was a large table, barely recognizable beneath the chaos strewn over its surface. Plastic containers of bones—both human and animal—were stacked high and carefully labeled with some unintelligible code not even the One Vision could untangle. A tray piled with blank sheets of parchment was set beside a decrepit-looking quill and inkwell.

Most intriguing, however, was that either side of the table was lined with glass bottles hovering over candle flames. Many of the candles had burned down to pools of white wax, drooling onto the floor.

My eyes lingered on the glass containers. They had been worked into delicate, almost ethereal shapes, many resembling flowers or moons, all of which had a pearlescent sheen. I couldn't place exactly why they'd captured my attention until I saw Olwen eyeing them with something like grief. One of her hands strayed toward the nearest one, her finger ghosting over its curve.

They were nearly identical to the ones she'd kept on the shelves of her infirmary.

The Bonecutter was quick to replace the melted candles with new ones, adjusting the heights of the bottles as needed. Muttering something to herself, she reached into a small burlap sack hooked onto the end of the table. When she dropped the tiny leaves from inside into the nearest bottle of simmering liquids, it belched up gray smoke as the leaf dissolved.

"Now," the Bonecutter said, clearing the center of her table by unceremoniously dumping piles of books onto the dusty floor. "What have you brought me?"

I set the basket down in front of her, pulling the blankets back to reveal the shattered skull inside. I bit my lip. It was worse than I remembered—some of the shards were so small, they wouldn't even qualify as slivers.

The Bonecutter retrieved a large pair of glasses from the drawer of her worktable. My own reflection stared back at me in the glossy amethyst lenses, gaunt and bruised. Her small hand shoved me back a step so it could swing the neck of an articulated lamp over.

Light flooded the scarred wood surface, revealing more than one dark stain I could only pray was ink. Her stool creaked as she pumped a lever to raise its height, and again as she turned to face the table.

At that slight movement, the workshop tore itself apart.

The explosion of movement sent my heart slamming into the pit of my stomach. The stones in the walls scattered like disturbed nests of roaches. Olwen leapt away in alarm as they clattered up toward the ceiling and revealed the line of Victorian glass display cabinets hidden behind them.

The dingy light fixture rattled, then bloomed into a full crystal chandelier. The moodier light suited the tapestries that unfurled in all their tattered glory to cover the small windows where the ceiling met the wall.

Smaller tables and chairs raced out from behind the shelves containing the pub supplies, forcing Emrys to dive out of the way to avoid being run down as they moved into position in front of newly emerged bookshelves. The shelves were, of course, stuffed to the gills with scrolls, notebooks, tomes, and even what looked like the occasional Immortality.

Having remade itself, the workshop stilled again. The sound of some unidentifiable, metallic jangling filled the long silence that followed.

"That was *amazing*," Neve gasped out. "Where did you hide all the sigils? How did you trigger them to cascade that way?"

The Bonecutter gave only a tight-lipped smile.

Olwen wandered the space with starry eyes, greedily drinking in the sight of it all.

"Should you be keeping the pub stuff this close to your . . . other stuff?" I asked uneasily.

The Bonecutter waved me off. "I've only ever had one incident, and the man was able to pass the adder out of his intestines eventually."

"No lasting damage with that, I'm sure," Emrys said. Our eyes met and looked away just as quickly.

"His tongue did, eventually, grow back," the Bonecutter said, lifting a piece of bone closer to the light.

"What is all this?" Olwen asked, studying the array of objects in the lit cases. They were displayed proudly, like prizes.

"Payment from satisfied customers," the Bonecutter said.

"Payment?" I repeated. "If you take goods in trade, why make

Cab—" His name caught in my throat. "Why make us agree to your mysterious 'favors' to get a key out of you?"

"I only ask favors of those who possess nothing much of value," the Bonecutter said.

My face heated with embarrassment. We'd been poor, not completely destitute. "We could have paid."

Her brows shot up above her glasses. "Not the price *I* would have asked."

I used the nearby shelves as an excuse to look away, fighting the flare of heat in my face.

"Is this all stuff you've found or traded for?" Neve asked, joining Olwen in front of one of the lit cases. They seemed entranced by a collection of necklaces, some ornate and sparkling with fat gemstones. Others were simple: A thin silver strand. A gold chain with an ivory locket. Gold rings and even a few earrings, one shaped like entwined serpents, were displayed beside them. But there were also gardening shears, books, and even a violin.

The Bonecutter looked up from where she had begun to lay out the shards of Viviane's vessel on the table. "Both. Do you see that puzzle box, the one no bigger than your palm?"

I joined them at the case, studying the warm-toned wood. On its lid, several tiles with painted sigils sat in various grooves.

"Does it look familiar, Dye?" she asked.

"Yes," he muttered, leaning against a shelf of stacked scrolls, just outside the glow of the table's light. He shifted, toeing the holes singed into the rug. The Bonecutter seemed to enjoy his discomfort.

"What does it do?" Olwen asked.

"It can trap a soul if you assemble the sigils correctly, but might just as soon trap yours," the Bonecutter said. Her gaze narrowed, slicing back toward Emrys. Assessing. "I'll sell it back to you, if you're interested. Seems you could have use for it."

He only lifted a shoulder in a shrug.

Olwen let out a soft gasp as she studied another section of the case.

Her expression turned distraught, and my heart all but leapt out of my chest.

"What?" I asked.

The Bonecutter's smirk was that of a snake circling another animal's nest of eggs. "You've spotted my apple, I see."

At the word, Caitriona was by Olwen's side in an instant, searching past her horrified reflection in the glass until her dark eyes landed on the small apple and its pedestal. The fruit looked sickly but hadn't lost its golden sheen.

"You cannot have this," Caitriona said, raising her fist as if to smash through the glass. "You *cannot*. This is . . . this is not *yours*."

"And it concerns you how, exactly?" the Bonecutter asked, fixing her with a gimlet eye.

"We took a vow to protect Avalon," Olwen began.

"And what a wonderful job you've done," the Bonecutter said. "Can you be a priestess of a place that no longer exists?"

"That's enough," I said sharply.

But Olwen didn't need protecting. She tilted her chin up and said, "Of course we can. We still serve the Goddess."

The Bonecutter turned her gaze toward Caitriona, a knowing smirk tucked into the corner of her lips. It was all the more unsettling on a child's face. "And do you agree, Lady Caitriona?"

Caitriona's jaw set dangerously. She barely seemed to be breathing.

Emrys's voice broke through the seething tension. "Did the apple come from one of the exiled sorceresses?"

The room's focus shifted to where he stood behind us, picking an invisible piece of lint off his jacket. Unbothered, as usual, by anyone's feelings outside of his own.

Still, that small redirect was enough to steer the conversation back to safer shores.

"Yes." The Bonecutter returned to the task in front of her, holding up the largest piece of the skull again. She lifted the amethyst lenses of her glasses to reveal red, then silver lenses beneath them. "I must admit, of all the things I thought you might bring me from Avalon, I didn't expect a druid vessel. I would have thought they'd be destroyed after the sorceresses stopped the druids from taking control of the isle."

"Do you know how to fix it?" I asked again. "I just thought, you know, you work with sorceress bones to create keys—"

"What?" Neve asked, horrified.

The Bonecutter lifted a brow. "Forgot to mention that to her, did you?"

Neve sent me an accusatory look.

"How do you think the Hollowers get into sorceress vaults?" I asked her. "The Veins are sealed with skeleton knobs. You need the bone and blood of someone in that family—if not the sorceress herself—to feed into the lock."

"You can see a sample of that work in the case on the far left," the Bonecutter said with a grim flourish of the hand. Always the consummate businesswoman.

"I think I'll pass," Neve muttered, eyeing both Emrys and me with outright disgust. "And for the record, I just thought Hollowers were talented at breaking whatever curses locked up vaults and tombs."

I shifted my weight, hugging my arms to my center. Cabell was the only person I knew with an innate talent for breaking curses.

The Bonecutter studied me, as if she'd had the same thought.

"Then you have greatly overestimated the capabilities of most Hollowers, including myself," Emrys said. "Half the time survival's a matter of luck and remembering to look down before you take your next step."

"Well, you've found yourself a bit of luck today," the Bonecutter said, leaning back and removing her glasses. "As it happens, I do know something of vessel-making and believe—after some consultation of a few books and journals—I will be able to fix it."

I drew in a sharp breath, moving toward the table.

"But again, I return to the same question," the Bonecutter finished. "Are you willing to pay the price?"

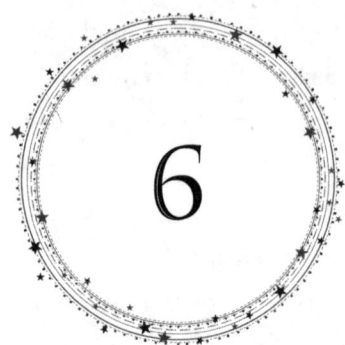

6

A weight built in my chest, dragging my heart into the pit of my stomach. "What do you want?"

The Bonecutter had been prepared for this moment—the ask was already poised on the tip of her tongue. "I would like your Hand of Glory, little Lark."

Panic fluttered through me. The lie was instinctive, born of a life with few possessions, and fewer true valuables. "I don't have it anymore."

The Bonecutter looked utterly bored. She jutted the small point of her chin toward the workbag at my side. "Yes, you do. I can scent it."

"Great." I grimaced. "Now I just feel bad that you've had to smell him this whole time."

"You should," the Bonecutter said. "He reeks of burned hair and fatty meat. Do we have a deal?"

I didn't move. My thoughts raced, trying to outrun my heart.

"That fetid thing crawled out of a dark pit," Caitriona said. "Get rid of it."

Defensiveness prickled my every nerve. "He's not that bad—"

Emrys let out a laugh of disbelief.

"No one asked for your opinion." I turned and glared at him.

He held up his hands. "Please, continue debating. We have all the time in the world to stand here while you attempt to process human emotions for the first time."

We'd bickered and fought countless times, and I'd certainly launched some magnificent insults his way in the past. But . . . the casual cruelty of his words stung like the kiss of a knife to my throat, and for a moment I couldn't speak. I stared at him, at his perfect, beautiful face, and felt a new cold gather on my skin.

His haughty expression dimmed, his eyes softening even before Olwen moved to slap him upside the head. I almost let myself believe he regretted it.

Neve grabbed my hand between hers, drawing my focus back to her face. The understanding only made me feel worse.

"Far be it from me to speak ill of your creepy little friend," she said, "but weren't you convinced he was trying to escape your bag to smother you the other night?"

"Okay, *fine,* he's horrible and may be some sort of cosmic punishment Fate has inflicted on me for wrongdoings in a past life," I said. "But he's still useful. He can unlock any door, remember?"

"You travel with a sorceress," the Bonecutter said. "Can she not unlock doors? Could the priestesses not be of assistance?"

"I have relinquished my magic," Caitriona said.

The Bonecutter, for the first time in our short acquaintance, seemed somewhat nonplussed. "I hadn't taken you for a fool. How does rejecting your gift punish the one who gave it to you?"

Caitriona didn't offer an answer. The Bonecutter's dark curls gleamed as she shook her head and simply moved on.

"The Hand of Glory?" she prompted.

"It's . . . ," I tried again, but couldn't think of any other word to express the apprehension swarming in my gut. "It's mine."

"Actually, it was *mine* to begin with," the Bonecutter said. "Your guardian bought it from me years ago."

My hands gripped my elbows. I could feel the others' gazes on me, waiting.

"Tamsin?" Olwen queried into the long silence that followed.

"I'm just . . ."

I drew in a deep breath. *Being an idiot,* my mind finished.

It was stupid—so stupid—to hesitate this way. We needed the Bonecutter to repair the vessel. We needed to know what memory Lord Death had tried to hide, and if it could help us destroy him.

So why was my stomach in knots? Why couldn't I slow my racing thoughts?

"I see fear in your eyes," the Bonecutter noted. "Curious, that. Are you concerned you may lose the One Vision and need him again? That you might return to who you were before?"

The questions gave my fear a name, a face, a razored edge.

"Impossible," the Bonecutter said. "You have passed through the threshold of the One Vision, and you cannot go back. Trust that the person you were was left behind at that door. You will never be her again. Forward, little Lark."

You will never be useless or helpless again, my mind whispered. *You will never be left behind.*

I rubbed my nose, swallowing. "Fine. You can have him."

I pulled Ignatius from my bag one last time, unraveling the purple silk to set him on the table. I didn't understand the small swell of sadness as I stepped back. I'd been a hostage to this lard-dipped fiend, forced to rely on him to survive.

The Bonecutter picked him up by the iron candlestick holder, looking distinctly unimpressed by that "improvement," as well as the state of him.

The bulging pale blue eye blinked open at the center of the palm, scanning the world around it until it landed on the Bonecutter. The eye widened, and then his whole being began to tremble—not with fear, but utter joy. *Adoration.*

And just like that, my sadness evaporated.

"Yeah, good riddance to you, too," I muttered. "Thanks for the memories, you wick-brained creep."

A bell rang upstairs—then rang again, and again, and again, more insistent the longer it went unacknowledged.

"Well?" the Bonecutter said, laying out her work instruments. "Is anyone going to get the door?"

I exchanged a glance with the others. Neve shrugged. I didn't see a reason not to either.

Emrys stepped aside to allow the rest of us to pass, lingering in the dark until the Bonecutter said, "Come here, Dye. I've use for your delicate hands. Little Lark, take that bag up with you—yes, the one staring you in the eye."

I picked up the brown paper bag on the nearby shelf, surprised by its weight. The Bonecutter murmured something behind me and Emrys answered, his voice low and rumbling.

At the sound of the pub door opening, I turned and raced up the stairs two at a time, and emerged from the workshop like a traveler returning from the Underworld.

The woman seemed to unfurl from the night itself, her heavy steps and walking stick banging out a loud tattoo on the floor. With her riot of silver-streaked dark hair knotted into a lopsided mound on her head and the withered leaves caught on her shabby cloak, it looked as if she had come stumbling out of some ancient wood.

Caitriona shut the door and locked it behind her, her hand hovering over the knife hidden under the sleeve of her shirt.

"They've got what you asked for, Hem!" the Bonecutter called from downstairs.

"The old bag can't be bothered to come up and give it to me herself, I see," the new arrival said, enjoying our reaction to the name *old bag*. She eyed each of us in turn, her face streaked with soil, as if she'd been gardening under the cold moonlight.

At last, she turned toward the bar and shouted down, "The whole list?"

"Yes, you withered bat," the Bonecutter called back. "I even strung the protective wards from the temple on Delos for you, not that you'll pay me for my time!"

"That it?" the woman asked, crooking a finger at me.

I handed it over, watching as she rummaged through the bag, nodding as she silently counted the items inside. Reaching into the inner pocket of her cloak, she retrieved a bundle of dried herbs. They had a sweet, floral scent, but I held them by the tips of their stems anyway, not letting any other part of the plants touch my skin or clothes. You never really knew with this kind of thing—it could just as easily be the starter for poison as a relaxing salt mix for the bath.

"Are you a sorceress?" Neve asked, unable to keep the note of eagerness out of her voice.

"Did the mystical aura give it away, or was it the wart on my nose?" the woman shot back. "Yes, child. Much to the Sistren's chagrin, I was once called the Sorceress Hemlock."

I opened the archive of my mind and sorted through it until I found the pieces of her story and began to assemble them. Her swift, glorious rise among the ranks of sorceresses to vie for High Sorceress . . . and an even swifter inglorious fall.

I snapped my finger, pointing at her. "The Mouse Shepherdess."

Neve whirled around, horrified. *"Tamsin!"*

"It's all right," Hemlock said with a deep chuckle, folding the bag's opening over. "I've been called worse for some of my ideas, and pushing for the Cunningfolk to have a voice on the Council of Sistren is one I take pride in. As good a reason as any to be expelled. The problem with being before your time is that you almost never get to see the moment you transform from fool to hero in others' eyes."

"You were expelled from the Council?" Neve asked, shocked. "For *that*?"

"Are you one of the Sistren?" Hemlock asked Neve. "You seem a bit too free-spirited for it, I must say. Unless they no longer seek to crush their maidens into the same mold."

"I'm self-taught," Neve admitted.

"Ah, no provable bloodline, or were they merely feeling especially callous that day?" Hemlock asked.

Neve toyed with the end of one of her braids. "The first."

"Well, you'll be better for it," Hemlock told her, with surprising sympathy.

"What do you mean?" Olwen asked, curious.

"Only that her learning won't be limited to what they wish her to know," Hemlock said. "Breaking away from their rigid system of sigils allows for the Goddess to manifest more strongly in our intuition, allowing new depths of power to be discovered."

Neve's expression sharpened with interest. I knew she was thinking of the light, and the way the sorceresses had reacted. "You really believe so?"

"I know so," Hemlock said. "That's why the priestesses of Avalon called upon magic in whatever way innately spoke to them—forgive me, I'm telling you what you already know, aren't I?"

Olwen smiled sadly.

"Even I get the occasional scrap of gossip thrown to me when it's juicy enough," Hemlock said. "Terrible trouble you've found yourselves in, my girls. Enough to win yourselves your own unflattering nickname."

It seemed we were all too tired and heartsick to explain ourselves again.

"Lord Death is hunting sorceresses," Neve said. "Wouldn't it be safer to see if you can rejoin the others?"

"I'll be damned before I leave the house I've built with my own two hands," Hemlock said. "I'll fight to defend it with whatever breath I've left in my body."

She held up the bag from the Bonecutter to emphasize her point.

"Then you'll die," Caitriona told her plainly. Leaning a hip against the bar, she crossed her arms over her chest.

"So I will," Hemlock said, turning toward the door. "Tell that fawn-faced ninny to burn my body when it happens."

"Don't say that," Neve said. "You can still go to your sisters. They need your help as much as you need theirs."

"It doesn't work that way with the Sistren, though I wish it did,"

Hemlock said. "I meant what I said before, about my body. You live as long as I have, and you'll find it best not to leave anything unspoken."

"Please," Neve tried again.

Hemlock stood in the doorway. Cold wind swept in around her, but the goose bumps on my skin had nothing to do with its icy kiss. "Have heart, sweet sorceress, but say your goodbyes while you have the chance."

7

It occurred to me as I stood at the window and watched Hemlock's shadowed form hurry down the path that Emrys still hadn't come upstairs.

As the minutes passed and we couldn't hear a word of whatever they were speaking about, I became even more suspicious. He could be getting answers to questions we didn't yet know to ask. He could be bartering for information, and we wouldn't know until it was too late.

Leaving Neve, Caitriona, and Olwen to find wherever Griflet was hiding and debate about where we'd stay that night, I took the opportunity to bring Hemlock's payment back down into the workshop.

I kept my footsteps light, the way Nash had once taught us, hoping to catch snippets of their conversation, but the last step announced my arrival with a squeal. The Bonecutter didn't look up from her work at the table, but Emrys did, his gaze skimming over me. He stirred the contents of the small cauldron beside her, careful to alternate clockwise and counterclockwise strokes.

In addition to the lamp, the Bonecutter had placed a large magnifying glass on a stand hovering over the remaining skull fragments. Using forceps and a remarkably steady hand, she picked up a needle-thin piece of bone and carefully placed it in one of the remaining holes of her puzzle. The jaw and the curve of the skull were starting to take shape.

When she finally looked at me, it was through the purple lenses of her glasses. I held out the bundle of herbs by the twine holding them together. "How come she gets to pay you in weeds?"

"Perhaps I like her better than you," the Bonecutter said. "All right, Dye, I've finished with you. Take the others upstairs to the flat—if you must sleep here, I'll not have you mucking about in my pub. And tell them if they want food, they'd best leave the money for it on the counter."

Emrys released the shard of bone he'd been holding, lowering the instrument onto the table slowly, as if waiting to make sure the piece would stay in place.

I stepped forward at the exact wrong moment as he passed by, and a flutter of warmth moved down my arm as it brushed his.

He stopped, drawing in a deep breath. "Agrimony, comfrey, and . . . violet."

"Show-off," I grumbled.

He left with a ghost of a smile.

"You can set the herbs down over there." The Bonecutter gestured behind her, and it took me more than a few moments to spot the table beneath a massive pile of rolled carpets, drapes, and tapestries.

I circled the workshop toward her, eyeing the way she dipped the edges of a bone shard into a black pot of something. She paid me no mind as I leaned over her shoulder to investigate it. The ground seemed to vault up beneath my feet. I drew back.

Silver.

The liquid was a glistening, molten silver. Exactly like the cauldron I'd found in the tower of Avalon.

"That's . . . ," I began, my mouth dry. "That's death magic."

"Of course," the Bonecutter said, looking at me like I was the child. "Vessels are created using it, and they must be repaired with it. What did you think I would use?"

It felt like there was a hive of bees in my chest. Like my tongue had swollen and turned to stone. The Bonecutter set her delicate instruments down, and her stool creaked as she turned toward me.

I saw my frightened face in the lenses of her glasses. My stomach knotted.

"Are you quite all right?" the Bonecutter asked. "Please sit before you crack your skull open and spill your brains onto the floor. I've only the patience to fix this one."

I shook my head, trying to catch my breath. "You work with him—you worship Lord Death—"

"And *you*," she answered, with an edge of irritation, "are being quite ridiculous."

She pulled a small, sweet-smelling sachet out of a drawer under the worktable and shoved it into my hand. "Take a deep breath, will you? Have a few, even."

I hesitated, but even without bringing it close to my face, the earthy scent was dulling the jagged edges of my fear and slowing the dizzying march of my thoughts. When I was sure I wasn't being poisoned, I inhaled deeply, letting its scent cool the fires that burned in my lungs.

"Better?" she asked.

I felt humiliated that she'd seen me react this way. I was still shaking like a damn mouse beneath a cat's paw.

"Listen to me closely, little Lark," the Bonecutter began. "I do not worship Lord Death. I am a servant to no king or god. Despite what he'd have you believe, he does not control access to *all* death magic everywhere, only Annwn's supply of it."

"So he really is a god?" I asked, my voice tight.

"No, but something like it," the Bonecutter said. "He's one of the Firstborn, the earliest race created by the Goddess. Immortal, and bloody difficult to kill, but not entirely impervious to death."

"I've never heard of the Firstborn before," I said, feeling calmer as my mind finally focused.

"You have, though likely by a different name," the Bonecutter said. Her voice, so melodic, was oddly suited to telling stories. "Some call them the Tuatha dé Danann, the Aes Sídhe, or, in this part of the isles, the Tylwyth Teg. I've even heard them called the Gentry by the especially superstitious."

"Aren't those all different kinds of fairies?" I asked.

"You can call them fairies, I suppose. They once ruled over all of the Fair Folk," the Bonecutter said. "They were given a special piece of the Goddess's magic to aid them. Yet they left our world to create their own—the Summerland—long before the tides of beliefs changed and hostility toward magic grew."

"Right." I knew of that Otherland, at least, and I already knew why Lord Death hadn't joined them there. "Lord Death was forced to rule Annwn as punishment for something—do you know what that was?"

"I haven't the slightest clue," the Bonecutter said, though that seemed impossible to me. "But if you're intent on understanding death magic, you must first understand that there is magic in all our souls. That is our spark of life. If nothing interferes with it, that spark will continue from one lifetime to the next, persisting. But the souls brought to Annwn are different—twisted, cruel, corrupted by darkness long before they arrive."

"And bringing them to Annwn takes them out of a cycle of reincarnation in our world," I finished.

"Yes, but they're brought there to serve another purpose as well," the Bonecutter continued. "When you call on death magic, you sap that power from the wicked dead—their souls. As long as those malevolent souls exist in a world, as they do in ours, anyone can call on death magic, provided they know the rituals involved."

"And you know them," I said.

"I do," the Bonecutter said. "And the knowledge will die with me. While no magic is inherently evil, death magic has a corrupting effect with too much use."

"So Lord Death wasn't always like this?" I asked in disbelief.

"The Goddess saw fit to give him her power to manipulate shadows, as if recognizing the way they called to him," the Bonecutter said.

"But that inclination toward evil has only grown now that he commands the full might of Annwn's power."

A cold kiss of ice touched my skin as realization set in.

"That's the real purpose of the Wild Hunt," I said quietly. "He needs to collect the wicked dead to add to his power."

Tales of the hunting party of ravenous spirits and other supernatural beings roaming the world in search of souls to spirit away existed across many cultures, with good reason.

"Yes, his Winter Host," the Bonecutter said. "The whispers say its horn echoes again through the night. That the wrath of winter has returned to this world once more."

I pressed the back of my hand to my mouth, staggered. The night before, in Boston, we'd heard it, hadn't we? That strange, unearthly bellow that had dug its claws into my awareness, that had sent the man claiming to be Nash running with a warning for us to do the same.

The night the Sorceress Stellamaris and four others had died by Lord Death's hand.

"Have you heard it?" the Bonecutter asked quietly. "The herald of death? It has been centuries since he assembled the last ride, leaving countless wicked spirits to roam free."

Likely owing to Lord Death's imprisonment in Avalon during that time.

"Yes," I said. "But the Wild Hunt isn't collecting the dead. It's hunting sorceresses."

"Then what was prophesized has finally come to pass," the Bonecutter said, stirring the small pot of molten silver with a glass spoon.

I nodded toward the pot in front of her. "In Avalon I saw that same silver inside a cauldron. What is it?"

She motioned me closer. "What you see is death magic distilled into physical form."

When I looked up from it, I caught her studying me, her expression pensive.

"Why can I see it, but others can't?" I asked.

"That question," the Bonecutter said, "you'll need to ask your guardian."

I blew out a hard breath, trying to avoid thinking about Nash and what he'd told me back in Boston. "I'd have better luck interrogating the wind."

She arched a brow. "Where is he, anyway? I heard he was knocking about again, and I would have thought he'd keep you close."

I shook my head. "All I know is that he's doing what he always does: taking care of himself and leaving me to take care of everything else."

"Ah. Including your brother," the Bonecutter said, taking up the next bone shard.

I looked over sharply.

"The Dye boy told me."

Of course he did.

"Now, now, none of that," she said. "He owed me a favor and it was that or disposing of a gentleman who is past due on payment."

I perched on the edge of the worktable, knowing it was pointless to ask her to elaborate, but also scared that she might. The floorboards overhead creaked and squealed as the others moved around.

Her words from earlier drifted back to me like the dust raining from the ceiling. *Cursed child.*

I crossed my arms over my chest, looking to the floor until I finally managed to dislodge the aching lump from my throat. "Do you know anything about my curse?"

The Bonecutter set her tools down and turned the vessel on its wooden pedestal, inspecting her work. The hairline cracks of silver gleamed in the candlelight. "Not much, I'm afraid. Just the implications of it."

I watched, almost mesmerized, as she dipped the edge of a bone shard into the molten silver and placed it, using a whisker-thin paintbrush to smooth and spread the magic. Using the other end of it, she etched in several small sigils and flowing patterns that had been covered by the silver or damaged as the sculpture broke. She was making quick work of it, but there were still hundreds of pieces in front of her.

"How long do you think this will take?" I asked.

"The reassembly will take the rest of the night," the Bonecutter said. "But it'll need another few hours to set, and for the magic to take hold."

I bit my lip. She was working faster than I could ever have hoped, but the thought of spending another day here made me want to slide down to the floor and cry like a child. With every hour that passed, Cabell moved further and further out of my reach.

"You and the others may stay here and keep watch on the pub while I run errands," the Bonecutter said. "It'll be closed tomorrow."

"What? Where are you going?" I asked.

"I've a delivery to fetch," she said simply.

"You're just going to leave us?"

"I didn't realize you required constant supervision," the Bonecutter said.

"When will you be back?" I pressed.

"No later than suppertime tomorrow," she said. "The workshop will seal itself once I leave so you're not tempted to test the vessel before it's ready and ruin my work."

"I wouldn't."

"You would," she said. "You're as impatient as an asp."

All right, yes, I would. "And if the vessel doesn't work?"

"Then no repair will ever fix it," the Bonecutter said. "And you'll have to find a new way forward."

"Great," I said drolly, sliding off the table. If there was no helping the amount of time it would take, I'd claim what few hours of sleep I could. The fact that I couldn't remember the last time I'd gotten more than an hour of rest was reason enough.

"Little Lark." Her voice interrupted my thoughts. "Do you know why this pub is called the Dead Man's Rest?"

"I didn't realize I was supposed to wonder about it."

She hummed again, this time with a warning edge.

"There's a legend in this village that goes back hundreds of years and is still used to frighten children," she said. "On nights when the sky is free of clouds and the moon is high and bright, they say that the dead who perished at sea can find their way to shore again. They can seek a favorite drink they cannot taste, wander the streets with unfamiliar names, and visit the homes that now belong to someone else."

For a moment, just one, I could have sworn I saw a shadow of her true age cross her face. "It's a tale of caution—the very caution I would give you now. We can visit the past, but nothing good can ever come of lingering there."

"I know that," I said sharply.

"Do you?" the Bonecutter asked. "Sometimes we are asked to leave behind not just others, but our dreams of the self we thought we might be, and the life we thought we might have."

"Was that your riddle-me-this way of saying that I should abandon my brother?" I demanded. "That we shouldn't go after Lord Death? I can't do that. Not after everything."

"No," she said. "I mean the life you thought you might have. When you find yourself in the darkness, you cannot stop or turn back, not without losing sense of which direction was once ahead. You must never stop moving forward."

I bit my lip, saying nothing.

"Grieve it, little Lark," the Bonecutter said. "Grieve what's been lost and keep your gaze fixed on what might yet be. But in the meantime, I must kindly ask that you get the hell out of my workshop."

8

The second floor of the pub was an empty apartment with a few broken antique chairs, begging the question of where the Bonecutter actually lived.

The bathroom, at least, had running water, allowing us to wash both ourselves and our clothes before changing into the spare sets we'd brought. After Olwen took a long soak in the claw-foot tub, her cheeks regained some of their color and she seemed more like herself.

I emerged from a quick shower to find that someone had lit a fire and gone down to get food. Caitriona and Neve sat in front of the hearth, a basket of assorted pub snacks between them. There were dinner rolls, the remains of the day's fish and chips, and cakes, along with pitchers of water on the table. At my questioning look, Neve popped a cake into her mouth and jutted her chin toward the window.

Emrys lay on the floor beneath it, his back to us. He was wrapped in his blanket, his head resting on the crook of his arm. His face was reflected in the window's glass, strange and ghostly. He could have been feigning sleep, the way he seemed determined to fake everything else, but his eyes were shut and his breathing slow and even.

I was tempted to shake him awake and send him to sleep downstairs, or preferably outside in the bitter cold, but there was some truth to that old saying about keeping your enemies close. At least here, we'd have an eye on him.

Eventually, my hunger overcame my pride and I helped myself to one of the rolls.

"Does he seem . . . ," I began, my voice low, "different to you?"

"Different how?" Neve asked. "He seems his usual backstabby, annoying self." Her gaze slid sideways to me. "We *are* still mad at him, right?"

"Right," I said quickly. "I don't know what I meant." I really didn't. My head was a mess. "Just . . . forget it."

"Can and will," Neve said, brushing the crumbs from her lap as she rose. "I'm going to see where Olwen got off to."

Caitriona tracked Neve's movement down the stairs, her silvery hair glowing in the firelight. Griflet idly toyed with the small bit of string that had pulled from the hem of her shirt. She said nothing, but I could tell by the crease between her brows that some thought was haunting her.

We hadn't really spoken about the argument in the apartment; it had been shoved aside by the sorceresses taking us, Emrys's appearance, and our journey here to find the Bonecutter. But now that we'd found a moment of calm, it didn't feel fully settled among the four of us.

What would happen if the vessel couldn't be repaired and we were faced with that same question of what to do next? The sorceresses might not want our help, but Neve wouldn't give up on trying to work with them—all of us knew that. Olwen would try to keep the peace, I wouldn't give up on saving Cabell, and Caitriona would never retreat from her promise to kill Lord Death. A seed of discord had been planted between us, and if we didn't uproot it now, its poisonous vines might push us apart.

Growing up, I'd only ever fought and made up with one person; I knew how to do this with my brother, but the thought of saying something wrong, of messing up my friendship with any of them, left me terrified.

Caitriona rubbed absently at the hollow where her neck met her shoulder, massaging the muscle there. Guilt burned in me all over again; she'd been bitten by Cabell's hound form while trying to protect me, leaving a grievous injury that it had taken the best of Olwen's magic and knowledge to heal. Sometimes, she pushed her physical pain down so deep inside herself, it was hard to see how badly she was truly suffering.

"Does it still hurt you?" I asked. "The wound?"

She shook her head. "No, it's only sore now and then. The skin's knitted back together so well that there's barely a scar."

I nodded, processing that.

"I'm not particularly great at this," I began again quietly. "But are we . . . all right?"

Caitriona turned to me, her face softening with surprise. "Of course. Why would you think otherwise?"

"It's just, things got a little heated . . . when we were talking about what to do?" Why did I feel like such a kid right now? Trying to get the words out felt like the game I used to play with Cabell, where we tried not to step on any cracks on the street.

She braced her hands behind her, leaning back. "I apologize for the harshness of my words in the moment. My focus may be on hunting Lord Death, but I don't want you to think I don't care about helping you find your brother. That I won't do everything in my power to pull him away from Lord Death's influence."

"Oh," I said, releasing a shaky laugh. "Because I feel the same way—I want to help you in whatever way I can. It was only that—and I know this is stupid—I just worried that you might want to leave. Do your own thing, I mean."

"Tamsin," she said, waiting until I looked at her before continuing, "no quarrel will ever be so bad that I'll turn my back on you. None of us would. If we didn't fight, it would mean we didn't care."

I smoothed my hands over my jeans, letting the crackle and snap of the fire speak for me.

"Are *you* all right?" she asked.

"Of course. Why?"

"Your guardian," she said carefully. "What he told us about the curse. Anyone would be anxious to learn such a thing."

Up came the memory, and down I shoved it again, with vehemence.

"I'm fine," I told her. "Nash has always been a liar, and I have no reason to believe he wasn't trying to manipulate me yet again. Even if there's the faintest *glimmer* of truth in what he said, even if I am cursed . . . talking about it won't fix anything. It'll just be a distraction from what really matters."

"You and I are a lot alike, then," she said, rising onto her knees as Olwen and Neve came up the stairs, their heads bent together over something. "Not everyone will understand."

Whatever they were talking about, it seemed a hell of a lot more pleasant than our current topic of conversation. Still, a small measure of relief filled me at knowing that there was at least one person who would never ask me to bare my feelings.

"No," I agreed. "They won't."

Griflet abandoned the string for his two favorite people, nestling between them as they sat down in front of us, forming a circle.

"You may hate this," Olwen began, her voice hushed.

"Tamsin absolutely will," Neve added.

"Wow, already selling it," I said.

Olwen turned her fist over and opened her palm to reveal four bracelets. Four different fabrics had been braided together in a thin band of color—I recognized the blue from the blanket we'd wrapped Viviane's vessel in, and the faded green from the dress Olwen had been wearing when the worlds merged; the white might have been a bandage, but the red . . .

"I traded a piece of information about Avalon for a red scarf the Bonecutter had," Olwen explained. "I wanted the colors of the elements woven in, the way they are when we perform high magic. Braided together, it's stronger than a single strand."

Caitriona's lips flattened.

"I just thought . . . I know that you all have different things you're hoping to achieve, but I think it's important to make a promise to each other that we'll see it through together," Olwen said. "To remind us that no death, no man, no darkness can break us."

Neve held out her wrist, letting Olwen knot the bracelet tightly. She held it up to the light, admiring it, and Olwen beamed.

I went next, watching as Neve carefully tied mine. A warmth spread in my chest at the foreign feeling of it. After a moment, I took the last bracelet from Olwen's hand and tied it around Caitriona's waiting wrist, doing the knot the way Nash had taught me, for extra security.

"Together to the end," Neve said softly.

"Beyond that," Olwen answered.

The lingering worry in my mind eased. We were fine, all of us. And we would see this through as one.

"I'll take first watch," Caitriona said. "The rest of you should try to sleep now."

"Are you sure?" Neve asked.

Caitriona rubbed at her mouth, saying gruffly, "I slept some earlier."

"Well . . . all right," Neve said. "Wake me up in a few hours and I'll take over."

Then we settled in for the night, and our agonizing wait.

The hours ambled slowly by, keeping time with the slow, hibernating pulse of the village. The floor was hard, but there was a fire in the hearth and a roof over our heads, and after years of being made to sleep outdoors with Nash, I would always be grateful for that.

At one point, well after the fire had turned to embers, the pub's door unlocked, scraped open, and locked again as the Bonecutter set off on her "errand."

There would be an assortment of protective wards hidden around the building—maybe even scattered through the entire village. We were safer here than almost anywhere else in the world.

I lay on my back, staring up at the wooden rafters. Neve had been out within seconds, snoring softly—one of those lucky people who could sleep anywhere, under nearly any condition. After a while, I gave in to the urge to look across the room, where Emrys still had his back to us, truly asleep.

And, somewhere between breaths, a dream slipped past my lowered guard and stole through the murky edges of sleep.

The forest tore itself free from the dark mist ahead of me, the thin bodies of the trees edged with moonlight. My bare feet padded forward on the damp earth and I relished the feel of my weight sinking into it, grounding me. Mud and flecks of leaves spattered against my skin and the white satin gown that swirled around my feet.

The world breathed around me, alive. Unseen life watched from the trees. I felt tiny heartbeats as surely as the cold brush of mist against my cheek. The darkness that lay just beyond the edge of sight stalked forward through the ferns and roots like spilled ink.

My steps hurried forward.

The path opened into a clearing and revealed the creature waiting for me. It was as white as the starlight, as the mist. The unicorn's eyes were dark pools as it watched me approach, its horn pearlescent against the night air.

I reached out a hand to stroke its shimmering mane, but it turned away, inviting me to follow.

I knew where we were going then, even before the lake came into view.

The small island at the center of it was partly hidden by the shifting whorls of mist, but I could still make out the barrow. The burial mound of the High Priestesses covered in a blanket of pristine white flowers.

A disorienting calmness overtook me at the sight of it, as if nothing had ever happened here to warrant the flicker of dread in my heart.

The unicorn stopped at the edge of the lake; the water glittered with the reflection of the sky, as though it had stolen the stars and trapped them just below its dark glass surface.

I knelt in the muddy shallows, letting cold water wash up around my knees, turning my dress translucent.

I leaned forward over the water slowly, no longer in control of my body.

My face stared back at me, my eyes wide with terror. I reached up, touching my face in confusion, and my reflection began to scream, to shout something I couldn't hear, couldn't read upon my own lips.

In the distance, through the trees furiously shedding their leaves, a blue-white light billowed up toward the sky.

Protect her, the wind begged in my ears, *protect her, protect her—*

The water roiled, bubbling furiously as if something was surfacing. A hot, sharp pain ripped down my forearm.

Blood covered my gown, dripping into the water and the dirt. My skin fell away in strips, revealing the pure silver bone beneath it.

I gasped, but no sound passed my lips. A bloodcurdling scream split the night. I scrambled back from the water, colliding with something hot and reeking—the unicorn.

Its body was splayed out over the ground, its belly ripped open, viscera spilling out onto the earth. It rotted away before my eyes, the skin crumbling to dust, the muscle withering, its eyes hollowing. And from beneath it, brown vines rose, winding through the exposed bones and braiding back together until something began to take shape there.

A face.

It opened its mouth of thorn teeth and howled.

9

I jolted awake, momentarily disoriented by the firelight and the blur of my surroundings. I pressed a hand to my pounding heart and tried to catch my breath. My shirt was drenched with sweat, but my face and hands were icy to the touch.

A second piercing howl tore through the silence.

A dream, I pleaded as much as thought. *I'm still asleep.*

I might have been able to believe that if Olwen hadn't reached out to touch my shoulder. The pressure of her fingers grounded me fully in the moment and whatever horror it was about to show us.

Caitriona and Emrys were already at the window, pushing the curtains aside to search the night-cloaked street.

"Was that . . . ?" Neve began groggily, rising onto her knees.

"A wolf?" Olwen suggested.

"There aren't any in this part of the world," Emrys said.

The howl came again, and this time, it was answered.

Tenfold.

The baying creatures worked one another up into a feral frenzy. Each yelp and cry clawed at my ears. The reaction in my body was visceral, nurtured by centuries of inherited fear. Wolves had been hunted into extinction in this region; it couldn't be a wild pack. And that first howl . . . There was something about it—something that made my body want to lock up and my throat close.

Cabell.

I shoved up onto my feet, grabbing the jacket I'd hung from a hook on the wall, and my boots, and launched myself toward the stairs down to the pub.

"Tamsin—*wait!*" Emrys moved to catch me, but I dodged his grip and burst into the dark pub. Thunder roared in the near distance, shaking the building in its fist. Glassware rained down from the shelves behind the bar, shattering.

The Bonecutter had warned us to stay inside, but if Cabell was out there, I had to try to find him. I might never get another chance.

I tugged my boots on, not wasting the second it would take to lace them. Throwing the door open, I ran out onto the path. A blistering wind slashed through my clothes as I tried to determine which direction the howls were coming from.

They echoed off the pub's stone walls, heckling, only to disappear again as the wind kicked the snow and loose earth up from the ground.

Caitriona took a running leap down the pub's steps, Neve and Olwen close behind her. I fell in line beside Caitriona, trusting in her tracking ability over mine. We ran off the path where it curved toward the village and instead continued along the rugged line of the coast. The knife in her fist glinted like a fang in the early-morning light.

Loose stones and ice bit at my feet. My eyes stung as beads of hot tears dripped down my cheeks. Caitriona slid to a sudden stop ahead, throwing an arm out just in time to catch Olwen. I forced myself to slow as I came up behind them, panting.

The fierce landscape looked as if it had been cleaved with a giant's sword. At our feet, the ground dropped precipitously in a sheer cliff, whose base eased into a gently sloping hill. Halfway down was the thatched roof of a small cottage. The whole structure struggled against the billowing wind, quivering like a rabbit in the teeth of a wolf.

I shielded my eyes, searching for the way down to it—if I ran left for maybe half a mile, it looked like the slope was less severe and I could wind my way over and down. The howls deadened into a low roar in my ears.

Someone grabbed me from behind before I could run. I hit the ground hard, drawing snow and dust into my lungs. Pain flooded my already aching body.

"Let me go!" I cried, trying to twist away.

Emrys only held on to me tighter, his arms locked around my waist. "Believe me, I wish I could, but for once you're going to have to trust me and just—*look!*"

He spun us both to face the coastline, where the sky over the sea had turned an ominous green. Thick gray clouds there unfurled, spilling out high above the raging water onto the cliffs.

The sky opened, dumping hailstones and ice shards sharp enough to cut my arm and Emrys's cheek. He swore under his breath, releasing one hand to dab at the cut, even as another split open his brow. "Damn, the pretty face was the last thing I had going for me—"

His body was shockingly warm against mine, and in the biting cold, I was too aware of every place we touched, his chest to my back, my arms against his—

"Take your hands off me," I snarled.

And damn him, but to prove his point, he loosened his grip. I felt the change in my balance immediately; without our combined weight my boots slid through the mud and ice toward the cliffs, and the churning clouds.

He shook his head, shouting to be heard above the wailing wind. "You really want to see if you can fly, Bird?"

Bird.

Ice pelted me, catching my chin, my cheek, and still, it took a moment to remember to raise an arm to protect my face.

"*Lark.*" Emrys squeezed his eyes shut, anger sharpening the lines of his face. But it wasn't directed at me, and I didn't understand it. He held out a hand to me.

"*Tamsin!* Over here!" Neve waved her arms above her head until I caught sight of the movement through the blinding storm.

It was the wind, blowing from every direction at once, that made the decision for me. At least, that was what I told myself as I clasped my hand around Emrys's wrist and let him close his around mine. He hauled me back toward him, only shifting his grip so we could both face forward as we fought our way toward Neve.

She'd found shelter behind an outcropping of rock, letting it take the brunt of the battering winds. Emrys held on to me as we ran toward it, and for once I didn't mind—without our combined weight, the wind would have had an easier time of blowing us off the cliffs to our right, into the sea.

"Not to question the immaculate logic of running out into the middle of an ice storm in pursuit of terrifying noises," Emrys said, "but what the hell are we still doing here?"

Neve and I reached out, guiding Caitriona and Olwen to us. Caitriona tried to shout something to us, but it was lost as the whole sky flashed with lightning. A horn sounded, the fathomless call of an ancient horror.

If you hear that sound again, closer than it is now, run as fast as you can.

But it was too late.

They had already appeared.

They rode out from the dark heart of the cloud hanging low over the sea, their ghostly steeds burning with the cold light of distant stars. One by one, they galloped through the air, whooping and shrieking like raiders as they fell upon the cliffs below us.

The breath choked out of me—they weren't men, but hideous creatures in their mold, spun from bone and shadow. The metal of their grotesque spiked armor glowed with the silver magic radiating from their eyes.

A pack of spectral dogs wove between the legs of their horses, foam dripping from their maws as they barked and yapped in wild anticipation, captives of their own bloodlust. The one at the front was larger than the others, its coat a silken black flecked with ice. It was real.

Cabell.

I would have lunged forward, screaming for him, had Emrys not grabbed me again.

"I swear to every god, if you don't let me go—" I began, trembling with anger. Emrys had taken the one thing that would have helped me save Cabell from this fate, and now he was going to block me from reaching my brother?

Like hell he was.

I shoved against him, but his grip tightened, and this time, he forced me to look at him. Forced me to meet his bright eyes. The hail had receded, softening to a heavy curtain of snow that crusted in his dark hair.

Then he struck the fatal blow. "Would he even recognize you? Or would he just tear out your throat?"

He already knew the answer. He saw what had happened in Avalon, when Cabell's curse was triggered. We'd barely survived it.

"You have to stay alive to keep hating me, Lark," he reminded me, close to my ear.

I poured every ounce of my fury into my gaze, even as his grip eased. Even as my body instinctively softened at his nearness, seeking comfort he'd never give. I gritted my teeth as I pulled back, catching Neve's eye, and the unasked question there.

For all the storm's wrath, for all the riotous exhilaration of the hunters, the world went suddenly silent around us.

The final rider had appeared.

Like the others, he was clad in armor, but it seemed to absorb all light, drinking it deep rather than reflecting it. The animal pelts at his shoulders flowed behind him as his horse surged forward. Lightning bolts flashed with every strike of its hooves against the cloud, their jagged shapes mirroring that of his horned crown.

My heart sped until I was sure it would burst. The next roll of thunder felt as if it had been torn from my own chest, the most powerful of screams.

The Bonecutter had claimed he wasn't a true god, but he was a king of another world, and he wore the body of one who had ruled in this one. High on his terrifying mount as he was, that regal bearing was borne out. Here, with his host, he was at his most powerful. He was master and conqueror.

Lord Death.

Caitriona dove forward, but Olwen and Neve gripped her arms, forcing her back from the edge of the cliff. She grappled with them, her face burning red with fury and the belting wind, but the others only held her tighter.

I reached out, gripping her wrist. Keeping both of us there, alive.

"Release me . . . ," she begged. "He's there—I can—"

The hunting party formed a line behind Lord Death. Their horses danced with impatience, whinnying. The hounds circled, snapping at the feet of the riders and tearing up the dead grass beneath the snow. Their sole focus seemed to be the stone cottage at the bottom of the hill.

My whole chest tightened as I realized who they'd come for.

A dark figure that emerged from the front door, wand in hand.

"Oh, Goddess," Neve breathed out. "What is she doing?"

The one thing the Sorceress Hemlock wasn't doing was running. She strode out into the wild tangle of her snowy garden, wand in hand as she squared up against the riders.

"No!" Neve began, instinctively starting to rise.

Lord Death lifted the horn to his lips again, and that eldritch bellow exploded with the first touch of dawn. I covered my ears, but there was no escaping it. I felt its dread deep in my body.

The riders burst forth in answer, their horses' hooves falling upon the earth like drums of war. They kicked up clouds of snow as they barreled past their master, toward the cottage.

The hounds raced alongside them, saliva foaming at their jaws as they bounded across the stones with terrifying ease. The Sorceress Hemlock held her position, her wand at the ready.

"Come on, come on—" Neve closed her eyes and tried to gather the scattered melody of a spell. Her first instinct, as always, was to help others, but mine was to help ourselves.

"There are too many of them!" I told her. "Any spell will lead them right to us!"

And the riders had already reached the fence line of the property.

A scorching light erupted from the boundary, singeing the air with the smell of raw magic and burned leather. I squeezed my eyes shut, feeling the magic of the sorceress's protective wards surge and billow out past us in a blinding wave.

But when the light cleared and I opened my eyes, the riders were still there, their swords slicing through the fence, through the shimmering wall of magic, sending sparks flying with the snow. With taunting shrieks and whoops, they broke through and began galloping toward Hemlock with unearthly speed.

I wanted to look away, but I couldn't—if we couldn't save her, we owed it to her to witness her end.

Cabell broke from the other hounds to snap and claw at her, cutting off her sole path to escape, but there was no need. Hemlock chose to turn and meet her end.

She brandished her wand, slashing the beginning of a sigil into the snow.

Then Lord Death was upon her in a heartbeat, as if even the distance between them had bowed to him. He towered over her on foot, raising a fist toward the sky. The last vestiges of night wrapped around his hand, smearing like ink against the snowy air. She carved her spell in furious strokes.

A strangled scream tore from me as he drove his hand into her chest. Hemlock's body arched back, locking with pain. The air, already sharp with the scent of snow, turned acrid with foul magic as Lord Death ripped his hand back. There was no blood, just a swirl of dark magic as he hoisted something pale and shimmering in the air like a standard.

The sorceress's body collapsed to the ground in a dark heap at his feet.

The riders and dogs alike howled with glee as they circled the cottage. One of the horses kicked down the door and three of the riders galloped inside. When they appeared again a few moments later, a familiar face led the other two back out.

Emrys's hand fisted in the fabric of my shirt, his breathing turning ragged.

"That's . . . ," I began, barely a whisper.

The wickedness of Endymion's hideous visage didn't become him so much as it revealed him for what he was and always had been: a monstrosity of entitlement and unending rage. And in death, he had only become all the more powerful.

If I believed nothing else, I believed the terror mauling Emrys's perfect features. Once so like the man his father had been.

Endymion—whatever he was now—shook his head at Lord Death, saying something beyond our hearing. Lord Death's top lip curled in a sneer as he threw the soul to the ground. When it rose again, it was Hemlock—but not. There was nothing familiar or warm in her face, her features elongating ghoulishly, the way Emrys's father's and the other riders' had.

Lord Death bent to retrieve a piece of the broken fence. A silvery fire sparked at the wood's center as he threw it on the thatched roof of the cottage. It didn't matter that it was coated in ice. Within seconds, the whole structure was engulfed in flame. Dark smoke rose, devouring even the white of the snow.

Lord Death climbed back onto his horse's saddle, signaling to Hemlock and the others. She went mindlessly, falling in line among the others on foot. A sword materialized in her hand.

Snow thrashed against my face as the air whitened. The riders and Lord Death disappeared into the churning storm and were gone.

The smell of smoke finally reached us, and I breathed it in deep, needing to remember everything about this moment.

There was the sound of thunder, of the ever-crashing sea, and when the snow settled, only the body of the sorceress remained to tell of the Wild Hunt's return.

PART TWO

THE MIRROR OF BEASTS

10

The cup of instant coffee in front of me was growing cold, but I still couldn't muster the energy to lift it to my lips to drink. Not even knowing how few packets were left in my bag to waste, not even to drive out the ice in my blood. One last breath of steam rose from it, curling in the morning light. I watched it as I dripped melted snow and mud onto my chair and the floor.

Neve pulled pieces of long grass out of her hair, then braced her head in her hands, drawing in several steadying breaths. Caitriona and Olwen weren't in any better shape; after fighting through the remnants of the storm, and a perilous journey down the steep path, we'd burned the Sorceress Hemlock's body in her own garden.

"Shall we say a few words?" Olwen had asked, once her magic had devoured the last of the mortal remains.

"What's the point?" Caitriona had said, brushing ash and snow from her face.

"She deserves respect," Neve had said sharply.

Rather than slice back with a cutting remark, Caitriona had let out a soft sigh. Her whole posture seemed to relax as she spoke, as if she'd unfastened a piece of armor. "I only meant, the prayers for the dead are to help their souls find the Goddess and be reborn. Lord Death has taken hers. She doesn't need a prayer or song, she needs to be freed of him."

"Then we'll make her a promise," Neve had said. "I vow in the name of the Goddess, on the bones in my bag, on all the fungi in the forests, on the stars that blaze in the night sky—"

"Neve," I interrupted.

"Right," she said. She pressed a hand to her chest and leaned forward. "We'll get him, Hemlock."

"We will," Caitriona said.

"We will," Olwen echoed.

"We . . . are definitely going to *try*," I'd said. Seeing their looks, I'd added, "Just hedging our bets a little here. I have enough guilt about this as it is."

I wanted to be as brave as they were, boldly declaring that promise for the wind to carry to the four corners of the world. After seeing the way Lord Death had bent the storm to his will and had torn the soul out of Hemlock's body, it was nearly impossible to keep my rising doubts at bay. But if they believed, then I could rely on their strength until I did too.

If they believed, I wouldn't run from the pain or struggle the way Nash always did.

"All right," I'd agreed. "We will."

We broke apart, moving through the burned-out wreckage of the Sorceress Hemlock's life in search of anything that could be useful to us. But what hadn't been destroyed by the fire had been shattered and torn to shreds by the violence of the morning.

I stepped out of the remains of her cottage with a heavy sigh. The stench of smoke clung to the air and my skin as I surveyed the property.

A short distance away, Neve and Olwen crouched over something in the snow, their heads bent together in discussion. When I came to stand behind them, I saw what it was: the unfinished sigil.

"What does this part of the symbol mean?" Olwen was asking the sorceress, pointing to several straight lines that jutted from its curling center.

Caitriona's heavy footsteps crunched through the snow behind me, joining us as Neve explained, "You'd include something like that to summon light, but this part, where it curls into itself and then continues straight? That looks like the sigils you'd use to create a weapon. You'd add on a little tail here for arrows, cross through it for a sword . . . so, a weapon made of light?"

She glanced back over her shoulder at me, looking for confirmation. Tilting my head, I could see it. "Agreed. Would it really have done anything, though?"

"If Morgan and the other sorceresses couldn't destroy him with magic alone . . ." Neve's voice trailed off. "Why light, though?"

The Bonecutter's earlier explanation circled back to me. I'd told the others about our conversation, but with everything that had happened, I'd put it out of my mind, even as I watched threads of darkness wrap around his fist.

"He can manipulate shadows . . . ," I said. "It was the unique gift given to him by the Goddess. Maybe it's related to that . . . ?"

"Right," Neve said, her shoulders drooping. "Right . . ."

I knew the feeling, but the sight of her, so uncharacteristically despondent, left me scraping my low reserves of positivity for something to say.

"He *can* be killed," I said. "We can stop him. Hemlock didn't die in vain."

"Is that . . . a note of optimism I detect?" Neve said. "From our adorable doomsayer Tamsin Lark?"

Botheration. I grimaced. "I prefer *misery goblin.*"

"In the meantime, though, what should we do about him?" Olwen asked, nodding toward the lone figure at the edge of the property, gazing out over the cliffs.

The wind ruffled Emrys's hair, wrestling with his soaked jacket, but he stood there taking it. His shoulders hunched, as though he were curling into himself.

"Was that rider really his father?" Neve asked.

I nodded, swiping a loose strand of hair out of my face. If I let myself think about it, if I let myself replay the memory of Hemlock's death, I recognized other faces too. Other Hollowers from our guild.

I just didn't know what any of it meant, other than the universal truth of assholes always seeming to find one another.

"He has reached the end of his usefulness," Caitriona said. "I say we cut him loose now."

Neve glanced at me. "I can't tell what you're thinking."

I sighed. "That's because I don't know what I'm thinking."

I could have said, then and there, that it was time for him to leave, but I couldn't seem to summon the words from the icy depths of my chest.

Where *could* he go? Back to his mother, maybe. Into hiding. Certainly not back home to the Summerland estate, where his father could find him.

Hours later, the question was still circling my mind as I watched him from across the pub. He sat near the head of the bar's dragon, his head braced against his hand. He'd helped himself to some whiskey, but by the look of it, he'd had as much of his drink as I'd had of mine.

"What's on your mind, Olwen?" Neve asked, finally breaking the thick silence.

The priestess straightened in her chair, trying to put on a reassuring smile as she fed Griflet a bit of fish we'd scavenged from the pub's refrigerator.

"I've been thinking about death magic," Olwen said. "The way it transformed Hemlock's soul—it corrupted it, didn't it? I thought he could only collect the souls of the wicked dead, those bound for Annwn."

"He might not be able to harvest death magic from them," I said, "but it looks like his crown allows him to control all souls. Including those belonging to the living."

Seeing the way Lord Death had manipulated the riders and

Hemlock's soul had only deepened my certainty that Cabell was under the sway of his magic.

"Then why didn't he control all of us in Avalon that way? He went to so much trouble to get us to perform the ritual . . ." Neve trailed off as she took in my expression. "I'm not saying Cabell isn't in his thrall. I just don't understand his choice."

"Cabell wasn't . . . he wasn't himself," I said. "He might have been more susceptible to that magic."

"He couldn't have influenced the Avalonians without one of us noticing," Caitriona said, running a finger along the grain of the tabletop. "Especially one of our sisters."

The ghost of that word, *sisters,* haunted the silence that followed.

"I don't know," Olwen said, with an apologetic look at me. "If he could master souls within our living bodies, why would he need to kill Hemlock to add her to his ranks?"

The question left a queasy feeling in my stomach. "Because he wants revenge. He wants to humiliate the sorceresses the way they humiliated him. He wants to kill them. There are a million reasons."

Caitriona's skeptical grunt carried just as much meaning as if she had put her disbelief into words.

"What?" I pressed her, that same sinking feeling from our last argument returning. "You don't agree?"

Caitriona jolted with a sharp *"Ow!"* as Neve not so subtly kicked her shin under the table. The sorceress lowered her brows and gave the other girl a look that made *my* soul shrink inside my skin.

"I only meant . . ." Caitriona cleared her throat. "That perhaps there is something in the hunt that . . . calls to the nature of his other self. The hound. And that is how Lord Death keeps his hold on him."

"No," I said firmly. I knew in my bones that wasn't right. "His humanity would rebel against that."

But Caitriona didn't look convinced.

"Are you giving up on him?" I asked quietly, trying not to let her expression crush me.

"No—*no*," she said quickly. "Of course not."

The locks on the pub's door clicked open, finally ending the grim line of questioning. The bundled-up Bonecutter was swept inside by a gust of freezing air, followed closely by a human Bran.

She stamped the snow from her boots and unwound her woolly scarf with one hand. In her other fist was a velvet sack with a dark stain spreading across the bottom of it. The liquid dripped to the floor, but more alarming, the bag's contents were still wriggling around.

I really, truly did not want to know.

Her purple-lensed glasses fogged with the sudden warmth. She lifted them, assessing each of us in turn.

"Got old Hemlock, did they?" she asked, not unkindly, handing her coat and scarf to Bran to hang up. "A shame, that."

She dismissed her companion with a flick of her hand, and he transformed again, scaring Griflet beneath the table. This time, the Bonecutter held the door open for the raven, letting it slam shut behind him. The locks clicked back into place.

I asked the question I should have thought to ask last night. "Do you know what he's looking for? What he thinks the sorceresses have?"

"I'll trade you the answer for a question of my own," she said. "I know that Lord Death's original mortal form was destroyed by Morgan and the others. And so I wonder: Who'd he skin for this one?"

Something in our expressions must have given it away, because she let out a shocked laugh.

"Really? Arthur?" The Bonecutter twirled one of her ringlets in thought. "I always imagined he'd be swollen like a rotten berry ready to burst. Or moldering at the very least."

"No moldering," Neve said. "Unfortunately. Do you want me to get you a mop for that?"

The Bonecutter startled, looking down at the puddle of inky fluid draining from the bag. "I would recommend not touching it, or breathing the fumes in, if you can help it." She held the velvet sack aloft. "I'll sort this out and be back up shortly."

"And the answer to my question?" I demanded.

"Is *no*, I don't know." Her childish voice all but sang the words with glee.

I gritted my teeth. "That vessel better be ready."

"And you better have paid for that food and those drinks," she called back.

Emrys lifted a folded fifty-dollar bill in the air for her to see and slid it toward the cash register.

"I knew we kept you around for a reason, Trust Fund," I said.

A mordant smile touched his lips. In the past, when we'd sparred like this, his eyes would glow with the challenge—it was one of the most maddening, distracting things about arguing with him, the way he seemed to enjoy it. But now, as he gulped down half of the brown liquor in front of him, something in his expression shuttered.

I don't care, I thought. *I don't.*

"Didn't realize your affection could be so easily bought," he said. "Or else I might have thrown a few pity dollars your way sooner."

My hatred was a living thing inside me, but like all living things, it could be hurt, it could bleed. And what he was implying . . . That word—*pity*. It was anathema to my whole existence. In all our sparring, he had never gone so low.

"Do you have a death wish?" Neve asked him without an ounce of warmth in her voice. She rose slowly from her seat. "Because I would be *more* than happy to oblige."

"Shed a drop of blood here and you'll be banned from my pub until the other side of eternity," the Bonecutter warned, but not before Neve had turned and mouthed the word *maggots* to me.

The trapdoor behind the bar swung open as the Bonecutter brushed a hand against the dragon's eye. I tracked the sound of her heavy steps on the stairs, drumming my fingers at my side. A smell like pickled fish wafted to us from the dark pool congealing on the floor. Griflet scampered over, eyeing it with clear interest.

"What is that evil stench?" Caitriona asked, tentatively approaching. "Poison? Venom?"

"We're not going to find out," I said. We'd brought our borrowed blankets downstairs to warm up, and not knowing what else to do, I threw mine over the spill. I leapt back as the liquid tore through the fabric, consuming its fine weave like a flame devouring parchment. A heartbeat later, the entire wood plank collapsed in on itself. A single tendril of smoke rose pitifully from the hole, like a spirit cut loose from its body.

Neve and I leaned over the singed opening.

"Whoa," she said.

"Whoa," I agreed.

I'd half expected to see the Bonecutter's angry face looking up at us from the workshop, but there were only old cobblestones and dirt.

"I'll have you know that blanket was a gift from a Bavarian prince," came the Bonecutter's irritated voice.

"I'm sure your prince can replace it," I said finally.

"That would be difficult, seeing as he's been dead for two hundred years," the Bonecutter said.

Viviane's vessel appeared first from behind the bar, carefully balanced on the wooden pedestal. My heart sped at the sight of it—and stopped dead in my chest as the pedestal tilted and the vessel slid toward its edge.

The world blurred around me, slowing. I felt like I was moving through water, lunging for it. Too far—I was too far.

But Caitriona was there, with all her finely honed reflexes. The skull hovered an inch above the floor, balancing on the tips of her fingers. The rest of us stared, eyes bulging.

"Well." The Bonecutter gave her the once-over. "I suppose I should thank you for that."

But she didn't.

"Allow me," Caitriona said coolly.

"Set it down here," the Bonecutter said, gesturing to the closest table.

She placed the pedestal there and stepped back, allowing Caitriona to carefully, carefully, set the vessel down at the center of it.

Reassembled, the skull looked more silver than bone.

This isn't going to work, my mind taunted. Pessimism rose in me like a drowning tide, and after the night we'd had, I wasn't sure I could keep my head afloat much longer.

"Here," the Bonecutter said, pulling a small votive candle from the pocket of her dress. Today's choice featured a full skirt, this time made of black silk. It only enhanced the feeling that a haunted Victorian doll was staring back at me.

Caitriona's fingers lingered at the curve of the skull a moment before she took the small candle.

Once Caitriona had placed it inside the vessel, Olwen lit the wick with magic. Both drew in a sharp breath as the sigils on the vessel illuminated on the walls around us.

"So far so good," Emrys said, still seated at the bar.

Olwen shared one last look with Caitriona. She stroked the curved edge of the pedestal, closing her eyes with a soft hum, starting the echoing spell the way she had in Avalon.

The pedestal creaked, wobbling slightly as its top piece revolved in slow circles. Glowing sigils passed over Neve, the walls, the Bonecutter, until, finally, it began to spin fast enough that the mysterious language of spellwork turned to rivers of warm, streaking light.

The hair rose on my arms as Olwen's humming turned deeper, raspier. The haunting melody pulled at me, as much a lament as a prayer. Soon the edges of each sound became distinct, turning to words with no true origin or meaning. It was as if Olwen herself were the vessel, conducting the sound up through the ages.

Or from a far-off world.

My heart turned to stone in my chest. I glanced to the Bonecutter, searching for some sort of reaction, but her face was impassive.

The vessel had been created using death magic and a cauldron born of Annwn. Yet Olwen was using Goddess-born magic. It was strange to see the two magics work in tandem, but then again, the druids had once practiced the magic of the Goddess. With vessels, they'd found a way to align the two powers, and that collision—the meeting of death and living memory—was as terrible as it was beautiful.

Olwen opened her eyes, her face etched with an aching hope.

"How do we ask to see the missing memory if we don't know what the memory is of?" I frowned. "There are only a few reasons Lord Death would go to such trouble to take the skull fragment, right?"

"And fewer reasons still why he wouldn't want to crush the bone outright," Caitriona said. "I assume he would have if it had specified how to destroy him. It must be something he believed he'd need to reference again."

"You guys are thinking about this way too hard," Neve said. Leaning down so the vessel was at eye level, she asked, "Will you show us the most important memory of Lord Death you hold?"

The light continued to stream around us, the pedestal's little squeaks the only reply she received.

Nothing. I leaned a hip against the table and sighed. Olwen's lip turned white as she bit it. Caitriona only scoffed, shaking her head.

"Are you sure you repaired it correctly?" Emrys asked the Bonecutter. Rather bravely, given the way she glared at him.

"Oh, my work was perfection, as always," the Bonecutter said. "You, however, have asked the wrong question. Your phrasing is too subjective—a spell can't make that determination. You need to be more precise."

"What memory or memories were you missing until now?" I suggested.

"It's not sentient enough to know that," the Bonecutter said. "Thankfully."

"We could ask to see all of the memories that relate to Lord Death," I tried again.

"There would be hundreds of them to comb through," Olwen said. "He was mentioned in many of our lessons and in song, and I'm still not sure I'd be able to tell which one was missing."

"Oh," I said. "Right."

"What memory is Lord Death most afraid of?" Emrys offered. "No, that's subjective too."

"It is," Caitriona agreed. Her brows lowered in thought. It looked as if she might say something, but she held her tongue in the end.

"What is it?" Olwen asked.

"Viviane was very pragmatic," Caitriona said. "She used to tell me that she and Morgan were one being—her the mind and Morgan the heart. And she always cautioned against acting out of emotion alone, and encouraged us to not be too prideful to ask for help when needed."

"Sage advice," the Bonecutter said.

"Yes, that's all true," Olwen said, "but I'm not sure I'm following."

"By the time the darkness came to Avalon, all of the elder priestesses were gone," Caitriona continued. "And the pathways were closed to the remaining Otherlands. We know she at least suspected it could be Lord Death regaining his strength, but she didn't know how to stop him. She would have consulted the only other being alive who might."

A grin broke over Olwen's face. "Oh, aren't you clever? We'd asked about it before, but there were no memories to echo through."

"Precisely," Caitriona said. "If we find one now, we'll know it's the one Lord Death tried to hide."

"This all sounds very exciting," Emrys said. "But can you please share with the rest of the class?"

Caitriona turned back toward the vessel. "We would like to see all of Merlin's prophecies about Lord Death."

"Close your eyes," Olwen instructed us.

My gaze drifted toward Emrys, drawn by some self-destructive impulse, but his eyes were already shut and I followed suit.

When Olwen began to hum again, the song seemed to sink through my skin, echoing in the marrow of my bones. A warm trilling sensation raced up my spine.

The shadows behind my eyes lingered. My fingers curled at my sides, until my ragged nails bit into the flesh of my palms.

This isn't working, I thought miserably.

Which, of course, was when I heard it.

The sound of footsteps scuffing along stone. The drip of unseen water. A wick catching fire and flaring to life.

The underpath below the tower revealed itself in silky brushstrokes all radiating from that single shivering light. Then came the ivory hand that held it, the skin fragile enough to see blue veins running over the back of it. And, finally, the woman herself. Olwen made a pained sound at the back of her throat.

Her face was only partly visible beneath the hood of her midnight-blue cloak as the woman strode forward down the dark corridor. Her features were handsome but had been softened by time. Strands of snow-white hair had escaped the long braid over her shoulder.

The tangle of roots along the floor and walls retreated in her presence, slithering back along the stones like humbled serpents. She hastened her steps toward her destination.

Drawing in a deep breath, she waited for the wall of roots guarding the entrance to the side path to part and made her way toward the dark shape ahead. The bark of the Mother tree shifted as the body trapped inside twisted, pushing out against the softened wood and sap to face its visitor. The white orbs of his eyes flashed in the dark. The snap of the bark as the creature forced his mouth open sent a shudder down her spine.

"Is it the shadows . . . or do my eyes deceive . . . ," the creature rasped. "Is it Viviane of Avalon . . . stooped and weary with age?"

"Merlin." Her tone was withering. "My, how you've . . . festered."

"I have called before . . . and yet you did not come . . . ," Merlin continued. "I spoke your name . . . to the shadows . . . but they did not . . . bring you to me."

"I've had better things to do than listen to the last of your mind rot," she said primly. *"But I've use for you now."*

He gave an awful, wheezing laugh.

"What knot can . . . the great Viviane . . . not unravel . . . that she must now . . . seek the help . . . of one . . . such as me?" Merlin grated out. *"Perhaps the darkness . . . that seeps through the isle . . . ? The poisons drunk deep by the roots . . . ?"*

Viviane was a tall woman and she held herself like a queen. But the question made her shrink back in alarm. "It has already reached the Mother tree?"

Merlin said nothing.

"Do not be a fool," Viviane said. *"If it reaches the heart of the isle, you yourself will be consumed by it."*

"It . . . will be . . . an end," he said.

Viviane's expression hardened with anger. "Is it him, then? Your former master?"

"Not master . . . guide . . ."

"I haven't the time to debate your doomed choice to worship at the altar of a false god," Viviane said. *"I am asking you, as High Priestess and the last protector of Avalon, if you—shepherd of kings, keeper of stories, and prophet of dreams—have seen visions of what is to come."*

Merlin let out a harrumph *that expelled several beetles between his crumbling teeth. But the flattery and deference coaxed him into speaking again.*

"I have seen much . . . when the paths turn to ice . . . when the world shakes and weeps blood . . . when the sun is devoured by darkness," he said, closing his terrible eyes.

"More of your infernal riddles," she fumed.

"The worlds will sing of the coming, chains of death broken . . . new power born in blood," he finished. *"You know . . . of what I speak. The end . . . has come. He will have . . . what was once promised . . . to him."*

Viviane drew in a sharp breath. "It will not come to that. Not if you tell me how to stop him. Did you not hear something whispered on the wind? Did the answer not come to you in a dream? You are too clever not to have divined a way to escape him."

Merlin's eyes remained closed. His lips unmoving.

"You have had centuries to ruminate on the way you betrayed this isle," Viviane said, "the very one that welcomed you, when the mortal world would just as soon have cut the heart from your chest. Do you not have any desire for atonement?"

Still the druid remained silent. Viviane wore her disgust plainly, all but trembling with barely suppressed fury. She pulled a knife from her belt, drawing closer to him. "Then I'll carve you out and burn you to cinders, the way I should have done an age ago—"

With a flick of the blade, a gnarled chunk of bark stripped from his cheek and fell to the floor. An oozing pocket of pus and sap opened on his face.

"Is that . . . all?" The druid's laugh was low, pitying. "You never possessed . . . the stomach to do . . . what must be done. That is why you lost . . . Lady Morgan . . . and why you . . . shall now lose everything else . . . you hold dear . . ."

Viviane drew back at Morgan's name, her nostrils flaring with anger. With pain.

"I will find the answer another way," she vowed. "And you—you will continue to be nothing more than a husk of what you once were."

Her cloak whirled over the floor as she turned to go, taking long strides down the corridor.

"Look . . . upon me with despair . . . ," Merlin continued in his harsh, labored voice. "For I am . . . the Mirror of Beasts . . . my silver sings of eternity. . . . as I capture all . . . in my glare."

Viviane's steps slowed, but only for a moment.

"The mirror lies . . . beyond your reach . . . forevermore," he roared after her, malice and spittle dripping with each word. "And you . . . you shall die screaming . . . with all the rest!"

My eyes snapped open as I surfaced from the memory.

I braced a hand against the table as a spell of dizziness passed over me. My mind needed more than a moment to accept the sight of the sun-streaked pub after lingering in the darkness of the underpaths of Viviane's memories.

Olwen wiped the tears streaming down her face, turning for a moment to compose herself. Caitriona looked more rattled than I'd ever seen her.

"Was that the only memory?" Neve asked as the pedestal rattled and slowed to a stop. The vessel stared back at us with its hollow eyes, the manifestation of Merlin's final promise.

"I think the better question is," I began with a calmness I didn't quite feel, "what, in all the many hells, is the Mirror of Beasts?"

11

There are few things more vexing in life than questions without obvious answers, and stories without ends. When confronted with such a mystery as this, there was only one place I wanted to go.

The guild library was hushed with night, lit by the cozy glow of the fireplace and lamps scattered across the worktables and bookshelves. With the time change, it was just past midnight—my favorite time of day to visit.

It wasn't unheard of for the other Hollowers in the guild to stay into the small hours of the morning conducting their own research, drinking to the good old days, or showing off their latest finds, but after what we had seen of the Wild Hunt, the emptiness of the old town house was telling, and ominous.

"Oh, *wow*," Neve breathed as she stepped out of the atrium and into the main collection. The dark wood around us had been recently polished and now had a princely gleam.

I felt proud myself, and strangely happy to show them another piece of my life, regardless of the circumstances.

Olwen studied the stained-glass windows along the back walls, fascinated, but Caitriona only had eyes for the central display case.

"That's Goswhit," Emrys said, hovering behind her. "The helmet that King Arthur inherited from his father, Uther Pendragon."

Scarred and dented as the helmet was by an untold number of

blows, it was hard not to feel disappointed by how shockingly ordinary the relic looked. Whatever magic had once been attached to it had been removed or faded in time.

"Found by Eos Dye," she read from the placard. "Any relation?"

"Grandfather," Emrys said. "Got clobbered by a skull-crushing curse while retrieving it, ironically enough."

"Shame you weren't with him," I muttered.

Every rational part of me had screamed to ditch Emrys back at the Bonecutter's pub, but I couldn't bring myself to fight another losing battle. He'd know where we were headed, and he'd follow. If nothing else, at least I'd be able to keep an eye on him.

There was no doubt in my mind that he had another purpose in all this, and I was going to find out what it was and block it if it was the last thing I did in this world.

"Are these all Immortalities?" Neve asked from behind a nearby shelf. "Your guild has been hoarding all this knowledge for *how* long, exactly? Do the Sistren know?"

"Those are actually Hollower journals, but if you'll allow me, I'll give you the grand tour of the place, including where to find the Immortalities," Emrys said. His courteous flourish set my teeth on edge.

Olwen and Caitriona went with them, disappearing past the shelves of folklore and fairy-tale compendiums, around the fireplace and plush leather chairs, and vanished into the stacks of the next room.

I didn't have the heart to tell them they wouldn't find anything about the Mirror of Beasts in those Immortalities. I'd read all of them, even the delicate ones on the verge of crumbling to dust, and the name didn't appear anywhere.

To my surprise, the Bonecutter had seemed just as perplexed by the mirror as the rest of us. Or maybe she knew we couldn't afford to pay for her help. The vessel hadn't contained another memory about the Mirror of Beasts—because of course not. Not having a safe place to keep it, and using the opportunity to cross off one of the many favors I owed her, we let the Bonecutter keep Viviane's vessel in her workshop to explore the High Priestess's memories, with the promise that we'd have access to it as needed.

The library cats hissed ominously as I passed, their eyes glowing from the darkened shelves. Two of them, Titan and Duchess, leapt down from the stacks of seventeenth-century maps, their tails flipping back and forth with unspoken threat. Griflet burrowed as deeply as he could into the pocket of my jacket, trembling.

"Oh, lay off, you demons," I told them. "I bottle-fed you when you were barely bigger than my thumb."

They jumped onto a nearby table and sat, their tails lashing, as I followed the sound of a vacuum cleaner in an adjacent room.

I slowed as I passed the wall of wooden lockers. Someone, correctly assuming the worst, had put up the customary black crepe mourning panels on Septimus Yarrow's and his men's. I ripped them down and stuffed them into the nearest trash bin.

Librarian was vacuuming happy little circles into the carpets, blissfully unaware that the majority of the guild appeared to have joined an undead host.

Seeing me coming, Librarian switched the device off and began to wind its long power cord around the handle. It occurred to me that we could probably afford to get the automaton a better, nicer one without the nuisance of a cord, but he'd never take it. Librarian liked to preserve traditions, not reinvent them.

I warmed at the sight of him, my throat thickening. It was silly, but I hadn't realized how badly I'd wanted to see him until this moment, and what a relief it would be after what we'd been through. His forever-unchanging bronze body, his placid expression that felt understanding at times, and absolutely murderous when you broke a rule. The consistency of him in a world determined to turn itself upside down and inside out made my eyes sting.

"Good evening, young Lark!" he chirped.

It was still a shock to hear his voice rendered in English by the One

Vision after years of conversing with him in ancient Greek—though I was still sore about being the only one in the damn guild who'd had to learn it the hard way.

"Good evening, Librarian," I said. "I hope you don't mind, but I've brought a few visitors with me to do some research?"

"Of course, young Lark," Librarian said. "You will have the library to yourselves."

Endymion's wraithlike appearance flashed in my mind.

"Oh?" I said weakly. "Have people not been coming in?"

"Many in the guild have gone to England," he said. "To see what they might find in the ruins that appeared in Glastonbury."

Of course they'd gone to Glastonbury—to the ruins of Avalon. *Of course*. They wouldn't respect any boundaries set up by investigators or researchers as they studied the site. I could see them now, circling the remains of Avalon like the jackals they were, waiting to rip whatever meaty relics were left among the bones. Them, and every other Hollower guild in the world, no doubt.

The thought inevitably stirred up the bloodstained memories of the isle's final days, and made me sick to my soul.

"Are you well?" Librarian asked. "It has been some time since I last saw you."

It had. In the short time we'd been in Avalon, three months had passed in this world.

I cleared my throat, trying to collect myself as I took the vacuum and walked back toward the tiny office he kept. Stashing the device in its usual corner, my heart swelled at the sight of his tidy desk and the shelves of objects lining the wall. Feathers, interesting crystals, lucky charms—all things Cabell and I had collected on jobs and brought back for him.

"You kept them," I said softly.

"Of course," he answered. There was no emotion to the words, but I felt his confusion anyway. "They are treasures."

It was a moment before I could speak again. "I know this is a lot to ask, but could we possibly use the attic upstairs for the next few days—just for sleep?"

"This is your home," Librarian said simply. "It will always be your home."

The irony didn't escape me that an ancient automaton, unpossessed of a human heart and mind, had shown more compassion to two orphaned children than the whole of the guild's membership.

Instead of casting us out into the streets, he had allowed us to secretly live in the attic, had brought us food and water, and had even given us some basic schooling. Maybe he'd somehow intuited that, like him, we were not equal to the other members of the guild and would always be treated that way.

"It will be such a pleasure to sit and read with you beside the fire once more," Librarian said.

I smiled faintly at the thought. Each night, after the last Hollower left, Cabell and I would come down and help him feed the library cats, and then we'd sit in front of the hearth, the three of us, and read to one another. It had been an easy, peaceful sort of existence, the kind I would kill to one day know again.

The thought left me uneasy, but for Cabell, I knew I'd do worse.

He deserved to have that kind of life again too.

Librarian spotted the soft gray head peeking out from my pocket and pointed to it. "A new treasure?"

Carefully, I extracted Griflet from my jacket and passed the trembling kitten into Librarian's bronze hands. Griflet gave me a look of utter terror, but I knew Librarian wouldn't hurt him. He'd never harm an innocent creature.

"The other cats don't seem to like him, so I'm not sure he can stay," I told Librarian.

He gently stroked a single finger down the kitten's back. "It is very difficult when others only see our differences."

"Yes," I agreed.

The quicksilver that flowed in his body whirred softly through the veinlike glass tubes visible at his joints. I stared at it—that liquid—and felt my breath snag as I realized for the first time how similar it was to the molten silver I'd seen in the cauldron in Avalon.

Not similar. Identical.

What you see is death magic distilled into physical form, the Bonecutter had told me. *It can be used for more specific purposes this way, such as the creation or repair of a vessel.*

Or, perhaps, to animate a man made solely of metal parts.

The Bonecutter had claimed that death magic wasn't innately evil, despite its source and the corrosive effect it had on your soul. Seeing the tenderness Librarian showed to Griflet, I was starting to believe her.

"Librarian, have you ever heard of something called the Mirror of Beasts?" I asked. "It would have some connection to Annwn and its king."

"An intriguing phrase, *the Mirror of Beasts*," he said, his head tilting as far as it could on its neck. "In what context have you heard or read it?"

I repeated the prophecy—the riddle, really—from Merlin.

"Though many divinations do not speak in literal terms," Librarian said, "this one does appear to describe a mirror. Would you like me to research it for you, young Lark?"

"I would appreciate any help you can give us," I told him, accepting Griflet's delicate weight back into my hands. "Thank you."

"Young Lark?" Librarian queried as I started to head back to the others. "Is your brother here as well? I would be quite glad to see him, too."

"No," I said quietly. "He's not."

I wound my way back through the stacks, retracing a path I'd taken thousands of times. The smell of varnish and old paper filled my chest, easing some of the tightness there. I slowed for a moment, leaning against a shelf, trying to gather my thoughts. A warm light filtered through the bookshelves to my right, demanding my attention.

The mass of amber had been the entry fee for a member of the guild a century ago, who was remembered only for dying on his first vault job. I wandered over to it, drawn, as always, by its honeyed glow. Instead of sitting on the floor, the way I had as a kid, I stooped down, examining the bodies of the spider and scorpion, imprisoned forever by their fate.

Merlin's words rose again, whispering through my mind like smoke. *As I capture all in my glare . . .*

I straightened, electrified by the realization. I looked at Griflet, who stared back up at me like I'd grown snakes for hair. "It can't be that easy . . ."

The library blurred around me as I hurried back into the central chamber, shooting across the room like an arrow. I was almost breathless by the time I reached the others.

They made for a cozy scene in front of the fire. Neve had taken up one of the oversized leather wingback chairs, her feet tucked up to the side as she pored over an Immortality, devouring each word, oblivious to the way Caitriona was watching her from the tufted couch, *A Journey through Welsh Legend* unopened in her lap.

Olwen sat cross-legged on the floor, three separate books open in front of her, but she was far more interested in playing with a nearby lamp cord, marveling as she clicked it on and off, on and off, on and off.

"*Remarkable . . . ,*" she whispered. "Oh!"

She jumped, first at the sight of me, and then at Librarian as he clomped by across the room. Headed, I knew, to tidy up the atrium before retiring for the night in his office. "When you said he was very human-like, I didn't—"

The words burst out of me. "I think I know what the Mirror of Beasts is."

Neve blinked. "Librarian knew?"

"I do occasionally—like, once in a blue moon—actually figure things out on my own," I said, ignoring the way the library cats were gathering in the shelves above us, hissing again. Griflet burrowed down in my jacket pocket and stayed there.

"Uh-huh," she said. "So what is it?"

"I think it's something we call the Mirror of Shalott," I said. I honestly couldn't believe I hadn't thought of it immediately. "The frame is carved with beasts, of this world and of the Fair Folk."

"Shalott?" Neve glanced at Olwen and Caitriona, who looked just as confused. "Why do I know that name?"

"There's a famous story—a poem—about a woman, the Lady of Shalott," I explained impatiently. This was why Cabell had always been the better storyteller—I just wanted to get to the point. "She was trapped in a tower, cursed to view the outside world only through a mirror's reflection. When she escaped the tower, the curse killed her, and she was later found by Lancelot floating down some river toward Camelot."

"Has anyone ever told you that you have a real way with words?" Neve asked wryly. "I'm so moved, I could cry."

Olwen, however, looked genuinely distressed. "What an awful tale."

"Oh, don't worry. As per usual, the real story is even worse," I said. "Unlike the poem, this all happened shortly after the death of Arthur and the fall of Camelot. The titular lady was a love rival of a sorceress. They both had their hearts set on the same knight, so the sorceress trapped her in the mirror to get rid of the competition."

Caitriona's face darkened. "Oh, really."

"Maybe Miss Lady of Shalott deserved it," Neve said, holding up a finger. "Did you ever think about that?"

"She deserved to be trapped in a mirror's cold void?" Olwen asked, aghast.

"Considering most Immortalities refer to it as 'that regrettable Shalott affair,' the consensus seems to be that she *didn't*," I said. "And that's why someone came around and released her."

Eventually.

A few centuries later.

"Think about it," I told them. "What if there is no way to destroy a soul after all, and that's why the corrupted ones are sent to be imprisoned in Annwn and why Morgan and the others were only able to destroy Lord Death's physical form? Wearing the crown of Annwn grants him unlimited access to death magic there to sustain his soul. Maybe the only way to truly stop him is to imprison him."

"What's so special about the mirror?" Olwen asked.

"What do you mean?"

"What is it about that mirror that can't be replicated by placing the same spells on other mirrors or objects?" she asked.

"Well, if you believe the Immortalities, it's been lost long enough that no one's been able to figure out and replicate the spellwork on it," I said. "It might have been made by the Goddess, or created in—"

I barely stopped myself in time.

But they knew.

"In Avalon," Olwen finished softly. "Or one of the Otherlands belonging to the Fair Folk. They have superb craftspeople."

I nodded.

"*Ooooh,*" Neve said suddenly, slamming the Immortality shut. "What if *this* is what Lord Death believes the sorceresses have? He doesn't know what the mirror is either; he just thinks it can destroy him, so he needs to destroy it first?"

Olwen let out a thoughtful hum. "But Morgan and the others offered him something he already knew about—something he desired so greatly he was willing to let them kill his most loyal servants."

"Good point," Neve said. "Maybe it'll become obvious when we find the mirror—I can write to the sorceresses about it and have them start searching too. Maybe Madrigal would be willing to help again?"

"Absolutely not," Caitriona said. "This is something we do on our own."

"But why?" Olwen asked. "Why not get more people searching for it?"

"And risk them betraying us?" Caitriona sent me an imploring look.

"Sorry," I said sincerely. "But I do think the sorceresses have just as much reason to want him trapped in the mirror as we do. Whether or not they'll actually help is another question entirely, though."

Caitriona sat back against the couch, crossing her arms over her chest.

"Together to the end," Olwen reminded her.

Caitriona sighed and nodded.

I understood her worry. I *did*. But the sooner we or the sorceresses found the Mirror of Shalott, the sooner I'd be able to extract Cabell from whatever magical hold Lord Death had on him.

And never see Emrys Dye's face again, I thought, though it was cold comfort.

"Talk to Librarian," I told Neve. "He has a way of sending letters to the sorceresses."

"Do you have any idea of where to begin looking?" Olwen asked me.

"No," I said. "I've heard rumors that one of the European guilds has it, but nothing concrete."

Puzzling it all out felt good—like we were finally accomplishing something after two days of desperately trying to get off the back foot. But there was a nagging feeling at the edge of my mind that something was missing.

Or not something, but some*one*. The person I'd gotten so used to bouncing ideas off in Avalon, when everyone else had turned their focus elsewhere.

"Uh," I began. "Where's our traitorous not-friend?"

"Emrys?" Olwen asked. "He said he was going to do some of his own research."

"Did he," I said darkly, handing Griflet over to Neve. "I'll be right back."

12

I'd only been down in the library's lowest level once, while playing a game of midnight hide-and-seek with Cabell.

After he'd caught us slinking back up the stairs like the tiny fiends we were, Librarian had explicitly asked Cabell and me not to go down there again. Truth be told, the guilt had been less of an impediment than the steel lock he added. The stupid thing had been vexingly impossible to pick.

This time, the door was left open.

A knot in my gut I hadn't wanted to acknowledge began to tighten. If the little weasel wasn't down there . . .

What does it matter? Let him have run back to Madrigal with Merlin's prophecy. Good riddance. It would only show this had never been about amends. I would gladly be proven right.

I shook my head and stepped through.

Seven years ago, the basement had been crowded with towering stacks of wooden crates and wilting boxes with empty shelves waiting to be filled. I hadn't been able to stay long enough to explore; the chamber stank to high hell of the poison they'd recently used to annihilate the dynasty of rats battling the Hollowers for ownership of the building.

Back when the library was a sorceress's vault, this had been the central chamber, and it still bore some signs of that: the clawed-out curse sigils on the walls, small alcoves where each treasure had been carefully stored, a chandelier made of unidentifiable bones, and a long, winding staircase in the shape of a massive serpent.

I descended slowly, taking a quick look around to get my bearings. It was just as cold and dank as I remembered, but the Dyes had improved the space, throwing old, faded rugs over the cracked mosaic floors and installing candle-like sconces on the walls that flickered on when I passed a motion sensor.

Gone were the boxes and crates, and the empty shelves were now aligned in neat rows, filled to bursting. Immortalities—leather-, skin-, and scale-bound—were chained to the shelves. The air was choked with the smell of decay and old blood.

And there were . . . *so many*. So many more books and Immortalities down there than I remembered or imagined.

The tension in my stomach released with my exhale.

Emrys stood at the far side of the room, his hands braced against a gorgeous old desk. His lips moved silently as he scanned the book in front of him, assisted by the light of a Tiffany lamp.

"You . . ." I stopped on the bottom step, outraged. "You *bastards*."

"That's practically the family motto at this point," he said idly. "You're going to have to be more specific with your grievance."

The sheer amount of material they were hiding down here was staggering, but it was all the more infuriating to know that this collection was just overflow from the even larger one at their estate. Immortalities and relics completely lost to the rest of us.

I snaked through the shelves, trying to capture in my memory the names listed beneath the Immortalities.

"Haven't you been down here before?" Emrys asked, leaving his work to walk along the far end of the shelves, watching me. "I would have thought you'd sneak down here just to prove a point."

"Not since its esteemed days as a rat graveyard," I said. "Was the point of keeping this collection here just to remind the rest of us that we're powerless peasants?"

"I'll try to remember to ask my father that before I eradicate whatever is left of his shriveled soul," Emrys said.

He returned to the desk, and with one last, long look around me, I joined him.

"You can't kill what's already dead," I reminded him. That had been one of Nash's favorite lines during ghost stories.

"I know," Emrys said, running his finger down the book—some sort of log—in front of him. "That's why I think we're looking for the Mirror of Shalott."

My lips parted, annoyance stinging me like a wasp. I moved to the other side of the desk, facing him. "You did *not* figure that out."

He only smirked.

"When did you know?" I demanded.

"I suspected it right away because of all the creatures on its frame," he said, turning the record around and leaning toward me. "But I wanted to find out who currently has it before I brought it to the group."

Liar, I thought, the word echoing in my bones. If I hadn't come down here, if I hadn't seen what he was looking for, would he ever have told us his theory? Or would he have slipped away before we'd realized he was gone?

I held his gaze, suddenly aware of how close our faces were. "Are you sure it wasn't to beat us to it?"

His frown deepened, and for a moment, just one, I could have sworn his gaze dropped to my lips.

I felt that glance everywhere, a flush of heat spreading from my core. Shadows gathered around us until the Immortalities, the walls, the desk, everything but him, faded.

"Were you worried I'd left again?" he asked, his voice low. *Warm.* He was watching me through his lowered lashes, his throat bobbing as he leaned that little bit closer. I barely heard him say, "And here I thought you didn't want me around . . ."

His breath mingled with mine. My heart fluttered in my chest, like a small bird trying to break from its cage. His lips moved, shaping a word without giving it voice.

Real. The word winged through my mind, breathless. *Real.*

But then Emrys straightened, pulling back. Tapping a finger on the open book in front of him, he returned his attention to the page, letting out a thoughtful hum—as if it had never happened.

As if I weren't right there in front of him, like a discarded thought.

In that moment, with the color burning high in my cheeks, I wasn't sure who I despised more: him, for all his little games, or me, for letting him win that round.

I blew out a hard breath through my nose and looked down at the page. It was labeled MIRROR OF SHALOTT at the top, and two different hands had written dates and names beneath it.

January 1809—June 2000 Laurent Perreault, Paris Guild—Attic of home?

Sold August 2000 to Edward Wyrm, London Guild— Rivenoak

"My forefathers may have been at home here with the rodents," Emrys said, "but even I can admit they kept good records."

"God's teeth," I said. *"Wyrm?"*

"Good old Wyrm," Emrys confirmed. "I seem to remember he and Nash had some kind of tiff . . . ?"

"That's a very nice way of saying that Nash used him as a human shield while opening a vault and cost him a kidney," I said.

"Is that all?" Emrys asked dryly.

"It was such a stupid thing for Wyrm to be upset about," I said, glaring at the paper. "He has a second, perfectly fine one."

A smile ghosted Emrys's lips. I forced myself to look away.

"Don't you dare laugh," I warned him. "He banned us from entering Rivenoak in front of his whole guild."

"I know," Emrys said. "I remember."

"You *remember*?" I repeated, feeling the mortification of that moment wash over me anew. "You were there?"

He nodded. "And for the record, he later got drunk and admitted it wasn't Nash's fault at all. He triggered the curse and wasn't fast enough getting away. And Nash let him lie to spare his pride. He's an arrogant ass."

Emrys could have knocked me over with a flick of his fingers. Nash not being at fault for once was one thing, but Emrys telling me that was almost . . . kind, which made it all the more confusing coming from him after the day we'd had.

Well, I consoled myself, the gods might have hated me enough to allow him to witness that first degrading moment, but at least they'd spared me the second.

Emrys's brow furrowed, as if he sensed my thoughts. ". . . Why do I get the impression that's not the only reason you despise him?"

"I need another reason?" I shot back. He didn't really care, and I wasn't about to give him another little dagger to gut me.

I hadn't let myself think of what had happened with Wyrm in years, content to let it melt away in the bitter sea of resentment I felt toward my own guild after they'd abandoned Cabell and me as children.

I was grateful, then, that I hadn't let my guard down enough to tell Emrys the full story of the years we'd lived in the library. How, a few weeks after Nash's disappearance, Wyrm had contacted Librarian, asking if he could come and speak to Cabell and me. How he'd shown up in all of his finery, smelling like expensive wood, and sat with us in front of the fireplace. How Wyrm had told us in a revoltingly gentle voice that we would be coming to live with him at his palatial estate, and wouldn't that be just wonderful?

At the time, at all of ten years old, I'd been willing to overlook everything that had happened in the past because I was so angry at Nash myself, and because Wyrm was promising all of the things I couldn't: that we would never go hungry, that we would never have to sleep rough out in the bitter cold, that we could go to school and not have to travel from town to town every few days. That I wouldn't have to watch my brother suffer, and see every day that I was failing him.

Looking back, I knew better than to believe in the fairy tale he was selling. I really did. But I'd been so desperate for it to be true, to believe that someone could care, and that things could get better for us, that I'd gone along with it. I hadn't noticed the subtle line of questioning about where we'd recently traveled with Nash, about what he'd been looking for, that Wyrm threaded through all of his promises. I didn't know back then that he had been looking for Arthur's dagger too, and that he'd have no qualms about using two children to dig for information about it.

What I knew was that he'd told us to pack our things and wait for him to return in the morning, and we had. We waited all morning.

All day.

All night.

In the rare instances I let myself think about that day, I had to relieve the deep, unbearable burn of humiliation that arrived when I'd finally accepted we'd been tricked. I had to remember the way Cabell had tried so hard not to cry as we carried our things back up into the attic. I swore to myself I'd never let any man make a fool of me again.

And yet there I was, standing in front of someone else who'd played me like a fiddle.

"You know what this means, right?" Emrys began, interrupting that unwelcome descent into memory.

"Oh, I can't wait to hear this," I muttered.

"You've never been inside the estate, have you?" he continued, as if to really rub it in.

"Didn't we just establish that?" I snapped back. Wyrm's personal home also served as the guild's headquarters and library. We'd been banned from ever doing business there.

"Well, *I* have, and I think I know exactly where they keep the mirror." There was an edge of triumph to his look. "So you're not quite rid of me yet."

My lips parted as I scrambled for an argument. The air around me grew colder with each second, as if to help trap me there. "You think we can't figure it out ourselves?"

Even as I said it, my inner logic, rarely heard, whispered, *This is for Cabell.*

"There are only nine days left until the winter solstice," he reminded me. "And you have no idea what Lord Death's plans are. You're—"

He broke off midthought, his head snapping back in alarm. The air spiked with a depth of cold I'd felt only once before, when the White Lady had appeared in the field of blinding snow. Instinct and terror collided, begging me to move, but the death mark flared with such acute pain it felt as though I'd been stabbed there, straight to the heart.

I couldn't move, couldn't breathe, even as the shadows behind me snarled.

Emrys reached out and grabbed me by the jacket, hauling me over the top of the desk to his side as the ghost materialized from the dust and darkness where I'd stood only a second before.

The sight nearly made my bones jump out of my skin.

The woman's long ropes of hair drifted around her, glittering and translucent. Even the dim light seemed to shy away from her, flickering over her face but refusing to linger more than a moment on her hideous expression of hunger.

White, glowing eyes fixed on me with recognition, her lips silently forming the word. *You.*

"What . . . the hell . . . is that?" I breathed out.

The heat of Emrys's body was the only relief from the iciness that filled the air.

"*That* would be the sorceress this vault belonged to," Emrys said, drawing us back. "Enora, what's gotten into you?"

Her features sharpened like a knife, more wraith than human. Dust, grime, loose parchment, scraps of fabric, and fragments of tile rose to form her like clay in a sculptor's hand. They encased her in a hideous skin of filth and decay. Giving her a body.

A phantom wind blew through the basement, rattling the chains on the Immortalities and slamming the door at the top of the stairs. I jumped at the noise, gasping at the sudden stench of ash and a rancid sourness. Flecks of dead earth and wood splinters were still finding her, scratching at our own skin as they tore through the air.

The ghost opened her maw, revealing fangs of stone and tile shards.

Revenant, my mind screamed. She was becoming a revenant.

Her arms stretched out like twining vines, her talon-like nails raking through the air toward my chest.

One of Emrys's hands released me, fumbling with the desk drawer to retrieve something—a clay talisman, with a sigil for protection against the dead.

"Noooooooo," the creature wailed, turning the air rancid with her misery. She lunged toward us, but her hands dissipated as they reached the talisman, clumps of dirt and ash from the fireplace raining down on the desk.

"You *knew* this thing was down here?" I squeezed out.

"She's a shade," Emrys said, bewildered. "She's just a shade . . ."

A shade was a soul that remained in the mortal world, refusing to pass on. It didn't possess the kind of malice or corrupted pain that would produce a more terrifying specter like a wraith or White Lady. Shades were stubborn, not monstrous.

At least, they were supposed to be.

"I've never seen her like this before," Emrys said. "She's helped me do research in the past. She was *charming.*"

"Great," I said. "Now she's a charming revenant who wants to claw our faces off."

He exchanged a worried look with me. When he nudged me behind him, I realized he still had a grip on me. I was too harried, too distracted by the hard throbbing of my death mark, to object as we took a long arcing path around the shelves, heading for the stairs.

The revenant stalked behind us, leaving a trail of grime and soot smeared in her wake.

"That's a good Enora . . . stay back now," Emrys said, holding the talisman out in front of us like a shield. She snarled and snapped like a wounded animal. Her hands hovered inches from my throat, stroking the air, as if imagining how it would feel to shred my soft skin instead.

"Noooooooo," she wailed, almost sobbing as we made our way up the stairs backward, not daring to turn our backs on her.

Her body contorted into grotesque shapes as she climbed on hands and knees behind us, the ridges of her spine rising like thorns. Her jaw unhinged itself like a snake's. *"Noooooooo!"*

Nash's words shuddered through me, throbbing in time with the death mark.

Like spring, you are cursed to die young.

"—sin?" Emrys was talking to me. "Tamsin!"

I forced myself to respond. "What?"

"Can you get the door?" he asked. "She's not going to get out, I promise."

I was embarrassed by how hard my hand was shaking as I felt for the knob behind me. It took another beat to get a good enough grip on it with my sweat-slick palm.

I all but fell backward into the library's marble atrium. The impact knocked some sense into me, and I scrambled back. The statues kept watch as Emrys struggled with the door, with hanging the talisman around the handle.

With a scream of rage and seething magic, the revenant blew it open, throwing Emrys back into the nearby statue of Athena with enough violent force to stop the heart in my chest. The talisman flew the opposite way down the hall, clattering as it hit the floor. My mind tracked the sound of it, screamed at me to retrieve it, even as I scrambled toward Emrys's prone form.

There's no blood, I thought, rocked with relief. I gripped the back of his jacket, shaking him. "Emrys!"

He groaned, but the sound was swallowed by the revenant's mournful wail; she sobbed and screamed until I had to cover my ears. My stomach turned as her cries echoed against the cold white stone, as inescapable as her path toward us.

Toward *me.*

The stench of rot poured from her as her eyes fixed on my face once more, her grasping claws trembling as they stretched toward me.

"*Tamsin!*" Neve's cry carried down the hall a moment before she appeared, her face etched with fear.

"Run!" I shouted back.

The revenant spun toward her, snapping her teeth at the sight of Neve summoning a spell. As her otherworldly song rose, a blue-white light gathered around the sorceress. The words from my dream echoed back to me, haunting and otherworldly. *Protect her, protect her—*

The revenant went utterly still, as if caught in some unseen web. When she spoke, there was none of the mindless rage. There was only terror. "No . . . no . . . not *you*—!"

Neve balked, taking a step back in alarm as ash and dirt dripped off the revenant, crumbling onto the pristine white marble floor. Beside me, Emrys forced himself to sit up, shaking his head as if to clear it.

Ash and dirt and debris fell away from her form as it crumpled, until only the ethereal outline of the ghost remained. *"Not you, not you—forgive me!"*

The spirit flew back toward the door to the basement, singeing the air with the scent of raw magic. The commotion had drawn Caitriona and Olwen, and the sight of them just beyond Neve's shoulder finally spurred me to action. I released my grip on Emrys and ran for the talisman.

"What was that thing?" Neve gasped out as I slammed the door shut and hung the talisman around the handle.

As if sensing me there, the spirit surged forward again, rattling the door, straining it against its hinges. For a moment, I was terrified the talisman had cracked when it had fallen.

But it held. The sigil lit with a cerulean glow, forming a seal around the door, imprisoning her, but not her voice.

Emrys stood slowly, his gaze catching mine as the revenant's screams turned to a lament of desperation.

"Great Mother, I did not see! I did not know! Forgive me—forgive me—!"

Neve's shocked face mirrored my own. She brought a hand up to her chest, touching the pendant hidden beneath her shirt. I knew what she was thinking. I was thinking it too.

What are you?

But when silence finally came, there were no answers to be found there, either.

13

Rivenoak Manor was as impossibly grand as I remembered it, made more so by the dusting of snow and the shimmering lights upon its towering facade.

The palatial home had been an exercise in delusions of grandeur by some Elizabethan courtier who'd had no way of knowing his descendants would be brokers of stolen relics, not power.

We weren't Rivenoak's only visitors that evening. The lit torches lining its long drive and the parade of sleek cars heading toward the house had been our first sign of trouble. It only got worse from there.

Douglas firs had been hauled in to decorate the entryway. Their sweet smell filled my chest as I took in a deep breath. The glow of the party fluttered like golden wings against the house's many windows. Entering its light was like crossing into an Otherland—as tempting as it was forbidden.

My attention narrowed onto the man in a white tuxedo collecting invitations at the base of the marble stairs, at the very center of the circular drive. The arriving guests were kitted out in formal wear, glittering with jewels and warmed by dead animal skins. A black-tie affair.

I glared at Emrys through the velvet curtain of night, shifting so the boxwood hedge was no longer poking my cheek. "Did you know about this?"

"Yeah, of course," he whispered back. "I always try to show up when I'm most likely to be caught."

"Should we . . . come back?" Neve ventured, daring to peek over the bushes we'd ducked behind. Having been able to use the hedgerow along the drive to shield ourselves from the view of passing headlights, we'd finally reached the end of it.

"Can we just go around to the back of the house?" Caitriona asked.

Emrys considered the idea for a moment. "No, the only way to access the library is from a door inside, or by climbing through that window there—" He nodded to the third-to-last one on the house's face. "We have a better chance with the window. We just need to wait for the last guest to arrive—"

Neve let out a soft, pitchy hum, her eyes fixed on one of the decorative trees on the left side of the door. Within seconds, it went up like kindling.

As the man in the white tuxedo and several security guards turned their backs to rush toward the fire, Neve seized the initiative and leapt ungracefully over the hedge, leaving the rest of us to rush after her.

"—or a distraction works too," Emrys whispered, pained.

By the time we heard the hiss of the fire extinguisher, the five of us had managed to crawl into the narrow space between the wall and the wild thicket of rosebushes—though not without a cost.

"Why did it have to be roses?" Olwen whispered, carefully removing thorns from her hands and jacket sleeves. My own neck looked like I'd been in a losing fight with the library cats.

"Ooh," Neve whispered, sliding a hand under one of the bushes to pluck something from the ground. "Herald of winter!"

Emrys whirled around the best he could in the cramped space. "Really?"

Neve held the small yellow-bodied mushroom out for him to see. I snapped my fingers, drawing their attention back to me. "Fungi later. Focus."

A hint of "Greensleeves" drifted through the windows above us, played lavishly by a string quartet. When I turned back to face front, I saw that I'd lost both Caitriona and Olwen, too. They'd stuck their heads up just enough to see through the lustrous glass, to the world of the massive stone hall beyond it, and the sparkling contours of the candlelit party swirling inside.

Several revelers blocked our view, their raucous laughter animated by the light, fizzy delirium of champagne. Their glasses clinked carelessly together as they toasted themselves.

I knew from Nash's journal that the west wing of the grand country home was reserved for Wyrm and his family, the east for the members of his guild, but Cabell and I had been made to wait outside like street dogs, blocked by the pig-faced butler from even glimpsing the foyer. As sweeping and immaculate as the exterior of the house was, it was an appetizer to the feast awaiting our eyes inside.

I drew in a breath as the partygoers drifted apart and the soaring height of the hall revealed itself.

It was impossible to take it all in at once. The hoarfrost clinging to the glass gave everything a dreamy, unreal quality. Guests danced around the frothy towers of champagne glasses, tucked safely beneath the ostentatious stonework bracing the hall like a rib cage. A giant Yule log burned in the hearth, the flames gorging themselves on the last of the ribbons and dried berries tied to it.

"All of this for one family?" Olwen whispered.

I understood her horrified amazement. The tower of Avalon had been enormous, but served a purpose as the heart of the isle and had housed dozens of families by the end. Here, the size of the house was only meant to make the rest of us feel inferior.

Here and there, I saw faces I recognized, from my own guild and the London one—more intriguing were the collectors, the black market traders, and the auctioneers who served as the connective tissue between what a Hollower found and their payday.

I caught a glimpse of lanterns and fur-draped seats, but once my gaze landed on the feast, I couldn't tear it away. A long serving table nearly the length of the hall was laden with immense platters of fruits and cheeses, festive cookies, and bright sweets. My stomach gave a pitiful moan at the regiment of roasted turkeys being carved by the chef. She offered each fresh cut to the line of guests, who carried their heavy plates over to one of the smaller round tables that dotted the space.

Most guests, however, had forgone the food and were gathered around a well-lit case at the center of the hall.

As in my own guild's library, the London guild had chosen to display the relics submitted for membership. A dozen display cases lined either side of the hall, interspersed with windows and full suits of armor. My lip curled in annoyance as I recognized Pridwen, King Arthur's shield, in one; the girdle of Brynhildr in another; and what was rumored to be Merlin's druid spoon in a third. All, however, paled in comparison to the hooded cloak.

It had been carefully displayed on a faceless mannequin, swept out to reveal the woven image of a stag in a flowering forest. The fabric looked unbelievably delicate—as finely woven as gossamer. Certain threads glimmered silver and gold in the light, like winks of magic.

"Arthur's mantle?" Emrys whispered. He met my look of disbelief with one of his own. "They found it? *Wyrm* found it?"

"Why would one of Arthur's old cloaks be worth finding?" Olwen asked. "Unless—you mean the one Morgan gave him?"

"The very same." I sighed. "It renders the wearer invisible. Allegedly."

"I guess we know what the party's for," Emrys said. "And here I was thinking it was just a night of festive fun, when it's actually an expensive excuse to show off his latest find."

"Ugh," I muttered, almost too disgusted to keep looking. "Botheration. I *hate* that he's the one who found it."

"I thought you didn't care about the bigger relics?" Neve said pointedly.

"I don't," I answered, fighting the urge to punch a fist into the ground like a child. "But I don't want him to have it either. He's awful, and not just by my standards. The first time I met him, he told me to look him up in a few years and he'd show me a good time. I was *seven*. And believe me, he only got worse from there."

It wasn't worth going into more detail when that appeared to have sufficiently repulsed everyone. I tried not to notice the way a shadow seemed to cross Emrys's face, or how his hands clawed at the near-frozen soil.

Stop it, I thought. To myself. To him. Once we had the mirror and I was sure Emrys hadn't found a way to swipe it out from under us like he had the ring, I'd never have to see his face again.

"So what you're saying is, you would trap him in a mirror if given the means to do so," Neve said after a moment. She held up her hands at my expression. "Just making a point."

The crowd parted around the glass case, and the man himself appeared.

Edward Wyrm pushed through the guests like a cannonball, throwing his arms out as he regaled them with some highly exaggerated tale of how he'd found it. The din of the party music was too loud to make out much. His white tuxedo shirt strained over his barrel chest, but the manner with which he carried himself was immaculate, as if centuries of noble breeding and besieged nannies had gone into the making of this moment.

His face was even rounder and redder now, and the once-red ring of hair around his head had faded and thinned like a shedding rug. The deep scar across the bridge of his nose, however, was exactly as I remembered it. As he turned toward the fire, a silver pin on his lapel flashed.

As I watched the party whirl by, shining and carefree, a strange melancholy crept up on me. I wondered if this was how the Lady of Shalott had felt, forced to watch the world passing by through glass.

"Come on," Emrys said from the front of the group. "And try not to brush against the wall—there are a few curse sigils carved up near the roof to protect the house from intruders."

We scurried along the edge of the house like mice, until Emrys stopped beneath the window he'd pointed out before. It was higher and smaller than the others along the hall. I looked back over my shoulder, but the arrivals seemed to be winding down, and much of the staff had gone back inside.

The small pouch on Emrys's belt had been hidden by his jacket until he unclasped it and dug around for the crystals he needed. Arranging the amethyst, quartz, and tourmaline in a pattern I'd seen Cabell use hundreds of times, he sat back, resting his hands on his knees. Neve leaned over his shoulder, trying to get a better view of what he was doing.

"When they're in the right grid formation, the crystals work to absorb some of the magic and deflect most of it away," he whispered to her.

"Yeah," she said, "I have eyes."

Cabell was the only known Expeller in hundreds of years. Unlike the rest of us, he was able to use his own innate magic to break the curses in sorceress vaults. Though the work took enough out of him that he often relied on crystals as well.

Hang on, Cab, I thought. As soon as we had the mirror, we'd finally be able to confront Lord Death directly, and end this.

Protective magic hugged the white stone wall so tightly, it was all but invisible, even with the One Vision. It was only when it flowed up and away from the crystal grid on the ground that I saw its iridescence.

I didn't bother to hide my smug smile. Some sorceress had probably charged Wyrm an arm and a leg for this so-so cursework. If anyone deserved to have his finds hollowed from his possession, it was him.

With one last look toward the entrance, Emrys turned his gaze to me. "You can pick a lock, right?"

"You can't?"

His expression turned exasperated. "Are you going to hoist me up there?"

I was tempted to hoist him directly into the middle of the rosebushes—though, knowing him, he'd probably have liked it.

"Olwen and I can help with that," Neve whispered. "We can just manipulate the air to lift us, right?"

She turned to look at the priestess for confirmation, but Olwen's attention was on the long driveway, the darkness between the torches. She fiddled with her braided bracelet.

"Olwen?" I said, touching her arm. "Can you use a spell to get us up to the window?"

"Yes, but . . ." She trailed off. "Are we certain about this? Should we not wait and try another night, when there are fewer eyes upon us?"

"We don't have time," Caitriona said. "The winter solstice is nine days away."

Olwen drew in a deep breath, steadying herself. "You're right. Here, Neve, I think if we focus on creating an upward wind . . ."

Olwen began the quiet song, letting it rise from within her chest like an exhale, as if to demonstrate to the magic what she was asking. Caitriona stayed on her knees, staring down at where her hands were pressed to the earth, as Neve's voice joined Olwen's.

Their songs seemed to dance with one another, harmonizing in a way that might have been arresting, had the air not suddenly vaulted me up toward the window like a springboard.

My rib had been feeling better, but the dull pain stabbed me again as I gasped. The others watched from below, Caitriona and Emrys moving into position beneath me, as if worried I'd drop as quickly as I'd risen.

"A warning would have been nice!" I whispered down to them. It felt like riding a strong sea current; all you could do was surrender and accept the bobbing rhythm of the air. Leaning forward, I could just make out the tops of bookshelves on the other side of the dusty window.

An old window in England generally meant an old lock, and I could tell this one hadn't been upgraded since it was first installed. My smirk returned. There'd barely be any picking involved. Wyrm really had been relying on the curse wards to protect him.

"Idiot," I muttered.

Leaning forward to make sure the library was unoccupied, I pressed my hands flat against the windowpane, shaking it within its frame. For once, luck was on my side. The sash lock dislodged itself on the third try.

The window was as long as it was narrow, swinging in and up. At its terrible creak of protest, I froze, waiting for someone to come running.

When no one did, I turned and gave the others a thumbs-up. Caitriona and Olwen stared blankly, but Olwen lifted her thumb back, clearly having no idea what it meant.

Somehow I managed to go horizontal and drag myself through the window frame. The air released its grip on me, and my body dropped heavily onto the top of the bookshelves, breaking off a chunk of the delicate floral molding.

I winced, holding my sore rib as I carefully climbed down.

One by one, the others entered behind me.

I crept along a section of Immortalities and books of lore. All four walls were lined with bookshelves, and a few rows had been placed at the center of the room.

Their library was smaller than I'd imagined—about half the size of our own, with only a single worktable in front of the cold hearth. A display of old, rusted swords hung above the floral stonework of the mantel.

At first glance, it all seemed typical of what you'd expect from a guild library: its walnut shelving and green velvet cushions, displays of relics proudly stolen. But the London guild was older than mine by hundreds of years, and had twice our numbers. Unless they'd sold the majority of their books and Immortalities, or their members kept them at their own homes, their collection was looking a bit thin.

Suspicion bit at me. This library felt more like a museum than a working space.

They had a number of relics on display in the hall—maybe they kept the bulk of their collection there as well, and set up tables where the light was better and they had more room to breathe?

I brushed a hand along the shelf beside me, frowning as it came away coated with dust.

"Great Mother," Olwen breathed out behind me, studying the statue of the Venus de Milo—the real one. Some gutless reptile in their guild had swapped it with a fake when the Louvre's treasures were removed for their protection during the Second World War, and even after Nash—no doubt inspired by jealousy and not chivalry—reported it, no one came looking for it.

Caitriona bent over a large case displaying one of the earliest known maps of Great Britain. I leaned over it too, unable to resist committing it to memory. The muted carousing of the party on the other side of the wall was a constant reminder of how close we were to being caught.

"What are we looking for, Trust Fund?" I asked Emrys, voice hushed.

"A copy of Tennyson's *Idylls of the King* with an emerald-green spine," Emrys said, still negotiating with the stubborn window to shut it. Neve, betrayed by her own kindness, climbed back up the shelves to help him.

Which was, of course, the moment the library's door opened.

14

The darkness of the library gave us only a moment's grace to find cover before the lights snapped on.

Caitriona and I dove behind the map case, tucking ourselves behind its bulky stand. Olwen slipped behind the statue, pressing flat against the alcove's wall.

"—just take a second—" came a man's voice. The sounds of the party, music and laughter, flowed in behind him. His tone changed in an instant. "What the devil are you doing in here?"

Caitriona gripped my wrist, her gaze meeting mine in silent question. I shifted, risking a quick look out from behind the stand.

"What does it look like?" came Emrys's drawl.

My heart leapt into my throat, fingers curling against the plush rug beneath us.

"Oh— Gods, I'm sorry, I didn't realize—" Judging by his accent, the Hollower was one of the London guild members. "I didn't recognize you there, Mr. Dye."

He was all but bleating with deference, one terrified heartbeat away from bowing and scraping.

"Does Wyrm know you're here?" he continued, his voice growing faint at Emrys's cold silence. "He told me that your father hadn't sent his regrets, so we weren't . . . sure."

Emrys stepped out from behind the shelves, his arm looped around

Neve's shoulder. She leaned her head against him, her arm wrapped around his waist. "It's always fun to keep a bit of mystery, isn't it?"

"Oh, well, yes," the man said, eyeing them—Emrys dressed for a vault job, and Neve in jeans, her sweater, and a dark purple jacket, both a far cry from the black tie the invitation had clearly called for.

I just barely held in a shocked laugh; they'd mussed up their hair and clothing, as if they'd been caught midfumble in one of the library's many dark corners. The Hollower was either too polite or too scared to comment on it.

"This is—" Emrys covered his hesitation with an adoring gaze at Neve, and suddenly, I didn't feel like laughing. "This is Violet."

This is what he does, I thought. *Play pretend.*

Neve took the moment with a cool confidence, dismissing the man's outstretched hand with a single devastating look. "Enchanted, I'm sure."

When the Hollower looked down to collect his thoughts, having clearly forgotten what he'd come in for, Neve shot Emrys a look. She motioned to her jacket, mouthing, *Violet? Seriously?* He gave her a helpless shrug.

"Shall I take you to, ah, greet our host, then?" the man said. "I'm certain he'll be overjoyed to see you again. And he'll want to show you the mantle, of course . . ."

"Fine," Neve said, feigning irritation. "I was getting bored anyway."

Emrys's brows lifted as he swallowed a laugh.

"Right, then," the Hollower said. The silver pin on the man's tuxedo flashed as he opened the door, and Emrys startled. He drew Neve in closer to his side, his hand tightening around her shoulder.

"Some pin you've got there," Emrys said, raising his voice ever so slightly. Meaningfully.

I looked again, squinting to see the pin as the man turned back toward Emrys in surprise. It was a hand holding a bare branch, cast in silver.

The breath stilled in my chest.

It was the very same one I had seen on both Emrys's father and Septimus Yarrow in the weeks leading up to our journey to Avalon.

But the pin and my growing uneasiness were pushed to the back of my mind when Neve caught my eye over her shoulder. As the door closed behind them and they were swallowed up into the festive scene, she tilted her head with a clear message. *Go.*

The lights automatically shut off, throwing us back into darkness. After a beat, Caitriona leapt to her feet to go after them, but I grabbed her arm.

"Come on," I whispered. "Now's our chance."

Caitriona whirled toward me, whispering furiously, "And leave her alone with them?"

"We have to," I told her. "I don't like it either, but she can handle it."

Caitriona remained unmoved.

"The sooner we find the mirror, the sooner we can return for them," Olwen reasoned, though she didn't quite sound convinced herself.

"Emrys said to look for Tennyson's *Idylls of the King*," I said. Unfortunately for us, we had no idea why.

With a hard breath through her nose, Caitriona finally relented, and forced herself to join us as we searched the shelves.

"Oh—here!" Olwen called. She was in front of the bookcase just to the right of the fireplace. Her fingers skimmed along the old cloth spines. And somehow, even before she tried to tug the book free, I knew what would happen.

With a horrible scraping groan, the fireplace—swords, mantel, and all—slid down into the floor, and behind it were the very modern silver doors of an elevator.

"Great Mother," Olwen breathed out, leaning around the bookcase with wide eyes.

"Okay," I said begrudgingly. "That was a little cool."

It was a small lift, big enough for two people at most, and only had a single button.

"I'll meet you down there in a second," I told them, bundling a hesitant Caitriona and Olwen inside. I stepped back to keep watch on the entrance to the library. The elevator doors closed.

Why did he point out the pin? I thought, circling back to that moment, to the unguarded look of alarm on Emrys's face.

The elevator doors opened again. Caitriona and Olwen stood there, flummoxed. I stared back, equally confused before I realized my mistake.

Caitriona stomped a foot to the ground.

"Down!" she ordered in an imperious tone.

"Please?" Olwen offered, staring up at the ceiling, in case that helped.

Flipping the book back into place, I managed to leap over the fireplace before it closed the elevator off from the room again.

"Sorry, sorry, I forgot." I squeezed in with them, weight limit be damned, and leaned forward so the sensors would allow the doors to shut. I reached behind me, and after assessing the various emergency and call buttons, hit the one labeled CELLAR.

Caitriona's hands shot out to steady us as the elevator rumbled to life and began its descent.

"So this is what we call an elevator," I told them, watching their expressions transform from fear to curiosity. "An alternative to stairs. It also rises."

"Oh," Olwen said, looking all too tempted by the panel of buttons in front of her. "Marvelous!"

Caitriona looked ready to pry the doors open by force. "This is unnatural."

"But convenient!" I said, a bit too cheerful.

The trip down into the cellar was mercifully short. Before we spilled out into the narrow stone hall, I twisted toward Olwen. "Can you take out the little red velvet bag from the front pocket of my jacket?"

"What is this?" Olwen whispered, holding it up. "It feels . . ."

"Dark," Caitriona finished.

I took it from her, letting the spent crystals spill out into my palm. The magic trapped inside thrummed against my skin. "Take one."

Olwen held hers close to her eye, studying the rippling light trapped inside the quartz.

"They've absorbed the magic of curses," I told them. "They'll interfere with any electronic security system down here, including cameras."

I might as well have been speaking in tongues.

"Electronic . . . cameras?" Olwen repeated, testing the sound of the words.

"I promise I'll explain it later, when we're not about to commit theft," I said. "Follow close behind me, and let me know if you see any strange symbols on the wall—"

Caitriona immediately pointed to the glowing emergency exit sign, a man running from fire toward an open door.

I clarified, "Any strange symbols that look like curse sigils you've seen before."

"Got it," Olwen whispered, beginning an eager search.

With the crystals interfering, any automatic sensors for lights didn't switch on, leaving us in darkness until Olwen let out a soft hum and snapped, creating a small blue flame at her fingertip. We followed the short hall into the main chamber of the cellar.

Barrels of whiskey and shelves of wine bottles greeted us. I did a slow lap around the room, scanning the stone walls for doorways or curse sigils. My frown deepened.

"Are you sure we're in the right place?" Caitriona asked.

"Not even a little," I said, annoyed all over again that Emrys had managed to get both himself and Neve caught. So much for him being useful.

"At least it's warm down here," Olwen said, rubbing her arms.

It really wasn't. There were no vents to bring in heat, allowing the winter cold to seep in through the foundations. But as I circled back toward her, I felt it too. The air warmed like a breath around us.

I backed up toward the nearest wall, keeping a hand outstretched to follow the trail of warm air. I checked the floors for sigils and this time saw what I had missed before. Half of a sigil was carved into the floor at the place where it met the stone wall and had been painted to blend into the tile.

"Oh," I said. "What a clever little Wyrm."

"What is it?" Olwen asked.

I couldn't resist showing them. I walked back toward the wall, keeping my hand out in front of me. Instead of meeting stone, my hand passed through the wall, as if it had been nothing but air.

It *was* nothing but air. The other half of the mirage sigil was visible as I stepped through the doorway, into the actual storage room.

"God's teeth," I whispered.

It wasn't a room, it was a *warehouse*—not just for relics, it seemed, but artwork, statues from antiquity, and furniture that looked like it had been scavenged from some beheaded king's palace.

I was so used to crawling around dusty old vaults and researching the past that it was disorienting to see such a modern, almost futuristic setup. Everything was sleek metal and clean shapes. The storage cases that contained relics were lit by dim lights and temperature controlled, covered by both locked steel cages and protective wards.

As my eyes adjusted to the low light, I scanned the walls and floors for any other sigils that might trigger an alarm, a trap, or worse.

"Don't step on any of the rugs," I told them. "There could be curse sigils beneath them."

"What is all of this?" Olwen asked, holding her flame higher to better see. Rows and rows of tables and chairs were scattered throughout.

"Their real library," I said. "And storage for their finds." Most of the guilds focused exclusively on legendary, magical relics rather than priceless antiques and mortal-made treasures, but it seemed that the London guild was branching out.

"Hello?"

The faint voice was as soft and sweet as a songbird's. For a moment,

I thought it had come from upstairs or the wine room, but Caitriona held out a hand, stopping us.

"Hello? Is someone there?"

"Yes," Olwen called back before I could stop her. "Where are you?"

"H-Here."

The voice was already faltering, as if swallowed by the gloom. We moved toward it, past the barred cases, past the shelves of Immortalities, to the unlit end of the room, where a tall object was hidden by thick fabric. Caitriona gripped it, pulling it away with a single hard tug.

The mirror revealed itself in all its towering glory, its silver frame adorned with beasts of every kind—dragons, unicorns, lions, falcons, stags. We saw none of it. Not at first.

Not when there was a trembling, pale-faced girl staring back at us from the other side of the glass.

15

The girl had a dreamy quality to her; what light touched the silvered glass made her image ripple with iridescence. She was small, but not a young girl, her hair as dark as a raven's feather and her skin bone white. It was her eyes that held me there. Large and round, they were of a pale blue that seemed as endless as the sky itself.

She dropped her palms from where she'd pressed them against the glass and wrapped her arms around her waist. The style of her pale green gown was more at home in Avalon than our world—a glimpse of the past you would only see now in costume, or portraits.

Caitriona was the first to recover her senses. "Who are you?"

"My name is Elaine," she said. The words were hoarse, as if she'd spent a lifetime screaming for help that never came. "Please, you must assist me. You *must* let me out. They have kept me here so long."

"Great Mother," Olwen said, horrified. "No one has helped you in all this time? How can that be?"

Yes, I thought. *How* could *that be?*

Now that the shock was wearing off, there was room for suspicion to slip in. Judging by Caitriona's uneasy stance, she was following a similar, more coldhearted line of questioning in her mind.

"Elaine of . . . Shalott?" I ventured.

"Yes!" the girl said, her breath fogging the glass as she drew close again. "You know of me?"

Olwen turned to me, her eyes pleading. "There must be a way to get her out?"

"Sure," I said, trying to keep my tone neutral. "But how were you trapped in the mirror in the first place?"

I'd read the faces of enough tarot customers at the Mystic Maven to know what the quick pursing of Elaine's lips and the angle of her head meant. Annoyance. Impatience.

"A sorceress by the name of Lavina ensnared me when I did not bow to her wishes," Elaine said. "I beg of you, release me. My family must miss me terribly and I so long to return home."

I leaned closer to the mirror's frame, searching the design of animals. "I'm not seeing any sigils . . ."

"They wouldn't be on the frame," Olwen said. "Metal is an inorganic material."

Oh. Right.

"So is glass," I said, thinking. Covering my hand with my jacket, I gripped one side of the mirror. As expected, the backing was wood. As I leaned closer to it, I saw that the glass wasn't glass at all, but a layer of magic meant to mimic it.

"Cait, can you help me pull this away from the wall for a second?"

"Wait—what do you mean by this?" Elaine asked.

Caitriona obliged and had a far easier time of straightening the heavy mirror than I did. But even that small bit of space was enough to see the sigils written in crimson on the back of it. Blood, it seemed, to further intensify the power of the spell.

"Are they back there?" Olwen asked, trying to lean over my shoulder to see.

"Yes," I said faintly. There were five words written beneath the curse marks. Caitriona met my gaze from the other side of the mirror. Carefully, so carefully, we leaned the mirror back against the wall.

"Did you not remove them?" Elaine said. "Surely taking a blade to them and scratching them out would be enough?"

I took several steps back from the glass. Caitriona followed.

"What—what are you doing?" Elaine asked, looking between us. That twitch of her lips was back, and in her agitation, her eyes had darkened to black.

"Here's the thing, *Elaine*," I said. "Your first strike was the name. The real Lady of Shalott was freed centuries ago. There were several sorceresses present for it, and they recorded their memories."

Now Olwen was the one to back away.

"No—" the girl began.

"The second was the name of the sorceress," I said. "The sorceress Honora was the one who trapped the Lady of Shalott."

"You're wrong," the girl protested. "It was Lavina, I swear it."

"The *third* strike," I said, "and my favorite of all, is the fact that there's a warning written on the back of the mirror. Do you want to take a guess at what it says?"

"This woman is a creature of dangerous beauty?" the girl whispered hopefully.

"No. *The beast within devours all,*" I said. "So, again, who are you?"

The girl shrank back into the misty shadows of the world behind the glass, until she became darkness itself. Her face lengthened into more of a snout, her eyes glowing as she watched us, unblinking.

"It wasn't *all*," she said, her voice taking on a hissing, if not prim, tone. "I have discerning taste in man flesh, you know."

"I'm sure you do," I said.

"Creatures born of magic are always more enticing than mortals," she said. "It was not my fault there were fewer and fewer of the former, and more and more of the latter. Mortals breed like fleas."

Her features shifted again, her dark hair lightening to silver, her face rounding, softening, and her eyes assuming a distinct shape and color.

For a moment, it looked as if all our reflections had merged into one.

"Stop that," Caitriona barked.

"Stop what?" the creature asked innocently. She glanced at Olwen, then placed her hands on her hips in a mirror of her pose.

I sifted through the archives of my memory, through the hundreds of thousands of book pages I'd consumed, searching for a creature who ate flesh and mimicked the forms of others. A pooka, maybe—they were omnivorous, but the few that remained in our world tended to shy away from humans. Those who weren't sorceress companions kept to forests and cliffside dwellings.

Feeling the creature's gaze shift onto me, I looked up at her again. Before I could ask about my theory, she had a question for me.

"What is it that your heart desires?" the creature began, the question ending in a hiss. Her gaze flicked over to Olwen before returning to me, pity burning in her eyes. *My* eyes.

"It must be difficult to travel with one so beautiful as she," the creature said softly, nodding to Olwen. "To know you will never be desired by another so long as she is near."

"Oh dear," I said dryly. "How will I ever survive?"

"It *is* a wonder," the creature agreed with a pitying look. "In my time, they would have been quick to shove you into some convent so they wouldn't have to tolerate looking at you."

"Hurting someone's feelings only works when they have feelings," I told her. "You would have been better off trying to start your negotiation with endless riches or eternal life."

"If you release me, I can make you into what you wish to be," the creature said, eyes glinting. "Your hair will no longer look like withered wheat. Your toady face will blossom with beauty."

"We like our Tamsin the way she is," Olwen interjected, more annoyed than I'd ever heard her. Something in me warmed at the word *our*. "And besides, if we're picking the most objectively beautiful member of our group, it's Neve."

Caitriona and I nodded in agreement.

"But you're very lovely too, Olwen," I said, "by any standards. And extremely clever and brave."

The creature sputtered as she looked between us.

"Oh, Cait is by far braver," Olwen said, her cheeks warming with color.

"You are all—" the creature tried to interject.

"That's not true," Caitriona insisted. "You *are* brave, and better yet, openhearted."

"*Listen to me—*" the creature growled.

"And extremely talented with magic, too," I added.

"Your cunning nature has saved us more than once—" Caitriona said to me.

"*Enough!*"

The word echoed through the storage facility, drowning out even the distant sounds of the party above.

"There's no need to be rude," Olwen told the seething creature.

"You *will* release me!" she roared. "Right this very moment! Or—or I shall drink your blood and whittle your bones into picks for my teeth!"

"How do you intend to do that from behind the glass?" Caitriona asked.

The scream that followed was pitiful enough that I almost felt sorry for her.

Almost.

"Olwen, do you think you could figure out a way to reduce the size of this so we can carry it out?" I gestured toward the mirror. "I don't want to leave Neve up there alone for any longer than we need to."

"I'm with you on that," Olwen said. She pressed a hand against her cheek as she considered the mirror, thinking. The creature slid over to her, resting her face against her hand in the same way.

"What is it you intend to do?" the creature asked. "You came to find my mirror, did you not?" Her lips stretched wider, contorting into a serpent's smile. "Do you intend to trap another with it?"

"Don't you want a playmate?" I asked. "Or, I don't know, a hearty snack?"

The creature floated behind the glass, drifting my way. "It is impossible. The mirror's magic is only powerful enough for one."

"You lie," Caitriona said.

"Do I?" the creature replied. "The master of the house tried, oh, how he did. Pressing an enemy up to the glass, wanting to give me that plump little morsel . . ." She salivated at the thought. "But if one goes in, one must come out."

The others looked to me, but I had no answers for them.

"Who is your enemy?" the being asked. "Perhaps if you let me go, I can eat them for you?"

"The King of Annwn," I said. "Lord Death. Still hungry?"

The creature's face swirled, magnifying her disgust. "The usurper?"

"Yes," I said, though I had no idea what the being was referring to. I wasn't about to give her something to dangle over us. "The very same."

"Has he come, then? The new Holly King and his ravenous host of hunters?" the being asked. "Has he escaped Avalon?"

The Holly King. The personification of winter in the old tales. If those stories were true, his power would be at its greatest at the winter solstice, the longest night of the year. After, it would wane with each day, until summer rose again.

But . . . that didn't make sense, did it? Not knowing what I did about Annwn's death magic.

I studied the creature again. She was just haughty enough that my fishing expedition might work . . .

"Yes, he'll remain in this world until the winter solstice," I said, putting on an air of confidence. "Until his power is at its greatest and he can slay his enemies."

"Poor fly-brained mortal, devouring every lie fed to you," the being said, the words dripping with arrogance, correcting my guess as I'd hoped. "That is merely the day the boundary between the mortal world and Annwn is at its thinnest and a pathway can be opened. The day the Wild Hunt carries its bounty of dark souls to their prison."

The realization braided itself together so quickly, it took my breath away. It was a leap, I knew that, but nothing else made sense. The threat wasn't that he would open the door and pass through . . . it was that he would leave that gateway open, allowing the malevolent dead to escape into this world. And when they began to kill the living as they craved to do, it would only add to Lord Death's power.

Caitriona made a questioning noise, but I couldn't bring myself to speak.

"They aren't just hunting dark souls," Olwen told the creature. Then, catching on to the game, she added, "Oh, I forgot that you've been trapped in there for *so* terribly long, you'd have no idea what his true aims are, or what he's desperately searching for."

"I was there at the dawn of the world, and I shall be there at the end, when the last light of the Goddess fades and you mortals return to the stardust and clay that bore you," the being sneered at us. "I carry the knowledge of the ages, and I will bear it still when time extinguishes you from memory."

"You know nothing," I said, fighting to hide the way my hands had begun to tremble. A sickly fear was making its way through me, a dread that had no name.

"I know what Lord Death seeks, as do all those who saw the blood spilled that day, who heard the last lamentations of the Goddess," the creature said.

The world grew hushed around us again. The creature's strange eyes glowed, a lure that drew me in, made me step closer to the rippling surface between us.

"He seeks that which was denied to him centuries ago," she said at last. "He seeks the soul of his lost beloved."

16

I knew my little game was at an end when a victorious smirk slithered across her amalgamation of our faces.

His lost beloved. I'd heard her clearly, but it was as if the words couldn't fully take root in my mind. *Beloved.* The word felt hideous in that context. Impossible.

"Oh?" she crowed. "Perhaps there *is* a deal to be made, then? For it seems you do not know who, exactly, it is you face."

Her words became a spider in my mind, weaving its web, trying to connect all the various pieces of information I'd been carrying with me since Avalon.

"He is incapable of love," Caitriona snarled. "He seeks only power and pain."

"Perhaps as Lord Death," the being taunted. "But that was not always his name. He was not born a king."

"Tamsin?" Olwen began, uncertain. I knew what she was thinking. Any sort of deal would involve releasing this creature into the world again, with no doubt more deaths to follow.

"How do we know we can even trust its word?" Caitriona demanded.

The creature drew herself upright, her expression livid. Blue lightning crackled along the surface of the glass as the creature strained against it, the magic activating in an instant, throwing the being back.

She wailed pitifully, pounding her fists against the dark air.

But Caitriona's question had given me an idea. I licked my dry lips to hide my smile.

"All right. I'll release you if you tell us the truth about the man called Lord Death—"

"Tamsin!" Caitriona interjected.

I held up a hand, hoping my eyes were enough to convey the message. *Trust me.*

"You have to tell us everything you know about him," I continued, "and the soul he's after."

When the creature smiled, it was with all her ragged teeth. "First, you must give me a taste of your blood. Just a droplet, to bind our promise and ensure that I can hunt you and your kin should you fail to release me."

Being the only blood member of my family that I knew of, it was an easy yes. Using the pocketknife in my back pocket, I made a small cut at the tip of my index finger and let the blood run down my hand, into my palm.

Caitriona caught my wrist. "Think about this . . ."

"Together to the end, right?" I said.

After a moment, she nodded.

Coming as close to the mirror as I dared, I flicked a droplet of blood at the glass, watching in horrified fascination as the blood seeped through the magic to the other side and the creature greedily lapped it up with a soft sigh of pleasure.

I wrinkled my nose, disgusted, but the creature's own face did the same, her mouth twisting at the taste.

"It's . . . sweeter than I remember," she said, rubbing her tongue against her teeth, as if to dispel the taste.

"Well, you're the one who asked for it," I answered, offended. "Sorry it's not to your usual standards."

A strangely contemplative look crossed the creature's mockery of a face. She licked her gray lips again, as if seeking the last traces of the taste.

"The information?" Caitriona cut in.

Whatever the creature had been stewing over vanished like mist in the morning sun.

"Oh, yes. Lord Death, the King of Annwn."

"That is hopefully the one and only Lord Death," I said flatly.

"He is the second of that name," the creature said, drifting lazily back and forth behind the glass. "He killed the first and stole his crown—but that is getting ahead of myself."

As she spoke, the echo of another voice stirred in my mind. A man's voice, murmuring and indistinct, layered over hers. A ghostly image, of a bed, of a glowing candle on the table beside it, flittered through my mind. A thought slipped in through the shadows, unbidden. *I know this.*

No, I didn't.

I sat back on my heels, hugging my arms to my chest. A sharp prickling began at the base of my spine, clawing its way up my body to grip the back of my neck.

"His true name is Gwyn ap Nudd," the creature said, "son of Nudd Llaw Ereint, whose own father was one of the Goddess's Firstborn."

Nudd of the Silver Hand. An ancient king of Britain and legendary hero.

"Never content with what great good fortune had been given to him," the creature continued, "Gwyn saw only what others were given, heard only what praise his father offered to his brothers, tasted but the bitterness of every fruit. It is little wonder, then, that he desired a young woman already promised to another . . ."

The dark scene—the bedroom, the frail candle's light—painted itself in bolder strokes, refusing to be ignored. There were two children in the bed, a fair-haired girl, a boy with hair so dark it looked like a spill of ink on the pillow. The man who sat at the end of it, drawing the covers up over them, wore a leather jacket, his eyes somber as he spoke.

It was me. It was Cabell. It was Nash. But it had never happened. I would have remembered it. I would have remembered it before now.

When had Nash ever tucked us into bed? It seemed almost like a little inn, but I didn't recognize it.

"Who?" Olwen's voice intruded on my spiraling thoughts.

"Who indeed," the creature said. "For this was no ordinary girl, but the divine child of the Goddess herself. A daughter she had created to be hers alone. Her name was Creiddylad."

I know this. The thought filled me with a strange panic. I knew this story, but I couldn't place how. I couldn't draw up the pages I'd read it on in my mind's eye. I couldn't remember where we'd been, or who had told me. There was only that impression of the room, of Nash sitting at the edge of the bed, darkly shimmering.

"A daughter?" I heard Olwen repeat incredulously.

"Impossible," Caitriona said. "We would know of such a being—"

I focused on that image, holding it there at the front of my mind, refusing to let it go.

I know this. How do I know this?

The prickling at the back of my neck rose, spiking through the bone at the base of my skull. I drew in a sharp breath, my shoulders tensing as my mind gave a physical jolt, like the clunk of a key turning in an old lock.

I pushed through the dull ache building at my temple, the detritus of half-formed, fragmented memories that littered my mind like dying leaves, digging and digging through the layers of chaos until I found the clear jewel of a memory buried underneath.

I remembered.

The inn in Helmsley, Yorkshire, after another fruitless day searching for Arthur's dagger at the nearby castle. Winter's frost kissing the window. The bone-deep cold that had lingered after an entire day outside, one no fire or blanket seemed to be able to drive out. I curled my knees up to my chest to trap in some warmth, fuming silently as I pretended to sleep.

"Will you tell us a story?" Cabell whispered.

His side of the narrow bed dipped as Nash sat down. I kept my back to them, eyes squeezed shut. After the day we'd had, I wasn't in the mood to go to sleep.

"What sort of story, my dear boy?" came Nash's rumbling reply, the words warmed by the ale in his hand.

Cabell thought about it a moment. "A winter's tale."

"Ah." I felt the pressure of Nash's gaze as he glanced my way. He was quiet for a moment. Normally there'd be a story already perched on the tip of his tongue, waiting to unfurl itself, but now, he took his time, as if needing to think through his selection. "The story of that old heel Father Christmas soft-shoeing around houses, snooping on children, perhaps?"

I could imagine perfectly the face Cabell made. "No. A new one—one you've never told us before."

I bristled. Nash was always telling Cabell things he wouldn't tell me—they were always going off, leaving me behind, telling me I wouldn't understand.

"I think that ought to wait until your sister's awake," Nash said, after taking a long sip from his bottle. "Hardly seems fair otherwise."

Cabell wasn't deterred. "Tamsin's never liked a scary story. Tell me one of those."

I glowered at the window in front of me. He wasn't any braver than me. Cabell wouldn't like it either if the monsters followed him into his dreams.

"I think I know the one, then," Nash said, his voice hushed as he began to weave his tale. "Long ago, before Arthur ruled man and the Fair Folk alike, the Goddess began the great work of her creation. Her children, the Gentry, came first, then beasts of every kind, and man—but few know the story of the child she bore for herself..."

The present came into focus again as the creature stroked a long nail over her cheek in thought, then seemed to find her place again in the tale. "As much as the Goddess desired to keep her daughter by her side, Creiddylad was a curious child, and asked to live among the mortals and know their world. The Goddess entrusted her to Nudd, who swore to return her to her mother in a year's time."

Nash's lyrical telling flowed into the river of the story as it passed through my mind. *"There in the house of Nudd, Creiddylad fell in love with a young man, one of the Gentry, and though her mother was reluctant to part with her own heart, she allowed them to be betrothed . . ."*

"Gwyn, having lived with her in his father's home, was said to be taken by her beauty and set his heart on her," the creature continued.

"One night, Gwyn, in an act of foolish pride, spirited her away," Nash continued, his voice far-off in my mind. *"He tried to force her hand in marriage. Her intended, however, caught up to them and a duel ensued. And in the end, Creiddylad's love fell to the power of Gwyn's blade."*

"Poor Creiddylad." Olwen, with her kind heart, looked close to tears.

"Oh, yes," the creature said, smirking. "You see, Creiddylad had relinquished her divinity for a mortal life. Before Gwyn could claim his prize . . ."

". . . she raised her lover's blade to her heart and killed herself rather than submit to him."

Cabell gasped.

"That was my reaction as well, lad," Nash said. "But her end is not the end of this tale."

"Well!" the creature continued, articulating the word with a flare of her fingers. "The Goddess was devastated, but it is not in her nature to kill."

"She punished Gwyn by sending him to Annwn as a prisoner, and so great was her grief, the Goddess herself receded, accepting the final form of a god—the incorporeal soul of the world she created," Nash continued in my mind, his telling harmonizing perfectly with the creature's telling. *"It fell to the Lady of the Lake, one of the Gentry and the first priestess of Avalon, to ensure the soul's protection, when the day came for her to be reborn. For it was her destiny to protect the Goddess's heart—the sacred isle of her worship, and the child born of her being."*

"And was it reborn?" Olwen asked.

"It is beyond our knowing, for a spell was cast by the Lady of the Lake to ensure she would remain hidden," the creature said. "It is meant to stay lost, child, that is the point. For a seed of evil was planted in Gwyn's soul that day, when he was denied what he felt he had won rightfully in that contest to the death."

"He burned with fury at being sent to the world of the dead," Nash continued. "Being of noble blood, he ingratiated himself to Arawn, the true King of Annwn. Seeing the death magic at the king's command, a terrible notion overcame him, and Gwyn killed Arawn and took his place on the throne."

"Industrious of him," I heard myself say.

"Gwyn ruled when Arthur and his knights came to Annwn, showering them with gifts in exchange for any morsel of information about the soul," the creature said. "And so he began his hunt again."

"So great was his desperation to find Creiddylad's soul, Gwyn destroyed Otherlands with the Wild Hunt, tearing through them with sword and claw." Nash's voice was fading, the memory sinking back into the same dark morass I'd pulled it from. "All because he believed the soul had been hidden there. Then one year, when winter arrived to haunt the world once more, the Wild Hunt did not accompany it. Many believed the hunt had ended for good, but there are those who know better, who believe Lord Death will one day ride again . . ."

Cabell had fallen asleep long before then, carried into the darkness of dreams. I'd felt his breathing even out as certainly as I'd felt Nash reach over and brush my brow, whispering, *"But do not worry yourself with such things . . ."*

Dread walked along my skin, stinging. I was sure the others could see the pulse jumping in my throat—that they could hear it thundering in their own ears. But Olwen and Caitriona had looked to one another, as if to silently debate the truth of it between them. A story they'd never been told.

But I had.

Nash had known it, had spoken it. He prided himself on collecting little-known legends and stories, but this . . . I'd never read any record of it. Hadn't even been able to summon the memory until something the creature had said cracked the forgotten archive open and allowed it to come spilling out again.

How did Nash know this story?

And why had I forgotten it?

"And so I end my tale, having told you the whole of it, from head to hind," the creature said. "Now release me—"

"*Wait!*" Emrys's voice sent a warm frisson racing up my spine. My body turned toward his of its own accord, trying to chase the almost unbearable fluttering sensation in my chest.

Beside me, Caitriona relaxed her blade-straight posture ever so slightly, drawing in a deep breath as Emrys and Neve ran across the warehouse.

"Do we hate him?" the creature whispered to me. "Is his meat stringy with greed? Is there malice in his marrow? Which one is the pretty one you spoke of? They both have such succulent flesh and delicate bones . . ."

I ignored her, scanning Neve to make sure she was all right. The priestess only stared wide-eyed at the creature, her lips parting in surprise.

"You can't let it out," Emrys told me, breathless.

"And why not?" the creature sputtered, asking for the both of us.

"That's Rosydd, Hag of the Bogs," he said.

Caitriona, Olwen, and I all turned back toward the mirror, at the creature sputtering with outrage. Somehow the fact that we were speaking with a primordial monster was the least surprising part of this turn of events.

"Hag of the *Moors*," the creature growled. "Moors!"

It didn't seem like the opportune moment—or the right audience—to point out that bogs were just wet moorlands.

"How do you know that?" Olwen asked Emrys.

"One of the Hollowers told us—well, bragged is probably the more accurate description," Neve said, rolling her eyes. "They're all drunk as skunks up there."

"Sounds delicious," the creature noted to herself. "They've marinated their meat."

"You can't let the hag out," Emrys said, a new edge to his tone. One that sounded suspiciously like fear. "She'll devour all of us."

"I wasn't planning to," I told him.

"What?" the hag roared. "You swore it! You made a blood vow!"

I looked back over my shoulder. Almost a decade of bargaining with sorceresses had taught me a thing or two about slippery language. "Yes, I did promise to release you. But you never asked me to specify *when*."

Emrys's brows rose. "Not bad, Lark. Did you even know that a hag can't break a sworn vow, or were you rolling the dice on that one?"

I glared at him. "Of course I knew that." Just now, after he told me.

"Uh-huh," he said, crossing his arms over his chest.

The hag drew near to the glass, electrifying the protective layer of magic. "You think yourself cunning, little fox, but there are bigger teeth in the forest."

"Good thing we're nowhere near a forest, then," I said.

"As much as I'm enjoying this face-off, we need to get out of here," Emrys said. "Right now, and I think we should leave the mirror and come back for it another day. There's supposedly an exit out of here hidden behind one of the cases."

"Don't be ridiculous," Caitriona said. "We're here, aren't we? We just need to carry the accursed thing out."

Neve looked torn. "Yes, but Emrys is right, there isn't time."

Emrys reached into the inner pocket of his jacket for something. "This isn't just a celebration of the season, or a party to show off the mantle."

When he opened his fist, a small silver object glowed in the dim light.

The pin. The hand holding the branch.

Sweat broke out along my neck and back. The hair on my arms rose, pricking with the sensation of a growing electrical charge in the air.

And above us, the deep blare of a horn sounded.

17

An explosion of shattering glass rained down inside the manor house, shrill enough to be heard through the heavy layers of stone. Laughter rose like wind, the hooting and whooping drowning out even the terrified screams. At the wild drumbeat of horse hooves, I bit the inside of my mouth hard enough to taste blood.

I gripped Emrys's arm, drawing his focus back to me. "You said there was a way out of here?"

"I don't know where it is—" He spun around, searching. "It opens to the Avon River—where they used to bring the relics in—the river's east of here—"

"Where's east?" I asked.

Caitriona pivoted, trying to orient herself. "I think . . . that way?"

I saw only a bare stone wall.

"Perhaps this is a forest after all," the hag sneered. "What will you do, little fox?"

"You, be quiet," Neve said, throwing the fabric cover over the mirror again.

And in the merciful stretch of silence that followed, the elevator dinged.

A moment later, before I could even think to move, three shadowed figures burst into the warehouse, their chests heaving, reeking of blood and sweat.

"Oh gods," one was chanting, his body shaking, "gods—"

Their tuxedos hung from them in tatters, the once-white shirts splattered with enough gore to make me gag.

"Hey!" Emrys barked at them. "Where's the—"

When they turned to us, it was as if that last veneer of humanity had been ripped away from them and what was left in their haunted eyes spoke to their most basic, primal instinct. *Survive.* And through the dark veil of pain and terror that had them in its grip, they reacted like the wounded animals they were.

One had a work axe in his hand, and I watched in slow horror as he threw it directly at Caitriona's head. As she leaned back, dodging it, he limped forward with a ferocious scream. *"You won't take me!"*

"We're not hunters!" Olwen cried. One of the men lowered his head and charged toward her with death in his eyes. She threw out a hand with a sharp grunt, and the blunt force of wind knocked the man back into the nearest case. The glass fractured as he struck it, shards slicing into him as he slumped to the ground.

I leapt back as the third man tried to swipe the jagged stone across my chest like a dagger, spit flying as he screamed at me—just *screamed,* as if he could breathe his desperate rage into my body and infect me with it. I backed away, bumping into one of the worktables, feeling across it for something to protect myself with.

Emrys appeared behind him, a vase in his hand, and smashed it into the man's skull. The man's scream died with a whimper as he collapsed, the whites of his eyes flashing as he sank into unconsciousness. I stared at Emrys, my lungs working like bellows, and he stared back, his eyes lit with fear.

"You—" I began. A clatter rose from down the hall—the sound of hooves against stone.

I swung my gaze toward Caitriona as she caught her attacker around the neck and held him in the crook of her arm.

"Where is the hidden escape path?" she demanded. *"Where?"*

The sound of horse hooves thundered in my ears, rattling the ceiling, shaking the furniture in the room like a cup of dice.

It didn't matter what the man told us. We were out of time. Caitriona caught my eye, understanding even before I did. She released him and he fled to the far end of the room, disappearing into the shadows. He moaned, frantically running along the walls as he searched for a doorway that never appeared.

I barely had time to get the word out. *"Hide!"*

We scattered to the four corners of the room, Olwen and Caitriona running for stacks of empty crates, Neve for the small fleet of covered antique cars. But Emrys was gone. The warehouse shrouded itself in shadows around me, my heart pounding so hard it was painful.

"Run, little fox!" the hag sang out, her voice barely muffled by the thick velvet thrown over the frame. "Wherever shall you hide from the hunters?"

Adrenaline gave me the last burst of speed I needed to reach a baroque armoire painted with scenes of fairies.

All the modern cabinets around me would be locked or be storing something. But this—this was open. The lower half was filled with drawers, but I could dislodge the upper shelf and climb up into it, curling my legs in tight to my chest.

I had only just got the doors shut when one flung open again.

"Seriously?" I whispered.

Emrys's pale face hovered in front of mine, just as shocked to see me. But there was no choice; at the sound of approaching voices, I gripped his wrist and hauled him up beside me, narrowly avoiding being kneed in the face as his long limbs tangled with mine. The wood groaned beneath our combined weight.

But the old wood somehow held.

"This feels familiar," he breathed out. I elbowed him a bit harder than I'd meant to trying to shut the doors again, but with both of us inside where no human was meant to be, there was no way to completely close them. We had a clear line of sight to the entrance as the first of the hunters arrived.

"No," the last man moaned, sinking onto his knees. "Please—please—I have a family—I can pay you—"

I held my breath, suddenly terrified that the slightest rustle of fabric would alert them to our presence. The bracelet on my wrist pressed into my skin, and I forced myself to concentrate on that, not on worrying about whether or not the others had found a safe enough place to hide.

A hunter stepped forward. The sunken, sinewy planes of his face made it impossible to tell who he was, but the moment he spoke, it was like I'd been caught in a net of stinging holly.

"Looks like we've caught ourselves some little mice who scurried off before the fun was over," he sneered.

I bit my lip, heart sinking.

That was Phineas Primm, one of the Hollowers from our guild. I'd recognize the old man's smarmy, nasal tone anywhere.

Emrys lifted his head, meeting my gaze in alarm.

I squeezed my eyes shut at the sound of the man's final screams, the wet rending of flesh as the hunters fell upon the other men we'd left there, unconscious. My stomach turned violently, horror and guilt flooding my veins.

I tried to focus my thoughts on the past, filtering back through my memories to find that night in the library. Primm, Septimus, and Hector had dogged my every move, keeping a close watch on the books I'd retrieved as I was trying to puzzle through the mystery of the Servant's Prize. Septimus had been wearing the pin of the silver hand holding the branch—had the others?

Yes. Yes, they had.

It couldn't be a coincidence. They were all connected to Endymion Dye in some way, even Wyrm and the Hollowers of his guild. The pin was more than a mark of belonging, it was a vow of allegiance.

More and more of the hunters poured into the warehouse behind

Primm—a dozen, if not more, their spectral glow a sickening shade of poison green. If they searched the warehouse . . .

Emrys's hands came up to gently grip either side of my face, turning it away from the carnage and toward him. His own expression was calm, but I could feel a slight tremor in his fingers.

"Help!" came the hag's voice, as sweet and crisp as it had been when we'd first arrived, when she'd pretended to be Elaine. "Help me, please!"

"Ignore whatever the beast says." Endymion's clipped voice shredded the last of my nerves. "The hag will say whatever she must to convince you to release her."

"He lies," the hag moaned. "My name is Elaine. The Sorceress Lav—ah—the Sorceress Honora imprisoned me for daring to love the man she set her heart on—"

Well. Let it never be said you couldn't teach an ancient hag a new trick—or a new story.

"Start with the cabinets on the far end and work your way toward the center," Endymion ordered. "Tear the place apart if you have to, but make quick work of it."

This time, I was the one holding Emrys's face still, forcing him to look at me, not the twisted remnant of his father's soul.

I'd never seen his eyes like that before, his pupils dilated so that the green and gray were barely visible. I pressed my fingers against his cold, clammy skin. Even in the darkness of the armoire, his pulse was visibly fluttering at the base of his throat.

I started at the chorus of smashing glass and cackling glee. Alarms squealed, each screech like a knife in the ears. The flaring of fire, of cracking and splitting stone—one of the hunter's screams turned to bloodcurdling laughter from the others.

"A curse's not going to hit the same if you have no bones to break," Primm sneered.

They've set off the protective wards, I thought, wincing again as something crashed to the floor.

Emrys bent his head, letting it rest against our knees, his breath shuddering. The way his dark hair curled against the nape of his scarred neck, the vulnerability of his posture, made my whole chest ache.

"Why did he think it'd be down here?" one of the hunters asked. "Did he get a feeling or something? Or did Wyrm claim to have trapped it for him?"

"If he wanted you to know, he would have told you," Endymion snapped.

My body went rigid. He was close. Somehow, despite his being incorporeal, I could have sworn I heard the clip of his boots against the stone floor. A cloth *whoosh*ed as it was tugged free of something.

My head came to rest against Emrys's. I closed my eyes, breathing in the comforting scent of him—greenery and traces of fire smoke.

Please don't let them find the others, I begged. *Please just go—*

"Let me out, please!" the hag cried. "I do not deserve to be punished in such a way!"

"Do they really listen to this racket every time they're down here?" one of the hunters asked. "How do they shut her up?"

"I'll do whatever you want—I'll tell you whatever it is you want to know," the hag tried. "Perhaps you'd like to find some special sword to slay your enemies?"

"Oh, damn me, the Helm of Awe?" one of them said. "I'm taking it."

"Then I'm taking Chrysaor—I spent years of my bloody life looking for this blasted sword, and they've had it all along," said another.

The Hollowers did what Hollowers did best. The scavenging turned feral, the smashing and plundering frenzied. Death had only unleashed their darkest instincts.

"I'll tell you about the others hiding down here!" the hag cried. "I'll let you feast on their flesh instead!"

My blood turned into ice. Emrys's fingers tightened around my wrist.

"Keep searching," Endymion barked out. "Leave nothing of value behind!"

"There are—there were four girl whelps, and a boy," the hag continued. "His name was—it was Emrys!"

I lifted my head, and that slight movement, that shift in weight, sealed our fates. The armoire creaked loudly in the heavy silence, and my heart stopped dead in my chest.

A heavy, oppressive feeling of malice neared, turning the air noxious. I stared out through the cracked opening between the doors, too scared to even draw in a breath.

"What did you say?" Endymion asked, his voice hushed.

Emrys's breathing grew shallow, as if recognizing something in the tone. He released his hold on me, pressing his fists against his eyes. I didn't know what to do—the plans wouldn't come. There was no way to get either of us out of here without one of the hunters seeing.

The terrifying sensation released as Endymion stalked back across the shadowy warehouse, kicking aside broken chairs and crunching through shattered glass as he approached the mirror like a looming thunderstorm.

"What did you say?" he growled.

"Look!" The hag retreated in the glass, until I could no longer make out her eerie shape. "His face was like this—look, *look!*"

He fisted one hand in the velvet cover, ripping it away from the rippling surface of the magic. Whatever Endymion Dye saw there drew him closer. Closer.

His profile, barely visible through the darkness, wasn't of the man who'd exercised such careful control over the perfect image he'd cultivated as the de facto leader of our guild—charming one moment, cutting the next.

And there, staring into the depths of the mirror, the last trace of the man he had been shattered.

"You lying *bitch!*"

He gripped the frame with a scream of pure animal rage, throwing it to the ground. He whirled, upending the nearby table with a single hand, kicking in the oak legs, unleashing the deadly edge of his sword on its body until splinters exploded from it.

He fell upon the armchairs with the same mindless fury, shredding them, ripping out their stuffing as if they were entrails, before turning to the racks of wine and champagne bottles. The air was stained red with the spray of wine and fizz, a river of it snaking through the shattered remains of the warehouse.

The other hunters stood by, watching silently. Unwilling to disrupt his rampage, unwilling to risk joining him in case that scalding anger rebounded onto them.

Emrys lifted his head, but the set of his mouth, the look in his eyes—that wasn't fear. It was a bone-deep weariness. Recognition.

The ache in me deepened.

Nash had been a real bastard at times. He'd subjected us to curses and the elements when we slept rough. But even when I'd riled him up until he saw red, he never raised a hand to us. *Never.*

I watched Emrys, not his father tearing the paintings down from the wall, punching through the priceless canvases with his fists. How many times had his son been on the receiving end of them? How many times had his mother?

He lowered his head again with a shaky sigh. Trying to make himself smaller.

Above us, the horn sounded its thunderous cry, echoing through the levels of the house like a building quake. Then, and only then, did Endymion stop.

The destruction he'd wrought was still collapsing, shards of broken bottles still dripping champagne. The transformation was terrifying for its swiftness. He straightened, the placid mask slipping back into place as he faced the other hunters.

"If it *was* a feeling our lord had, he was likely sensing the hag," Primm told him. "Waste of time, if you ask me—"

Endymion flashed across the room, his ghostly hand closing around Primm's throat. *"No one asked you."*

He threw the other hunter to the floor, prowling back toward the entrance, leaving the others to follow with their plundered treasures. Swords that cut through any surface. Shields that protected against any spell. Mantles that increased their physical strength. More, and more, and more relics that would make the dead beyond invincible.

The voices echoed back to us long after they'd left the room. *"To the next, to the next!"*

I counted to a hundred in my head before I dared to whisper, "Emrys?"

The heat of his body against mine, the pine-sweet smell of him—it all crashed into the adrenaline still screaming through my veins, with the horror at what I'd just witnessed. I was still so bad at this, but something in me *needed* to try. To comfort him. It was the only explanation I had for why I leaned forward again, listening to my own inexperienced instincts, and hesitantly pressed my lips against his upturned cheek.

Emrys drew in a sharp breath, sitting up so quickly his head bumped my chin.

"Don't," he breathed out shakily, his face stricken with a disgust that cracked me open. "Don't touch me."

He pushed the doors to the armoire fully open and climbed out, letting them shut behind him.

Heat burned in my chest, rising to spread over my face. The humiliation of it was so acute, the sensation of my heart shattering so violent, I actually thought I might vomit. Even as I tried to steel myself, to swallow the sour taste on my tongue, I caught myself hoping the darkness of the room would overtake me like a drowning tide and carry me into its depths.

You stupid, gullible idiot, my mind seethed at me, sinking deeper into the abyss of self-loathing.

All this time, I'd prided myself on being able to read people's feelings, to use those tricks to figure out the secret longings of their hearts—the dreams and possibilities they wanted me to weave for them as I turned over each tarot card. I had been the hustler, not the hustled.

Until Emrys.

Some part of me—some tiny, desperate piece of my heart—had still held on to a sliver of hope. That it wasn't all pretend. That his feelings for me had been as real as mine were for him.

But he'd disabused me of that notion swiftly and brutally.

Don't touch me.

I pressed my fingers against my burning eyes, hating myself, hating him. When the stinging sensation of needles passed and the blood returned to my limbs, I climbed down from the armoire and pushed past him.

Neve spotted me before I saw her, weaving through the debris at a full run toward me. The sight of her chased the clawing bitterness away, replacing it with a pure, effervescent relief. When she threw her arms around me, I didn't even try to squirm away.

"Is everyone all right?" Olwen asked, accepting her sister's help over the pile of downed display cases. All of us, I noticed, were careful not to look at the bodies of the men.

"Well, *I'm* fine," the hag said, her voice muffled by the floor.

I only nodded, keeping my arm looped around Neve's shoulder. She shot me a questioning look, one that I avoided.

"What now?" Neve asked.

"We give chase," Caitriona said. "Follow them back to whatever lair they've slithered off to."

Neve leaned over the back of the Mirror of Shalott, studying the sigils there. "The current spellwork is specific to trapping a hag." She pointed to the markings. "I don't know what sigils we'd need to use to trap something like Lord Death."

"I do!" the hag offered. We ignored her.

"I can write to Madrigal again and ask for the Council of Sistren's help," Neve said. "They have researchers—"

"No," Caitriona cut in. "We do not involve them."

There was a difference between being righteous and obstinate, and she had crossed from one into the other.

"Cait . . . ," I began. Something hot and wet struck my cheek.

I looked up, touching my hand to it, only for another fat drop to fall, striking my scalp. I looked down at my fingers, holding them to the nearest flickering light.

Blood.

18

A deep foreboding filled me as we climbed the hidden emergency stairs into the decoy library. It built beneath my skin like a gathering swarm of flies, buzzing in my ears and stealing my breath long before we came across the first body.

Caitriona emerged first, holding out a hand to us as she looked around. I pushed Emrys aside and joined her, letting the slow horror of the scene wash over me.

"Holy . . . gods . . . ," Emrys began.

The fine carpets squelched underfoot, blood soaking the hem of my jeans. The feel of it, the stench of it all—raw meat—was intensified by the sight of the human remains strewn like a wolf's uneaten carrion across the furniture, the low shelves, everywhere.

Some had tried to run for the display cases before the hunters had stolen the weapons inside, leaving only bloodied handprints on the stands.

The silence from the hall was absolute, the terror of it penetrating the library and spreading through us. The smell of smoke clung to everything, but still wasn't enough to cover the cloying stench of blood.

The world flickered around me, and for a moment, all I could see was the tower's courtyard. The bodies.

It's happening again.

We moved in different directions, searching for survivors, or anything that resembled a weapon.

As I rounded one of the bookshelves, my foot caught, and I fell. A scream clawed its way up my throat, lodging itself there. The headless torso shuddered as I staggered forward, heaving, desperately trying not to vomit.

I swore a blue streak under my breath, picking up one of the wooden chairs and slamming it against the worktable until the leg splintered and finally broke off. It was likely the best weapon I was going to find here.

Emrys tried to pull an old sword down from where it was displayed over the fireplace, yanking it with increasing frustration.

"It's bolted on, genius!" I snapped.

"You think?" he bit back. The whole plaque came tumbling off the wall with his next tug. He yelped as it hit the floor and the blade broke off from the hilt.

It was only then that I saw who was crouched beside the unlit hearth.

Olwen's knuckles were white as she gripped a piece of smashed shelving. Her hands trembled violently as she tried and failed to force herself to rise. Breath tore in and out of her. Her eyes were unblinking as she stared at a nearby body, her face devoid of color.

I gripped her arm, forcing her to look at me. "Olwen?"

Her gaze seemed to pass through me. She wasn't really here—and I knew her mind was in the past, in the courtyard of the tower.

"Olwen!" I gave her a hard shake, finally breaking through. She turned with wild eyes. She might have been a healer, she might have dealt with broken bones, pus, and jagged cuts, but you could only heal the living.

"You should go downstairs," I said. "Stay with the mirror while we see what happened."

"What?" Olwen said. "No—no, I can handle this."

"Please," Caitriona said, crouching down on the other side of her. "It's all right. We'll rejoin you in a moment."

"What if someone needs help?" Olwen breathed out. "And I can heal them."

"Dear heart," Caitriona said, holding her hand gently. "They didn't leave anyone alive."

Indecision warred on Olwen's face, but in the end, she nodded. We waited until she was safely down the stairs before turning back to the carnage around us.

"Why would they do this?" Caitriona asked me.

I lifted a shoulder in a helpless shrug. This wasn't the bloodless death of the Sorceress Hemlock, when her soul had been ripped out.

"Maybe the violence is the point?" Neve said, looking faint at the scene around us. "Violent death creates more death magic, doesn't it?"

Glass crashed just outside the door to the hall, ripping me out of the haze of fear. Caitriona pivoted toward something in the far corner of the library—a pale spear half buried beneath a pile of Immortalities and the remains of one of the Hollowers.

"That's—" Emrys choked at her manhandling of the weapon, following her as she strode toward the door leading into the hall. "That's Gáe Bulg, the spear of Cú Chulainn—made of the bone of a sea monster—"

She threw a single glance back over her shoulder as she pulled the door open. "Now it is the spear of Caitriona."

"It splinters—" Emrys began, but she was already gone. "Never mind. She'll figure it out."

I followed, narrowly avoiding the body splayed in front of the door, his face torn away to reveal bone. Static rose in my ears, until the crackle of it burned away all the sound in the room, save for my own galloping heart.

Somehow it was worse than my dark mind had imagined.

The hall was almost unrecognizable. The windows had been blown in, leaving gleaming spikes of glass scattered over the floor like deadly ice. Several of the Hollowers had tried to rush toward the library, only to fall, smearing blood across the stone as they'd tried to crawl to safety. Their chests gaped open, as if skewered.

The long feast table was on fire. One of the burners beneath the trays had been knocked over, and now gorged itself on the once-pristine tablecloths. Emrys came to stand just behind me. He'd picked up someone's axe and now spun the handle in his grip, surveying the slaughter with a hard expression.

Neve wandered out through the bodies, a hand pressed to her mouth in horror. I would have gone to her, if I hadn't caught sight of a smudge of darkness moving at the edge of my vision.

The lanky figure strode around the long drive, the shape of him black against the heavy snowfall. Something glimmered in his hands—the shimmering fabric of Arthur's mantle.

I couldn't make sense of the sight of him here. *Alone.* The exact opportunity I'd been too afraid to hope for.

His shape grew smaller and smaller as he headed down the drive, his long strides eating up the distance.

No, I thought. *I'm not letting you walk away again.*

Not when he was within reach. Not while he was away from the distorting magic of Lord Death's influence.

"Stay here!" I shouted to the others, ignoring their own cries as I ran for the cold air and drifts of snow blowing in through the broken windows.

Smoke clogged my mouth and nose, heat burned against my face, but everything else—the fighting, the screaming—it all fell away as I vaulted over the remains of the elaborate window frames and gave chase.

"Cabell!"

Somehow, through the wind and relentless snow, my brother heard me. He turned just enough for me to see the silhouette of his profile, but he didn't stop. His strides only lengthened. Quickened.

So did mine.

I wove through the maze of cars still parked on the circular driveway, barely conscious of their cracked windshields and smashed roofs.

One SUV had managed to make it halfway down the long drive and was still rolling forward despite the lack of driver and passengers. The broken, blood-streaked windows told the full story.

The torches had gone out, leaving only the moon to illuminate the snowy landscape. The snow flurries danced with the ash drifting from the house.

With his dark hair and even darker clothing, my brother seemed to drift in and out of the fabric of the night—until, I realized, he'd drawn Arthur's mantle over his shoulders and disappeared entirely. But while the relic hid him from even those with the One Vision, it didn't disguise his footprints in the dirt and snow or stop his breath from blooming white in the air.

His steps slowed as we came to the end of the drive and the empty road intersecting it. Clusters of trees swayed with the wind, their bare branches shivering in the silence.

I lifted my eyes from the last of his visible tracks, staring into the dark air where he ought to have been. There was a whisper of fabric against fabric, and for a moment, I thought I caught a glimpse of his profile again, as pale and thin as a crescent moon.

"Cab," I said, my own chest burning for breath. I fumbled for the right words—the ones that might cast the spell to keep him here, if only for a little longer. "Can we talk? Even when we fought, we were always able to hear each other out."

He said nothing, but I felt the anger radiating from him like a wraith hovering between us. It seemed Lord Death had fed it, nurtured it, in those days since I last saw him.

"Are you okay?" I asked him, trying to keep the tremor out of my voice. "Has he . . . has he hurt you?"

"No."

The word was colder than the snow gathering in my hair. It iced my veins.

But at least he was talking. That was something. If I had been bigger, or stronger, or had even an ounce of magic, I would have knocked him out and dragged him away from all this death and darkness. Even still, I wasn't convinced it would do any good. Distance alone wouldn't be enough to break the hold Lord Death had over him, not when Cabell refused to fight it.

"No, you're not okay, or no, he hasn't hurt you?" I clarified. "I'm just trying to understand—what did he do to get you to turn your back on us? Did he promise you something?"

The silence was back, festering. I bit the inside of my cheek, my mind racing. The last few days had conspired to rip every last shred of pride I'd had away from me, to tear at my sense of self. When we were children, I'd fought to hide my tears from him, to be the strong one. I couldn't do it anymore. The pressure built behind my eyes.

"I know . . ." It felt like I was ripping the words out of my chest. Tears burned down my frozen cheeks. "I know I wasn't there for you. Not the way you needed. Tell me how to fix this. Tell me how to fix us, and I'll do it, Cab. I'll do anything."

"Why wouldn't you listen to me before, then?" he said. His cold mask cracked, revealing the frustration simmering below.

"Before?" I asked, startled. "In Avalon?"

"I told you what he's doing is to *help* all of us, to rid the world of creatures like the sorceresses," he said. "Like the Hollowers who turned up their noses at us and would have let us starve."

I stared. "You saw what the hunters did in there. How is that *helping* anyone but himself?"

"He only wants what the sorceresses kept from him," Cabell said. "All of this will stop when he has it."

"Will it?" I pressed, daring to take another step forward.

"Come with me," Cabell said, an edge of pleading to the words. "We won't be helpless ever again. We'll never be the orphans hidden away in the attic, or prey to men like Wyrm ever again. Everything we need, we'll have. Power. A home. *Respect*. We can have it—but only if you come with me."

Until that moment, I'd seen the conversation going one way: me begging him to come with me. To hear him turn the question back on me flipped my world inside out. I couldn't make sense of it. These weren't Lord Death's words. They were *his*.

Maybe . . . maybe I was breaking through. And if I just pushed a little harder—

"We don't need Lord Death for any of that," I said. "I know you think you're in control of what's happening, but the depths of his magic, Cab—what he's given you isn't power. He's taken away your freedom."

"Is that what you think?"

The words were a punch to my lungs. Panic raced through me, trembling and terrible. I reached out a hand to search for him. "Please. It's not too late—it's never too late. You can come back."

I really was a fool, because I almost let myself believe that the silence that followed meant something. That I was starting to bring him around.

"There's no going back. All I see now is what lies ahead." His tone was rough and low, as if he didn't quite trust the wind not to carry the words to more distant ears. "You can come with me now and see the truth of what's unfolding around you, or you can stay here in the dark and die."

"All of those people, Cab," I said. "In Avalon, tonight—how can you stand it, knowing what he did? How could you stand there and do nothing to stop him? Some part of you, deep down, the part of you his magic can't touch, knows all of this is wrong. Knows that what he's doing to you, to everyone, is *wrong*."

He scoffed, his laugh cruel and baiting. "Am I supposed to believe you actually care?"

When I didn't answer, his boots crushed the gravel as he made to cross over the road. I had one last card to play, and I threw it down between us.

"Nash is alive," I told him. "He came back."

His steps stilled. I heard his sharp intake of breath. "You're lying."

"I'm not," I told him. "We can go to him together. He'll explain everything."

I held my breath, as if any small movement might tip us off the knife's edge we stood on.

Damn Nash, I thought. *Damn him for leaving again.* If he'd just stayed with us, if he had come here, if Cabell could have seen him with his own eyes . . .

If, if, if, my mind echoed, singing the refrain of my entire life.

"It's too late for that," Cabell said, barely a whisper.

"It's never too late," I told him again. So close. He was so close.

"In ages past, in a world that was full of darkness and curses, there were two children," I said softly. "And all they had—all they ever had—was each other—"

"Stop it," he hissed.

Cabell's low noise of distress was almost too much to take. In a single, powerful move, he unsheathed his blade and whirled on me. Its cold steel point hovered over my heart, where my death mark still ached.

My eyes slid from his face, hollowed and pale, down to the unfamiliar sword. My agonized expression was mirrored back to me in the silver blade. An inkling of a thought dripped through my mind, only to disperse before it could take shape.

"There's nothing you can do to stop what's already begun," Cabell snarled. "I'll only warn you once—if I see you again, I'll kill you myself."

He lifted his sword and I instinctively reared back. My chest seemed to be caving in on itself; the death mark throbbed sharply, as if pierced by broken bone. He strode through the underbrush and trees, sending rivers of snow falling from their branches. I struggled to draw in my next breath, my body hollow with grief.

"*Tamsin!*"

Through the slant of snow, Emrys appeared. His expression blazed with concern, eyes flashing as he searched the darkness.

The sight sent an unwanted flutter of warmth through me, as if some unconscious part of my mind or heart had summoned him.

Don't touch me.

The twin flames of shame and anger lit within me, not even half as terrible as the deep longing that followed in their wake. The desperation to feel something other than loss was all-consuming, sawing me open from the inside.

Don't touch me.

Why had he even followed me out here? Why was he doing any of this—seeming to care one moment, ripping it away the next? Was it just to hurt me, to have yet another little laugh at my expense?

"Was that Cabell?" Emrys asked, trying and failing to catch his breath.

I nodded, keeping the distance between us even as he took several steps forward. He stopped then and just watched me, his hands curling and uncurling at his sides. No doubt trying to work some warmth back into them. The snow pelted me, my eyes stinging and watering.

He raised his hand toward me, as if to grab me, hold me—only to let it fall back to his side. On another day I might have had the strength to cut him back in some way, but just then, I couldn't overcome the quiet cruelty of it. My nostrils flared.

"Why can't you just leave me alone?" I half begged, half raged at him. He'd taken the ring, taken my trust, taken my deepest secrets. What more could he want? What else was left? To see me break?

Emrys's expression shuttered again as he started to turn away.

"I wish I could," he said, "but you need to come too—we found a survivor."

19

Of all the people who could have survived the Wild Hunt, it had to be Edward Wyrm.

I read the scene in a single look. True to his name, the man had somehow managed to slither his way into a small hidden compartment disguised behind one of the decorative wall panels not far from the massive hearth.

The snow blowing in through the shattered windows had smothered the fires burning on the tables, but it had also subdued the last of the Yule log. Without it, there were only the pitiful flickering of the grand chandeliers and the moonlight to illuminate Wyrm cowering on the floor, his face and balding head smeared with blood.

"—I didn't know it would be this way!" he was telling Caitriona. She glared down at him, her expression merciless as she held the point of her spear to the loose skin of his neck.

Neve looked on, her hands on her hips. "Then what was the party for?"

"It was—"

His eyes bulged as they landed on me, as if I were another unwelcome ghost. He mouthed the word *Lark*.

I'd be all too happy to haunt him until he drew his last miserable breath. "Lovely to see you again, you steaming piece of rat excrement."

He swung his gaze to the safer choice of Emrys.

"Emrys, my boy, tell them! You know how these women can be when they get something in their heads. I've been a friend of your family for years. I had no idea they would—they would—"

"Murder every last one of your party guests and take their souls?" Emrys finished coldly. He pushed past the others, hauling Wyrm up by the blood-splattered collar of his shirt and forcing him toward the bodies littering the floor. "*Look* at them, you coward! Then tell us again you had no idea this would happen!"

The fury in his voice took me aback. Maybe his had been living as close to the surface as mine. Maybe, before today, I would have cared.

Wyrm began to weep, his sobs pitiful and heaving. "It was supposed to be a gathering to greet him! To present him with the mantle! This wasn't supposed to happen!"

"You knew the Wild Hunt was coming?" I asked in disbelief.

"Yes," Wyrm moaned.

Emrys ripped the silver pin from his lapel, then released him, letting Wyrm's body fall limp to the floor. Blood and champagne sprayed up around him and the old man gagged.

"Tell them what this means," Emrys demanded. When the other Hollower struggled to find the words to speak, Emrys threw the pin at him, hard enough for Wyrm to whimper like the mewling child he was. "Tell them!"

"But you know—you know, don't you?" Wyrm insisted, wilting under Emrys's gaze. "Your father was the one who started it all back up again."

"*Tell them,*" Emrys said through gritted teeth, more furious than I'd ever seen him. The others looked on in shock.

"It's . . ." Wyrm tried to regain his composure, smoothing a hand over the last wisps of his hair. "It's the Order of the Silver Bough."

"Why do I already hate the sound of this?" Neve asked.

Of course. I pressed a cold hand to my face.

I didn't know why I hadn't put the meaning of the symbol together before. A silver apple branch symbolized an invitation to journey to an Otherland.

"And the 'Order' is what, exactly?" I pressed. "A little fraternity of power-hungry toads?"

Wyrm bristled. I wondered when had been the last time a woman had spoken to him like that—given the sputtering indignation, probably not in the last three decades. "The Order has been around for hundreds of years. For as long as there have been sorceresses in this world."

"Ah," Neve said darkly, cracking her knuckles one by one. "That would be why."

"The Order is meant to uphold the knightly virtues of Arthur and his court—to protect the world from the destructive magic of sorceresses and their hellish nature," Wyrm continued.

"Hellish nature, huh?" Neve said. I threw out an arm to block her path.

"We need to ask him a few more questions before you tie his tongue in knots," I told her.

Wyrm whimpered.

Neve feigned a reluctant sigh. "Oh, all right. I suppose I can wait a few more minutes."

"She's . . . one of *them*?" Wyrm whispered in horror. He dragged himself across the floor, making as if to escape. Emrys planted a foot on his chest, kicking him back down.

"You're working with a sorceress?" Wyrm cried. "What hold does she have on you, my boy?"

"I'm not your boy." Emrys leaned down, bringing his face in line with Wyrm's. "And you'll be lucky if a hold is all she puts on you."

Wyrm's plum-red face blanched as he looked between the two of them. Neve's smile made the hair on my arms rise.

"What business does this Order have with Lord Death?" Caitriona asked, swinging her spear back around toward him.

Wyrm held up his hands, as if he had a face worth protecting. "Many of us are descended from the druids. We only desired to renew our worship of him—to summon him back into our world to defeat our enemies."

I leaned down, resisting the urge to spit in his face. "You wanted death magic."

"Well . . . yes," Wyrm said. "Is that really so wrong? Why should the sorceresses be the only ones with true power?"

I shook my head in disgust. Wyrm and so many of the dead around me were Cunningfolk. They *had* magic, abilities no mere mortal had. Just not enough, clearly.

"You really expect us to believe you didn't know what would happen tonight?" I asked.

Wyrm sent one last desperate look Emrys's way. "Your father wrote to me that I should host the celebration, to offer our allegiance. I didn't know what had become of him—what had become of all of them . . ." He trailed off, twisting around to survey the hall. "D-Do you hear that?"

A moment later, I did.

The crackling felt eerily familiar, enough that it set my teeth on edge as I looked up toward the ceiling, expecting to find the plaster splitting. But it was a wet sound, like footsteps in a marsh, a gurgle—

Neve sucked in a sharp gasp. I spun, following her gaze until it landed on the bodies near her feet. Something moved beneath their skin, slithering.

Caitriona bumped into me from behind, trying to escape the remains that were twitching, the limbs slapping against the floor, their teeth chattering.

"Oh gods, *oh gods!*" Wyrm cried, scrambling onto unsteady feet. Using the distraction, he fled for the open library door without a backward glance, twisting away from the rattling bodies. At the first *snap* of bone, I knew, with horrifying certainty, it had been a mistake not to follow him.

That sickening sound, the gurgle of entrails shifting, of cartilage stretching and remaking—that was one I recognized.

From Cabell's transformations.

"What in all the hells . . . ," Emrys breathed out.

Spidery limbs and blood exploded out of the man's chest at my feet, his skin stretching and tearing as his spine pulled apart, spiking through his flesh, through the ragged remains of his tuxedo jacket. His back curled up like an animal stretching after a long sleep, and when he lifted his clawed-off face, it had become a familiar gray mask of death.

He—it—rose on long, sticky-wet legs, bringing its glowing white eyes level with mine. My mind screamed for me to move, but I couldn't. My feet had turned to stone. The stench of rot billowed around me as the creature's jaws broke and remade themselves into a snout, as its remaining teeth became silvery knives beneath its bloodless lips.

The heat of its baying screech blew my hair back from my face, splattering me with foaming spittle that burned everywhere it touched.

Terror, as it turned out, was its own kind of thrall. It held me there like a helpless prisoner as the corpses rose as Children of the Night.

They moved as one, circling us with a predator's delight. They had woken starving—many devoured the discarded flesh or the half-transformed monsters, shredding them before they could fully rise. The hall shifted before my eyes, smearing into that of a dead forest. Smoke became mist.

I couldn't move.

Time unspooled violently around me. At the edge of my vision, Neve lifted her hands to cast a spell, her lips barely parting before she was knocked back to the floor with a single blow. The sound her skull made as it collided with the wood echoed in my ears as she lay unmoving beneath the monster.

"Neve!" Caitriona launched her spear into the back of the monster. The weapon splintered as it soared through the air, embedding itself like a spray of arrowheads in the writhing body.

If she was shocked, Caitriona took it in her usual stride, leaping forward to rip the largest piece of the spear out of the monster's convulsing body. The scattered pieces flew toward that largest one, reassembling in her hand in the instant before she threw it into the next creature that tried to claw Neve away from us. Caitriona slid across the distance between them on her knees, covering the sorceress with her body.

It was the last thing I saw before I was falling too.

The hard shove knocked me sideways, robbing the breath from my lungs even before I slammed into the floor and a heavy weight collapsed on top of me. A ragged shout of pain blossomed like a blood-red rose.

Everything came into sharp relief as Emrys tried to stand again, one hand clutching the ragged claw marks slashed across his chest from shoulder to hip, as if he could hold the skin together by force.

Blood spilled out between his fingers as he gasped for breath. He staggered, dropping to a knee. He met my horrified gaze with one of total resignation. The Children skittered toward him from all directions.

"*No!*" The word tore out of me as I leapt to my feet, flinging broken furniture, discarded weapons, anything I could find. Nothing held them back for more than a second. Nothing would, but fire.

"Cait, please!" I shouted. "Please, you have to!"

She knew what I was asking her—it was the only option left to us.

Her fingers worked furiously, creating a flow of symbols, calling the magic of the Goddess in the way that was uniquely hers. Summoning fire.

But none came.

Her head shot up in disbelief. I watched in growing fear as she tried again, alternating between striking the Children and trying to eke a single flame out of the darkness around her. Her shoulders shook as the movements grew more and more frantic.

Emrys collapsed to the floor, blood flowing out of him in dark rivers. One of the Children bent over him, ripping the collar away from his shirt to get at his exposed neck.

A thunderous roar and flash exploded from behind me, and the creature's head was blown clean off its body. Oily blood sloshed out from its torso as it collapsed to the floor, thrashing in the throes of death.

Nash emerged from the whirling smoke, a hunting rifle raised to his eye, firing at the creatures again to drive them back. He turned the barrel up toward the chandeliers, firing at their chains until they crashed down around us. The twinkling crystals shattered, slicing through the Children who couldn't jump away in time.

More rose, screeching with the rage of the newly born. They were drawn to the thunderous sound of the gunfire and bounded away from us, toward him. Their claws tore the freezing air, primed for his own flesh.

"Nash!" I screamed.

His cool expression never wavered. He lifted the gun's sights again and, this time, kicked one of the large barrels strewn across the floor toward them. The Children vaulted over it, but the bullet was faster, igniting the whiskey inside.

The explosion flashed hot and bright. My ears rang as I tasted the burn of it with my next gulping breath. The Children scattered back toward the window, stopping only to feast on the severed limbs of those caught in the blast.

Nash was splattered in enough blood to look like a monster himself as he shouted to us over the shrieking of the Children. "Get to the library, you wee idiots!"

We did not need to be told again.

Caitriona scooped Neve up in her arms, her first uneven steps quickly turning to a flat-out run for the door.

I knelt beside Emrys, hesitating again. His skin was ashen.

Don't touch me.

Well, right now, I couldn't give either of us that choice, because I'd be damned before I'd let him die for me.

I looped his arm around my neck. His blood flowed, heavy and unrelenting, soaking into my jacket as I struggled to get us upright.

"*Walk*, Trust Fund," I told him, clutching the hand at my shoulder to try to get him to focus. His eyelids were drooping, his face going as lax as the rest of him. "Don't make me carry your sorry ass—"

As if I could. He was *heavy*.

Dead weight, my mind whispered.

"Leave . . . me . . . ," he gasped out.

The words pissed me off enough that when the next surge of adrenaline came, I started fully dragging him. The sound of gunfire was the only confirmation that Nash was still behind me.

"Come on, come on," Nash said, reaching Emrys's other side and gripping his waist. With him balanced between us, we were able to drag him through the library in a few short steps. Nash kicked the door. Relinquishing Emrys to me again, he moved to pull and kick bookshelves down to block the entrance.

"Emrys?" I said, his weight dragging both of us to the floor. "Can you hear me?"

He gave no acknowledgment at all. His lashes fluttered as he fought to open his eyes again. I pulled off my jacket, pressing it against his open wounds, for whatever little good that would do.

The Children battered at the door from the other side. Flakes of plaster shook from the ceiling and walls.

"Vexing vexations—*Tamsy!*" Nash shouted. "A little help here!"

I tore myself away from Emrys's side, placing his hands over my bundled jacket. I tried not to think about how cold his skin was to the touch.

"You don't get to die a hero," I told him sternly, pushing up off the floor. *You don't get to die at all.*

I threw a panicked look over to where Caitriona had set Neve down on one of the love seats, but the sorceress was awake now, her eyes darting around the room.

"What . . . ?" came Neve's faint voice.

Caitriona gripped her arms, searching her for injuries, saying something I was too far away to hear. Neve's gaze shot to the other girl's face—Neve looked momentarily stunned.

"Tamsy!" Nash bellowed. He'd dug his heels in to try to hold the quaking bookshelves in place as the Children savaged the door. Their eyes flashed through the gouges they'd raked in the wood.

I mimicked his positioning, throwing my weight back against the bookshelves until my muscles quivered with the effort. The bookshelves thumped against my back and my palms with bruising force, and I only pushed against them harder.

It's really him, I thought. This was the Nash I remembered. Desperately reckless, always finding himself in the thick of things, but armed with an impossibly good sense of timing.

"Did I, or did I not, tell you to stay in that apartment?" Nash got out through gritted teeth.

"Is this really the moment for a lecture?" I snapped. "You would've had to lock me up—"

The idea that came to me was as reckless as it was breathtakingly stupid—but that had never stopped me before.

"I'll be right back!" I jumped away from the bookshelves, leaving a startled Nash in my wake. Caitriona dove forward to take my place, eyeing the shuddering door uneasily.

"Tamsin!" Nash shouted after me, but there was no time to explain.

I ran for the stairs and flew down them, my arms pumping at my sides as I burst into the cellar. The magically cloaked opening to the warehouse buzzed against my skin as I broke through it.

This is stupid, I thought, bending to pick up a large fragment from a champagne bottle. *So, so stupid* . . .

Olwen had lifted the mirror upright again and was pacing anxiously in front of it, her hands tangled in her ink-blue hair.

"—if you release me, I won't eat mortal flesh for a year," the hag was saying, watching the priestess. "All right, you have me. A fortnight, then. Well, perhaps three days."

Olwen stopped. "I don't think that's how bargaining works."

"I'll take that deal," I said, rushing toward them.

Olwen gasped in horror at the sight of me. "What's happened?"

"Neve and Emrys—they're hurt, they're in the library—"

She didn't need to hear anything else. Pressing her bag to her hip to keep the bottles inside from rattling, she ran back the way I had come.

Leaving me alone with the hag.

The primordial creature eyed me, licking her lips at the blood staining my skin and clothes, edging ever closer to the surface of the mirror. The shard of glass cut into my palm as I drew in a deep breath and curled my fingers.

"You said you prefer the taste of magic-born creatures, right?" I asked.

The hag nodded eagerly.

"If I let you out—right now, right this second—will you swear not to eat any humans—any mortals—for at least a year?"

"A *year?*" the hag bellowed, her breath fogging up the glass between us. "I'll swear to three days—"

"A fortnight," I countered.

"Fine, a fortnight, I agree!" the hag countered quickly.

"Do you vow it?"

"*Yes!*" Saliva was already dripping from her eager fangs.

"Good," I said, reaching around the back of the mirror to claw through the sigils there with the glass. "I hope you're hungry."

20

Upstairs, in the aftermath of the hag, it was frighteningly quiet again.

I moved slowly, as if walking through yet another nightmare. The mirror pulsed beneath the velvet cover I'd wrapped it in. After the hag had wrenched herself free of the glass, the floor-length mirror had shrunk down to the size of a handheld one, solving the smallest of our problems. Its insubstantial weight was a relief to my exhausted body.

Rosydd had scorched the air with magic as she'd fled the warehouse. The power was different than the others' I had felt. This was a deep, ancient magic, one that gave birth to worlds and tore others asunder. It vibrated in my bones, my teeth, as I traced its path up the stairs and back into the library.

I counted the others as I saw them.

One—Caitriona standing on the remains of the bookshelves, staring through the missing door into the hall. A glob of viscous blood fell from the ceiling onto the floor in front of her, and as I neared, I could see where that same monstrous blood had painted the ceiling. In the grand hall, only a scattering of bones was left of the Children.

Two—Neve sat beside *three*, Nash, watching as he bent over *four*, Emrys. His shirt had been torn open, exposing the horrifying wounds and the way the claws had reopened some of his scars. The bridge of Nash's nose was still swollen from where I'd hit it, and the bruise only seemed to add to the seriousness of his mien. His brow furrowed in concentration as he used a needle and thread to try to sew the gashes shut.

I'd seen him stitch himself up countless times after run-ins with unhappy business partners and close calls with curses, but seeing him do it to another person—and a Dye at that—only added to the surreal quality of the moment.

"There, dove, you can apply it now, just be quick and gentle with it," Nash murmured.

Neve screwed a small jar of ointment open, and its soft, minty fragrance somehow cut through even the vile stench of death around us. Her fingers shook as she dabbed it onto the row of stitches Nash had just finished before moving on to the next.

I chewed on my lip as fear swallowed the rest of my thoughts. Emrys's skin looked like wax, as if all the life had drained from it. But somehow his heart was still beating. Somehow he was still breathing.

Nash finally looked up, his eyes scanning me quickly before returning to his work. "You've had some real harebrained ideas in your short life . . ." He looked up again, the corner of his mouth twitching. "That, however, was not one of them."

That rare bit of praise caught me off guard.

"Are you okay?" I asked Neve, despising the emotion overtaking my voice, the strain. She waved off my concern, still looking a bit worse for wear. "Next time you think about being that brave, remember that no one's going to take care of your weird bone collection. *And* I'm going to be very upset."

She struggled to smother her smile. "Are you . . . mad at me for getting hurt?"

"Of course I am!" I said huffily. "You're not allowed to bail on us—"

I clamped my lips shut, glaring at Nash as he pretended not to listen.

"And *you*," I said. "You couldn't have shown up five minutes earlier?"

He scowled. "If you'd just done what I asked, the four of you—"

I stilled, letting the rest of his words roll past me like the rumble of thunderclouds.

Four of us. *Four.*

I scanned the wreckage of the library again, fear spiking my pulse. The mirror slid from my hands, hitting the floor with a dull *thump*. Neve sent me a questioning look.

I counted *five,* but there should have been *six.*

"Where's Olwen?" My voice sounded like I was speaking underwater.

Caitriona was in front of me in the space of a moment. "What do you mean? She's downstairs."

My pulse sped and sped, until I thought I would double over. "No. She came up to help you—"

Caitriona pushed past me. Her silver hair streamed out behind her like a banner as we bypassed the open doors of the elevator and made for the stairs again. By the time we reached the warehouse, the magic that had burst from the mirror with the hag had settled, and the room was cold and silent again.

"Olwen?" Caitriona called out. "*Olwen!* Where are you?"

"Maybe she hid when she heard the Children?" I thought aloud. But even I knew that made no sense. She would never abandon the people she loved, even to a losing fight. "*Olwen!*"

Caitriona went right, heading in the direction of the armoire Emrys and I had hidden inside. A new thread of cold weaving through the air drew me left, and as I made my way through the shattered remains of shelves and cases, I saw something that hadn't been there before.

Snow.

White flakes floated in the standing crimson pools of champagne, then melted away. More and more of it was scattered over what was visible of the floor, over furniture that had been kicked over and out of the way.

I followed the trail of it, gaining speed with every step, tracing that same icy thread through the darkness of the room until it brought me to a stone wall. There, the snowflakes were drifting into the warehouse not from a crack between the stones, but *through* the stones themselves.

I held out a hand, pushing it forward, feeling the magic crawl over my skin toward the hidden passage on the other side.

"Cait!" I shouted.

Emrys had been right after all. There *was* a way out of the warehouse—a little smuggler's tunnel that opened to a storm-whipped river. The snow shrouded much of the surrounding landscape. I could only make out the scattered trees by their shadowed outlines. The sigils carved into the stone near my feet were the same spell that had concealed the entrance to the warehouse.

I shielded my eyes and, bracing my front foot, leaned out from the edge of the tunnel, wary of the steep drop down to the water. "Olwen!"

The sharp smell of snow filled my lungs, undercut by the river's earthiness. There was no dock, but the river's dark water lapped up against two wooden posts marking either side of the tunnel entrance. Loose ropes twirled from each.

"She fought," Caitriona said quietly behind me.

I spun around. She gestured to the wall beside her, sweeping her hands down to the ground, revealing what my untrained eye had missed. The gray stone was charred black, and chunks of the smooth surface were scattered around her feet. She took a careful step toward me, crossing one foot over the other. Her mouth tightening with concentration as she knelt to touch a groove in the dirt, where something—someone—had been dragged.

Her eyes followed its path, stopping at a spot near my feet. It was only then that distress settled over her expression, carving deep lines in her face.

I forced myself to look.

Buried beneath a layer of snow, painted brown with the tunnel's grime, was a bracelet of braided fabric, torn apart at the knot.

I picked it up with trembling fingers, holding it out for Caitriona to see. The tunnel seemed to press in around us, suffocating.

Only two alive in Rivenoak had known about this way out. One was upstairs, unconscious. The other . . .

Caitriona's eyes met mine, burning with rage, and I knew she was thinking the same thing.

Wyrm.

Bath, England

His heart was still racing when he broke through the last thicket of trees and found himself in a clearing near the river.

He forced himself to stop, steadying his breath as he listened to the ambling river carve its path through the earth.

His skin itched with the urge to shift. To give in to his riotous pulse and feed his mind to the beast prowling inside him. In the hound's mind, there was nothing but instinct—to hunt, to obey, to kill.

Instead, he tugged the mantle off his shoulders and hastily folded it. The magic woven into the fabric whispered against his fingers, tempting him with warmth and power. Inviting him to disappear.

The problem was, he couldn't escape his thoughts.

Nash is alive. He came back.

He braced a hand against a tree, struggling to control his breath. To master himself. He could not go before his lord like this—weak and trembling like a child.

How had Tamsin managed to find the exact lie that would bring him back to that pathetic, sniveling boy he'd been?

We can go to him together. He'll explain everything.

The seneschal grunted as he felt the bones of his spine elongate, the first of hundreds of fractures that would remake him, if he let them. The pain steadied him, breathed fire into his soul.

Seeing her had caught him off guard, and he was repulsed by how cowardly he'd been, slipping Arthur's mantle on to evade her. But he knew her—knew Tamsin would follow, because she was too damn stubborn to be reasonable and accept his choice. He hadn't been in the mood for an argument he knew would only end one way.

If she had just *listened* to him, if she hadn't been so convinced of her own truth . . .

He didn't understand it. She'd spent their whole godsforsaken lives longing for magic, to have what he did, and she still turned her nose up at this? At the chance to be someone in a world that had rejected her at every turn?

But she hadn't just rejected his offer. She'd rejected *him,* twice now.

It's the third chance you give that makes you the fool, Nash used to say.

He hadn't lied or embroidered the truth to frighten her. It was as simple as the choice he'd had: if she didn't join them, there was only one fate left to her.

"I see the evening has been an unbridled success."

The silken voice slipped out from the shadows between the nearby trees. His lord appeared a moment later, and though King Arthur's body was slighter than the seneschal had always imagined, his lord's presence still managed to blot out the snow around him.

Snow melted through the thin fabric of the seneschal's trousers as he knelt and held out the folded mantle in offering. He bowed his head, both in respect and to buy himself a moment to control his expression.

The snow creaked beneath his master's boots, but the seneschal didn't look up. The tendons in his neck strained with the effort of holding himself still when every part of him was screaming to shift, to run through the woods until the sun rose and burned away the darkness of his thoughts.

The mantle was carefully removed from his outstretched hands.

"Cabell," Lord Death said softly.

He looked up at the name and inwardly swore as he realized his mistake. His body tensed, spine curling as he anticipated the blow.

"That is not your name," Lord Death said, his voice low and lethal.

His icy hand closed over the back of the seneschal's neck, tightening. "That was never your name."

"Yes, my lord," the seneschal whispered, licking his dry lips. "I'm sorry, my lord."

"Bledig," Lord Death said, his fingers tightening, as if to imprint the name on his servant's pale skin. "I feared that this would prove too much for you."

Bledig. Yes. That was his name. His true name. The one he'd forgotten in his human life.

"No, my lord. I was pleased to serve you," he said. "I remain your seneschal."

He hated the way it sounded less like a declaration and more like a question.

Lord Death's laugh was like a blade running down his spine. "Is that so? Then why did I witness you engaging with that wretch of a girl? Have you forgotten her callousness toward you? Her dismissal of all that you are?"

"No, my lord," he said, his chest aching as he remembered. She had chosen her own ignorance over him—her hatred and fear of him. "She was . . . she is nothing."

"You told me that you would kill her if you met her again," Lord Death said. "Was that a lie?"

In ages past, in a world that was full of darkness and curses, there were two children . . .

At the edge of his vision, a flash of blond hair moved past a nearby tree. He kept his head down but shifted his gaze, his heart battering his ribs.

But it wasn't her.

The little girl was nothing more than an apparition—a fading memory. Her skin shimmered with translucence as she returned his look with a menacing one of her own. Her tangle of hair was half tucked into a knit cap, her tunic rumpled.

Her name . . .

Flea.

Flea of Avalon.

"Well?" Lord Death prompted, the word barbed. "What do you have to say for yourself?"

"I . . ." The seneschal licked his lips again. He had never been a good liar. He'd always left that to his sister.

She's still lying. About all of it, he reminded himself. *Even Nash.*

"I simply did not want to risk her taking the mantle," he said, inwardly cringing at the poor excuse, "or harming it in some way."

Lord Death let out a huff. "If she could defeat you so easily, perhaps I have chosen the wrong sibling."

The chill of the wet snow bled into the seneschal's human skin as he waited for whatever his lord would do next. But something made him look again—made his eyes shift back toward those same trees, where the little girl stood.

He inhaled sharply, having to steel his body to keep from flinching. Bright blood flowed down her face, her clothing, collecting in the snow at her feet. Her lips moved, but no words reached him. And her eyes . . . they were horrendous. Cold, with no flicker of life.

"Rise, Bledig," Lord Death said.

He did, forcing himself to obey. To keep his head bowed, so as not to cause his lord any more offense than he already had. The blood—it became a river in the snow, winding around the roots and rocks, cutting a path straight toward him.

"Gather the riders," Lord Death said. "The night is still young."

The seneschal let out a shuddering breath. "Yes, my lord. Where will we go now?"

A single gloved finger touched the hollow beneath his chin, tilting his face up to meet his master's. For a moment, he saw himself reflected in a former king's eyes.

"That, young one, will depend entirely on you," Lord Death said. "And who you wish to be."

21

When Cabell and I were kids, the library's attic had felt like a vast amount of space—like our very own kingdom. That was the trouble with living mostly out of nylon tents on windswept landscapes or uninhabited forests; it made everything else feel secure and comfortable in comparison.

With five grown people and all our belongings, though, it was feeling less cozy and more cramped.

"Let's set him down here—oh, for the love of—" Nash swore a blue streak as he knocked his head against the low, slanted ceiling. I hastily shook out a blanket for Emrys, and Nash dropped him onto it unceremoniously, mewling pitifully as he rubbed his own aching head.

"Why are we *here*?" Caitriona demanded before she'd even fully set Emrys's legs down, spinning up the same fight we'd had leaving Rivenoak. "We should be going after Olwen—"

"Oh?" Nash interrupted. "And you know where it is they're going? Are you that eager to swing your sword around and fight shadows?"

Caitriona's anger only deepened; her head drew back, the way a snake's did before it struck. "Are you mocking me?"

"No, dove, I'm trying to make a point, however unwelcome it may be," Nash said.

I sat beside Emrys, too exhausted to try to join the argument. I'd felt my heart break before, in the armoire at Rivenoak, but looking at him now, hovering just out of death's reach, it was as if someone had reached into my chest to rip out each jagged shard. His face was too pale, too slack, but he was breathing, however faintly. I brought my thumb to my lips, biting at the hangnail there, trying to smother the scream that had been threatening to tear out of me all night.

"He could be taking her to Lord Death!" Caitriona tried again.

"Would he?" Neve said. "He seemed terrified of the hunters . . ."

"He's got the courage of a mouse but the scruples of a rat," Nash said.

He ran a bruised hand back through his sandy hair, his sky-blue eyes soft. He spoke in a gentle tone I hadn't heard in years—not since the last time Cabell had fallen ill. It was startling that, after everything, it could still have a comforting effect on me.

"If you hear nothing else, hear me on this, Lady Caitriona," he began.

"Don't call me that," she said sharply, swinging a fist up.

"Are you not a priestess of Avalon?" he asked calmly.

The memory of her trying to summon fire burned me all over again. The thought was cruel, but if Caitriona had voluntarily abandoned her vow . . . what was to say that the magic hadn't abandoned her in turn?

"Avalon is gone," she said, her jaw clenched.

"So it is," Nash said. "But you are not, and neither is Lady Olwen. I understand why you want to go rushing after her—"

"You could not possibly understand," Caitriona said, a tremor running through her words.

Neve hovered behind her, her hands outstretched, as if she might try to draw the other girl away, but in the end, she didn't. When Caitriona was fighting, nothing could stop her, not even us.

"—*but,*" Nash continued, "do you know where Lord Death resides in this world?"

"Why don't you ask your son?" Caitriona's words had their intended effect. Nash's brows shot up, as if he was surprised she'd managed to land a hit.

"I intend to," he said.

Caitriona spun, the full weight of her ire bearing down on me. "And *you* didn't think to demand those answers from him? You allowed him to escape. Or did you finally—*finally*—see what has been obvious to the rest of us for so long: that he serves Lord Death by *choice*?"

"Cait—" I began. I looked to Neve, but the sorceress turned her face down, not denying the other girl's words.

They don't believe he can be saved, my mind whispered. I looked to Neve to deny it, but she only pressed a hand to her mouth.

"He's a *monster*, Tamsin, and you know what must be done," Caitriona continued. "There is only one way to stop a monster."

My heart froze in my chest, finishing what Caitriona had left unspoken. *Kill it.*

"That's enough," Nash said sharply. "Inflicting pain on another won't ease the pain inside you."

Caitriona's nostrils flared with her next sharp inhale, but she held her tongue.

"Now," Nash continued, "you're certain Olwen and Wyrm didn't merely escape together?"

"Olwen would *never* leave us behind," Caitriona swore.

"Even still," Nash said. "Wyrm could be up to anything. Perhaps he only wanted to use her as a shield to escape and he's already let her go. Perhaps he's brought her to the next guild over in Edinburgh to try to get information out of her. Perhaps she's beat the snot out of him and is now searching for *you*."

Caitriona's chest heaved with the force of her ragged breaths, but this time, she didn't answer.

"Say he did bring her to Lord Death . . . where is the sense in going to confront him when you have no weapon to defeat him or his hunters?" Nash asked. "You'd end up killing yourself, not saving her."

"So be it," she said.

"Cait," Neve said, horrified.

"Don't you dare say that," I told her, my shock finally slain by anger. "It would devastate Olwen to hear you say that."

I knew because it killed me, too, and I didn't know how to make her take it back.

"This world is appalling, full of horrors. Even the air tastes poisoned, but it's alive and Avalon is in ruins," Caitriona said, her voice trembling. "There's no place in it for me, except to protect my sister, and if I cannot do that, then what is the point of any of this? What is the point of *me,* when all the others are gone?"

A hush filled the attic.

Caitriona's shoulders slumped, her arms hugging tight to her center, as if she was afraid of what else might slip out. Days without sleep, with little food, and even less hope had worn through her armor and revealed the wound that had been growing for days, tearing open again and again.

I closed my eyes, hands curling against the fabric of my jeans.

"Caitriona," Nash said into the silence. "I cannot give you purpose, or a reason to persist. That you must give to yourself. Have patience with your heart. There's no steel that can be forged without fire. What you have faced before this moment has prepared you to meet it."

Caitriona swallowed, looking down at her mud-stained sneakers. The words were almost . . . fatherly. If it hadn't been for the look on Caitriona's face, the way she was absorbing the words, I would have made a snide comment.

"I know what it is to have what you believed was meant for you ripped away, and to find yourself on a path you never imagined," Nash continued.

My already dark mood worsened, and I had to fight everything in me not to scoff. He knew nothing of the sort. All he had ever done was follow his own whims and fancies, to the ultimate ruin of our family. I almost couldn't take this.

"But there's still good left to be found in this world," Nash said. "Olwen is not lost to you, but we cannot risk endangering her by going in without a plan to destroy Lord Death."

"We have the Mirror of Beasts," Caitriona pushed back. The raw anger was gone, but the desperation in her eyes was still there.

Nash's brow furrowed as he took a sip of his cold coffee. "I don't see how that's possible, unless you mean the Mirror of Shalott." Understanding dawned on his face. "Is that why you were at Rivenoak?"

"Right place at the wrong time," I said.

I couldn't bring myself to revisit the memories of the last few hours, not yet. But one was circling at the back of my mind, and had been since we'd arrived at the library. There had been that one moment, when I'd faced Cabell, that a thought had come to me, as sharp as the sword in his hand.

Please let me be wrong, I thought, releasing a deep breath. *Don't let it all have been for nothing.*

I forced myself not to look at Emrys's unconscious form. His deathly pale face.

We couldn't lose this one small win, not when we'd already lost so much.

Please let me be wrong, I pleaded. But I knew no gods were listening.

"I'm sorry to tell you that's not the true Mirror of Beasts," Nash said, his words stealing the last glimmer of hope I had left. He straightened, puffing himself up for whatever tale he was about to weave.

The words were bitter on my tongue. "It's a sword, isn't it?"

"Wait," Neve began, startled. "What makes you say that?"

The floor squeaked as Nash shifted his weight. I couldn't tell if he was proud or annoyed. "Yes, I believe it's a sword, Tamsy. How did you figure it out?"

"Look upon me with despair, for I am the Mirror of Beasts. My silver

sings of eternity as I capture all in my glare," I said softly. "The blade is the mirror. You glimpse your reflection in it the moment before your death."

Nash seemed even more astonished. "Well, yes, that's what I suspect. But where did you hear that riddle?"

"The better question is, how do *you* know about it?" I asked. The memory of him recounting Creiddylad's story flooded back to me, as disorienting as it had been the first time. "How do you know so much about Lord Death and the Wild Hunt?"

"I've spent my life sticking my nose in places where it doesn't belong, collecting bits and bobs of lesser-known histories, and trading gossip with sorceresses," Nash said. "You think I haven't heard a scary story here and there?"

Nash lied as easily and naturally as he drew breath.

"So . . . what sword is it?" Neve asked.

"I believe it's one of the magic blades forged by the Goddess," Nash said. "Lord Death is nearly a god himself—and the crown he wears allows him to call upon the full might of Annwn's magic. It would take something divinely forged to kill him."

"Avalon was once home to all of the Goddess's gifts," Caitriona intoned flatly. "That included a number of finely honed weapons."

"Merlin told Viviane the mirror was out of her reach forevermore, which, by the way, is *such* a good word," Neve said. "So it was removed from the isle at one point or another. But, I mean, how many magic swords have come out of that place? Even Tamsin found one."

Nash turned to me, eyes alight with almost boyish excitement. "You did?"

I gestured toward our pile of things at the far edge of the attic. I'd found the sword—or maybe it had found me—at the bottom of the lake near the High Priestesses' burial mound. Even thinking about it was enough to draw the dream from the other night back to the front of my mind, and I hadn't wanted to touch it since.

"Is this . . . the sword of Rhydderch Hael? Dyrnwyn?" Nash said incredulously. "*White-Hilt?* You left behind a bloody fire sword when you went to Rivenoak?"

"What, am I supposed to walk around with it and wave it at people like a cool party trick?" I snapped. "How was I supposed to know what was going to happen?"

I'd left the sword behind because I hadn't wanted to believe there was any use for it. At least, that was what I'd told the others, but it had been far harder to lie to myself.

It was a piece of Avalon and the person I'd been there—the person I'd let myself believe I could be.

Someone who cared.

Someone worthy.

I'd only brought it to the library because Neve had made me, and because I didn't want it to be taken from the apartment while we were gone. But I couldn't shake the fear that when I pulled it from its scabbard, the blade would no longer catch fire in my hand.

The truth was, it *had* been a mistake on my part not to bring it. I knew Children of the Night had crossed into our world with Lord Death. It was inevitable we'd face them again, and if there was one thing a fire sword was useful for, it was scaring off monsters who hated light.

"I should have suspected something like this would happen," Caitriona said. "Avalon's dead underwent the same transformation into Children when we didn't burn the bodies."

"Is this happening to all the people they kill? Was that why Hemlock wanted her body burned?" Neve asked, horrified. "I thought the curse with the Children was connected to the isle, not to the way they died—or who killed them."

Nash pulled the sword from its scabbard, but only an inch. It was enough to spark the white flames on the exposed steel, the air whining and singing as the fire licked at it.

I stared at it in disbelief. Him? *Really?*

"Now I know that thing is busted," I bit out.

"Was it forged by the Goddess?" Neve asked hopefully.

"Sadly, no." Nash slid it fully back into its scabbard and handed it to me. "The first Lady of the Lake enchanted it with protective magic for a mortal king who swore to aid her in protecting the isle. I'll talk to Librarian and poke around in the stacks to see what I can find about the isle's divinely forged weapons. There's a bathroom downstairs I'd advise taking advantage of, and I'm sure we can rustle up some food from the lockers."

It was strange, in a way, to feel relief at someone else taking charge of the situation and telling us what to do. But even after Nash vanished back down into the empty library, none of us moved.

"Are we really going to leave Olwen in Wyrm's hands?" Neve asked softly.

The thought tore at me. "She's strong. As much as it pains me to say, I think Nash could be right about this—she might have already gotten away."

"And if she hasn't?" Caitriona asked. "If that despicable man brings her to Lord Death and he kills her and makes her one of his riders, or worse?"

"We can't think like that," Neve said. "Olwen is useful to him. She'll find a way to stay alive until we can get to her, wherever it is they're hiding out. But I think we're only going to get one good chance to strike at him before the solstice."

Less than nine full days. That was all we had left to find this sword, and with every night that passed, he created more hunters, and more Children. And as the Children killed innocent people, more and more would appear until they overran the mortals of this world.

"The sorceresses can help." Neve seemed galvanized at the thought of having something concrete to do. "They must have a sense of where Lord Death is hiding, and where we can find the sword. I'll write to Madrigal again and ask."

Caitriona lingered even after Neve went downstairs, still caught in that painful trap of indecision.

"Cabell won't let anything happen to her," I said, and instantly regretted it. She didn't believe me, and her certainty shattered mine. In the quiet that followed, my own thoughts began to turn traitor.

He stood by and let it happen, my mind hissed. *At the tower. At Rivenoak.*

"We have to find the sword," Caitriona said. I heard the tears in her voice, but didn't turn around. Didn't try to comfort her. That wasn't what she wanted.

She wanted her sister, and if I couldn't give her that, I could at least give her privacy.

I ran a thumb along the braided bracelet.

"Together to the end," I whispered.

"Beyond that," Caitriona answered, her tone hollow.

We'd made our choice, but the problem with choices wasn't in the making—it was in learning to live with them. And that was a poison without an antidote.

22

After Caitriona went down to wash in the library's bathroom and Neve busied herself looking for wherever Librarian had stashed Griflet, the attic had fallen silent again.

Only Emrys, still unconscious, was left for company. I sat beside him, listening to him struggle for each wheezing breath, staring into the night air.

A single word escaped him, a low murmur rippling with terror.

"... *don't* ..."

"Emrys?" I whispered. I moved to brush his dark hair from his forehead, to see if I could rouse him. Then those words, *Don't touch me,* the memory of him pulling away like what I'd done had repulsed him, lashed at my raw muddle of feelings.

I brought my hand back into my lap.

"He'll be all right."

Nash stood in the doorway, hunched slightly to accommodate the slant of the roof. In his hands were two steaming mugs of coffee. The smell of it all but purred through me, setting off a deep longing.

"How would you know?" I muttered.

"Fever hasn't set in yet, which means the ointment's doing its job staving off infection," Nash said, hesitating a moment before he sat down next to me.

The coffee mug was right in front of my face, my exhausted body was begging for it, but my petulance was stronger. "I don't want that. I won't be able to sleep."

Nash raised an eyebrow.

Okay, no, my body and mind had hit the point of exhaustion where not even caffeine was powerful enough to keep me upright. My words were starting to slur.

I took it from him, but I wasn't happy about it. I rummaged through my workbag, bracing myself for Nash to comment on the fact that it used to be his.

Instead, he eyed Emrys's scars with a look of curiosity that made me feel protective against my will. "Don't remember Endymion's favorite toy being quite this banged up."

"He's the one who did this to his son," I said, fighting the knot building in my throat. The thick scars were darker, more pronounced against Emrys's ashen skin, crisscrossing his body like a map of suffering.

"Ah" was all Nash had to say to that.

"Is that why you warned me to stay away from him?" I asked. "Endymion?"

"The man had ice for a heart long before he joined the Wild Hunt," Nash said. "When I heard he was spinning up the old Order of the Silver Stick nonsense, I made it a point to keep us away from the guild as much as possible."

Nash watched as I ripped open a soggy instant coffee packet from my bag and dumped that into the mug—drip coffee alone had never had enough flavor for me. Gripping the handle, I gave it a few careful shakes, trying to swirl the powder into the liquid. Nash looked on, horrified.

"Bloody roses, you still drink that stuff, Tamsy?" he said with a startled laugh. "You'll give yourself a heart attack."

"If you didn't want me to drink it, you shouldn't have given it to me when I was a kid," I said. "And anyway, it tastes better."

"It tastes like it was brewed in a festering wound," he said, taking a long drink of his own. "You need to eat something."

"I'm fine."

Next to me, a small bowl of dried fruit and nuts sat untouched. I'd never had a problem with it before, but the thought of eating a dead Hollower's food just then turned my stomach.

"You're not fine. You're all skin and bones," he said. "You'll need your strength if you're planning to run off and do something foolishly brave."

I scowled, knowing he had a point.

"Is this supposed to be your version of parenting?" I bit back.

"Just common sense," Nash said, drinking his coffee. He looked down at Emrys again, rubbing a hand over his mouth. This time, he kept his thoughts to himself.

"It really is you, isn't it?" I said, hating the throb of emotion in my voice.

"Of course it's me," he said, exasperated. "Ask your questions, Tamsin, I can all but hear them knocking around your mind."

"Fine," I said. "How are you alive?"

"You found the coin," he said. "You already know."

"The one you said to bury with bone and ash?" I pressed. Emrys and I had found it hidden beneath a stone at the ruins of Tintagel, but nothing had happened when we'd followed Nash's note with instructions on what to do with the silver coin.

Apparently something *had* happened after all.

Nash nodded. "And I thank the gods you did. When you got the fixings just right, the coin's magic was triggered. It made my body anew and called my sorry soul back from the darkness between worlds."

"I am the dream of the dead . . . ," I said quietly. The inscription on the coin whose meaning had eluded us.

It seemed so obvious now. The dream of the dead was . . . new life.

"You could read it?" Nash asked sharply. His eyes widened almost imperceptibly, his skin taking on an ashen quality. It wasn't the anger I'd expected.

"Yeah, I solved that problem myself," I told him. "And gave myself the One Vision, since you refused to find a way."

He seemed to relax at that, though he hardly looked pleased.

"Why not just bury the coin yourself if you thought you might die?" I asked, unable to keep the bitterness out of my tone.

"Well, for one thing, I didn't think old Myfanwy had it in her to cut me with a poisoned blade so she could keep both the ring *and* Arthur's dagger," Nash said ruefully. "Should have seen that coming, considering I was going to kill her for the ring."

I started at that. "You would have . . . you would have killed a sorceress?" *For me?*

He grunted. "It was the only way to take full possession of the ring; you—"

"—have to kill the bearer," I finished. "I know."

Nash nodded, rubbing his mouth again. "The original plan was that I'd get the ring, have you kill me to take possession of it, and your curse would be broken, and I'd be revived with the coin, good as new."

My horror was so acute, I was momentarily speechless. "You expected me—at ten years old—to be capable of killing you?"

"You hated me enough for it, didn't you?" he asked quietly.

I drew in a sharp breath.

"Didn't matter in the end," Nash said. "I was prepared to kill the sorceress, and I was prepared to have her kin come after me for it. But the ring . . . the moment I touched it, I knew it needed to be purified. Only the High Priestess of Avalon was capable of such a feat. But the poison from Myfanwy's blade started to take hold shortly after I crossed into Avalon . . . Should have known something was wrong when the Hag of the Mist wouldn't take my blood offering."

"And you just . . . expected me to find the coin you buried at Tintagel and put all of the pieces together with the barest of clues?" I continued in disbelief.

"It was my last coin—I had to take certain measures to protect it until the time was right," he said. "I also thought you might find it a trifle faster, given all I'd taught you."

I all but heard the *snap* in my ears as the last fraying thread of my patience gave way. "I was a *child*!"

"An incredibly clever child," Nash said. "Too clever by half, even. I didn't want to involve you until it became necessary, and I couldn't leave a message for someone else to find. I thought you'd work it out."

"How was I supposed to do that when you didn't even tell us you were leaving?" I demanded, the words like knives. "You never gave us any indication you were coming back!"

Nash's hand lowered, setting his coffee cup down. His Adam's apple bobbed as he swallowed. "You . . . thought I meant to leave you . . . forever?"

I didn't answer. I didn't have to.

The man drew in a sharp breath, pressing the back of his hand against his forehead.

"You said it was your last coin," I said. "How many did you have?"

"Nine," he said, and I scoffed. Of course. It was almost too perfect. "And before you ask, I got them from a sorceress whose mother smuggled them out of Avalon. Fair trade."

"What, you didn't go into that one planning to kill her, too?"

This time, he scowled at me.

"And all this because you're convinced I'm cursed, when there's absolutely no evidence of that," I said, shaking my head. "You really are something."

"Your curse exists whether you believe it or not."

I didn't want to talk about that. I'd come close enough to death these last few days to actually start believing it too.

"Where did you go when you left the apartment?" I asked.

"To Rook House," Nash said. "I got in a mighty tussle with Madrigal's pooka. Not exactly a fair fight when one of the participants can turn into a lion, now is it?"

"So you didn't get inside," I said. "And you didn't get the ring back."

"Course not. I ran for my life, and it was still a damned near thing," Nash said. "Then I got word from the Bonecutter you'd gone to see her, asking me to come get you out of her hair."

I bristled. "We weren't just dropping in. We had business."

"I'm sure you did. I've never known her to like unwelcome drop-ins, though. I could have told you that, if you'd just stayed put and waited for me to come back."

I wasn't about to get into this argument again.

"Is she still under that curse?" he asked, scratching at his stubble. "The one that makes her look like an ever-so-slightly demonic child?"

So it is a curse, I thought. Pride would never let me reveal I hadn't found a way to confirm that myself.

"Looks like it," I answered.

I drank down more of the thick sludge of coffee, letting its bitterness fill me. The old bones of the library's town house groaned as they shifted and settled again.

A hard wind was blowing in from the harbor, and a ghostly choir of moaning bled through the cracks in the walls. Sadness stole through me once more.

The first night we'd heard the wind, wrapped up in our blankets, terrified about what our lives would become, Cabell had started giving each of those "voices" a name—Philbert, Grumbleton, Moorna—and suddenly, we were laughing and crying and laughing.

"This is where we lived," I heard myself say. "After you . . . left."

Nash lowered his mug, resting it against his knee as he looked around, absorbing the cobwebs, the exposed beams, the beginnings of dry rot. "Librarian took care of you, then? He's always been a sweetie."

I nodded, my jaw sawing back and forth as I bit back resentment. It was awful, all of this—sitting here like it was one of our old campfires, hearing the rumble of Nash's voice, taking in his familiar earthy, leathery smell. His old jacket, the one my brother had worn for years, had been lost to Avalon, and his new one didn't have that same softness, the lived-in quality that only came after decades.

"You took care of your brother," Nash said. "I'm proud of you."

He could not have hurt me more if he'd ripped the heart from my chest.

For years . . . *years* . . . I would have killed to hear him say those exact words. But there was no truth to them now. I hadn't been able to protect Cabell when it mattered most.

"I saw him," I told Nash. "Twice."

"Hmm? Once with the hunt, I suppose?"

"Yes," I said. "And again at Rivenoak. I tried to talk to him there, but he wouldn't hear me out. Cabell . . . he . . ."

"Go on," Nash said. His pale eyes were clear, focused, and for the first time maybe ever, I felt he was truly hearing what I was telling him.

"Cab ran alongside the hunt as a hound, and he seemed so . . . natural. *Free.*" I traced a finger over the chipped rim of my mug. "Was his curse that he was forced to shift into human form?"

"He's not cursed at all, Tamsy," Nash said with unbearable gentleness. "He never was."

I stared down into the bottomless black of my coffee.

"Is that his true form?" I asked.

"What is true but what we choose to be?" Nash mused. "When I found him on the moors that night, he was a pup, but I recognized him for what he was—one of the Cŵn Annwn."

Despite the heat of the coffee, a chill prickled my skin. The hounds of Annwn.

"Why didn't you just tell us that?" I demanded. "Why pretend like the curse was on him?"

"You may not understand it," Nash said, "and I know you think I'm about as trustworthy as an eel, but you were children at the time. And I thought—well, I didn't want him to long for a place he could never return to. There's an unkindness to that, too."

Crossing my arms over my chest, I glanced at him out of the corner of my eye, some part of me still in disbelief that the bastard was here, sitting beside me.

"Gods forgive me, I know I was harsh on you at times," he said. "That I could be a distant, moody old bastard when it came down to it. I didn't always know how to give you the affection you might have needed, or how to console you . . . I'm not a soft man, I know this."

"I'd say that's an understatement," I said, my hands curling into fists in my lap.

"But I didn't realize how distant I'd been," Nash continued, "because I never imagined in all my worst nightmares that you'd believe I'd left you on purpose. That you weren't wanted. I look at myself now and realize I've become that thing I always feared most: an old man with regrets." He shifted, looking down at his hands in his lap. "I'm sorry."

I drew in a deep breath, not trusting my voice to speak. It was all of the things I'd been so desperate to hear—that I'd felt starved for, that had shaped me as surely as any knife.

There was a time when I'd believed he would come back, and I'd rehearsed what I'd say to him over and over, carefully carving my anger and devastation into arrows. Now that I had the chance to shoot them . . . I couldn't.

It hurt. It still hurt so badly.

"Cabell will return to us in time," Nash said. "But he must choose that form again. That life. He is drawn to Lord Death because of what he is, but he will step away from that darkness because of *who* he is."

"He won't," I said. "You haven't seen him. And after what he's done . . . the others might never forgive him."

"Forgiveness isn't meant to be easy," Nash said. "It's got to be earned. But it has to start somewhere. Look for the sign, it'll come."

"What's that you used to say? One swallow doesn't make a summer?" I said. "You didn't see what I saw."

"Maybe so, but I know the boy," Nash said. "I raised him from the time he was a pup, same as you."

"If he's a Ci Annwn, how did he get to this world?" I asked.

"I assume his line was left behind when the pathways to the Otherlands closed," Nash said. "And he was the last of his kind here."

"And what about me?" I asked. "Where did I come from?"

Nash's face hardened. "I've told you the tale. It's not one I'm fond of repeating."

"You told me you won me in a game of cards in Boston," I said.

"Who were my parents? What's my family name? If I'm old enough to know about my curse, I'm old enough for that piece of truth."

"You want the truth?" he said, drawing himself up and off the floor. "The truth is, I don't know. I never thought to ask."

"You're lying," I said incredulously. "Why are you lying?"

I could have screamed at the sound of footsteps coming up the stairs. The others seemed to realize they'd wandered into a private moment, because they froze awkwardly midway through the door.

"Should we . . . come back later?" Neve asked carefully.

"Ladies," Nash said. "Come on in and settle down for the night."

"We're not done with our conversation," I told him.

"Aren't we?" he shot back. "I think you should all—"

Whatever he'd intended to say cut off with his sharp gasp. His face turned livid as he dropped his empty coffee mug and launched himself toward the stairs. Caitriona lashed a protective arm out in front of Neve.

"What are you doing?" I shouted.

But Nash hadn't been going for Neve—his focus had been on the kitten nestled between her hands. Gripping him by the scruff, Nash freed Griflet and, with a guttural growl, flung the kitten toward the center of the attic.

Neve's scream was strangled off as the cat's shape exploded into bands of light and pressure, becoming little more than air until it began to reassemble itself into different forms—a bird, a snake, something like human, his face striking as he turned toward us with dark, feverish eyes that gleamed like flecks of obsidian. That form was still burned in my mind as it shifted one final time into a spider.

"Grab it!" Nash barked.

He and Caitriona lunged forward, but the spider had already darted past their feet and scurried down the stairs. Caitriona rushed out after it, her steps pounding down into the foyer.

I knew there was no point. The creature was gone.

23

"What," Neve managed to get out, "was *that*?"

Nash whirled on me, spitting mad. "Of all the foolish things, Tamsy! Did I not teach you how to spot a pooka years ago?"

"Uh, no," I said when I found my voice again, "you didn't."

"Oh—" His anger deflated, only to surge again. "Well, I meant to!"

"That was . . . what?" Neve began. "That was a pooka?"

"Blistering boils," Nash said, tugging a hand back through his hair. "I should have known they'd be spying on you lot."

"Who?" Neve asked. It came to her a moment later. "You mean the Council of Sistren?"

"Who else deploys pookas as spies and companions?" Nash said. "How long has that cat been with you?"

"Since Avalon," I said. "Before the merging."

He swore and began to pace, his face twisted with indecision.

Neve stomped toward the stairs. "That *thing* slept with us, and ate our food, and—he watched us change! I'm going to squish that little spider until he's a splat on the ground—"

She stopped, shaking her head. "I mean, no, I'm not going to do that, it's still a living creature. But I *am* going to trap him under a glass until he suffocates—no, I'm not going to do that, either." Neve considered it another moment, then snapped her fingers. "I'm going to have Tamsin catch and release him over the ocean so the wind can decide his fate . . . and I'm probably not going to watch."

"I'd be happy to," I said.

Caitriona came through the door a moment later, breathless. "I tried to follow him, but he scaled a wall and disappeared up over the roof."

"Ah, don't trouble yourself," Nash said, retrieving his coffee mug. "If it wasn't a pooka, they would have found another way of assessing the situation from afar."

The thought was too chilling for his cavalier tone. "How did *you* know what he was?"

"The way the light caught in his eyes," Nash said. "There's a hint of aquamarine in the gleam."

"Is it possible the pooka was sent by Lord Death?" Neve asked, her face anxious.

"He'd use a ghost, more like," Nash said. "Something he can completely control."

Caitriona had been silent until now, her face reddening as she absorbed what it meant.

"That kitten was a gift to my sister Mari," she said, barely mastering the fury in her voice. "Are you telling me that the pooka took its place?"

"I think it's been with you all along," Nash said. "Since Avalon."

"That would make sense," I said carefully. "I wondered how it had survived when the Children—" I couldn't say the words. "It could have shifted into something else and escaped, returning when we did."

"Let me ensure that I understand what you're saying," Caitriona began, trembling with the force of her quiet fury. "They had a way of sending this shapeshifter through the boundaries between the worlds to gather information for them. They therefore knew Lord Death had returned. They knew Avalon was dying. But they did nothing . . . *nothing* . . . to help us."

It was a damning assessment, but likely true.

"We don't know that," Neve tried. "By the time they found out, it could have been too late—"

"Don't." Caitriona held up a hand. "These beings left Avalon to wither and *die*. There is nothing you can say to redeem them."

"*I'm* one of those beings," Neve said, squaring up to her. "After all this time, you're still so quick to see sorceresses as the enemy—well, then, maybe I'm your enemy too."

Caitriona took a step back, her lips parting.

"Ladies," Nash said, smoothly inserting himself between them. "I'd remind you that what's said in the heat of the moment cannot be unsaid."

He put a hand on Caitriona's shoulder. "I need to have a word with Librarian, but after, I'd like to bring the Mirror of Shalott to the Bonecutter, to ask for her thoughts on how to adjust the spellwork to trap the hunters. Perhaps you should join me and catch your breath?"

It was the best advice he'd given, but the thought wrenched something deep in my chest. "I don't think we should separate—"

"Fine," Caitriona said to Nash, turning her back on us.

"*Fine,*" Neve said. "Then go."

Nash stooped to pick up his bag, waiting as Caitriona did the same, tucking the covered mirror under her arm. That feeling was back, grinding me down into someone smaller, someone helpless.

"When are you coming back?" I asked, following them out to the stairs.

"Stay here, Tamsy," Nash said. "You and Neve will be safe. We won't be gone for more than a few hours."

That's what you said before, I wanted to scream.

Neve's hand gripped mine, drawing me back into the attic and shutting the door behind us, as if to cut off the temptation to follow.

"What just happened?" I asked faintly.

"I cannot *believe* her," Neve raged, hugging her arms to her as she strode across the attic, angrily laying out her blankets. "After everything, she still believes the worst—"

"Neve," I said, unable to move from that spot near the door. "What just happened?"

She looked up, her hands stilling. She understood, the way she always did. "It's all right, Tamsin."

"How is it all right?" I asked, rubbing at my throat, trying to dislodge the pain there. "We lost Olwen and now we just let Caitriona go?"

"They'll be back by morning," she said, as if she had any way of knowing that for certain. She patted the spot on the blanket next to her. "Come here." Seeing me hesitate, she added, "I'm not going to hug you. Unless you want a hug, in which case . . ."

"A hug's not going to fix anything," I said.

"It's not supposed to," she answered.

I sat next to her, looking to where Emrys lay prone on the floor, oblivious to all of this.

". . . Do *you* want a hug?" I asked finally.

"Yes," she said.

I tried my best, looping an arm around her shoulder and giving it a gentle squeeze. Neve leaned into me, resting her head against my shoulder.

"I don't understand her," Neve said quietly. "She'll act like we're strangers one moment, and the next . . ."

There was a faraway look to her eyes, as if she'd gone back to that moment and wanted to linger there.

"What did she say to you?" I asked. "When you came to at Rivenoak?"

Her cheeks warmed with color.

"Now you have to tell me," I insisted.

She drew herself upright, mimicking Caitriona's intonation. *"Don't ever do that again, I cannot bear it.* What does *that* mean?"

Finally, something I was an expert in. "I believe that's Emotionally Repressed for 'I care for you and love you.'"

Neve groaned, pressing her face to her hands. "I thought she hated me . . ."

I gave her an incredulous look. "Are you serious? I have the emotional intelligence of a toddler and even I can see that when she's not keeping a protective eye on you, she's gazing at you with wonder. It would be sweet if we weren't in danger of being killed by undead hunters at any given moment."

"She doesn't love me," Neve whispered, more to herself than to me. "How could she love me when she doesn't even respect who I am?"

"I think she sees you separately from the other sorceresses," I said. Out of the corner of my eye, I saw Emrys's limp hand curl against his stomach. "And as far as I can tell, hearts can be total idiots."

"I don't know if I can accept that," Neve said. "I can't change what I am any more than she can—no matter how hard she tries."

"Something's changed, though," I told her. "When you were knocked out and we were surrounded, she tried to use her magic and it wouldn't come."

"What?" Neve gripped my arm, forcing my gaze back to hers. "When were any of you going to tell me that?"

"When we weren't lurching from crisis to crisis," I said. "So . . . now."

Over the last few days, I'd watched the light that always seemed to radiate from her face dim, and now it was happening again. She looked troubled, but more than that, devastated.

"What does that mean?" I asked.

"I don't know," Neve said. "Nothing good. The Goddess isn't cruel. She wouldn't take it from Cait the moment she needs it most, or when she's in pain. But we call our magic from the heart, and if she can't summon it . . . I'm worried about what that means. If the walls she puts up are so high that none of us can climb over them . . ."

She trailed off, sighing.

"I can't stop thinking about Olwen," she said. "The fact that we aren't going after her *right now* feels like a knife to the heart. I told Madrigal what had happened to her, asking if the Council could try to find her, too, but she's never written back. I don't even know if she's receiving my letters."

I didn't really know, but I nodded for her to continue.

"It's just . . . everything is moving so fast around us, it feels wrong to stop, to be here sitting still."

"Morning will be here soon enough," I told her. "And we can start looking for the sword then."

"There it is again, that note of hope in your voice," she said.

"A little mawkishness is good for the worms that live in my rotting heart," I told her. "Gives 'em a reason to squirm."

I managed to get a small smile out of her. "And you think I'm the weird one in this friendship?"

"Just trying to get on your level," I told her.

She looked down at Emrys, pressing the back of her hand to his forehead. Checking for fever. She drew the blanket down over him, inspecting the loose bandages we'd wrapped around his chest.

"Caitriona told me what happened," she said. "That was very, very brave of Emrys to push you out of harm's way."

I grunted in acknowledgment, resting my chin on my palm.

"Just checking in on if we still hate him," she said casually. "And if we're angry because we still can't trust him, or because he broke your heart."

Heat rushed to my face. "He didn't break my heart—"

"Tamsin," she said. "He *did*."

I swallowed, fighting the burn in my eyes. "He didn't."

"He did," she repeated. "You asked me before if I thought he was acting differently, and now I see it too. Something's going on with him, and if it's confusing me, it has to be confusing you."

"No," I said, feeling the sting of his endless rejections yet again. "This is who he truly is."

She looked doubtful.

"He did it to ease his conscience," I said. "That was his whole purpose in coming back. To make himself feel better about what he did."

"I doubted his motivations in Avalon," Neve said. "But I never doubted his feelings for you—"

"Please," I interrupted before I threw myself down the stairs to escape this conversation. "Can we talk about *anything* else. Fungi. Your creepy bone collection. Anything."

Neve looked disappointed by the dodge, but she didn't push. "How about Nash? Did you have a chance to talk to him?"

"Yeah, a bit," I said. "He's still being cagey. But you're going to love his explanation for how he beat death."

And she did, hanging on every word of the story.

"What about your parents?" she asked. "Did you push him on that?"

"I tried," I said.

Neve nodded, one hand drumming her fingers against her crossed legs, the other absently slipping beneath the collar of her T-shirt to grip her pendant. "Do you ever try to imagine what your parents looked like?"

"All the time," I said. Sometimes I genuinely envied the ease with which people could point to their eyes and say, *I inherited them from my father,* or brush their hair and know it had been a genetic gift from a grandparent.

"Come on," I said, hauling us both up from the floor. "Let's get washed up and try to steal a few hours of sleep."

I led her downstairs to the bathroom, and the single shower stall that had been preserved after the town house had been converted to the library. Listening to Neve sing a low, soft song, I let the hot water and thick steam welcome me into their comforting grasp.

The clock in the foyer said it was half past two by the time we emerged, clean and settled. For a moment, I was tempted to check in with Librarian, to see if he'd found anything about the Mirror of Beasts in his research, but Neve drew me back toward the stairs.

"No," she said. *"Sleep."*

It was a relief to return to the scratchy wool of my rumpled blanket, to lie out across even a hard floor and know I was safe.

Neve tapped my shoulder from beside me, offering me one of her earphones. I scooted closer to her so I could press it to my ear and she could keep the other pressed to hers. The disc player whirred softly to life, and the ethereal synthesizers of Cocteau Twins drifted through us, making my whole body feel like it was floating.

Eventually, I found sleep.

But not before the dream found me first.

24

I couldn't escape Emrys Dye, not even in my own mind.

I would have known the shape of him anywhere. The cut of his clothes, his broad shoulders. His chestnut hair. I followed him as he made his way down a darkened hall. It brought on an unwelcome wave of déjà vu. I'd lost count of the times we traipsed through the bleak underpaths of the tower together just like this, flashlight beams our only source of light.

But this wasn't the tower. This was a home—a grand estate, complete with portraits of glowering ancestors and mahogany furniture. Windows took shape, water streaking down them. Rain drummed against the roof high overhead.

Summerland House, I thought. *It had to be.*

He faced a set of imposing doors just off the entry, crystals and iron nails hammered into their faces in swirling patterns of lethal beauty.

Instinct revolted. I didn't want to follow him there. I didn't want either of us to. I knew, with the certainty of the sun's path across the sky, that this was a bad place.

But I didn't have a choice. I tried to catch his shoulder as he strode toward the door, but my fingers passed through him, and then it was too late. He reached for one of the silver door handles and, without knocking, stepped inside.

Refusing to follow him inside the study didn't work; the dreamscape shifted around me, drawing me into the waiting viper's nest. A silk canopy covered the room, as red as a sliced belly.

But my body had no form. Thunder raged overhead, drumming like a call to war. Garlands of holly and oak leaves were twisted into an unfamiliar shape around us.

Emrys took a step back, his pale face cast in eerie bloodshot light. "What in the hell . . . ?"

Behind you! *I tried to shout.*

I gasped as the first hooded figure slipped through the room's fabric shroud, a horrible, expressionless mask covering his face.

Emrys backed toward the door. The man stalked after him, with the slow confidence of knowing there'd be no escape. I didn't know how Emrys knew, how he figured out who it was, only that horror bloomed in his expression.

"No . . . ," Emrys began. "Dad—"

He spun around, searching the door for a handle. There was no resistance as the blade slid into Emrys's turned back. He staggered to the right with a gasping cry of surprise and pain.

A silent scream tore out of me.

Wake up! *I begged myself.* Wake up!

I couldn't watch this—I didn't want to see this—

More and more hooded men in their wooden masks appeared, their blades gripped like prayer candles. The chanting began as a deep, uncertain rumble but gained strength as the next knife pierced Emrys's shoulder.

"Come now, night, come, thy king—"

"Don't," Emrys begged, twisting away. But there was another man there too. Another knife. "Don't—!"

I couldn't breathe. It felt like my chest was being crushed as Emrys lunged one last time for the door. I ran toward him, desperate to stop them, but my hands were as insubstantial as smoke.

A knife lanced between his ribs.

Another in his back.

Emrys coughed up blood as he collapsed to the ground. Even then, he was trying to fight, to pull the door open, to survive. He screamed, ragged and fading, as they fell upon him in a frenzy. His body rocked with the force of their clumsy, rough blows.

My knees collapsed under me as I turned away from the violence, pressing my hands against my eyes, but there was no escaping that sound—that wet suck of blood and skin.

In the sudden silence, I lifted my head from my hands and turned. My eyes burned with my sobs, but no tears came.

Emrys stared back at me, his gaze empty, his face streaked with his own blood.

I screamed and screamed and screamed, trying to launch myself at the men, to tear them apart with my own hands—

"Tamsin!"

Waking felt like my soul had suddenly returned to my body. I sat up with a sharp intake of breath, searching the dark air around me.

The attic. We were in the guild library's attic.

The cold stroked my face, soothing. Every part of me was shaking, and, with a start, I realized I was sobbing. My throat burned.

"Tamsin?" Neve queried softly. "It's okay, it was a dream—you're okay."

I threw a desperate look to my right. Emrys was still unconscious, but his chest rose and fell, his breathing finally evening out.

Alive. A surge of relief, of desperate joy, overcame me. There was a spark of life still burning in him, and suddenly, nothing else mattered.

"What happened?" Neve asked, wide-awake now. "What did you see?"

I swallowed and swallowed and swallowed, trying to get the burn of bile out of my throat. "It was . . . it was nothing."

"Well, that was an awful lie, which is only more proof that whatever it was has you rattled," Neve said. "You haven't had a normal dream since Avalon. Was it about Olwen?"

I shook my head, drawing in a shuddering breath as her words sank in. My dreams in Avalon had all of the uncanniness of a sleeping mind trying to piece thoughts and memories together, but what I'd seen in them . . .

It had all come true.

Emrys's expression was peaceful; if *he* had dreams, they were at least kind to him.

"Emrys," I said loudly, my hands twisting in the fabric of my shirt. *"Emrys."* I turned to look at Neve, still feeling my heart race with the remnants of adrenaline and fear. "Why isn't he waking up?"

She could only shrug helplessly.

"I saw him die," I whispered.

"What?" Neve touched my shoulder, trying to focus my attention back to her. "Are you sure?"

"They kill him." The flash of the knives was still too close to the surface; I couldn't let myself wade back too deeply into those waters. "These . . . masked men. His father. It . . . They must have been the hunters. They were at the Dye family estate. They caught him by surprise."

"Do you think that's where they've based themselves?" Neve said. "It would make sense, especially if the property had a lot of land and few neighbors."

I pushed my still-damp hair off my face. "It does."

"Tamsin," Neve said. "Just because you had a dream, it doesn't make any of it real."

But it felt that way, I thought, clenching my hair hard enough to pull it out at the root. I'd experienced it on such a visceral level, it felt like part of me was still trapped inside the nightmare.

A sound like a steaming kettle filled the dark attic. Neve and I both looked up toward the roof, only to realize, at the same moment, that it was coming from below.

The library cats, I thought. They only hissed like that when there was a curse present.

Neve tilted her head in silent question. I motioned to where there was a decent-sized gap in the boards—wide enough, at least, to be able to see a sliver of the central chamber of the library.

Alarm trilled through my entire body, fraying the last of my nerves.

The shadowed figures stood at the very edge of the room below, just outside our limited range of vision, but I heard them all the same. The sharp intakes of breath, the restless shifting.

Everywhere, the library cats were scattering through the stacks of shelves, climbing up into their higher reaches. One cat, an orange tabby named Midas, was sent flying across the room, as if someone had given him a hard kick. He rolled and recovered, darting away with a hiss.

"We've come, as you have requested. What do you ask of us?"

Endymion Dye.

I pressed a hand to my mouth to keep from making a noise, holding myself as still as the statues in the atrium.

Endymion and the other former members of the guild drifted into view, casting their sickly glow onto the nearby shelves of Immortalities. They were laden with stolen weapons and shields, looking like the worst of the fell creatures that prowled inside the pages of the books around them.

The book spines shivered against one another as they passed, as if stroked by the death magic that had remade the riders.

"I have but one command to make."

Neve's gaze shot to mine, the voice stripping away every other emotion in them but fear.

Lord Death stepped forward out of the dark air, lowering the hood of Arthur's mantle to reveal himself to the others. I recoiled at the sight of him here, in such a sacred, safe place, even before Cabell's head of dark hair appeared beside him.

Cabell leaned against the nearest bookshelf, his eyes on the ornate rug. At the sound of a cat spitting nearby, his own hackles seemed to rise, and he crossed his arms over his chest in a defensive posture I was all too familiar with.

The riders, a dozen in all, knelt to receive Lord Death's orders. It became a terrible game to match their mutilated forms, the grisly alterations of their faces, to the Hollowers they had once been.

"It has come to my attention that you have all been keeping the knowledge of this library from me," Lord Death said, his gaze sliding over to Cabell, who bowed his head, shamed. "That you hid this supply of powerful weapons."

A rush of ice pushed through my blood as I understood what Cabell's expression meant.

He led him here.

And there my brother stood, saying nothing as this monster strode through our home as if he deserved to be there, and there I was, unable to so much as breathe.

"I wondered to myself why," Lord Death continued, "when you proclaim such fealty."

"My lord—" Endymion began.

"Silence." The word rose toward us like smoke, soft and silky, with a promise of something darker.

"I am left to assume that you do not believe that I can provide for all of your needs," Lord Death continued, "that you do not trust in me, do not have complete loyalty to our cause. Rather than destroy the scourge of sorceresses, you have preserved their memories. You have retained relics they have created."

He began to pace, using a finger to tip Immortalities off their shelf. One by one, they slammed to the floor.

"We only used their memories to find the treasures they stole," Endymion protested.

Lord Death stopped, turning his grizzled face toward them. "Then I'm sure you will feel no pain in destroying this shrine to them."

I sucked in a sharp breath, pressing my hand tighter to my mouth.

"Of . . . of course, my lord," Endymion said, bowing his head. The attic receded around me as Lord Death held out a hand and a silver-black flame appeared there.

Endymion knew what his master wanted and raised both of his palms, as if in supplication. The flame danced as it passed between them. Endymion rose to his feet and turned toward the shelf on his left.

Heavy footsteps sounded from the other side of the library.

No, I thought desperately, *don't do it—don't come out.*

But Librarian had been trained to defend the library and all its occupants, whether they had a heartbeat or not, and he wouldn't falter in it. Not even when he stood against the very same people who had tasked him with the role.

"Stop!" Librarian's tinny voice rang out. "Destruction of library materials is strictly forbidden by the guild's code!"

He had come prepared, a sword in one hand, a fire extinguisher in the other. The riders surrounded him, blocking his path to Lord Death. Even cast in jointed bronze, his face a mask of divine perfection, Librarian looked more human than the ghouls circling like a pack of ravening wolves.

Endymion held the flame to the nearest book, his face the very portrait of veneration as he looked to Lord Death for approval.

The dark flame caught with ease, racing along the edge of the shelf in a terrifying *whoosh*. Within moments, the entire shelf was ablaze.

As the fire spread, it wasn't any protective ward or spell that activated to protect the library, but the modern-day sprinklers. They dropped from the ceiling, raining water down over the fire, and the smoke detectors joined the cats' piercing yowls.

Do something, I thought, *do anything . . .* But I didn't know who I was speaking to—myself or Cabell.

The silver flames leapt from one shelf to the next with ease, spreading their caustic fingers over the varnish and old, brittle volumes. The air filled with a dizzying chemical stench.

Lord Death bestowed flames on all of his servants with a look of cold pleasure. Others, like Primm, took it upon themselves to smash the display cases of the relics, feeding the invaluable instruments, the scrolls, the fabrics, the weapons into the fires, or battering them with their sword pommels until they were beyond recognition.

The sound of pain that bellowed from Librarian was so human, so utterly tortured, that it felt like my body had caught fire too.

The automaton broke from the ranks of the riders, dropping the fire extinguisher and clasping his sword in both hands. He faced Lord Death like the last soldier left to defend his keep.

"Desist," Librarian said. "Or you and your ilk will be dealt with."

Lord Death laughed, reaching beneath the folds of his cloak to retrieve his sword. Instead of brandishing it, however, he held it out to Cabell.

The same dark magic whined and hissed over its blade, dancing like lightning.

No. The word became a stone in my throat. *Please.*

Cabell looked up through his curtain of dark hair, then straightened.

"You seem surprised," Lord Death noted.

Cabell spoke, but it was too quiet to hear over the cats, the roaring fire, and the alarms screeching like untuned violins. When he didn't move to take the blade, the pressure on my chest eased.

My brother was still in there, somewhere. Even as the fire raged around him and the cats fled the shelves, searching for safety, he resisted.

But, a small voice whispered in my mind, *he's not stopping them either.*

I read the words as they dripped from Lord Death's lips like venom. *Look at me.*

Cabell did.

The last, fading hope in me dimmed. His expression wasn't that of a devoted servant, unfailingly obedient. Indecision creased his brow, and he hesitated just long enough to force me to see it. To truly understand.

He was only my brother. He was only Cabell.

Someone imprisoned by another's magical influence would act without question. Someone struggling against an all-consuming tide of power would be desperately clawing for any moment to break free. They wouldn't take several unsteady steps toward the automaton, jaw clenched, spine rigid. The debate painted on their face in shadow and flame.

He was only Cabell.

"Young Lark . . . ?" Librarian queried softly, lowering his own sword.

And he made his choice.

Cabell drew in a breath—and drove his blade through the automaton's chest.

25

He's gone.

My brother stood watching as Librarian's heavy body staggered back, the quicksilver liquid that gave him life gushing out through the open cavity of his chest. He stumbled back once—twice—struggling to regain his balance.

Librarian stood a moment longer, lifting a hand toward Cabell, letting it hang in the air like an unspoken question. Then, with a harsh clatter, the automaton's body finally collapsed, quicksilver seeping from every joint. Finally the rattle of his struggling limbs stopped, and he was still.

As Cabell stood there, his face impassive, that same wrenching thought returned to cut me again and again. *He's gone.*

The brother I'd grown up with, the one who had been sensitive and funny and prone to dreams . . . He hadn't been chained by Lord Death's magic. He'd been free this whole time. Every decision . . . every life lost . . . he'd done it knowingly.

And the pain I felt was unspeakable.

Lord Death placed an approving hand on his shoulder. Smoke rose, spreading its delicate fingers up through the floorboards around us, seeking. Through the haze, I saw Cabell and the others escape.

I pushed up from the ground and ran for the door. Neve, at least, seemed to know exactly what to do.

She planted herself at the entrance to the central chamber, facing the radiating heat of the magic flames. Her spell sang out, as strong as it was unhesitating. The sprinklers had done nothing to halt the fire's path, but as the priestess spread her arms, the flames seemed to acknowledge her, standing at attention.

They might have been sparked by death magic, but it was Neve's magic, drawn from the Goddess's source, that smothered them. The fires went out with a last gasp as she drew her hands sharply together in front of her.

The moment the raging heat abated, we ran through the choking cloud of smoke and the maze of worktables for the windows at the back. Coughing, I struggled with the lock leading out into the fire escape; its metal warped with the heat.

"Botheration," I gasped out, picking up a nearby chair and throwing it through the glass.

Whatever wards had protected the guild library had only protected it from outside threats, I thought bitterly, not those coming from inside. The terrified library cats clustered around my feet until, finally, they were able to jump out onto the fire escape and flee into Boston's dreary winter.

"Wait!" Neve stuck her head out of the window to call after them. "Come back! You're indoor cats and those are mean streets!"

The thought of them out there, without any true shelter, was just as sickening to me as the sight of the smoldering black clumps that had once been books.

I dropped down onto my knees beside Librarian, pressing the back of my hand to my mouth. The death magic painted his bronze body with cruel silver stripes. For a moment, I didn't know if I should even touch him. What the point would be.

Those with magic believed the Goddess would allow them rebirth in another life, in another form. Even the vilest souls among us experienced a second dark existence, in a different world. The promise of their deaths was life.

But what of those beings like Librarian, for whom death wasn't merely the first step of another journey, but an end? How could he have been so morally upright, so pure of intention, and never be reborn, simply because he didn't have a human soul?

How could he just . . . cease to be?

Maybe I'd been the biggest fool of all, believing, in my desperation for some sort of parental figure, that an automaton was capable of things like love. It was equally possible that Librarian had merely seen Cabell and me as an extension of his duty to the guild, and to the library itself. Small nuisances who were worse-behaved than the cats and harder to keep fed.

Maybe I'd imagined a life that never really existed at all. But it had been real to *me*.

My eyes burned from the smoke and lingering heat. I stroked my fingers gently down Librarian's arm. For the first time that I could remember, it was warm. And even though I knew that was because of the fire, it let me keep pretending, just for a moment longer.

But then a voice, small and fading, rose from inside his ruined chest. "Young . . . Lark . . ."

"I'm sorry!" I cried. "Please don't go. Please, tell me how to fix you."

". . . I have chosen . . . one you will . . . enjoy . . . ," he said, his voice flickering like a guttering candle. ". . . It will be . . . such a pleasure . . . to sit and read with you . . . beside the fire . . . once more . . ."

Librarian fell silent, and did not speak again.

"Tamsin?" Neve knelt behind me, touching my back.

One of the nearby shelves buckled, sending charred Immortalities and atlases of the ancient world tumbling to the floor. Neve winced at the noise, but I barely heard it. It felt like the smoke had wrapped me inside a mantle of my own and nothing could penetrate its numbing touch.

"Do you . . . do you have a bottle?" I asked, swallowing hard. "Just a little one?"

"I'm sure I do," Neve said. "Why do you need it, though?"

The idea already felt stupid, but somehow, hearing myself say it aloud made it seem childish too. "I want to preserve some of the quicksilver. The death magic."

"What are you talking about?" Neve asked.

"The death magic," I said. "It's all over him. You can't see it?"

Neve shook her head.

My earlier conversation with the Bonecutter came back to me in a rush. I'd tried to ask her why only I could see death magic in its physical form. She'd told me to ask Nash.

"Are you thinking that it may contain some of his memories?" Neve asked. "Some part of his essence?"

"I don't know. Maybe." I shook my head. My thoughts no longer felt clear, and it was too much effort to try to understand them. "Is that stupid?"

Neve gave a sad half smile. "Not at all. We'll go get our things, and then we can leave when you're ready."

I'd seen so many ruins in my life, it hollowed me to my core to look around the library and see that it had become yet another one.

The rich wallpaper, the ornate rugs, the worktables that had borne the weight of countless books, were all scorched black. The loss of knowledge contained in this collection was staggering. Even if I dedicated my whole life to it, I wouldn't have enough years to transcribe their contents from my own memories.

Ash and scraps of burned paper fluttered by me as I collected as much of the silver liquid as I could stand to. While I worked, Neve combed the shelves, searching for any injured cats. As I rose to my feet, a new feeling rose in me too.

The library had been our only true sanctuary in this great, vast world. It had been a place to escape to, to travel from, to learn, to be alone with one's thoughts. Inaccessible to the outside world, it had been safe. It had been ours.

And Cabell had led his master right to it.

He'd turned his back on me, on all of us. He'd stood by and

watched as others died and had done nothing to help them. The truth was agonizing in its clarity now, and I felt foolish and ashamed all over again.

He wasn't under the sway of Lord Death's magic, and he was never coming back.

When the anger came, I welcomed it. I let it fill the part of me that had held on to forgiveness, let it burn my hope away until it joined the ashes at my feet.

Because the next time I saw my brother, I would make him pay for what he'd done.

"Tamsin?" Neve called.

I found her in Librarian's closet of an office, somehow mercifully untouched by the spread of the fire. She was bent over an open book there, one I recognized by the stained edges of its pages. The covers were two sheaves of oak bark with a layer of living moss coating them.

It was one of the earliest known records of the hidden magical world within Great Britain, and one of the Library's oldest tomes.

I have chosen one you will enjoy.

Neve shifted, allowing me to squeeze in beside her. My eyes strayed to Nash's empty coffee cup, with the faded CATCH OF THE DAY restaurant logo, left just beside the historical record on the desk. A slow, simmering fear began to build in my gut.

"Look," Neve said, drawing my attention back to her. She was braver than I was, running her finger down the open page. The brittle paper was torn in places, as if insects had eaten away at it. The whole thing seemed like it would disintegrate if I dared to breathe in its direction.

In the illustration, a woman in long, flowing robes stood at water's edge, brandishing a sword above her head. Light billowed around her, and in the dark shadows bordering the scene, I could just make out monstrous faces.

The first words beneath the illustration had been lost to a tear and an inkblot, but the rest was still legible. While the One Vision could translate the words, it was still difficult to parse the writer's old-fashioned, spidery hand.

"Something something . . . *light of the Goddess drives out the plaguing darkness. As the first priestess and protector of the isle, the Lady of the Lake wields the divine Caledfwlch, the mirror of mortality, judge and executioner of the pitiless wicked, savior of the ensorcelled, and the mercy of the innocent.*"

I leaned in closer to the page, holding my breath. A woman's face, ever so faint, was etched into the light radiating from the Lady of the Lake. The Goddess herself.

"*The mirror of mortality,*" Neve repeated, visibly fighting to keep her hope at bay. "You don't think . . . I mean, it fits with your theory that it reflects you at the moment of your death . . . ?"

I let out a light, breathless laugh. Being forced to learn the other languages had taught me to think about the changing meaning of words over time. "Mortality can also refer to humanity as a whole. The mirror of humanity. Of beasts."

"Then we just have to find it," Neve said. "This . . . Caledfwlch."

"It's better known by another name," I began, feeling some of that hope drain from me. Our already difficult quest to stop Lord Death had just become that much more impossible.

Neve's lips pressed together, her eyes questioning.

"We call it Excalibur," I said. "And it's been lost for centuries."

PART THREE

THE DROWNED KINGDOM

26

"You again?"

The Bonecutter looked neither surprised nor irritated at our sudden appearance in the doorway of the pub. Her eyes moved over us in quick appraisal before settling on Emrys's pallid form. Neve and I struggled under his weight, lowering him to the floor as soon as it was safe to do so. I turned around and locked the door behind us.

In the late-afternoon hour, only three figures sat at the bar: Bran, endlessly polishing the pint glasses; the Bonecutter, making notes in her massive ledger; and Caitriona, glumly swirling a spoon through porridge.

At the sight of us, soot-stained and reeking of smoke, her spoon clattered against the counter as she leapt from her stool. "What happened?"

Neve stared at her a moment longer than I think she meant to, as if seeing her again for the first time.

"Well," I began weakly. "What *didn't* happen?"

The Bonecutter's brows rose.

"Sorry for dropping in again uninvited," I said hoarsely, my throat still feeling singed from the heat. "We'd hate to deprive you of our peerless company for too long."

"Like a balm to the weary soul," Neve added. "A cold glass of water on a hot day."

"Or finding a rat after weeks of starvation," Caitriona offered. She glanced toward Neve expectantly. The sorceress only grimaced.

"We probably could have stopped at the glass of water," I told Caitriona, "but you're not wrong."

The Bonecutter gave a wave of her small, delicate hand. "I know what happened at Rivenoak, including that you've released a hungry primordial creature back into the world." I couldn't tell if the Bonecutter was delighted or disturbed by this. "And that your kitten turned out to be a pooka after all. I told you to get rid of that thing, didn't I?"

My temper flared. "You couldn't have added a little disclaimer about why? Or given us a warning that the Mirror of Shalott was occupied?"

"I might have, had I known for certain," the Bonecutter said, reaching behind the bar for the velvet bundle. The frame glinted as she unwrapped it. "While it might beggar belief, I am not omniscient."

"The Hag of the Moors said it could only have one occupant at a time," Neve said. "Is that true?"

"It hasn't been tested either way," the Bonecutter said. "It seems as though the size of the mirror might shift to accommodate more. I believe the sorceress who enchanted the mirror created a sort of pocket dimension inside it."

"Like a little Otherland," Neve clarified for Caitriona.

"Yes, something like that," the Bonecutter said. "But clearly I am missing a chapter of this story. Why have you arrived looking as though you've run through the fires of hell?"

In a strange way, it had been easier not to talk about it—not to force myself to relive it again through story. I tried to draw in a deep breath, but I couldn't dispel the taste of smoke from my tongue.

"Because we did," I said. "Lord Death had his retinue of ghouls burn our library."

"He was there?" Caitriona asked, anguished.

"There was nothing we could do," Neve said. "Even if we'd had the true Mirror of Beasts, it wouldn't have done us any good."

"That's not what I meant," Caitriona said. She ran a hand back through her hair, clenching it in her fist. "I never should have left. I never should have . . ."

"They *burned* it?" The Bonecutter finally shut her ledger. "Surely not all of it?"

"They destroyed the relics, too," I said, strained. "Some of the books survived, but they're probably waterlogged and unreadable."

"We have seven rare books you can add to your collection," Neve began, gently patting the fanny pack slung over her chest, where the carefully wrapped Seven Sisters were stored at a shrunken size. "If you're willing to make the same deal you did with the vessel—that you'll hold them, but allow us to use them—and knock off a few of the favors Tamsin owes you."

"Certainly," the Bonecutter said. "I'll strike two favors from my ledger."

And leaving more than I could ever hope to fulfill in a lifetime, no doubt. I tried not to grimace; I knew it was pointless to negotiate with her on the matter of favors.

The Bonecutter's gimlet gaze was on me again, cutting through me to get to the truth. "If you've been allowed to remove these rare tomes, then Librarian is gone, I take it?"

I nodded. My mind was determined to keep playing back that moment, of Cabell lunging forward with the sword, of Librarian collapsing, as if once hadn't been enough to sufficiently torment me. To scar.

"Shame, that," the Bonecutter said, crossing her arms over the bar with as much regret as she was likely capable of. "I preferred his company to most humans', and he had the most beautiful penmanship."

I couldn't argue with her there.

The Bonecutter inclined her head toward Emrys. "And I suppose you want him to be my problem now?"

"Can you get him a healer?" I asked. "Feel free to add the favor to his tally. He just can't travel in his condition."

"Oh?" the Bonecutter said. "Are you also anticipating an interesting journey?"

"Something like that," I said, sitting heavily on the edge of one of the tables. But as her words replayed in my mind, they snagged on a single word. *Also.*

I looked up, scanning the room, but I already knew what I would find—or, rather, who I wouldn't.

"Where's Nash?" I asked.

I had gotten so accustomed to his absence over the years, my tired mind hadn't bothered to remember he was supposed to be here.

"Where is he?" I asked again, hearing the anger building in those words.

Caitriona looked as though she wished I'd asked her anything else.

"Son of a—" I blew out a hard breath. "He *left*?"

"I'm so sorry," Caitriona said. "I closed my eyes for just a few minutes, and when I woke up, he was gone."

"That rotten bastard," I bit out.

"One cannot handle a feral cat and not expect to get scratched," the Bonecutter said. "Do you truly have no idea where he might have gone?"

"No, I—" The words fell away from me. Seeing his coffee mug next to the book in Librarian's office should have been warning enough that he'd try something like this. "He knows where it is."

"Where what is?" the Bonecutter asked, too innocently.

"Excalibur," Neve answered. "The Mirror of Beasts."

Caitriona shook her head. "No—it can't be. The sword's been lost for an age."

"Are the rumors true?" I pressed the Bonecutter. "Is it in Lyonesse?"

The Bonecutter's lips twisted with thought, as if she was weighing the options in front of her now.

"Bran," she said slowly. "Retrieve young Master Dye, will you? Put him up in the flat where he won't be such a depressing eyesore."

"Yes, miss," the bartender squawked. And, sure enough, when his face passed through a beam of sunlight slipping in through the window, his eyes had an aquamarine sheen. My already bad mood worsened.

"Is it in Lyonesse?" I asked again. "What do you even want? You're a sorceress, aren't you? You're in danger too as long as the Wild Hunt is tearing through this world."

"I am *not* a sorceress, not anymore," the Bonecutter said coldly, watching as Bran lifted Emrys in his arms and lumbered toward the stairs up to the flat. "But if it's Excalibur you seek, I've uncovered a memory that may be of interest."

She motioned for us to follow her into her workshop. Her smile was too sharp, too knowing. "And perhaps it will answer yet more of the questions that plague you."

For once, that possibility frightened me.

It was a dagger to my soul that the Bonecutter, not Olwen, sang the echoing spell.

The pedestal creaked as it started its slow spin, Viviane's vessel throwing light onto our weary faces and tattered clothing.

"In your absence, I have scoured the High Priestess's memories for references to the sword or Lord Death," the Bonecutter said. "But with the damage wrought to it, many of them have been reduced to mere fragments. Useless for our purposes. But there was one complete memory . . ." She turned her small body to address the vessel. "Show me the memory discussing the daughter, and the fate of Excalibur."

That word, *daughter,* echoed in my mind, even as the memory dripped into place and the thought was drowned by smears of shadows and firelight.

Viviane stood at a table, her hands braced on either side of a large book. Her agitation was clear in the rigid line of her spine, the hunch of her shoulders. Her white hair glowed gold in the light of the small fire burning in the hearth.

She hummed softly to herself as she turned the page, but kept her thoughts in. A piercing screech tore through the night-dark chamber, forcing her gaze up to the opening of her window. The line between her brows deepened as she worried her top lip.

It was the cry of the Children of the Night.

"Who is the Goddess's daughter?"

Viviane straightened, taking a moment to compose her expression before she turned to greet the small elfin standing in her doorway.

"Mari," she said gently. "We are all daughters of the Goddess."

But there was a flicker of worry in Viviane's ancient eyes.

"Come, dear one," the High Priestess said, moving to one of the chairs placed before the fire. "Sit with me awhile."

Mari stepped inside the room, pulling the door shut behind her. The firelight adored her leaf-green skin, caressing it as she lifted her small form onto the other seat. Her eyes were eager as she opened the leather-bound book clutched in her hands.

"I found Morgan's diary stored in a chest, in the room beside the Sanctuary," Mari said, still bright with the excitement of her discovery. "In it, she writes of a girl named Creiddylad—the Goddess's true child, born directly of her being, not just her power, as the rest of us are."

Viviane's lips compressed. She took a moment before answering. "Morgan always did love fanciful tales."

Some of Mari's hopefulness dimmed. "Is it not true? If we could find her—her soul reborn—Morgan believes that the child would radiate the Goddess's magic. Her light. *Could she not use that purifying light to heal the isle?"*

Viviane reached out and gently shut the diary. Her thin fingers wrapped around its spine, and Mari allowed her to take it without a sign of protest.

"Even if this daughter—Creiddylad, did you say? Even if she existed, her soul would reside in the mortal world," Viviane said. "And we cannot lift the barriers."

"Could a soul truly be hidden, as Morgan wrote?" Mari asked. "To such a degree that it would evade the man seeking her?"

The chair creaked as Viviane leaned back. "If the caster of such a spell was powerful enough, yes, but the soul would possess magic difficult to suppress."

"What of Seren's suggestion to find Excalibur?" Mari pressed. "It can still break enchantments, can't it?"

"It is lost to us," Viviane said firmly. "As I told you all, Sir Bedivere confessed that the sword he returned to the lake was not Excalibur—that Arthur gave it to another knight, to continue to protect the mortal world."

"Maybe that knight's—Sir Percival's—descendants still possess it?" Mari suggested.

"Merely finding the sword would not be enough," Viviane said. "You know this."

Mari nodded, all her eagerness deflated.

"Rest, my heart," Viviane said, stroking her head. "We will begin our search again in the morning."

Mari slid off her chair. "May the Goddess bless your dreams."

The older woman smiled. "And yours."

She waited until Mari had shut the door before looking down at the small volume resting in her lap. Running a hand over its weathered cover, she opened it, flipping through the pages, her eyes devouring the sight of Morgan's bold letters.

She snapped the diary shut again, her face twisting with unexpressed feeling. Closing her pale eyes, she lifted the diary and inhaled the scent of it.

Then, rising, she pressed the small book to her chest, to her heart, one last time—and cast it into the hearth's fire.

My eyes snapped open, the world swaying around me as I reoriented myself to the present, to the living world. Caitriona had gone deathly pale beneath her freckles; I understood only a fraction of what she was feeling, how difficult it was to see her loved ones alive in the past, only to wake from it like a dream and find she'd lost them all over again.

"So Percival had it," Neve said. "We just need to find where he's buried, or what remains of his family, right?"

But the Bonecutter was watching me still, as if waiting.

That cold, prickling dread I'd felt upstairs had returned. She had shown us this memory to confirm my suspicion that the sword was likely in Lyonesse, where Percival was thought by some to have died, yes. But just as a word could have many meanings, choosing that meaning depended on the context of the words around us.

We'd gotten the answer to what Lord Death was searching for, but that answer had been a distraction from the bigger question that surrounded it all.

The Bonecutter's gaze slid to my left, to where Neve was still waiting for her answer.

And my world began to cave in, brutal and swift, stealing that last bit of light.

"No," I whispered, my heart racing harder, harder.

The key to hiding something in plain sight wasn't to lie, it was to distract. And when I had looked at the history Librarian had left for us, at the illustration on the page, I'd been so focused on the sword, I'd barely noted the Goddess's light at the center of it all. That telling shade of its blue-white glow.

Morgan believes that the child would radiate the Goddess's magic. Her light.

The light I'd seen at the edge of my dream. That soft, whispering voice that filled my ears. *Protect her. Protect her.*

No.

No.

My stomach turned violently as the full weight of the realization bore down on me.

"Tamsin?" Caitriona asked, alarmed by whatever expression I wore.

The soul of the Goddess's daughter, the one Lord Death had destroyed worlds to find . . .

"Now you're starting to freak even me out," Neve said with a nervous laugh. "What did I say?"

The Bonecutter caught my eye again, nodded.

I could barely bring myself to look at Neve.

"It's you," I whispered. "Creiddylad's soul was reborn in *you*."

27

Neve stared back, as if trying to translate my words into a language she could understand. Then, all at once, she burst out laughing.

"You had me there for a second—"

The Bonecutter sighed, pressing a hand to her face as she shook her head.

Caitriona's focus sharpened from confusion to fear. "How . . . how can you be certain?"

"Think about it," I said to Neve, hearing the quiver in my words. "You were left with your aunt for your protection, with a note not to let *them* find you. Maybe your mother knew, or she sensed it. Maybe *she* was the one who instructed your aunt not to teach you magic, in the hope that your power wouldn't manifest."

Neve wheeled back, her hand rising to her chest. To the pendant. "No, that's not—"

"And your power—the light," I continued. "It doesn't hurt the rest of us, but it destroys the Children. It came to you for the first time in *Avalon*."

She was still shaking her head, backing away. "I'd never been in a life-or-death situation like that before. That alone could have sparked my magic to manifest differently. It's not proof of anything." She held out a finger, insisting. "It's *not,* Tamsin."

Caitriona caught my eye, and I knew she understood. The mere possibility that it *could* be true was enough to upend our plans. Because Lord Death and his hunters weren't merely pursuing an ancient soul from a story.

They were searching for *Neve*.

"Where did Percival die?" Caitriona demanded, whirling on the Bonecutter. "Was it Lyonesse?"

The Bonecutter nodded.

"Wait—hang on," Neve said, trying to insert her body between them. Her shock was shifting to fear as surely as mine was moving to anger.

Of all the people in all the many worlds, why did it have to be *her*? Why was she the one at risk of being taken by Lord Death, because of an accident of birth?

"If it's proof you seek," the Bonecutter said, "you will have it once you find Excalibur. A weapon forged by the Goddess's hand, imbued with her power, would certainly recognize the presence of her daughter."

Neve's mouth opened. Closed. A small noise of frustration built in her throat.

"How do we get to Lyonesse?" Caitriona said, ignoring Neve's protests.

"I can certainly help you," the Bonecutter said, folding her hands in front of her. A pretty, prim picture. "For a price, of course."

"Can't wait to hear this," I muttered, standing from the table. "What do you want?"

"I would like the Mirror of Shalott," the Bonecutter said.

"What? No!" Neve said, outraged. "We can still use it—"

"Not without the right sigils," I said.

"I wrote to the sorceresses about it," Neve said. "I'm sure they'll help."

"All the more reason to move it out of their grasp," Caitriona said. "They deserve no easy solution to protect themselves."

The Bonecutter's lips curled. "I'm coming around to you, Caitriona of Avalon."

"But—" Neve sent me an imploring look.

"We don't want to trap Lord Death," I told her. "We want to destroy him and his hunt."

The Bonecutter let out a small noise of surprise. "Is your brother not running with the Wild Hunt now?"

"We want to destroy the hunt," I forced myself to repeat. Cabell was no different than the other killers.

Neve's disappointment was palpable; but we were past the point of countering Lord Death's moves—we needed to get ahead of him.

"There's only eight days until the solstice," I reminded her. "Even if we can prevent him from finding you—" At Neve's doubtful look I added, "Fine, from finding *the soul*—the hag said that the doorway to Annwn can be opened on the winter solstice. If Lord Death doesn't get the soul, what if this world's punishment is flooding it with more dark souls, more Children? Innocent people will die, and his power will only continue to grow."

"He's already begun," the Bonecutter said. She snapped her fingers and Bran materialized at her side again, making all three of us jump. He held out a stack of newspapers to me, his expression dour as I took them.

The headlines screamed back at us as I flipped through them. Papers from the United Kingdom, from the United States, even France— all showing countless images of snow-crushed homes and the desperate struggle to dig loved ones out of shops and streets.

HUNDREDS KILLED IN FREAK WINTER STORM

VILLAGE FAMILIES FEAR WORST AS DOZENS STILL MISSING FROM ICE STORM

LIVESTOCK LEFT RAVAGED BY SUSPECTED WOLF PACK

STRANGE SIGHTINGS HAUNT THE EAST

The black ink blurred in front of me. I tore my gaze away from the stack of papers. "They're attacking cities now? Not just the sorceresses?"

"The—what did you call them? The Children?" the Bonecutter

began. "The Children have been feeding, but I suspect Lord Death knows that the more souls he collects, the more riders he'll have to hunt the Sistren."

"And the more death magic he'll have at his fingertips," Neve finished.

"The Cunningfolk have been trying to hunt the creatures and keep reports of their sightings under wraps," the Bonecutter explained, "but some mortals do have the One Vision, even if they possess no other magic. It will not stay contained forever, and once magic is exposed to the wider world . . ."

I threw the newspapers down on the table. "You can have the godsforsaken mirror. Just tell us where Excalibur is."

"As I said, I'll do you one better," the Bonecutter said, motioning for us to join her as she moved toward her workshop. "I will give you everything you need to get there."

A small smile ghosted her lips as she added, "Of course, the problem isn't getting to Lyonesse. It's surviving it."

28

Within an hour, we found ourselves back on the ancient, hallowed land of Tintagel, awaiting midnight, and a journey down to Merlin's Cave at the base of the castle ruins.

If the Hag of the Mist had been able to manipulate the mist-shrouded magic barriers between Avalon and our world, the Bonecutter believed, there was no reason she couldn't also open a path to Lyonesse.

And just then, I was willing to borrow someone else's certainty, because it felt like I had very little of my own left. Including whether or not the Bonecutter would actually tend to Emrys.

My sigh streaked the air white as I gazed out over the desolate landscape.

Despite the lack of snow on the ground, I wasn't sure I'd ever known a colder night. The fire barely thawed the air. It brought me back to that strange vault, years and years ago, where we'd found Arthur's dagger. The walls of ice that displayed the mangled bodies of Hollowers like masterpieces.

The garlands of protective wards rattled as I tended to our small camp's fire. The rocky outcropping we were sheltering behind did very little to protect us from the wind when it seemed to be blowing from every direction.

To pass the time, and perhaps even to distract her, Neve had asked a surprised Caitriona to teach her a few basics on correctly wielding a sword. Caitriona, of course, had accepted with all the gravity of a woman taking a soul-binding sacred oath—though I was beginning to realize that was true of all the girl's promises.

Caitriona's gravelly voice filled the quiet night once more. "No, no—here—"

I propped my chin on my hand, watching with raised brows as Caitriona came to stand behind the sorceress to adjust her stance. I didn't miss the way Caitriona seemed to leave her hands wrapped around Neve's a moment longer than necessary, or the way Neve leaned back against the taller girl's chest.

"Like this?" Neve breathed out.

"Y-Yes." Caitriona coughed, trying to hide her stutter. "And remember, extend your arms first, then lunge. You'll work up to the movements being tied together."

Caitriona finally forced herself to take a step back. She crossed her arms over her chest, as if to trap the last of Neve's lingering warmth there.

"I mean, I get that the basic gist is just *stab-stab-stab*," Neve said, practicing the lunge, "but is it really as simple as this?"

They were using her wand in place of a broadsword, and the sorceress couldn't help but add a little flourish to the thrust, swirling the wand's knife end through the air the way she might carve a looping sigil. Caitriona sighed every time she did it but knew better now than to attempt to stop it.

"It only looks simple," Caitriona told her. "But good form will help you strike true by adding power to your thrust. It'll allow you to pierce armor, or bone—"

Or a metal body, I thought, trying to breathe through the pain of what Cabell had done to Librarian. Every time Neve thrust forward, all I could see was that moment. The decision my brother had made. How easily the blade had sliced through Librarian's chest plate.

"Yes, yes! Exactly!" Caitriona crowed as Neve executed the move correctly. "But don't tense your arms until nearly the end of the movement."

Neve clarified, "Just before I stab them?"

"You seem unusually eager to do that," I noted.

Neve lowered her wand and looked at me. "Aren't you?"

After what had happened at Avalon, and Rivenoak, and the library . . . yes. I was.

"All right, I think I'm done for the night," Neve said.

Unzipping her neon fanny pack, which had been enchanted to store larger items with ease, Neve slid the wand inside.

"But we've only just begun," Caitriona protested. "I haven't even taught you a proper half step!"

"You have to save something for the next lesson," I reasoned. Then added, with a meaningful look, "Don't you want there to be another lesson?"

She chewed on her lower lip, and I watched in amusement as Caitriona finally relented. She moved to sit next to me, but I nodded toward the open space beside Neve, with yet another look.

She looked tormented by the mere prospect of giving in to what she clearly wanted to do. Eventually, after a moment more of hesitation, she made her way over and sat, leaving a respectful distance between her and the sorceresses.

I let out a soft sigh of my own. It was hard to believe I'd found someone more hopeless at this sort of thing than I was. It was like the baffled leading the bewildered.

Neve retrieved a blanket and wrapped one end of it around herself before tossing the other end over Caitriona's shoulders. The fabric slid away as Caitriona startled at its touch.

"I'm fine," she insisted. She shifted awkwardly, clearing her throat. The moonlight stroked her hair like a mother's adoring hand, making the long braid glow white.

"Well, *I'm* cold," Neve said, and she persisted, this time wrapping her arm, along with the blanket, around Caitriona's shoulders, tucking them both into a little tartan cocoon.

Caitriona drew in a soft breath, then went completely still. She kept her face forward, her eyes fixed solely on the fire, with the kind of discipline I could only dream of. I leaned closer to make sure she was still breathing.

Her cheeks had been burned red by the cold, but now the rest of her face went pink; a glimmer of feeling seemed to move behind her eyes, there and then quickly stamped out—the only signs she hadn't become an ice sculpture.

I stretched my legs out, knocking Dyrnwyn into the dirt. I stared at it, at the pitiful wrappings serving as the legendary sword's scabbard, but was too cold to move to retrieve it.

Neve sorted through the rattling items in her pack before pulling out a small glass vial.

"What do you suppose is in this?" Neve gave the offering the Bonecutter had provided another shake, bringing it close to her ear to listen to the faint rattling. I tried not to think about the dark liquid sloshing around inside and chose to believe that the round objects nestled at the bottom of it were small pieces of moonstone and not, in fact, human teeth.

"I'd pull out the cork and give you a guess, if I weren't so worried it might bring on the hallucinations," I said. "But I am tempted . . ."

"Don't you dare," Caitriona told me.

"We could have figured this out on our own, you know," Neve said. I could tell exactly how tired and frustrated she was by the unusual sourness bleeding into her tone. "This is how we got to Avalon. We would have made the connection."

"I know," I told her. I'd been beating myself up over it since the Bonecutter handed us the offering. "It saved us some time, though." *Time we need to save you,* I didn't add.

"So, while we hopefully do not freeze to death," Neve began, "what can we expect from Lyonesse? Has either of you read anything about it?"

Unfortunately, she was asking two of the least romantic storytellers in all the many worlds.

"It once rivaled Camelot for agricultural output," Caitriona said. "They had very nice groves and a steady supply of fish. And their craftsmen made excellent wagons."

Neve drew in a breath, closing her eyes as she regathered her patience. "Anything that might be immediately useful while we look for Excalibur? I know the Bonecutter thinks it may be hidden in the castle with some other valuables, but what else?"

"We'd better hope it's in the castle, otherwise I have no idea where to start looking," I said. "All right . . . let me see if I can tell it the way Nash used to—leaving out the parts that I'm pretty sure he just completely made up . . ."

Neve's eager face was lit by the fire as she waited for me to continue. She'd be disappointed. I wasn't born to tell stories, not the way Nash was.

"Lyonesse was once a great kingdom—like Camelot's younger, less handsome sister, but still a marvel in its own right," I began.

Or, as Nash had put it: a land of kings, of star-crossed lovers, and servant to the sea that surrounded it.

"Shortly after the death of Arthur, a darkness fell upon it—a monster, still known only as the Beast of Land's End, plagued the city," I continued, remembering the fear Nash's words had brought when he'd told us this story one summer night. I hadn't liked it then, and I didn't like it now.

Tamsin's never liked a scary story. Tell me one of those.

I pushed Cabell's voice out of my mind and continued.

"It was said to devour anyone who tried to pass through the city's walls. It killed so many people, in fact, legend had it that blood flowed through the streets like waves. Very few escaped."

"Oh, *wicked*," Neve breathed out.

"It's going to be significantly less cool if that monster eats us, too," I told her.

"Do you really believe it's still alive?" Caitriona asked. "It's been centuries."

"If you believe the worst of the rumors, the thing has had a steady diet in that time," I said. "I've read that sorceresses have a way in, and they're fond of dumping the monsters they can't kill there."

Caitriona let out a huff and stood, slipping out from under both the blanket and Neve's arm. She began pacing, doing laps around our small camp. "Go on."

"With King Arthur and his best knights dead, the so-called age of heroes was at an end," I said. "And no one was brave—or foolish—enough to hunt the beast again."

"The priestesses of Avalon were the ones who splintered Lyonesse from the mortal world, using high magic," Caitriona said. "It was one of their final acts before the druid uprising."

"Exactly," I said. "Then, later, the sorceresses encouraged the tales of the city succumbing to a wave sent by some wrathful deity, repeating again and again that the kingdom had been dragged beneath the icy sea, until the story became legend."

With the story at its end, we settled back into tense silence.

Neve craned her neck, searching the sky. "It has to be midnight by now."

The stars seemed sharper tonight, glittering with cold fire as the moon climbed the vault of the sky. Based on the moon's position, I guessed there was still an hour before midnight, that liminal hour between one day and the next.

"Nearly there," I told them.

"Nearly where?" a warbling voice asked.

My stomach bottomed out.

Caitriona spun around, lunging for her spear. Slowly, with every curse in every language I knew streaming through my head, I looked back over my shoulder.

Rosydd, the Hag of the Moors, was floating lazily at the boundary of the protective wards, her head propped up on one hand. She was still wearing that disconcerting blend of all our faces.

Neve rose to her feet, shivering. "Hello, Rosydd, you're looking lovely this evening."

The hag preened. "Thank you. You're looking delectable yourself."

I glanced between them, holding my breath as the hag floated closer to the wards. They repelled her with a hard *snap* of light and pressure.

"*Ouch!* That was mean!" She scowled at us, rubbing her sore arm. "Take those down immediately!"

"How many days do you have left of not eating people?" Neve asked.

Rosydd smiled, baring all of her many pointed teeth. "None."

"Thirteen," I corrected. "At least."

"You couldn't have asked for longer than two weeks, huh?" Neve muttered to me.

The hag drifted over to her, inspecting her as closely as the wards would allow. Neve drew back a step, recoiling as the hag shifted her features again, mimicking the sorceress's wide, luminous eyes.

"Stop it," Neve ordered.

"Stop what?" the hag asked innocently, shifting out of her white velvet gown and into a replica of Neve's plum-colored coat. She seemed to prefer my boots and copied them down to the way I'd tied the laces. And, weirdly, I was flattered.

"Why can't you just look like yourself?" Neve asked her. "What's so wrong with who you are?"

"What's so wrong with wanting to look the way I want to look?" the hag asked.

"It's one thing to change your appearance," Neve said, "and

something else to try to become another person. Do you even remember what you originally looked like?"

The hag stared at her, her lips—Olwen's lips—parting. "You're mean."

"It's okay to change yourself to your liking, but it's also okay to be yourself as you are," Neve said. "You don't have to look or be a certain way for others to like you."

The hag glowered at her. "You don't like me?"

"That's not—" Neve threw up her hands. "Never mind."

"What are we doing here, anyway, meaty-pie?" Rosydd asked me.

My mind couldn't decide what to process first, that *we,* or *meaty-pie.*

"We're here to see the Hag of the Mist," I said. "Any relation?"

Rosydd drew herself upright, allowing her bare feet to settle onto the crust of hoarfrost covering the ground. If I'd thought she was capable of it, I would have said she looked hurt—as if we'd committed some grave, mortal offense.

"But why . . . *her*?" she whined. "You like me best, don't you? And to think, we had such fun."

"If by fun, you mean we witnessed unyielding horrors and you tried to turn us over to the Wild Hunt, then sure," I said. "Listen, Ros—can I call you Ros?"

"Can I call you Supper?"

I paused. "Touché."

She nudged at the wards again, just hard enough to spark a little jolt. Caitriona drew closer, her expression enough to send Rosydd gliding back a step. "What do you want with that batty old creature, anyway? I thought we were friends."

"Do friends eat their friends?" I asked her.

"When hungry, yes," Rosydd said. "Well, all right, no. But they *do* eat disappointing acquaintances."

"Important distinction," Neve said.

"We need the Hag of the Mist to open a path between this world and Lyonesse," I told her. "She was able to get us into Avalon before."

The hag's nose wrinkled. "Is that it? All of my sisters and I can do that."

"Really?" I asked. "I thought she was the only one who could manipulate the mists that border the Otherlands."

Rosydd put her hands on her hips. "*Of course* she'd want you to believe that. So conceited. She's not any more powerful than the rest of us just because some soggy corner of the earth coughed her up first."

"So . . . ," I began. "You'd be willing to open a path for us?"

"It depends . . . ," the hag said. One of her curved fangs poked out as she bit her lip. "What did my sister ask for?"

"An offering, and a few strands of my hair," I said.

"Your hair?" Rosydd looked just as puzzled as Neve and Caitriona did.

"What's wrong with my hair?" I asked, tucking a strand behind my ear.

"She's always been the odd one in the family," Rosydd told us. "Never met a cave she didn't want to skulk around in, likes to be as slimy as a frog. She's probably sniffing those strands as we speak."

A small part of me died at that thought. "What do you want, then?"

"A good question . . . ," Rosydd said, sounding eminently reasonable. "What about your toenails? Surely they're easy enough to pluck out."

"What if," Neve cut in, before I could say something I regretted, "she gives you three eyelashes? They're what mortals use to make wishes on."

Rosydd looked intrigued. "Go on."

I'd never been more grateful for Neve's love of whimsy.

"Three eyelashes, for three wishes a god may answer," Neve said. She held out the bottle, letting the contents slosh around. "And this wonderful offering."

"Is that what smells like ruptured warts?" Rosydd asked, wrinkling her nose. "What am I supposed to do with that?"

"Whatever hags do with weird bottled mixtures," I told her. "You're the one with centuries of mystic knowledge."

"Well . . . all right," she said. "Maybe I'll throw it at an unsuspecting mortal and have a laugh."

Neve gave a pained smile as she passed the bottle over the wards. "Try not to aim for their heads, please."

"But it never shatters right when it strikes their flanks."

"In a moment, we will give you the eyelashes and the bottle," I said, careful to lay out the full deal, "and you vow you will open a portal to Lyonesse there for us right now, and keep it open to allow us to return when we are ready."

The hag pouted, and I knew then my instinct had been right. She would have turned my own trick back on me if I hadn't worded it as a vow.

"I'm going to take the wards down now," I told her. "And you're going to keep your vow moving forward, right?"

Caitriona took that as her cue to smother the fire, and Neve to gather our things. Rosydd held out her hand eagerly.

"I swear it," the hag said.

At the vow, I unwound the garland of wards from around the camp. Then, with some effort, I managed to pluck three eyelashes from my right eye. "Don't spend them all on one wish."

Her hand was shockingly cold as I wiped the pale lashes into her palm. The hag closed her fist around them, bringing them close to her mouth to whisper her wishes.

"Now blow on them, or let the wind carry them away," Neve said, handing me Dyrnwyn. I draped the strap of the hilt we'd made for it over one shoulder, and my loaded workbag over the other.

The hag did as she was told, releasing the lashes with childish pleasure. In that unguarded moment, her false face slipped, just for a second, revealing her true one. The blue-gray tint of her skin, the rugged planes of her face so like the nearby cliffs, the golden glow of her bulging eyes—and there was nothing frightening about her. Except, maybe, the razored teeth.

"The passage?" I reminded her.

Her mask slipped back into place as she turned to me. "Oh, all right, yes. You'll bring me back something tasty, won't you?"

"We'll certainly try," Neve said. "Do you have any preferences?"

I tried not to groan as the hag took her time deliberating.

"Something that isn't too hairy, or dead longer than a day," Rosydd said, finally. "Too much fur gets stuck in the teeth, and too-dead meat is tough to chew."

"Well, that's a mental image I'll never get rid of," Neve said.

"I can't leave the portal open willy-nilly," Rosydd said. "One of the big meanies might get out, and as much as it disappoints me, my jaws simply aren't big enough for some of them."

"Oh . . . dear," Neve managed.

"When you're ready for me, call out, *Dark the night, dark the moor, part the mist, open the door,*" Rosydd said, beginning to spin her hands in front of her, as if winding string.

"Why that?" I asked.

"Because it's *amusing,*" the hag snapped.

I held up my hands. "*Dark the night,* got it. Can you really hear us across worlds?"

"I can if you say my name first," Rosydd said. "Give it a nice big shout. Make it sound lovely and scrumptious, won't you?"

The hag raised her hands, then lowered them again, then raised them once more—only to stop and stroke the point of her chin.

"Is there a problem?" Caitriona asked.

"Grant me a moment, will you?" Rosydd said, cracking her neck. "It's been a while. I don't want to send you to the wrong place—believe me, you wouldn't like any of the forgotten worlds. Though I suppose you might like the one if you've ever wanted to bathe in the mouth of a god."

"Lyonesse will be just fine," I said quickly. "The castle, please."

"Really, take your time," Neve added.

Rosydd returned to her work with a satisfied snort. Closing her eyes, she inhaled deeply, and her body rose, hovering above the ground.

I hadn't been able to bring myself to watch her sister, the Hag of the Mist, open the pathway to Avalon. Now, I couldn't tear my eyes away.

Black threads appeared in the night air, braiding together, then slithering around and around like an ouroboros, the snake eating its own tail. Mist spiraled out of the darkness gathering at its center. As the portal opened, the smell of fir trees bled into the air like a promise.

"There," Rosydd said, sounding satisfied with herself. "Off you go, then. And don't forget—" She pointed at her mouth, chattering her teeth to mime eating.

"Believe me," Neve said, "we couldn't if we tried."

Caitriona gripped her pale spear as she made her way toward the door between the worlds. A breeze pushed the loose strands of silver hair away from her face. Dark tendrils of magic drifted out, wrapping around her, drawing her in. She didn't look back—she simply surrendered to it, and was drawn into its depths.

Neve followed, reaching into her fanny pack for her wand, pointing the knife end out in front of her as she stepped through. Remembering the first unpleasant trip, I hung back, trying to settle my nerves.

Go, Tamsin, I told myself. *Go.*

Squaring my shoulders, I stepped forward, waiting for the darkness to take me. One by one, its fingers stretched out, sliding around my throat, my wrists, my hips. I felt my hair lift from the back of my neck, and loud sniffing filled my ears.

The doorway tugged me forward, but Rosydd let out a shrill noise of panic, trying to grip the fistful of my hair again.

"No," she said, "wait—!"

But the passage had me, and I was already gone.

Greenwich, Connecticut

The sound of crashing glass and bellowing laughter rose from the floor below. Another moment blurring into the next in a tide of endless hours.

He'd been on benders before, but they were child's play compared to the way the riders of the Wild Hunt had unleashed themselves on Summerland House. They drank liquor, cackling as it ran through their immaterial bodies. They knocked candles over, hoping something interesting might catch and turn into an amusing blaze. They sang bawdy songs and retold stories of the kills they'd claimed—the way one sorceress had pled for her life, or how one had tried to hide within the walls of her decrepit house, the old one they'd run down in Wales who'd really thought she might escape.

Each hunt only sent them deeper into the frenzy. Even Endymion Dye had become something of an animal, eagerly clawing at the walls of his ancestral home as if to destroy that last tie to his humanity.

He turned over on the narrow bed, drawing his knees up toward his center, listening as they hacked at the chandelier in the entry. The roar of shattering crystal against marble made him curl his fists against his ears.

As the only living member of the horde aside from his master, he was the only one who required rest, a fact the hunters never allowed him to forget. Rather than take one of the stuffy guest rooms, he'd found a bare-walled room off the main corridor, barely bigger than a closet. It was clearly meant for a servant, which suited him fine. That was what he was. That was what he was meant to be.

But he had half a mind to find Emrys Dye's room and take a piss in his bed after what had happened at Rivenoak. When he hadn't appeared at the merging of the worlds, the seneschal had assumed the kid had died.

He'd said nothing about seeing Emrys to the others, especially Endymion. He was coming to appreciate that secrets were their own currency. Their own type of power. But as always in his life, he was barely scraping by. The hunters were circling ever closer to Lord Death, trying to bend his ear, trying to win his favor; he would have to work harder now to ensure that his place at his lord's side wasn't wrested away from him by another.

His hesitation to relinquish that final piece of Cabell in the library had cost him.

The pit of his stomach turned sour. Tremors crawled up and down his body and wouldn't stop, not when the sweat broke out across his neck and chest, not even as he heaved himself upright, setting his feet on the floor.

He doubled over, bracing his elbows against his knees, and his forehead against his fists. As the heat spread, his bones shifted, snapped, slipped like snakes under his skin. His lungs struggled for breath.

His hands reeked of metal, but it was the scattering of ash on the sleeve of his shirt that made him rear back, rip it off him, throw it into the shadowy corner of the room.

The house leaned in around him, creaking—he'd had the feeling it had been watching him this whole time, learning his ways.

"What are ye doing?"

The girl watched him from across the room, scowling. He could see through her translucent shape to the mirror behind her. She had no reflection, but his own face was chalk white.

He closed his eyes, rubbing at his temples, and when he risked another look, she was still standing there. Still eyeing him like he was scum to be scraped off her boot.

"You're not real," he said hoarsely.

He was exhausted. The nonstop raids, Rivenoak, and then—

The memory was a snake coiling around his throat. He flexed his hands over his knees, remembering the weight of his sword, the strength it had taken to drive the steel through the automaton's body.

Young Lark . . . ?

He growled, furious with himself. That wasn't his name. That had never been his true name.

"You're not real," he repeated, feeling suddenly feverish. An infection of unwanted emotion swelled in him.

"What did ye do?" she asked, her voice fluttering around the room like the frantic wings of a baby bird.

"Nothing," he whispered. "Leave me alone."

"Yer the one calling me," the girl sniped back.

"I'm not," he said. "You're not real."

He ran his hands back through his hair, ripping his fingers through painful knots. Like all of the others in Avalon, this girl had needed to die. His lord saw no other option.

And when his master had explained his plan, the seneschal had understood, finally, the bottomless ache in him. He saw how he fit into the great puzzle of it all. He had found someone who would never leave him, who saw what he was and didn't cower from it. He had belonged to something. Someone.

But the blood . . . There had been so much of it in the courtyard . . . And he'd quickly discovered that there wasn't a chamber beneath the tower deep enough to muffle the screaming.

Or had he imagined that, too? Somehow the things he knew were real no longer felt that way, and his nightmares walked in daylight. His lord's thinking had made so much sense on the dark isle, but the girl standing before him made all those reasons unravel, and he could no longer find that first thread.

"*What did ye do?*" the girl asked again. *Flea.* The girl's name had been Flea.

"Nothing," he grated out. His hands had been clean. He hadn't killed anyone himself. Not the Avalonians, not Wyrm's guild, not even the new Children they'd gathered from all across the Western world.

Not until Librarian.

Young Lark . . . ?

He choked on his next breath, welcoming the shifting, cracking bones of his spine.

Yes, he thought, *now.* There was peace in the shift. The hound didn't know the girl. Didn't care that Flea had died.

"Nothing," he said again. "Nothing."

"*What did ye do?*"

The question was as inescapable as his own reflection. Her voice turned singsong, mocking.

"*What did ye do?*"

"Enough, Tamsin!" he snarled, finally looking up. He realized his mistake immediately, heart hammering in punishment.

The girl stared back, her expression offering nothing. Not forgiveness. Not anger. Not even pity. It was the gaze of someone a hundred years older, not that of a child who'd lived only a handful of years. Who knew nothing about choices, or what it meant to live a lie.

And she never will, a voice whispered in his mind. *Because of you.*

He shoved up to his feet, letting the world sway around him. He'd get rid of her, and he'd ensure she couldn't come back. That her soul was well and truly sealed in his lord's gemstone with all the others.

His bare feet padded down the hall, avoiding the piles of broken glass and the plaster moldings that had fallen from the ceiling. The relics in the house had been destroyed the same way the ones in the guild library had: melted down into molten ore, rendered into ash. Each display of destruction an oath, a vow.

The wall sconces flickered feebly as he reached the stairs, following the din of the hollering and revelry from the dining room below, just off the front door. A flash of blond hair appeared in a mirror as he passed it, the small ghost trailing behind him, keeping pace even as he quickened his steps.

"—the next one will be a real beauty, mark my words—"

"—might keep her around a little longer for the hell of it—"

"Hear, hear!"

The ghouls lounged around the massive dining table and the map of the world that had been spread out over it. Little red pins marked the souls they'd claimed, now in the hundreds.

"A bunch of snot-nosed knaves," Flea noted.

He whirled around, striding toward the study. If his lord was not with the riders, he would be there, keeping his own counsel.

Sure enough, Lord Death's voice reached the seneschal before he'd even set foot in the foyer. The time spent as a hound had sharpened his hearing, and he only had to draw a little closer to the oak door to hear the murmured conversation inside.

"—of course, that can be easily arranged."

His skin prickled, a growl curling in his chest. *Endymion.*

He hadn't noticed that the rider wasn't with the others, but he should have known. Endymion desired power above all; it was inevitable that he'd weasel his way in closer to Lord Death to position himself as the most faithful deputy.

He might have been the lead rider, but he was not their master's seneschal.

"How fare the searches?" Lord Death asked, his voice rumbling.

"I've set several of the men on Excalibur's trail, but I believe it is not in this world and may be no concern to you," Endymion said.

"Then you are an even bigger fool than I thought," Lord Death replied.

"My apologies, I should not have assumed to know your mind," Endymion groveled.

"The Lady of the Lake's sword is no mere weapon," Lord Death warned. "Not even demons escape its touch. Until it is in my hand, and I decide whether to wield it or eliminate its threat, remember that."

The Lady of the Lake. Yes. His master had mentioned such a blade to him.

"Of course," Endymion said.

"It's just as well I've another set of eyes searching for it," Lord Death said.

"My lord?" Endymion said, startled. The seneschal felt his own breath catch at that unexpected information. "May I ask who?"

"You may not," the king said. "But if I were you, I'd fear them finding it first."

"I will find it first, then," Endymion said quickly.

The seneschal's top lip curled into a sneer. Why hadn't he been tasked with this?

"And the other search?" Lord Death prompted. There was the sound of clinking glassware, and the smell of Scotch bloomed in the air. "For the soul I tasked you to find?"

Yes, the seneschal thought. *The soul.* The woman who had been taken so cruelly from his master.

"It continues," Endymion said. "I believe the next sorceress rat we catch in our net will have more information on its whereabouts. I'll keep her alive long enough to pry the information from her."

"Good," Lord Death murmured. "*Good.* Then you're dismissed."

The large gem he wore at the base of his throat pulsed with the light of the souls swirling inside. All those who hadn't been made into riders were imprisoned inside the dark stone—but, somehow, the little girl's soul had escaped.

Instead of alerting his master to it as he'd intended, the seneschal backed away from the door swiftly, crossing the foyer to the stairs. If she *was* a hallucination, it would only make his master despise him more.

"*Secrets, secrets . . . ,*" the little girl whispered behind him.

The taunt curled around him as he made his way up the stairs. The little girl trailed behind him, skipping up the steps as she sang.

"As the bud blooms to flower, as the moon passes to mark the hour..."

"Stop," he begged.

She didn't.

"As Lord Death rides upon his cold power, so the Goddess built the tower..."

But when he turned, there was only his own bleak face staring back at him in the mirror on the landing.

"Well, well, well!" one of the hunters cried from below. "Look who's finally turned up—"

The seneschal whirled, anger driving him to the railing to see who'd dared to say it. But none of the hunters below were jeering up at him. They were focused on two new arrivals being dragged into the foyer through the back hallway.

"What's this?" Endymion drawled. "Edward Wyrm, back from the dead?"

Wyrm was splattered in blood and dirt, his once-fine tuxedo hanging from him in tatters. The seneschal's nose picked up the stench of his sweat and piss. The look in the man's eyes was one of terror, even as he declared, in the way only these rich old men could, "I—I demand an audience with our lord! Immediately!"

"*Our* lord?" Endymion repeated, his teeth flashing with a cruel smile.

The hunters' excitement turned to outright hunger as Wyrm stepped aside, revealing the person behind him.

The seneschal's nails elongated into claws.

Olwen.

If it hadn't been for her usual soft smell of herbs and fresh water, he might not have recognized her. His pulse climbed, pounding hard enough for his teeth to chatter. Wyrm had knocked her around, if the bruise swelling on the right side of her face was any indication. Her hair was matted, half ripped out of its braid. Her clothing was in worse shape than his own.

"*No,*" came the little girl's voice beside him. "*No, no—*"

The seneschal's mind raced, his claws tearing away at the wood.

"Who is this?" Endymion asked, circling them.

"*Do something,*" Flea begged.

Wyrm had gagged Olwen and bound her hands behind her—but he'd taken further precautions too, hooking a ward with a sigil to repel magic around both their necks. Any spell she could have summoned against the Hollower would have glanced off both.

Endymion, with the precision and power of a raptor, lunged and grabbed Wyrm by the neck. "*Who?*"

Their master's voice emerged from the darkness of the study, and a moment later, he was in the doorway, watching all of it unfold with a small smile. "Why, that is Lady Olwen of Avalon."

The seneschal was already moving down the stairs when Olwen wrenched herself out of the hunters' hands, fighting against her gag to summon a spell. When one of the fools tried to grab her again, she lashed out with a foot and rammed into another with her skull.

"That's enough," Lord Death said coldly. "Bledig, bring her to me."

"My lord," Wyrm bleated out, already on his knees to grovel. "I apologize for the lateness of my arrival. I wish to serve you—as a mortal man, of course, who can move within this world and—"

"Endymion," Lord Death said, disappearing back into the study. "The Children haven't had their supper yet, have they?"

"Th-The Ch-Children?" Wyrm began. "Whose children?"

Endymion let out a throaty laugh as he gripped the other man by the back of the neck and hauled him out through the front door. Supper for the monsters.

Olwen was shivering—with the cold or terror, the seneschal wasn't sure. He grabbed her arm, narrowly missing her foot as it swung around. Her eyes widened at the sight of him, and despite her spit-soaked gag, he heard her shocked "Cabell?" all the same.

She fought every single one of the thirteen steps to the office. She writhed and butted against him as he forced her into the wooden chair across from the desk. Lord Death waved his hand and magic singed the air, sharp and sulfuric, as restraints twisted from the chair's armrests and pinned her in place.

"Hold her, Bledig," Lord Death said.

Olwen sent him a pleading look and the seneschal's chest tightened, the air squeezing out of him in a hard gust. There was no need. The chair had rooted itself into the floor and wouldn't move, even against the full might of whatever small magic a priestess could summon.

He is your master, he thought, watching Lord Death retrieve a small knife from the scabbard hanging over the desk's chair. *You must prove yourself again.*

"Cabell, please," Olwen got out around the gag. "Don't do this!"

"Don't!" Flea cried from the corner.

Olwen made a small noise of distress as Lord Death came toward her, the blade glinting in the candlelight.

"Go ahead," Olwen said, her expression hardening with defiance. "We already have what we need to stop you. Killing me won't change your fate."

Lord Death let out a laugh, bringing his face down in line with hers. "My dear, I have no plans to kill you. Not yet, at least."

He brought the blade down to her forearm, slicing it with a single stroke. Olwen gasped with the pain of it. Fresh blood burst across the seneschal's senses, and inside him, the hound growled.

"Now," Lord Death said, collecting the blood in the palm of his gloved hand. "Let's see what secrets are hiding in your memories, shall we?"

29

Between worlds, there was nothing but darkness.

It was unending, absolute. My first journey had been too chaotic to notice anything other than the sensation of being compressed and hurtled forward at a speed that left me breathless. Now, my mind was alive to what it was seeing—a despairing abyss, a void where no life existed. A place beyond the sight of gods.

Then the mist came, a hazy border.

Then the light.

The snow.

I burst out of the doorway, momentum carrying me even as I tried to dig my heels in to stop. But beneath the snow was a layer of hard ice, and even the spikes on my boots couldn't gain any kind of purchase. I was powerless to do anything other than fall.

The whipping winds snarled with disorienting rushes of snow. I staggered up, bracing my feet to fight back against the force of them. Snow—ice crystals—battered my face as I searched for the others in the maelstrom of white around me.

"Cait!" I shouted. "Neve! Can anyone hear me?"

Fear spiked through my chest. The portal had vanished. I couldn't even tell which direction I'd come from.

This doesn't make any sense, I thought. The others should be here. We'd come to the same place—I'd traveled through right after them.

"Neve!" I tried again. My face was stiff and aching from the cold. "Cait! Neve!"

The shouts were nothing compared to the howl of the blizzard. It seemed to laugh, sputtering ice and snow in my face until it became difficult to breathe. A growing panic simmered beneath my skin.

"Is anyone there?" I called, the words breaking at their edges. "Hello? Anyone!"

I turned in a slow circle, trying to shake the growing sensation that I was drowning in blisteringly cold light.

Alone . . . my mind whispered. *Always alone.*

"Anyone!" I pleaded. If something had happened to them—

A shadow appeared just ahead of me, emerging from the cloak of white like a drop of ink seeping through parchment. My heart leapt at the sight.

"Over here!" I shouted, waving my arms. Thank the gods, or fates, or whoever for sparing me this one single ordeal.

The shape came closer, and closer. Slowly, as if to figure out who I was too.

And then its eyes, a hideous, glowing yellow, found mine through the storm. As it came toward me, it wasn't walking on two legs, but four.

My arms fell back to my sides, limp.

"Oh . . . shit," I choked out, already backing up.

At my movement, it *yowled.* The pitch was like glass shards in my ears, and if it hadn't been for that pure, primal drive to survive, I would have doubled over and tried to cover them. Instead, terror turned into an iron band around my chest as my mind flipped through its vast archive of beasts and horrors.

The creature was the size of a horse—terrifying, even at a distance. Its tawny fur was encrusted with snow. Massive claws tore through the ice beneath it with ease. Dark spikes covered the tip of its tail like a mace.

Cath Palug, my mind helpfully supplied. A monstrous wildcat that had become the scourge of the Isle of Anglesey, claiming the lives of at least a hundred and eighty warriors before King Arthur, or one of his knights, slayed it.

Apparently *not*.

Maybe if the others had been with me, if there'd been someone other than my sorry self to protect, I might have stood my ground and faced the coming fight with courage. But I was alone, and there was a monster, and even though I knew—I *knew*—predators reveled in the chase, every instinct in me was screaming *Run*.

I took off like I was on fire, searching the horizon for anything, anywhere, to hide. The misty snow swallowed me, soaking through my coat and boots until both felt like they weighed a hundred pounds. My workbag clattered at my side until I pressed it to my chest.

My skin crawled, prickling as Cath Palug answered back with a loud noise like chortling—like all I'd done was amuse it.

Shit, shit, shit—!

Of all the creatures I had to come across, it just *had* to be the one that could outrun, outlast, and outsmart me.

The sound of its claws ripping into the ice as it ran made me look back. Cath Palug galloped toward me, its fanged mouth stretched into a hideous grin.

I pushed harder, fighting through the gathering snow until another shadow appeared ahead. A curse aimed at every god that was listening leapt to the tip of my tongue—but it wasn't another beast. It was a large formation of rocks protruding from the snow. If there were more of them, I might be able to lose Cath Palug amid them, or at least find some crevice to hide in until the creature grew bored and abandoned the hunt.

Yeah, I thought. *Good luck with that, Lark.*

Because, of course, there were no other boulders aside from the two standing upright and the third one, which lay flat. There was nothing but the unending blizzard.

I looked over my shoulder again, and Cath Palug had drifted farther back into the storm. The relief that washed through me was short-lived.

Only a few moments later, when some potent combination of hope and fear made me check again, it had regained lost ground and was running even faster, screeching with that same gleeful, monstrous laughter, *"Ha! Ha! Ha!"*

It was playing with its food.

That peculiar, horrible calm found me again as my death mark pulsed. This was my curse, wearing fur and fang.

The thought of the others coming across whatever remained of my body sickened me. I could only hope the snow would pile high enough to hide it.

No, the wind seemed to urge, easing into a soft whisper. I heard it as clearly as I had the voice that stopped the White Lady. It was the very same. *Fight. The sword.*

Dyrnwyn's hilt dug into my shoulder, the metal giving the exposed skin on my neck an icy kiss.

But I don't know how, I thought back, my muscles throbbing. Why hadn't I ever asked Caitriona to teach me even the most basic stances? How to hold the stupid thing—

I knew Cath Palug had gained on me when I heard its huffing breaths again. It had survived in this desolate Otherland for centuries against all odds. There was absolutely no doubt in my mind that my body would give out long before its did, succumbing to exhaustion, or the brutal cold.

With no other choice, I ran toward the rocks, knowing I could at least keep my back to them and stand my ground there. Reaching back to grip Dyrnwyn's hilt, I jumped toward the flat rock—

Only to miss, and crash down through the snow and a brittle patch of ice.

The impact on the ground below jarred every bone in my body, blanking my vision. Mounds of snow fell in from above, filling the gap my fall had created until the way out was completely blocked.

Or hidden, my mind corrected.

I threw a desperate look around me, confused. I wasn't in water—

I seemed to have found the true ground, and it was muddy and scattered with stones and dead grass and moss. Above me, like a ceiling, a thick shelf of ice groaned and crackled, shifting with each insistent gale.

There was just enough room to crawl, so I did, scrambling forward in the direction I'd been headed in before. Ignoring the scattered bones that lay around me, ignoring the thorned brush that tore into my clothing and skin. It was a few minutes, maybe more, when I heard the ice above me start to crack.

What began as a web of thin lines turned into longer white seams as weight was added to it. I could track each of Cath Palug's steps, even before I heard its shuddering breaths. The sniffing.

I stilled, trying to stop the tremors punishing my body and rattling the blade and the contents of my bag. My blood boiled in my veins, my pulse pounding in every muscle of my body.

And I forced myself to remember.

I wasn't who I'd been before. The Tamsin who had prized a quiet security over all else—the Tamsin who'd never been touched by magic, let alone fought for it. Who had never clawed back against death when it tried to claim her.

I remembered who I'd let myself become in that dark world. I remembered the friends who were somewhere out there in the whirling snow, just as lost.

I remembered.

Thin cracks spread over the ice as the cat came toward me. Cath Palug's enormous paws were just visible through the clouded ice and the powdery snow above it. I bit my lip, fighting my mind's desperation to run.

The beast let out a whine of irritation, and I wondered if I'd overestimated its intelligence.

But then its claws sank down onto the splintering sheet of ice. And one by one, the claws over my head began to tap out a little mocking song. *Tap-tap-tap. Ha! Ha! Ha!*

The calm was back, but this time, I seized hold of it. I let it guide me to whatever end the next moments would bring—mine, or Cath Palug's.

The snow shifted above me.

The ice fragmented, each fissure feeding into the next, multiplying faster than the eye could track.

I adjusted the angle of my body, reaching back to grip Dyrnwyn's hilt.

Cath Palug's face appeared above mine, even more hideously distorted by the barrier between us. Its yellow eyes glowed—but not as bright as the white fire that raced along Dyrnwyn's blade as I drove it up through the ice, straight through one eye and into its skull.

It screamed, thrashing, but I screamed louder—in rage and desperation, pulling the sword free only to hack at its neck, until its head rolled away from the body with a spray of blood.

Breath sobbed in and out of me. I let my sword fall to my side; the threat gone, its flames released with a hiss, leaving the steel to cool. I reached up, wiping the sticky blood from my face, spitting it out of my mouth.

"Ha . . . ha . . . *ha* . . . ," I snarled out, and kicked the creature's enormous head deeper into the snow.

But whatever thrum of victory I felt faded as the winds spun through the empty landscape and I was alone once more in a kingdom of monsters.

It felt like an eternity before another shape emerged on the far horizon.

By then, I'd had hours to agonize over what had happened to the others. To imagine that Cath Palug had come upon them first, and caught them by surprise, or how they'd each be wandering alone in a complete whiteout, desperately searching for the other, all the while stalked by monsters.

Over and over again, I tortured myself with it, until I finally had to accept that the others might have a point about my mind being an extremely unhelpful instrument of terror.

But whatever that was ahead—that was *real*.

I knelt, staying low to the ground until I was sure what—or who—was waiting ahead. But the dark form didn't change, and only grew as the storm eased the worst of its rage and settled into a gentle, rippling snowfall. The clouds surrendered enough of the sky to reveal a sunset that burnished the frosted land in a dazzling fiery gold.

"Oh, please," I whispered hoarsely. "Please, please, please . . ."

Ahead were what appeared to be dozens of hills, but each was too uniform in shape and size to have been fashioned by nature's hand alone. My body felt as heavy as a pillar of marble, but I forced it forward, riding that wave of incredulity and relief as I neared the hills and found round, slatted doors half hidden beneath a layer of hoarfrost and snow.

When I reached the first of the mounds, I scraped at the frozen edges of its door with numb fingers, trying not to focus on how blue the tips of them had turned. I forced myself to stop, to back up a step. There was a faster way to do this.

I kicked at the door until the sheaves of ice fell away, then dug it out from the snow, opening it to peer into the darkness inside. The other nearby doors were similarly sealed shut, but it didn't mean other creatures weren't hibernating inside.

Seeing nothing, I strained my ears and listened. Only the breeze whistling down through the small, sturdy hearth inside answered.

I shouldered the door fully open with one last burst of energy, then collapsed to the ground once I was through. A bed of browned leaves and rotting rugs scattered with snow softened my fall. For a moment, I did nothing but lie there and let the wind slam the door shut behind me.

"Get up," I ordered myself. *"Get. Up."*

The words were slurred by exhaustion and the shivering that overtook me. The Fair Folk who'd built these mounds had insulated them, and the difference in temperature was startling. My skin burned as sensation returned to it.

It would have been so easy to stay there, my legs throbbing from exertion. Just then, it was impossible not to consider it. But Nash, in all his limited wisdom, had taught Cab—

I drew in a deep, steadying breath.

Nash had taught the two of us the signs of hypothermia. The dangers of it. Exhaustion, disorientation, clumsiness, forgetfulness. The body using its last stores of energy to keep itself warm. If I let myself rest the way my whole being was longing to, there was a chance I'd never wake up again.

That alone made me crawl toward the hearth. Using a small broom, I jabbed up into the chimney, clearing the debris and ice until they crashed down onto the fire-scorched stones. It was a risk to allow smoke to rise—a surefire way to alert every nearby predator to my presence—but as soon as I was warm again, I could set up wards to disguise it.

The small pile of wood was damp and wouldn't light, even with a match and drier bits of leaves. The next burrow over, however, had shielded their woodpile with a waxed cloth, and the rug, with its bright floral woven pattern, had been saved by someone thinking to place a stone cap on the chimney. There was even a small bed, neatly made, at the far end of the room. The sight of it held me captive for a moment.

They expected to return home one day, I realized. The Fair Folk who had lived here, hundreds of years ago. They thought they'd return to their life one day.

Where had they ended up?

With my pick of the mounds, I stayed in this one, where it didn't feel like I was about to be swallowed by decay. A bundle of dried lavender in the corner still carried enough fragrance to soothe my nerves.

After trudging back outside to remove the stone covering the chimney, I set about making a fire. The room flushed with heat as it finally caught. I held my stinging hands over it, coughing from the smoke, but also clearing the last of the cold from my lungs.

When the color returned to my hands, I dug into my bag for the dried fruit and jerky the Bonecutter had provided. The water in my canteen had frozen solid; I set it near the hearth to melt, then went out and gathered snow in the small cauldron that had been left hanging from a hook on the wall. My arms, neck, and face still felt sticky from Cath Palug's blood, and while there'd be no hope of removing the stain from my clothes, I could perhaps rid them of the heavy metallic odor.

While waiting for the snow to melt and boil in the cauldron, I took another, closer look around the room. The Fair Folk who had lived here were child-sized, judging by the low ceiling and miniature everything. Elfins, maybe?

With food in my belly, and my mind no longer focused solely on survival, I came alive to the small details I'd missed before. Pails of shriveled berries. A little toy cat, carved from some pale wood. Four figures etched into the mud-packed walls.

The longer I sat there, the more the heat thawed me, the deeper my guilt became.

The others were still out there, somewhere—hopefully together, in some shelter of their own. There had to be more villages scattered around this Otherland. Homes built by humans. Caitriona had her spear and Neve her magic, however unpredictable it could be. They were strong. They would survive this, until we found each other again.

I sipped at my warmed water, then stripped off my coat and blood-caked sweater. My black T-shirt had been spared the worst of it and hid the now dry, stiff splatters. I kept it on. After refilling my canteen, I plunged my outer layers into the hot water and scrubbed at the stains. Hanging them to drip-dry near the fire, I set about unlacing my boots.

Only for my hands to still.

Outside, footsteps crunched through the snow. Labored breathing followed as if the creature had run the length of the world to arrive on the mound's doorstep. The door opened. Inwardly, I swore—I'd drawn the curtain back over the doorway to keep the snow out, but it also blocked the sight of whatever was out there. All I saw was a shaggy outline of fur.

Reaching back, I gripped Dyrnwyn and had started to draw it out of its hilt when the curtain was shoved aside and the beast gasped at the heat that assaulted it, shaking out its dark fur.

I rose onto my knees, the hilt in one hand, the sheath in the other, bracing myself.

Human, my mind noted.

Bent at the waist to avoid the rough scrape of the rocks and branches supporting the ceiling. Bundled up in a fur coat, a scarf wrapped around their face and neck, leaving only their eyes visible.

One gray, one green.

Emrys, my heart sang.

He stilled, looking from the sword clutched in my hands to my face.

"Well," he rasped out. "Fancy meeting you here."

30

It was a moment before the words came unstuck in my throat.

"What are you doing here?" *Alive. Whole. In Lyonesse.*

Just then, though, he only had eyes for the flames dancing in the hearth. "Oh, thank the gods you got a fire started."

He pulled off his snowy coat and stamped the clinging ice and mud from his boots. Kneeling, he tugged off his soaking boots and socks to reveal distinctly blue-tinged toes.

"This is my sheltering spot," I said. "There are a dozen other fairy mounds, get your own."

"But I like this one," Emrys said. He let out a sigh of pleasure as he pulled off his gloves and set them beside his socks on the hearthstones. Warming his hands and wind-burned face, he shut his eyes, his expression relaxing into one of pure bliss.

"This is the best damn hovel I've ever inhabited," he declared. "Truly, the greatest ever in any world."

"Spoken like someone who's never laid eyes on an actual hovel," I said, indignant on its past occupants' behalf. "This is a perfectly nice home."

I finally released my grip on Dyrnwyn and sat back on my heels, crossing my arms over my chest. Goose bumps that had nothing to do with the cold crept over my bare arms, spreading under my thin T-shirt, over my whole body.

The initial wave of disbelief gave way to a slow-growing elation that I was quick to stamp out. As my mind quieted, a single question rose like a trail of candle smoke.

How?

Emrys cracked an eye open and had started to turn back toward me when he noticed my drying coat. He raked his gaze over it and my dripping-wet sweater—over the dark blood still staining both. Fear sharpened his features as he swung around toward me, reaching out with both hands to gently grip my arms as he frantically looked me over.

"What happened?" he asked, his voice still scratchy from disuse. "Are you hurt?"

His hands were so warm, the calluses on his palms sparking a friction that made my stomach tighten and my pulse speed. I had to remind myself to pull away.

Don't touch me, he'd said. *Don't touch me.*

Now he was acting like he'd never said it? That he was content to touch *me,* as long as I didn't do the same to him?

"I'm fine—*Emrys.*" He finally looked up at my face, hearing me as I repeated, "I'm fine."

"All that blood—" he began.

"—belongs to the poor, unfortunate Cath Palug," I said.

Emrys pulled back, his brows rising. An unmistakable interest brightened his eyes. "Cath Palug? I thought Arthur killed it. . . ."

"Yeah, well, it turns out that men taking credit for things they didn't actually do has been an ongoing theme throughout history," I said.

"We are but creatures of fragile ego and beastly pride," Emrys said. "Do we need to worry about it tracking us back here?"

"Not unless it can reattach its head to its body, or it has little Cath Palug offspring to avenge it," I grumbled. Which, frankly, would be just my luck. "And *we* don't need to do anything. What the hell are you doing here, anyway?"

He sat back, swiping a hand over his rueful face. "Isn't it obvious?"

I hated the warm frisson his words sent down my spine.

"Last time I checked, you were half dead and unconscious," I said. "So no, it's not actually obvious."

"Wait," he said, holding up his hands. "Can we go back for a second to the part where you apparently beheaded a legendary monster?"

Emrys looked at me with something akin to wonder. I glowered back.

"No," I said. "We're staying on the topic of how you possibly tracked me here, to Lyonesse."

"Are you asking because you were worried I wouldn't recover, or because you didn't believe me when I said I wanted to make amends?" His voice was deceptively light.

My jaw clenched so hard that I was afraid I'd locked it in place. His eyes were soft as he watched me, and it was maddening and bewildering and painful, because I had *wanted* him to look at me like that. In Avalon, when he'd come back. Instead, I'd gotten harsh words and cold rejections, as if *he'd* been the wronged one. He'd pushed me away, before I could do the same to him. The confusion had to be the point—to keep me off-balance, to keep me guessing.

"I don't care if you die," I told him. "Or if you make amends."

"Well, that was a lie," he said, unimpressed. The edges of his lips curled—not that I was staring at them. "You have a tell, you know."

"I don't have a tell," I protested. My lying face had earned me a steady income through the Mystic Maven. It remained unquestioned and undefeated, even in card games.

"I'm sorry to break it to you, but you do," Emrys said. "It's subtle, though."

"What is it, then?" I demanded.

He smirked, revealing nothing.

"You are *impossible*," I growled. "Tell me!"

"And give up the only advantage I have over you?" he said. "Not a chance."

I blew out a hard breath through my nose. "Stop it."

"Stop what?" he asked, with all the innocence of someone who knew exactly what I meant.

"*This,*" I said, unable to check the ache in that word. "Why are you doing this? This—*game* you keep playing, where you act like nothing happened one minute, then you turn around and cut me the next like I'm nothing and *no one.* If you won't tell me what's going on with you, then just . . . *stop.*"

I didn't care anymore if he saw me upset. I could admit he'd won, because this was killing me more than the betrayal ever had.

His gaze lowered with his voice. "All right. I hear you."

The wind was stirring again outside, wheezing and whistling as it moved past the fairy mounds. With the darkness of night now firmly in place, it would be hours before it was safe to go out and look for the others.

"What the hell is that, anyway?" I asked, pointing to his enormous fur coat.

"That was the last coat the Bonecutter had available for purchase," Emrys said, scratching the back of his neck. "At least, that's what she claimed. I mostly just think she wanted me to look like the idiot I am."

"And you're . . ." I gestured toward his chest, where the jagged wounds were hidden beneath layers of cloth.

"Healed?" he finished. "Mostly. Bran's a jack-of-all-trades. Bird, bartender, stalker of enemies, occasional healer." He stretched an arm across his chest, only to wince. "Force-fed me some concoction that gave me the weirdest dreams about sailing on a leaf over the ocean, but the wounds are already starting to scar. Still not quite back up to full steam, though."

I picked at a hangnail, trying not to look relieved. He didn't deserve that.

"What happened while I was out?" he said, brows drawing down as he watched me. "I didn't have enough to trade the Bonecutter for the information."

"Mayhem, hungry primordial deities, your father and the others burning the library—it was a veritable bonanza of terror," I said.

"They burned the library?" Emrys stilled, horror sweeping over him. "What about Librarian?"

I said nothing. I didn't have to.

He swore. "I'm sorry, Tamsin. What else happened while I was down for the count?"

"Wyrm took Olwen," I whispered.

"What?" Emrys turned his back to the fire and faced me fully. "Why?"

I could only shrug. "We don't know. We don't know where she is, or if she's gotten away, or if she's—"

"Don't say it," Emrys interrupted. "She's not."

"You don't know that," I said.

"I do, because it wouldn't make sense," Emrys said. "Even if Wyrm brought her to Lord Death, he has other uses for her. She knows our plans."

I looked up at him, aghast. "Is the idea of him torturing her supposed to make me feel better?"

"No—yes—I mean—" Emrys breathed in deeply, finally collecting his thoughts. "I just mean that Olwen is extremely clever, and she'll find a way to stay alive until we can help her."

"We," I repeated. "There's that word again."

"Yes, *we*," he said firmly. "Please. Let me help you."

My frustration crested and broke over me.

"Why?" I asked. "*Why?* You've given us information. You saved my life at Rivenoak. Why can't you be done? What was the point of you following us here, still pale as a ghost—you said yourself you're not back up to full strength! So why?"

"Because," he said, with an almost fatalistic laugh. As if it were the most obvious thing in the world. "I would follow you anywhere."

"Don't," I warned, my breath hitching, "say that."

Don't give me hope and take it away again.

Emrys let his head fall back against the wall beside the hearth. He drew his knees up, resting his arms over them, watching me through a heavy-lidded gaze.

"I didn't ask you to come."

"You didn't have to," he said simply. "I meant what I said. I would follow you anywhere. Through dusty library stacks . . . into cursed woods . . . across drowned kingdoms . . . You've become the map of my life. There will never be any adventure worth having, any prize worth finding, that's greater than you."

My heart sped, even as the shadowy world around me slowed.

I didn't know what to say to that. It didn't make sense—nothing did. His words. Him being here. The way he kept looking at me like he used to. The fact that he was still so beautiful, his profile perfectly sculpted. He ruined all of my thoughts, threw all of my plans into disarray just by being here.

"I know I don't deserve it," he said, closing his eyes for a moment. "But if you'll let me stay beside you, just a little longer . . . just to make it right . . ."

His words faded in my silence. The knot tightening in my throat made speaking impossible. I'd felt he was keeping something from the rest of us, but this . . .

"Tamsin," Emrys said, his voice rough, "are we even now? Can we please be even?"

I didn't know how I found my voice again to speak.

"I thought you were done keeping score," I whispered.

"Yeah," he answered. "But *you* aren't."

I settled back against the wall behind me, staring at him across the narrow mound. My throat worked, as if trying to summon a denial, but it wouldn't come. Maybe I had been keeping score, but he was the one who kept changing the rules of the game.

"Is that why you did it?" I asked, that moment rising again in my memory to slash me to the quick. "Why you pushed me out of the way at Rivenoak? You wanted to be even?"

"I did it because if you die, there's no point to any of it," he said. "Not for me."

The words moved through me like lightning, shocking me into stillness.

"Gods, Tamsin," he said, pressing his fists to his temples. His words turned tortured. "I should never have left. I know why I did it. I can try to justify it a thousand different ways. But all of this . . . everyone who died . . ."

Every now and then, I felt the phantom weight of the bodies I'd carried to be cleaned and burned, as if it weren't just enough to have the memory of their dead faces, but my body needed to remember the trauma of it too.

Emrys drew in a deep breath. "I never should have left you."

"You . . ." The word felt like shards of glass in my throat, cutting me up from the inside.

"I can't take it back," he said. "Any of it. If I could give you the ring, I would. I'd let you kill me for it. It would be less of a punishment than your hatred."

"I don't hate you because you took the ring," I said, something tearing open inside me.

"If not that, then what?" he asked.

My fingers curled tightly against the dark air, trying to find anything to steady myself with. "You hurt me so badly because . . . it *was* different . . . it was different between us, and you broke whatever we could have been. And maybe none of it was ever real to you, but it was real to me, all right? It was, so congratulations, you really did win—you got that one over on me."

"Tamsin . . ."

"I don't *need* you," I told him. "I don't. But every time something's happened . . . every time I've felt lost . . . I wanted to be able to talk to you about it, the way we used to."

He looked shocked by my words, and I was terrified for a moment that my tone had revealed more than I'd meant to.

"I want that too," he said. "I want all of it, and all of you."

My whole body warmed at his words.

"You *don't*," I said, fighting back the burn in my eyes and throat. "You said horrible things to me—you told me not to even touch you, like I'm something disgusting to you—"

"No!" he said sharply, pressing his fist to his forehead again. "*Damn it,* no—that's not why."

"Then tell me what's going on," I pleaded. "Tell me why you've been acting like this."

He had a tell too, whether he recognized it or not. His gaze always shifted down before he was about to retreat, or lie. I could have screamed with frustration when I saw him do it again.

"Don't you dare lie to me again," I told him. "I understand why you took the ring. What I don't get is why you keep pushing *me* away. So why? Why did you leave?"

Emrys rubbed at his chest, wincing as he hit his wounds.

"The truth," I told him sharply.

His hand stilled over his chest, pressing against the place where his heart was thrumming beneath his skin and bones. Drops of sweat had broken out over his face, and for a moment, I thought he was going to be sick.

But still, he said nothing.

"We may be even now," I told him, feeling that familiar coldness settle in my chest. "But this is why it can't be what it was."

He barked out another humorless laugh, struggling to master his expression. There was something panicked in his eyes, like a cornered animal. "If I tell you . . . it definitely won't."

"What's that supposed to mean?" I demanded.

Emrys hesitated again. "I'm not . . . right. My father ensured that."

My eyes never left his face, even as my pulse leapt. I tried to understand. "Because he abused you . . . ?"

"No." Emrys drew in a deep breath, closing his eyes. "He didn't just hurt me, Tamsin. He killed me."

31

The fire spat and crackled in the hearth, burning through its dwindling supply of wood. Some part of my shocked mind recognized that it needed to be fed, but just then, none of it mattered. My lips parted but couldn't draw in air. The heaviness taking root inside my chest was a chimera of emotions—incredulity, anger, suspicion, and, finally, horror.

Emrys had lied countless times before. Smooth lies, charming lies, even protective ones. But the look of fragile hope on his face was truth. In it, I saw the child he'd once been, who must have come to his father never knowing if he might be accepted or rejected.

"I . . . what?" I got out.

Emrys reached down to grip his sweater and undershirt, pulling both off over his head. The firelight caressed the hard lines of his body, his strong shoulders and arms, his chest—but it also revealed the ragged scars that crisscrossed his skin. Even his more recent wounds, with their dark stitching, seemed less sinister.

The first time I'd seen the scars, in the light of Avalon's sacred pools, I'd thought he looked like he'd been shattered and hastily pieced back together, leaving evidence of the fractures that not even magic was powerful enough to erase. The sight of them now, the echo of his words in my mind, made me press a hand to my mouth.

"The night started like countless others," he told me, crossing his legs in front of him. He braced his hands against his knees and hunched forward slightly. "He'd—my father had hit my mother before I could get between them. When I finally got the bastard away from her, she fled up to her room and I left to try to cool off."

He snuck a look at me through the dark curtain of his bangs, as if measuring my reaction. Seeing I was still with him, he continued.

"When I got back home, I had a note to go see him in his study," he said. "It was the same routine as always. I'd apologize because he wouldn't, and we'd never speak of it again. Except . . ."

"Except what?" I asked roughly.

The dream, I thought, my heart hammering in my ears. It hadn't been a premonition.

I was already too late.

"The Order of the Silver Bough," he said. "When I opened the door to his study and stepped inside, they were waiting for me."

My breathing grew harsh in my ears.

"I didn't really understand it in the moment, because there wasn't time to," Emrys said, shuddering. "But when we got to Avalon, and we found that statue below the tower, when we heard what the druids had done, I started to piece it all together. There was holly everywhere, candles, chanting—it was a ritual, obviously."

"God's teeth," I whispered.

I couldn't get the images out of my head.

He nodded. "They were trying to summon the Holly King, and to do that, they needed a sacrifice. Someone to stand in for the Oak King, his enemy. It was over quickly. I didn't stand a chance. There were too many of them."

My hands covered my face now, trying to block out the words, trying to keep them from drawing out the memories of the dream. His lifeless body. The blood. I couldn't breathe.

"The next thing I knew, I woke up in Rook House," Emrys said, the words going thin. "Spilling out of a cauldron of some kind, naked as the day I was born, but . . . whole. Alive. I almost screamed at the feeling of the heart beating inside my chest. My mother was there, but she was so . . . changed. And Madrigal. She laughed when she saw me. She was *delighted* by it all."

My hands fell back into my lap. "What cauldron?"

"I don't know," he said quietly. "But it was death magic, clearly."

The wind let out a guttural moan as it battered the front door. I forced my gaze over to it as Emrys tugged his shirt and sweater back on.

"What did Madrigal do to your mother to age her that way?" I asked.

He rubbed at his arms, his expression strangely empty. "It was part of the spell to resurrect me. She had to give her own vitality, a piece of her soul. Mom had heard rumors about Madrigal and brought my . . ." He trailed off, but the word he hadn't spoken, *body*, fluttered like a moth's wings through my mind. "She brought me to Rook House. What was left of me."

The nausea was back again, rising swift and burning in my stomach. I wanted to clamp my hands to my ears like a child, to tell him to stop—but how could I?

"You're still you," I whispered.

"Am I?" he wondered. "I didn't even tell you the whole truth before, because I didn't want you to know the worst of it—that part that would make you scared of me, or see me the way I see myself."

"You don't scare me," I said.

He ran his hand back through his hair, gripping it in his fist. The look he gave me was pleading, as if begging me to make that true. "They didn't just kill me, Tamsin. As part of the ritual, they cut the heart out of my chest and burned it."

A terrible silence overtook us.

"That's—" I croaked out. "No, that can't be right—"

"It can, and it is," Emrys said. He looked down at his upturned palms. "I could tell something was wrong when I woke up. That *I* was wrong. But Madrigal waited until I brought the ring to her, when I thought I was finally free and could go back to Avalon. She waited until that exact moment, when I felt like my world had opened back up again, to tell me she had made me a new heart. With death magic."

"And you believed her?"

"I didn't have to," he said, rubbing at his chest. "My mother confirmed it."

Oh, my mind whispered.

"Madrigal laughed as she told me some part of my heart would always beat for her," Emrys continued, anger creeping into his tone. "And that if I ever crossed her, or displeased her, she could unmake it just as easily."

"But you brought her the ring," I said. "You repaid that debt."

"I know," he said. "She released me, but there's still a leash. I feel it every second of every day. I feel it when I run, when I try to sleep, when I look at you . . . Do you understand?"

His expression was almost desperate, as if he needed me to accept it. To believe it.

"I am never going to be completely free," he said. "I will *always* be under her control, in some way or another. I can live with the knowledge that she could yank the leash at any moment, or cut the thread of my life short, but I can't ask you or anyone else to. And if she asked me to hurt you . . ."

He trailed off, as if not wanting to give the idea life. "I thought it would be easier if you hated me. I tried to get you to despise me, the way I despise myself."

"Emrys, all of us could die at any time—" I began, but he didn't let me finish.

"I just keep thinking," he said, "death magic makes monsters, not men. We *saw* it. We saw what death magic does to the dead. A shadow lives inside me. A monster's heart. I'm so quick to anger, to succumb to those dark feelings . . . I don't see how it could be anything else."

I could barely summon the words through my shock. "Or it's just *grief.* Powerful grief. Because of what your father did, what your mother gave up, and what you lost. Because of what happened to us in Avalon."

Emrys's eyes remained on his hands, as if he could shape something out of the darkness, something that might make me understand. "I wish like hell that were true."

"Could a monster feel love?" I asked. When he looked up, I added, quickly, "You love your mother, don't you? Or regret? You regret what happened in Avalon. You wanted to help everyone there. We've seen monsters, Emrys. We barely survived them."

"Still . . . ," he whispered.

"You said there was nothing wrong about me, even after you saw the silver bone," I said stubbornly. "Do you still believe that?"

"Of course," Emrys said.

"I believe the same about you," I said. "Nothing about you is wrong, not to me."

He let out a shuddering breath.

"Irritating, sneaky, and a bit of a dork about plants, yes," I added. "But dark? No. You wish you had that much edge."

Emrys shook his head, but there was a small smile on his lips. "I prefer *playfully mischievous* to *sneaky*."

"Sneaky," I repeated, crossing my arms over my chest. My own heart was still hammering away against my ribs, as if the moment were spinning too quickly around me. If he had touched me then, if his fingers or lips had followed the path his eyes had taken down my face—

I drew in a sharp breath, shaking my head.

The fire sputtered out to its final few flames. I started to crawl toward the remaining wood in the pile, but Emrys beat me to it. By the way he took his time, carefully arranging the wood, I wondered if he'd needed a moment alone with his own thoughts.

It all felt too fragile; as if saying anything would shatter whatever this truce was between us, if it could even be called that. Nothing felt right, but I couldn't do it—I couldn't be the one to go to him when he was the one who had left.

But he's still here, I thought, dragging my pack over to me. The sleeping bag was decades old, but it would be better than suffering the indignity of trying to squeeze onto a toddler-sized bed. The rug at least provided some padding and protection from the hard-packed dirt floor.

Emrys unrolled his plush sleeping bag beside mine. I was about to point out a spot closer to the door, but I quickly realized that the mound was so narrow, we'd both have to lie lengthwise to fit.

"This feels—" he began.

"Don't say it," I said.

I settled down onto my side, keeping my face to the wall where I'd seen the etchings of the little family before. As Emrys lay down beside me, facing the other way, it was hard to tell what was providing more heat to my back, him or the fire.

"So . . . your dad's a ghoul of the Wild Hunt," I said, when the silence had finally become unbearable. "Appropriate."

"Yeah," Emrys said, turning over to lie flat on his back. I turned over too, as if pulled by some unseen tether. He caught my eye, and a sad, sardonic smile touched his lips. "Now he's as ugly on the outside as he was on the inside."

"Well, my not-dad is not-*dead* dead as well," I said. "So don't start thinking you're special, Dye."

"About that . . . ," Emrys began, his brow furrowing. I had to lace my fingers together over my chest to keep from reaching out to smooth the skin there. To run my fingers down the curve of his cheek. "How exactly is Nash alive?"

"I guess it's more like . . . reborn? Remade?" I said. "So far showing no signs of being interested in consuming blood or brains, but he remains an utter rapscallion."

Emrys seemed to process this in stride. "Death magic, then?"

"The coin."

His brows shot up as he found the right memory. I nodded.

"I hesitate to ask this, knowing how much you adore these touchy-feely conversations," Emrys began, "but are you all right?"

The stinging barb was right there, and so easy to reach for. It was a reflex now—the dagger of sarcasm or irritation flung back to avoid having to think about how I felt, or what I thought, on a deeper level.

"I'm . . . processing," I said finally.

For a long while, there was no sound but the duet of the pleasant, homey crackling of the fire and the moaning of the wind. I closed my eyes, trying to push the image of the others still wandering in the blizzard from my mind.

"I can practically feel you thinking," Emrys murmured. "Are you worried about the others?"

It should have unnerved me that he'd read my thoughts so perfectly, but instead, I found it almost . . . comforting.

"Yes," I whispered. "I don't understand how we got separated when we crossed into Lyonesse." That thought drew up another, and my eyes snapped back open. "How did you get here, anyway?"

"Same way you did, I assume," Emrys said. "The Hag of the Mist."

"Nope," I said. "Same method, but different hag."

At that, Emrys propped himself up on his elbow. "The Hag of the Bogs?"

"*Moors*," I corrected. "And yes. She was very helpful. Didn't even want our weird little offering bottle."

He shook his head, the waves of his fair falling into his eyes. My hands tightened around one another.

Stop it, I told myself. The friendly distance of the conversation was good. The distance between our bodies was good.

"You finally make a friend," he said in wonder, "and it happens to be an ancient monster. One with the tendency to eat any traveler she comes across."

"I have other friends too," I protested. "Neve and the others like me a solid sixty percent of the time."

"You know how they ended up trapping the Hag of the Moors in that mirror?" Emrys said, settling back down. "All they had to do was let her catch a glimpse of her reflection. She was so distracted by her own face she didn't even put up a fight."

"Well, that was rude of them," I said.

"You're defending the traveler-eater," Emrys reminded me.

"Everyone gets hungry now and then."

He actually laughed—a real laugh that rumbled deep in his chest. I wanted to gather the sound to me, to hold it close to my heart.

I wanted to remember it.

For once, I wasn't the one having a nightmare.

A low note of distress crept through the shadowed boundary of sleep, almost indistinguishable from the wind. If I hadn't been so primed to danger over the last few weeks, I would have drifted right back into the drugging pull of exhaustion.

"Please . . . don't . . ."

I sat up, the dark burrow spinning as my mind fought to grasp where I was. Who was next to me.

Emrys's voice was agonized. "Don't—"

His body thrashed violently, his legs colliding with mine as his torso contorted, threatening to rip open his stitches. My mind sharpened, fully awake now.

"Emrys!" I grappled with his arms, fighting to keep my grip on them as he wrested them away. His face was pinched with terror, his skin covered in a sheen of sweat despite the chill that had overtaken us.

Waking someone from a dream was like saving them from drowning. I pulled him back to me, managing to get my arms under and around him, trying to haul him up from the ground, to use the movement to wake him. *"Emrys!"*

His eyes fluttered open, the muscles of his chest and shoulder jerking against me as he slammed back into awareness. His gaze found mine in the dark, disoriented with fear. A feeling of almost unbearable tenderness filled me, more awful than ever now that I could name it. Now that I wanted to give in to it.

Every part of me was shaking. My throat burned as I released him. We both stayed there, suspended in darkness.

"Tamsin?" he said, his voice rough with sleep. "Is this real?"

I took his face between my hands.

"It's real," I told him, but the moment felt like a dream. A liminal place, where anything could happen. Where there were no consequences, no past, no future. Just . . .

The thought dissolved as his hand slid around my waist; the assuredness of it, the open look of wanting on his face, made me feel powerful. For once, I was in control of this—whatever this was.

I rose onto my knees, letting him draw me closer as I smoothed my fingers over his face, feeling the roughness of stubble growing in, feeling the muscles of his jaw relax. I would have been embarrassed, maybe, by how closely I was watching him, but he was watching me, too, his breath hitching as I straddled his legs.

I drew my face close to his, feeling his skin warm with my touch, smelling the earthy pine scent of him. I drew back ever so slightly, my breath mingling with his, giving him the opportunity to pull away and unravel this.

He rested his forehead against mine, his hand moving to cup the nape of my neck, his hand stroking the sweat-damp hair there.

"I don't want a dream," he whispered. I felt almost drunk with the sound of it, the husk of those words. "It's always been real to me."

Don't hurt me, I thought desperately.

Emrys had lied before, had lied and lied and hidden behind his veil of secrets, but his body told the truth and mine responded in kind. A feeling of liquid heat wound through my belly. I felt so dizzy with the sensation of him, I hadn't realized I'd said it aloud until he answered, his breath whispering against my ear, *"Never."*

His hand tightened around my hip, holding me there. "You know what I am . . ."

But I heard what he was really saying. *You can hurt me, too.*

I met his gaze, daring him.

"I know what we are," I told him, sliding a hand back to tangle in his dark, wavy hair. The word burned in me like a brand. *Even.*

Then his lips were on mine and I knew I was right—that the feeling in me, hot and desperate, that painful longing, echoed in him. I kissed him back, hungry for the sensation of his heart—*his* heart—racing. *Alive.* I rocked against him, careful not to brush against his chest, devouring the low, rough sound it drew from him, the way he moved against me in turn.

One moment blurred into the next, his tongue parting my lips as if we'd done this a thousand times, for a thousand years. He turned, easing me down onto the blanket, covering me with his body. The charge between us changed, that molten feeling in my belly spreading as it became a competition, that push and pull between us, that refusal to be the first to pull away.

He was everywhere, consuming all of my senses, erasing the fear from my mind, the painful ache of my battered body. My skin jumped as his hand slipped up beneath the hem of my sweater and skimmed over my skin, careful to avoid the tender spot on my ribs. I ran my hands up the muscles of his back, pulling his shirt free.

He leaned back to let me do it, capturing my face between his hands, holding me there in that stillness, even as I tried to lift my head and meet his lips halfway. He stroked my hair back from my cheek and I saw his fear play out clearly over his face.

"No," I whispered. "Stop thinking. You know what I am. I know what you are. It's just us here."

It was startling but also so completely natural to want him, the comfort of connection. Something in me, that voice that was so quick to cut, told me I was being a fool, that baring everything to him was an invitation to the pain that would inevitably come. But wasn't that the risk everyone took in opening their heart to another person? Closing myself off hadn't protected me. It had only kept me alone.

He drew in a sharp breath, his body trembling as I stroked his back, finding the waistband of his jeans. The button.

"Are you sure?" he whispered.

I'd been wrong to think he had nothing to lose in this, that he held all the power. His skin was as soft as mine, his heart just as vulnerable. If everything went to pieces around us, this at least would remain.

"Yes." For the first time in weeks, I felt calm, even if my movements were clumsy, needy. I was protected in the ways that mattered most right now and had been for years, since my first time. But this wasn't a quick fumble born out of curiosity. This was a promise.

Yes, I see you.

Yes, I want you.

The heat of him overtook me, burned away the world, burned away everything but the feel of him.

The silky night enveloped us, hushing the snowstorm to a whisper, leaving that sole thought singing through my blood as I kissed him again.

Alive, alive, alive . . .

32

"All right . . . this does feel familiar," I admitted. "Just a little."

Emrys chuckled as he surveyed the frosted land that lay before us. "Consider it a do-over, then."

My gaze slid sideways toward him, but he only looked ahead, pointing at a dark shape diminished by the miles between us. "That's the castle, isn't it?"

I shielded my eyes against the glare of the strange, milky sunlight. "Looks like it."

The storm had raged all through the night into the morning, and had only died down moments ago. The clouds gathering behind us, and the sharp quality to the air, made it feel like it had only temporarily retreated.

"That's where Rosydd was supposed to open the portal for us," I said, trying to rub some warmth into my arms. "Hopefully the others are headed that way too."

If something had happened to them in the night while I was safely tucked away with him beside a cozy fire . . . I drew in a deep breath, letting cold air clear the lingering fog of sleep.

Emrys swept an arm out toward it. "Shall we?"

I'd managed a few hours of sleep last night, in between watching his relaxed face and searching for signs that he regretted what we had done. My body felt relaxed but heavy, as if I were collecting little bits of exhaustion and carrying them around like stones in my pockets.

"Tamsin," Emrys said, his voice low. I almost laughed at the sight of the ridiculous fur coat he held out to me in offering. He smiled—one of his old smiles, too charming by half. "What? It's a *look*."

"You wear it, then," I told him, gazing out over the snow.

He grabbed my hand and pulled me back, tucking me into the soft depths of the coat, against the warmth radiating from him. The smell of him, pine and earth, lived on my skin now too. My senses were overwhelmed by a new awareness of him. The memory of his weight over me, the scratch of his stubble against my skin—my eyes drifted up to his lips again, my own still swollen. My hands curled against the warmth of his chest, against the feel of his heart beating fiercely beneath the layers of his clothes and skin.

Yet, little by little, as the night drifted further away from us and the world intruded, a knot of ice began to form at my center. I knew what it was immediately.

Dread.

I stared up at his face again, searching for those signs—the ones I had missed in Avalon, that would have told me what he'd planned to do. My pulse began to climb as the need for flight, for the safety of distance, kicked in.

I'm safe, I told myself, my hands sliding down to his waist. Holding on to him. On to *us*.

Emrys leaned down, brushing his lips against my cheek before whispering in my ear, echoing my own words back to me. "Stop thinking. It's just us here."

"What happens when it isn't?" I heard myself ask. My body responded to the proximity of him—how could it not, when those eyes were gazing so deeply into mine?

"Where do you want it to go?" he said, pulling back to study my face. "I'm not going to pretend like I don't want this to be something, to take it as far as you'll let it go."

I chewed on my bottom lip and he watched, captivated. I felt that warm power rise in me again.

The truth was, I'd never been a daydreamer. The way I'd lived until now, haunted by the past, living day to day on what small bits of money we could scrape together, I hadn't let myself.

But that wasn't Emrys. He was someone who lived for the future, who tried to shape it in whatever way he could. He wanted it as much as his next breath.

"I can only focus on right now," I told him. "That's all I know how to do."

He stole a quick kiss. "Then I'll meet you there, between today and tomorrow."

And that was enough for me.

A roar bellowed across the snow-laden hills, and we both dropped into a crouch. The wind was playing games with us, carrying the sound from every direction at once.

After that, we said nothing—we only quickened our pace, and kept our eyes wide open.

It was an hour, maybe more, before we encountered a strange, wavy imprint and the first splatter of blood staining the snow.

My hands curled into fists in my jacket pockets. Within my chest, my heartbeat began a traitorous refrain. *They're dead. They're dead. They're dead.*

"Tell me that's not the trail we're going to follow," Emrys began.

I only looked at him and continued on.

There was no way to avoid the bloody tracks; they were heading in the same direction we were, to the abandoned village at the foot of the castle walls. The fact that we could see the path the creature had taken at all meant it had been left this morning, after last night's snowfall.

If the others had come this way—

I shut the thought down and looked up toward the towering structure ahead. More than a mere home to kings, it was a citadel built into the side of a small peak. Four levels of outer buildings rose one after the next, to the pale stone castle at the peak. I counted four towers, and even through a dusting of snow, their turrets gleamed gold.

The village had been built out around the main road leading up to the castle gates. Aside from the blacksmith forge and a handful of structures with dilapidated signs announcing their trade or wares, the buildings seemed to be cozy stone cottages. Some with pens for animals that no longer needed them, others with snow-buried gardens. Our only welcome was the sound of a well's pail squeaking in the wind.

Like the fairy mounds, most of the stone cottages looked as though their occupants had risen from the breakfast table and never returned. Shutters clattered and snapped like twigs at the lightest of touches. Glimpses through fallen doors and uncovered windows revealed scenes that were almost heartbreaking in their domesticity. A straw doll left on a bed. Candles and hides left hanging to dry, forever unused. Frayed thread on a spinning wheel.

We slowed our steps, keeping close to one another as the tracks continued and pools of blood appeared. My pulse beat harder with each step. As we came around the corner of a collapsed stable, I reached back for Dyrnwyn's hilt, and held my breath.

Not Neve, I begged inwardly. *Not Cait.*

But there were no gods left in this world to hear me. There were only us, and the monsters.

Emrys sidled up beside me, giving me an encouraging nod. I released the air in my aching lungs and forced myself to lean around the crumbling stone wall.

My knees turned hollow. I braced a hand against the remains of the cottage, closing my eyes, trying to steady the wild beat of my heart.

"What . . . do you think could have done *that*?" Emrys asked.

A black serpent, the length of three of me, lay in pieces on the road. Chunks of its lustrous scales were riddled with holes. An unidentifiable, half-eaten mass of bloodied fur had been left near its gaping maw; tufts of white clung to the sticky blood on its swordlike fangs. My mind composed the story in an instant: the creature had gone hunting, found the day's meal, and was bringing it back to its den when another, deadlier predator had taken it by surprise.

I ran toward the castle gate, leaving Emrys huffing to keep up.

The main road served as an artery that climbed up past more homes, guild workshops, and armories. Covered markets protected from the snow revealed the last evidence of the carnage of the past. The stone road turned crimson there, still stained by blood that had never completely washed away.

"I thought . . . the rivers of blood . . . were only a story," Emrys got out between hard breaths. My lungs were working like bellows too, sending tremors through my body.

"There's always a seed of truth in every story's garden," I said. Another favorite refrain of Nash's.

God's teeth. I hadn't spared the man a single thought since crossing into Lyonesse, but he had to be somewhere in the kingdom too. Given his head start, there was a good chance he'd already beaten us to the citadel, and maybe to Excalibur.

"Come on," I said, steeling myself for the possibility. "We're almost there."

Emrys had turned back to survey the road behind us. The sight of his profile, achingly handsome, sent a bolt of warmth through my body. He would have been right at home here, I thought ruefully. A prince of a legendary kingdom.

The wind ruffled his snow-dusted hair, and as he turned back, his bright eyes met mine—and darkened in a way that sent heat washing up my throat to my cheeks.

"Don't look at me like that," he almost groaned. "Not when I don't have time to do anything about it."

My breath caught, and somehow—somehow—I forced myself to only reach for his hand.

"Later," he whispered.

A promise.

But by the time we reached the steps into the castle, there was nothing left in me but the desire to stretch out over the icy stones and cool my burning muscles. Miles of upward climbing through the streets had left both of us quietly gasping for breath as we made our way toward the waiting entrance.

The outer doors were nearly as tall as the building itself, decorated with iron flourishes and the symbol of Lyonesse, a roaring lion's head. And, mercifully, by wind or someone's hand, they were already ajar—just wide enough for the two of us to slip inside. Beyond it was a corridor that ran between two stairwells on either side of us, and beyond that, another set of doors that led into the great hall.

Exchanging one last wary look with Emrys, I released his hand and stepped carefully through the doors to the hall.

The smell of must and rot was overwhelming. The air itself seemed dead: unnaturally heavy and still, hanging over derelict feasting tables like a mourning shroud.

"Hello?" I called out. "Cait! Neve! Are you here?"

My voice echoed back to me, small and fearful. *Are you here? Are you here?*

"Do you want to wait here or go looking for them?" Emrys asked.

My gaze drifted over to the two thrones at the head of the hall. Carved from wood, embellished with gold; the velveteen fabric of the seats had been devoured by moths and damp. And any crowns had left the kingdom when its ruler did, dead or alive.

A section of the vaulted ceiling had caved in, and at some point, water had rushed in through the splintered stones like a cascade, creating a solid wall of ice along the grand room's eastern face. Tapestries.

My feet moved toward them of their own accord, even as my mind tried to pull me back toward the corridor connecting this room to the next. A breeze slipped through the open door and pushed at my back, encouraging me forward. The air hummed in my ears, low and soft, like a mother's hushed soothing.

Emrys pulled a flashlight out of his bag. I took out my own, moving to the first panel at the far end of the hall. Rubbing a hand over the frost, I shined the beam of light through it.

The scenes were distorted and magnified by the glasslike ice, but not even that could diminish their beauty. I walked slowly along, clearing the cloudy layer of rime as I went. After I reached the end of the panel, I stepped back to view it in full. Emrys stood behind me, his body warming my back, his chest rumbling as he made a thoughtful noise.

"The creation of the world by the Goddess?" he suggested.

"Looks like it," I murmured.

At the center of the panel was a pale-haired woman, her figure wrapped in silky white robes. Something about her face, the serenity of her smile, stirred a thought at the back of my mind, but I didn't know the right memory to reach for.

Around her outstretched arms, a garden was forming, and creatures of every kind gathered.

"And here we have men," Emrys said, pointing to the figures below the garden. "Struggling to spark fire, to harvest—"

"Not men," I said. "The Firstborn."

Emrys looked over, surprised.

"The Gentry. The Tuatha dé Danann. The Aes Sídhe. Tylwyth Teg," I said. "According to the Bonecutter, they're all names for the same beings. Born with magic and immortality, but not invulnerable to death."

He scratched at the stubble growing along his jaw as he moved to the second panel, revealing it with a few careful swipes of his arm.

There were the mortal men, with the Firstborn lording over them with magic and crowns. Swords appeared, and the scenes of duels became battles. In the third, a man with a silver hand reached out toward a group that looked to be his children. Three sons, with wheat-colored hair and gray eyes. To my disappointment, the next panels were too torn and darkened by decay to see what they depicted.

A thunderous clatter sounded above us, like a wall collapsing. We froze in place as dust shook loose from the ceiling.

"Please tell me we're not going to investigate whatever unthinkable dark horror that was," Emrys said.

But I was already running for the door.

33

The entry hall was guarded on either end by spiraling sets of stairs. I let my feet guide us to the one on the right, straining my ears for an echo of the sound we'd heard. Other than the clatter of small loose stone and drifts of dust, the castle had fallen back into deathly silence.

The stone steps were partially caved in and tricky to navigate, but when a sound like dry, scraping stones drifted down the stairwell to us, we hurried to climb them before we lost the trail again. The noises seemed to be coming from the third floor.

"Neve?" I called softly at the top step. "Cait?"

The hall was littered with filthy clothing and broken furniture, as if they'd been dropped in the rush to flee the castle, and the open doors revealed bedrooms in various states of disarray, from once-grand beds reduced to matchsticks to wardrobes caked with grime.

Emrys ducked into the first, giving it a quick search. I tried to stop him, but he mimed holding a sword, raising both brows.

I sighed. He was right; regardless of where the others were, and what had made the noise, we were here to find Excalibur.

I leaned into the next bedroom and took a quick look around. Inside I found little more than furniture draped in disintegrating cloth. Every time I lifted one of the sheets to search for signs of the monster or Excalibur, I could feel traces of the rot rubbing off on my skin.

Something built in me, room by room—an urge. Not to run, not to speak, not to fight. It had no name, but it haunted me with each step. Not even the reassuring feel of Emrys's eyes tracking my every move was enough to dispel it.

Halfway down the hall, we were greeted by one of the vilest smells I'd experienced in my life—like sun-roasted sewage. I shrank back from it, and despite my stomach being empty, it heaved.

Emrys coughed, covering his mouth and nose with the sleeve of his jacket. He sent a wary look my way. "You know, we *could* go back down and wait for the others."

I wanted that more than my next breath, but this was one of those incredibly rare moments in which purpose prevailed. "No, we have to keep going."

He took a step forward with obvious reluctance.

"Are you scared, Dye?" I whispered, teasing.

"Yes." He turned his big eyes on me. "Will you hold my hand?"

The air was bitterly cold, but it did nothing to stop the hot flush that overtook my cheeks. "No."

I hurried ahead of him, making quick work of the rooms on the right side of the hall as he searched the left. With his longer legs, he caught up to me easily as I reached one of the last doors on the hall. And, together, we discovered the source of the rancid stench.

It took all the restraint I had left to not rub the phantom feeling of itchy decay from my arms. The rot overwhelming my senses gave the horrifying impression that it was my own body that was decomposing. As we hovered in the doorway, I pushed up my sleeves to make sure skeins of dead skin weren't falling from my bones.

My silver bones.

The room's door was on the ground, forcing us to step on and over the stones piled onto it. It was as if it had been ripped off with such great force, it had taken the stones framing the doorway with it, leaving a jagged opening in the wall behind.

Emrys gave me one last pained look, then stepped through, his scarred hand brushing over the rough stone.

I stayed close to him. The stench of death flourished around me, the metallic tang of blood and hideous rot nearly sending me to my knees. With my free hand, I reached back to grip Dyrnwyn's cold hilt and we crept slowly into the room.

The chamber was vast, broken up by a few crumbling walls. As in the other rooms we'd seen, much of the furniture was dull shapes beneath the protective cloth.

A circular settee sat at the very center of the room, curving beneath the coarse fabric in a way that was surprisingly modern. The scale of the enormous four-poster bed in the farthest visible section of the suite suggested that whoever had once resided here enjoyed high status. The musty silk wall panels drew my eyes to tarnished suits of armor by the hearth. But only for a moment.

Emrys reared back, his breath hitching in his throat. Slowly, with agonizing care, he lifted his foot off a long yellow bone, having narrowly avoided snapping it in two.

More bones littered the ground, some so badly broken, their edges were spiked. The longer I looked, the easier it was to convince myself they'd once been animals—at least until I saw the first skull, carelessly tossed aside beneath a small table.

Human, my mind screamed.

I stepped forward, picking my way through the remains. With a look of extreme reluctance, Emrys followed, taking the opposite side of the room. I looked down the doorways connecting one room to the next, but most had been emptied of their possessions.

It was a moment before I noticed that the air was warmer in this room—almost steaming with that same rotten sewage stench.

While Emrys knelt to look beneath the bed and check under the mattress for the sword, I followed my nose to the source of that smell, gripping the cloth covering what looked to be a large settee. Taking the cloth in hand, I gave it a gentle tug.

It slipped off with a soft *swish,* meeting no resistance as it skimmed over the slick, gleaming scales of a mountainous spine and pooled on the floor at my feet.

Thunder gathered in my ears as my pulse beat against my skull. My head no longer seemed to be connected to the rest of my body. Out of the corner of my eye, Emrys moved silently, desperately mouthing something to me.

The beast huffed in its sleep, nestling its enormous head against the blood-splattered rug beneath it. It was smaller than I'd imagined as a child, only twice the length of the nearby bed. Its craggy scales reminded me of a crimson sunrise reflected on a distant mountain range. Every spine on every scale looked primed to slice flesh.

Draig Goch. Red dragon.

Its massive tail swished the way a cat's did as it slept. It scraped across the floor, making every piece of glass and tarnished décor shiver like terrified animals. The noise we'd heard before was the dragon shifting its massive weight, settling down in a more comfortable position. The floor rocked beneath my feet as the monster shifted again, bringing its head down to rest against its leg.

My stomach liquefied.

If this was the Beast of Land's End, it was now painfully clear why the kingdom had been abandoned. No blade could pierce the skin of a dragon. No spell, either. It was why Hollowers fought to source the material for their work gloves.

It was why we were going to have to find a way to leave this citadel *right now.*

The others, I thought, terrified all over again. If they'd come here and been taken by surprise . . .

Emrys held his hand out toward me, his panicked eyes flicking between me and the slumbering dragon. I took a slow step toward him, avoiding the bones scattered around us. Hot, smoky breath wheezed out between its teeth and through its nostrils, curling in a strangely beautiful pattern as it rose.

Another step.

Another.

I reached my hand toward Emrys, straining for his fingers, for something to steady me when my body was bursting with adrenaline.

The dragon let out another gasping huff, releasing a plume of ash.

One leathery eyelid lifted. A wet, clear membrane peeled back over the burnished gold iris. Both of our faces were reflected in the glistening surface as the dragon lifted its head. As it scented us.

Emrys's hand closed around mine, and, with one last desperate look, we ran.

34

The floor shook as the dragon barreled after us. Shards of stone exploded into the air as its great body slammed clumsily from wall to wall, its talons clawing for purchase on the slick stone floor.

The smell of smoke returned as the dragon let out a hacking cough, spraying flames from its mouth in every direction like buckshot. I slapped a hand against Emrys's smoldering sleeve before ripping the bulky thing off him entirely. The dragon wasn't going to mistake him for a fuzzy treat.

I pushed my body harder, faster, as a stairwell appeared through a parting cloud of dust.

The dragon's roar echoed off the walls like a deluge of untuned strings. It rasped and shrieked in turn, a quavering note of agony threading through every reverberation. The barking cough burst into a pure scream of fire.

The narrow walls funneled the maelstrom of flames right to us, and there was no other choice—we dove down the winding stairs. The steps battered my ribs, reviving the sharp ache of my earlier injury, and scraped at my legs. I had enough sense to protect my skull with my arms, letting them absorb the abuse as fire raged over our heads, spiraling down through the stairwell with us.

The river of flames scalded the air; I didn't try to breathe, knowing it would only damage my lungs and throat. As we hit the landing, I reached over, feeling for Emrys.

"I'm okay," he said, climbing unsteadily to his feet. "Let's go, let's go—"

The dragon screeched as it tried to force its body through the curve of the tight passage, straining, flooding the air with the noxious steam of its breath.

But between one heartbeat and the next, the red dragon suddenly stilled, as if in surrender. Loose debris skittered down the steps. Emrys's pulse sped beneath my fingers as my grip on his wrist turned to iron, but still, neither of us seemed capable of moving, not even to save ourselves.

My own heartbeat pounded everywhere in my body as a new gust of scalding steam billowed past us. The dragon, with all the grace and silence of a snake, stretched its long, sinuous neck down along the curve of the stairs until its horned head appeared behind us, and for one terrifying moment, the creature's mouth parted in an almost sinister smile. It flicked its forked tongue at our feet, taunting. Tasting.

My focus narrowed to those golden eyes glowing in the darkness. Pure blue fire began to gather at the back of the dragon's throat, illuminating every jagged onyx tooth.

"Tamsin!" Emrys hauled my stunned body up as blue flames intensified. Apparently, it liked to cook its meals before consuming them.

That delirious thought vanished as the dragon coughed and retched. The flames gathering in its mouth extinguished as it thrashed its head around the stairwell. Showers of dust and debris rained down over us as we fled.

We were halfway down the hall when the dragon finally rammed through the collapsing stairs and tore through the wall to reach the landing. An explosion of dust and rubble pelted us from behind. I glanced back, squeaking as the creature barreled toward us on all fours. Its wings were folded tight against its sides to squeeze through the corridor, but the left one jutted out slightly at an angle, as if it had been broken and hadn't healed straight.

Scars and missing scales pitted its face and neck. I noted each one, only to remember that the fact that I was close enough to see them was a very, very bad sign.

A deep draw of breath and the stench of smoke warned of coming fire. The dragon skittered to a stop, rising on its haunches, and spread its wings. A thick, veined membrane connected the bones and joints, and both wings were tipped with talon-like hooks that scored the walls as they beat the air.

The wind they created slammed into me like a tackle, knocking me off my feet onto the unforgiving stone floor. Emrys fell beside me with a harsh gasp.

Fire raced toward us, twisting and thrashing like an animal.

But it wasn't flame that blasted over us—it was a different, colder wind, blowing hard and furious, deflecting the fire back toward the dragon.

I looked up, shocked to find Neve standing a few feet away in the doorway, her hands still outstretched. A staircase to the main hall was behind her.

"Hi!" she said cheerfully. "Nice of you guys to show up! I was starting to get worried."

My relief turned to horror in an instant. "Get out of here!"

Heat gathered behind us again, the dragon hacking and snarling in fury.

It charged toward us again, bursting through the burning debris. I started to reach for the hilt of my sword, then stopped. Dragons were born from flames. They would never die of them.

Stupid fire sword, I thought, exasperated. It wouldn't even penetrate the dragon's skin.

"Let's go!" Emrys said, hooking my arm, then Neve's, to drag us away.

The beast raged forward, rasping and hacking. We ran down the stairs, each bone and joint in my body aching with the force of my pounding steps.

This time, however, the dragon didn't follow. As we reached the ground floor of the castle, I whirled back to find only shadows behind us.

"This way!" Neve panted. The cavernous hallway echoed her order. A distant dripping and the settling of rocks answered.

We found Caitriona standing at the imposing entrance to the castle, her back to the great hall. She waved a torch back and forth above her head.

"Here!" she shouted—but not to us.

Before any of us could react, she dropped the torch and turned to run into the great hall. Within the space of a second, the red dragon flew in low through the entrance, snow and ash shaking free from its scales as it gave chase.

"Cait!" I screamed, following at full speed. My feet slid over the loose stone and ice, crossing that last bit of distance to the doors of the great hall.

The dragon spewed flames as Caitriona ran alongside the wall of tapestries. As fire struck the ice encasing them, it evaporated into hissing steam that choked the chamber and stole Caitriona from sight.

The dragon's fiery breath died again as it hacked and choked, its spine curling up as it clawed at the floor.

I hadn't noticed Nash crouched in the crosshatch of the hall's rafters until he jumped down from them, landing on the dragon's back with a grunt. He slid down the smooth scales, grabbing one of its spiked shoulders at the very last minute to haul himself back up.

My scream was drowned out by the beast's as Nash used the dagger in his left hand to gouge the nearest eye. In his other hand was a rusted sword that he swung like a bat against the dragon's open jaws, sending fangs flying in every direction.

One came close to impaling Neve as she ran toward the fight.

"Now, Caitriona!" Nash shouted, struggling to keep his grip on the dragon's neck as it tried to flick him off with its wings.

Caitriona launched herself toward them, running at full tilt, even as she reached down to rip a long black fang out of a smashed table. The dragon lowered its head, its remaining fangs bared, but Caitriona was already sliding across the floor beneath it, slicing the dragon open from gullet to gizzard with its own tooth.

The beast gagged and raged, lurching forward, vomiting weak flames.

Of course, I thought.

Sword and spell had no effect; the only thing that could harm a dragon was another dragon's tooth or claw.

It collapsed heavily on the floor, the flames flickering out in its eyes. And as the great body relaxed, surrendering to death, a foul, steaming mass of entrails fell to the ground, followed by the vile contents of its stomach.

Bones, helmets, rocks, breastplates, statue heads, and silver pitchers spilled out in a sickening gush. I dared to take a step forward, only to have my path cut off as the last of it released: a cannonball, a crown, and a serving tray.

Nash spat on the dragon, sliding down its rough hide.

"Are you a complete idiot?" I asked him seriously. "Or did your brain not come back with the rest of you?"

"What?" Nash said, yanking his dagger out of the dragon's eye. He stepped over its lolled tongue with a look of disgust. "This old beastie ate its fair share of folks over the centuries, it got what it deserved. Worthy assist, Caitriona. Magnificent."

The praise stoked an ugly, jealous part of me, but it faded as Caitriona nodded in acknowledgment, looking deeply satisfied. Perhaps that was all she'd needed to release the anger building up in her.

Neve rushed toward her, gripping Caitriona by the arms. "That was both incredible and incredibly stupid, but mostly incredible."

It was hard to tell if there was a flush on Caitriona's cheeks, or if, like her hair, they'd been dyed pink by the spray of bloody viscera.

"I . . . ," Caitriona began, her tongue turning to stone as Neve took her face between her hands, inspecting that, too. "I'm fine."

"You," Nash said to Emrys. "If Your Royal Highness is done watching us do the hard work, perhaps you'd be so good as to look for something useful in that mess."

"Great, sure," Emrys said, looking a bit pale as he assessed the revolting offerings splayed in front of us. "Thanks for stitching me up, by the way."

"Well, I sure as hell didn't do it for you," Nash said, and at a warning look from me, added, "I'll not have that attitude from you right now, Tamsin Lark. I left you behind for a very good reason—I told you the beast was no mere story!"

I remembered my anger all at once, at being left behind, at nearly losing our lives before I got the answers I needed.

"Yeah, clearly you needed no help here," I said. "You could have done this job all on your own."

He gazed back at me, his jaw sawing back and forth.

"My job is to protect you, you peevish little imp," he said. "You don't have to like me, but you *have* to listen—"

"Oh, give me a break." Another thought occurred to me as I interrupted him. "And how did you even know the beast was still alive?"

Nash matched my glower with one of his own, then turned to Emrys, pointing at the dragon. "Go on, make it snappy, princeling. We still have to search for the blasted sword."

Emrys went about his task like a man headed to the gallows. I gagged at the metallic reek of blood and intestines as I went to help him, lifting my shirt over my mouth and nose. It seemed like the creature had eaten its share of the medieval world's trash.

"Oho," Nash said, reaching into its open chest cavity. Elbow-deep, he felt around before using his dagger to cut something away—what looked to my turning stomach like a piece of muscle. "I've got a treasure for you lot."

Caitriona came over, allowing him to plop a chunk of it into her upturned palms. She brought it closer for inspection, sniffing at it in a way that made me reflexively gag.

"Dragonheart's a powerful substance," Nash told her. "It can be used in a number of ointments and potions to amplify their effects. I think Lady Olwen would love to have some of this."

Caitriona's face fell at the mention of her sister, but she nodded. Neve took it from her, retrieving a plastic bag out of her bottomless fanny pack and wrapping it up. Undoing the buckle, she tossed the whole bag onto a nearby table, and I set mine down beside hers.

"What else should I collect for her?" Caitriona asked eagerly. "Some scales? More teeth?"

"Save one of the fangs for me, will you?" Emrys muttered from next to me. "I'd love a souvenir to remind myself of the terrifying experience I barely survived."

"Me too!" Neve said.

I grimaced, circling around the creature. The knot in my stomach tightened, and the creeping sensation of decay had returned, spreading through me like poison. Almost as if . . .

I can feel death hovering over it, my mind finished.

My hand rose of its own accord, fingers brushing the gleaming crimson scales.

"—sorry, great and ancient flying lizard," Neve was saying as she appeared suddenly beside me. She held up the tooth she'd selected for herself, and I shuddered at the sight of it. The thing was longer than my index finger, curving slightly.

Neve slid it into her jacket pocket, then patted the beast's neck. "If you hadn't tried to roast and eat us, we probably could have been friends."

I opened my mouth to protest, but even I had to admit that it wasn't unheard of. Dragons were cunning, fiercely intelligent creatures, and certain breeds were said to be docile enough to form friendships with mortals—though they were too stubborn to ever be trained.

That thought led to another melancholy one, a drifting memory of the dragon bones curled protectively around the snowy cottage in Avalon.

"Hey, old man," Neve called to Nash. "Didn't you say Excalibur has creatures carved into its hilt?"

"I surely did," Nash said, leaning around the dragon's barbed tail. "Why?"

Neve moved past me, kneeling beside the dragon's neck where Caitriona's cut began. I saw it then too—the silver metal protruding through the oozing wound, a blood-slick steel pommel.

The sword that had been lodged in the dragon's throat for an untold number of years.

"Found it!" Neve shouted back. "And, surprise! It's not reacting to me at all because, like I told you—" She gripped the hilt and pulled the sword free with a single tug.

A phosphorous blue-white light blazed around her, tugging at her hair, her clothes, her skin. I reached for her with a gasp, but in the next moment I was flying back, riding the pressure, the power, as it exploded around her like a dying star.

35

The light threw back the heavy curtain of shadow hanging over the hall, chasing the darkness to the very edges of the room. It undulated with a terrifying ferocity, its many arms tracing scorched patterns over the stone floors like lightning.

"Neve!"

As I struggled to pick myself up off the floor and shake off the disorienting punch of magic, Caitriona rushed past. She stopped just beyond the reach of the roiling magic, the fear etched on her face illuminated by its pure, unearthly power.

Neve's outline was just barely visible at the center of the growing orb; her back was arched painfully, her head thrown back as if caught in a soul-rending scream.

"Release it!" Nash shouted. The light hummed low and thunderous, as if displeased. "You must release the sword!"

A set of strong hands gripped me under the elbows, easing me up as my legs wobbled.

"What is that?" Emrys breathed out, drawing me closer to his side.

"Neve!" I called, struggling to hear myself over the thrumming vibrations. "You have to let go!"

As Neve and the light rose, the ground cratered beneath them, sending cracks racing over the stone floor and up the walls. There was a faint movement from within the depths of the magic—Neve turning her head ever so slightly to the right, where Caitriona stood, a decision flashing in her eyes.

"Don't—!" I warned, but Caitriona had already thrust her arm forward through the barrier of magic.

Rather than repel her the way it had with me, the light shifted and swallowed her whole.

Emrys cast an uncertain look my way, as if I'd know what to do now.

I took a step forward, shielding my face from the intensity of the light. Out of the corner of my eye, I saw Nash do the same. We fought our way forward, only to be shoved back again and again.

Silver flashed and sang as it sliced the air above me, and, all at once, the magic extinguished. Excalibur clattered loudly as it spun over the uneven rubble, sliding out through the doorway and out of the hall.

As the lingering sparks of light drifted around us and the magic's deep purr faded, Caitriona knelt in the center of the crater. Smoke rose off her silver hair where the long ends had been torched, and ragged strands now brushed her cheeks. Her dark clothing was torn and frayed, revealing bands of angry burns on her pale skin. She didn't seem to feel any of it—her whole focus was on the girl in her arms.

"Is she alive?" I asked, wild with panic as I ran toward them. "Cait, is she alive?"

"Stay back," Caitriona warned quietly. "The magic's not finished with her yet."

She was right. The same light that had gathered around Neve now ran beneath her skin like glowing rivers, illuminating her from within. The smell of burned flesh was almost overwhelming as I leaned over Caitriona, horrified.

There wasn't a mark, not so much as a scratch on Neve, but for a terrifying moment, it looked like she was breaking apart.

Sweat poured down Neve's face and she let out a low moan, her face twisting in pain. I could see the heat radiating from her, as if she were burning from the inside out.

"It really is her," I whispered.

"I think I've missed something," Emrys said, looking between Caitriona's crushed expression and mine. "Something else, I mean. Why did the sword react like that?"

"The sword was forged using the Goddess's power," I said. "The Bonecutter said it would have a reaction to the person who possesses the soul of her daughter."

The others must have told him the story at Rivenoak, when I'd first run after Cabell, or he sensed I didn't have the wherewithal to explain, because he only gave a shaky nod.

Nash muttered something to himself as he slid down the slope of the floor and came to stand beside Caitriona. "Let me carry her over to one of the tables, so we can look at her wounds."

Caitriona's fingers visibly tightened around Neve's shoulders.

"Lady Caitriona," Nash said, kind but firm. "I'll be careful, I swear it."

"She's still burning," Caitriona said hoarsely. The helplessness in her expression was shattering. "We need Olwen. Olwen would know what to do."

"Here, Cait," I said, kneeling beside her. "I'll help you."

Emrys moved to join us, but I held up a hand, stopping him.

Finally, Caitriona relented, shifting to allow me to take on more of Neve's weight. I tried not to flinch at the feeling of the scalding magic moving beneath her skin like fiery serpents.

"We need to cool her off," Nash said, guiding us to the last table standing in the hall. Emrys brushed the debris off it with a stroke of his arm before we set her down. "And you, Caitriona, take the salve out of my bag and put it on those burns."

"I'll get snow," I told him.

Neve let out another soft moan.

"I'll help you, Tamsy," Nash said. "You too, princeling, if you can stand a few minutes of actual work."

Emrys gritted his teeth, casting another worried look at Neve before answering. "I'll do my best to follow your heroic lead."

But the snow we packed around her seemed to provide no relief to Neve; it melted just as quickly as it touched her skin.

"That will not work," came a silky voice behind us. "Her body needs time to acclimate to the magic."

I turned slowly, my hand reaching back for the hilt of my sword, only to still.

Seven women stood at the entrance of the hall, some in long velvet gowns and fur-lined cloaks, others in more modern attire—down coats and boots so practical, I never would have imagined them catching a sorceress's eye.

But that was what they were.

I recognized the tall woman standing in front of the others instantly from the envy-ridden descriptions I'd read of her in the library's newer Immortalities. Kasumi had been the High Sorceress of the Council of Sistren for nearly a century now, though she, like so many of the others, had held on to her youthful appearance despite the vast number of centuries behind her.

Her fair skin seemed to drink in the last glowing embers of magic drifting around us. A curtain of long, smooth hair that draped over her shoulder was darker than the night itself. The sorceress to her right, a slight, nervous brunette, watched us through her lashes, her long wand out.

"Kasumi," Nash said, miming a slight bow over Neve's still form. "As radiant as the first day I laid eyes on you."

"How is it that you're alive?" she asked. "And here I'd so desperately hoped the stories of your demise were true."

"You know how I like to tease, Kas," he said.

I grimaced, opening my mouth to say something, but Emrys's hand suddenly found mine, drawing our linked fingers behind his back and giving them a squeeze. I followed his gaze.

The Sorceress Madrigal stood at the back of the group, glaring at all of us like a petulant child forced into doing something that bored her. Her waves of flaming red hair had been knotted in a low bun, and given that the last time I saw her, she'd been immersed in frothy black tulle, her crimson gown and matching overcoat, embroidered with all manner of bones, seemed unusually subdued.

"I told you they were here, didn't I?" Madrigal said. "Now can I leave this godsforsaken place before I freeze a tit off?" Her eyes skimmed over us, bored and irritated, until they landed on Emrys. "Oh. Hello, pet."

A small smile flicked up the edges of her lips, and if Emrys hadn't been holding on to me, I might have stalked over and clawed it off her face.

"Well, my sweet rosy-cheeked darling, I always enjoy our reunions," Nash said. "But I'd love to know what you're all doing here."

The cold air radiated off the stones around us, but nothing was icier than Sorceress Kasumi's expression. "I came for the girl."

"Oh?" Nash said, he and Caitriona shifting to block Neve from the sorceresses' view. "Well, we have a few here for you to choose from."

Kasumi's eyes flashed, but she managed to control her tone. "The girl who possesses Creiddylad's soul. She wrote to Madrigal seeking answers about her mother, describing her unique power."

Madrigal looked up from where she was picking at her clawlike nails. "Her letters were so pitiful I found myself moved to bring them to the Council."

"And buy yourself acceptance," one of the other women said snidely.

"Don't be jealous, Belinda," Madrigal said. "It's not becoming of someone with such a reptilian complexion."

"Enough," Kasumi told them. "Excalibur's reaction has proven my suspicions that she is the one Lord Death seeks. You must let me see the girl, Nashbury."

"No." Caitriona's voice was a blade that brought the leader of the Council of Sistren to a stop before she'd even moved. The other sorceresses raised their wands in response.

"Who is this?" Kasumi asked Nash, casting a steely gaze over Caitriona. She had taken his advice and applied the salve to the burns on her face and arms. The wounds were already starting to look better.

"That is Lady Caitriona, lately of Avalon," Nash said.

The other sorceresses shifted, clearly intrigued as they tried to get a better look at her. The slight brunette at the High Sorceress's side explained, "One of the two surviving priestesses."

"I'm no longer a priestess," Caitriona growled.

"And the rest of them?" Kasumi pressed.

"This is my daughter, Tamsin," Nash said.

A strange pang went through me at that word. It wasn't true, of course, but he'd never said it before.

"Great Mother, you reproduced?" Kasumi asked, aghast.

"Adopted," I clarified.

"And that is Emrys Dye, lately of the Dye family," Nash said. "Though we're trying not to hold it against him, as he seems less fond of his father than the rest of us."

Kasumi took the information in stride, her expression inscrutable. She gestured toward Neve's unconscious form. "May I?"

"Cait," I said. She looked to me, stubbornness burning in her. "Let her look. It could help Neve."

Caitriona didn't move, but she did let me draw her aside, just enough for Kasumi and two other sorceresses to approach the table.

"Don't lay a finger on her," Caitriona warned.

"I've no need to, sister," Kasumi answered.

"I'm not your sister," Caitriona snarled.

Nash made a soothing noise at the back of his throat, a hand clasped to her shoulder. The other sorceresses, including Madrigal, were starting to circle the table as well, and I suddenly felt like a lamb who'd woken up and found herself surrounded by wolves. I dragged both my workbag and Neve's fanny pack across the table, tucking the latter into my satchel for safekeeping.

Kasumi's face was impassive as she bent over Neve, studying her. Drawing the thin wand over Neve's body. Magic lashed out from under Neve's skin, crackling along the wood. "And this girl, she's of maiden rank?"

"No, she is unaffiliated with the Sistren," said the mousy brunette.

"Her name is Neve," I said. "And you rejected her when she came to you for schooling."

I wondered suddenly if Kasumi herself had been the one who'd turned Neve away—if she was the one who had mocked her lack of lineage and made her feel like nothing. Fury coursed through my blood.

Emrys's thumb stroked along my wrist, soothing. His eyes never left the red-haired sorceress as she leaned around Kasumi's shoulder, fighting to maintain her disinterested expression. Her perfectly arched brows rose at something Kasumi murmured to them.

"Well?" Nash asked. "What is it?"

"Yes," Kasumi said. "This is the power known as the Goddess's light. I believe it is her."

The words turned the castle around me, everything, to ash.

She'll never be safe, I thought, horrified. As long as Lord Death lived, she would never be able to return to a normal life. She would never be safe from him.

"She needs more protection than the four of you can offer," Kasumi said. "I must bring her back to the Council."

"Absolutely not," Caitriona growled. "You will not bring her into your nest of adders!"

"I see the Avalonian opinion of sorceresses has yet to improve," Nash murmured. "Think clearly on this, child. They are her own kind—"

"They are *not,*" Caitriona cut in sharply. "And they'll turn her over to Lord Death to save themselves."

"How dare you?" Kasumi's calm demeanor was more frightening than any of the wands pointed at us. "We are servants of the Goddess. We will not relinquish the soul of her child to that monster, nor one of our own."

"One of your own?" I repeated incredulously. "You sent her away in the cruelest manner possible. You refused to help her before, so why should we believe you'd be willing to do it now?"

"Child, are you under the mistaken belief that you have a choice?" Kasumi asked, the words edged with warning.

Nash held up his hands, paternally cajoling in a way that got my back up, even now.

"Between them, the Sistren have thousands of years' worth of knowledge," he said. "Would you rather risk having the magic burn her up? The poor dove was writing to them, *asking* for their help. Don't you think this is what she'd want?"

My hands clenched into fists at my sides, but I couldn't argue with the truth. Emrys squeezed my wrist in encouragement.

"There is another reason we will not give the soul to Lord Death," Kasumi said.

"That's—" Nash interrupted. "That's all hearsay, isn't it?"

She ignored him. "The soul possesses magic beyond our reckoning. If he were to kill your friend and take Creiddylad's soul to Annwn, both she and that power would be entirely under his command, and that would spell an end for all of us."

"More lies," Caitriona said, shaking her head. "You refused her before, just as you refused to help Avalon. You knew, didn't you? What was happening on the isle, how few of us were left. And you did *nothing*."

Kasumi's even stare was infuriating. "By the time we discovered what was happening, it was already too late. My only regret is not believing you'd be so foolish as to perform the ritual that unmade Avalon."

Caitriona surged toward her, only to be stopped by Nash.

"Easy," he crooned. "It's not a fair fight."

"Maybe if you had come yourself instead of sending your little spy, none of us would be standing here," I said.

"Spy?" Kasumi repeated, turning ever so slightly to me.

"Your pooka," I said.

Her head angled. "I sent no spy."

The others looked to Madrigal, who seemed offended by the

suggestion. "Why would I send Dearie to such a place when I had an errand boy already there?"

Emrys drew in a deep breath; I was mad enough to spit nails, but he was clinging to his composure with white-knuckled tenacity.

"If you didn't send it, who did?" Nash asked. "One of the other members of the Council?"

"No one would do such a thing without my explicit orders," Kasumi said. "It would involve dismantling all of the careful spellwork we've put into place. However that pooka got into Avalon, it was not our doing. Perhaps it was there all along. What matters now is ending this, while we still have breath in our bodies."

My thoughts whirled. You couldn't trust a sorceress, I *knew* that, but she seemed genuinely surprised by the accusation.

The other sorceresses don't like her, I reminded myself. We'd listened to them discussing her leadership in the vault, what felt like weeks ago. If the Council or other members were acting behind her back, what did that say about her ability to protect Neve?

Caitriona's thoughts seemed to follow a similar path. She moved toward Neve again, as if to carry her away from all of this. But Neve still didn't open her eyes, and when a surge of magic rolled over her, she cried out in pain.

And that was answer enough for me.

We have to, I thought, feeling my heart crack inside my chest. *There isn't another choice.*

I had to believe that this was the path Neve would choose for herself.

"This entire time," I told Kasumi, "all she wanted was to help the Sistren. To *save* you."

"Then let us return the favor and help her," Kasumi said. "We haven't the time to debate this. The hours pass swiftly in our world. When we return, there will be less than two days until the solstice—until he opens the pathway to Annwn and allows the dead to spill back into our world."

The thought sent terror skittering down my spine. "Time moves that slowly here?"

The High Sorceress nodded, though there was something victorious in her expression, as if she knew she'd played her trump card.

"Tamsin, you can't be seriously considering this," Caitriona said, her thick brows lowering.

"If you take her, we're coming with you," I told Kasumi.

"Tamsin," Caitriona pleaded. "Don't do this."

"I would expect nothing less." Kasumi cast a look of pure loathing at Nash. "I will even tolerate his presence."

"Cait," Nash said, drawing her off from us. "I understand, I *do*. But this is happening whether you will it to or not. Take a moment away to steady yourself. Fetch our things if you'd like. Just steady yourself."

Caitriona looked me straight in the eye as she said, "All of this was a mistake."

She sounded nothing like herself. It was as if the wounded animal we'd all sensed inside her, the very one we'd been trying to appease at every turn, had suddenly broken free of its cage. She looked utterly frantic, cornered—and in her pain, anger was the easiest thing to reach for.

I was surprised at how little her words stung once I understood what had fed them.

"Cait," Emrys tried, but she whirled on him, daring him to say something. He did. "It's only a mistake if we don't fix it."

She turned on her heel and strode out of the great hall, her footsteps echoing like hits to the chest. I started after her, only for Nash to catch my arm.

"Give her time," he said. "She needs a moment alone."

"She'll need more than that," Madrigal said. "I'd recommend copious amounts of wine, and, failing that, an hour or two in the iron maiden."

"Madrigal," Kasumi said sharply. "Isolde."

The slight brunette beside her straightened, eagerly awaiting her instructions.

"Go retrieve the sword so we can examine it," she continued. "Aife and Annalise—collect what you can from the dragon."

"You're welcome for that, by the way," Nash said.

Kasumi's lips compressed into a tight line. "Don't make me stuff you up its foul end."

The remaining sorceresses used their wands to carve sigils into the table beneath Neve. The top pulled free of its legs and hovered on some unfelt buoy of air.

"Oh, *look* at this," the Sorceress Annalise said, holding up the dragon's limp tongue. "The scholars will be thrilled."

A cackle echoed off the soaring stone walls in answer. Isolde was scurrying around the doorway, bent at the waist, her face becoming more and more frantic. But Madrigal only leaned against the wall, laughing.

And I knew. Somehow I did. It felt like the world was crumbling beneath me.

"What?" Emrys asked, then stopped, realizing it too. "Oh, gods. No . . ."

I hurried toward them, joining Isolde's frantic search, following the path I'd seen the sword take as it had spun away from us.

Instead, I found footprints. I followed the trail of them to the castle's once-grand entrance, down the stairs leading back out into the dead kingdom.

A scream clawed up my throat, but when I dropped to my knees, no sound came.

Caitriona was gone, and she'd taken Excalibur with her.

36

As it turned out, Nash's journey to Lyonesse hadn't involved bartering with ill-tempered ancient beings or breaking through the spell barriers of high magic that sealed our world off from the Otherlands. He'd slipped in like a spider through a crack between the worlds—the very one the sorceresses themselves used.

"How in hellfire did you know about this?" I demanded.

Kasumi and the other sorceresses looked just as vexed as they shuffled toward us through the icy snow, Neve on the tabletop floating between them.

"Yes, I should like to know that myself," Kasumi said.

As we'd walked the long path from the castle back to the abandoned village, the crunch of our footsteps in the snow the only sound between us, Nash had led us to the front door of what appeared to be a simple home.

The key Nash retrieved from his leather jacket's pocket looked similar to the skeleton keys we'd use to open a Vein and enter a sorceress's vault. This bone, however, was less a bone and more a claw, and it was longer than the hand that clasped it.

"Is this a Vein?" Emrys asked. "Or just a split between the worlds?"

"Give me that," Kasumi said, snatching the key from Nash. She held the razor-tipped end up in silent threat and he lifted his hands in surrender.

"After you, milady," he said, making a sweeping gesture as he pushed the door open.

Emrys had his answer. It wasn't like any Vein I'd seen—rather than a spiraling fabric of iridescent spellwork, the darkness ahead of us was shrouded in mist. It slithered out, searching.

"How?" I repeated, forcing Nash to stare at me.

"I'm a man of fewer and fewer secrets, my little imp," he said, with the smugness I knew so well. "Allow me to keep this one, won't you?"

"No," I said flatly. He pulled me aside to allow Kasumi and the others to pass through the doorway first, handling Neve with a gentleness that I begrudgingly approved.

"I traded a sorceress for it, all right?" Nash said gruffly, scrubbing the snow off his face. He looked weary as he followed my gaze.

"The girl made neat work of that snaky beast when she sent it to its death," he told me. "She'll be all right."

"I know that," I snapped. That was never my fear. Caitriona was more than capable of protecting herself. Nash had suggested searching the nearby rooms, on the off chance she'd fallen through some floor or gotten herself trapped, but we'd both known it was a waste of time. She'd probably called for Rosydd the moment she stepped out of the castle.

My disappointment stung so deep, it left me breathless. I tugged at my braided bracelet, trying to rip it off, but the knot held firm.

Caitriona was as stubborn as stone; only death would change her path now. A part of me hated her for this, and the longer I lingered there, in pain and resentment, the uglier my anger became.

We had chosen each other. We were supposed to see this through together.

Together to the end.

But I blamed myself, too. I'd felt her there on that precipice, all along, every moment since that last day in Avalon. I'd thought that if we were together, we'd be there to draw her back from the darkness that seemed to be gathering around us at every turn. To save her from her own fury.

"There are some journeys," Nash said, "we can only take ourselves."

"It's not right," I told him.

"No," he said, placing a hand on my shoulder. "But it is necessary."

None of us were who we used to be. The Caitriona I knew would never abandon a sister, or a friend. She would never seek revenge, as the sorceresses had so many centuries ago.

You weren't enough, came that old voice inside me. The one that had ruled over my heart for years like a tyrant. *You were never enough to save the people you love. To keep them with you.*

"Life is a mirror," Nash said. "There are times we must stare into its depths and face what we have become. The true fight is in saving ourselves if we cannot accept what we see there."

I am enough, I thought. *I am enough.* I wasn't going to be the one to let go of us. And maybe that made me a fool, and pathetic, and all the things I used to be afraid of, but I knew now that choosing hope was the braver thing than letting go first to avoid being hurt.

I chose them, and I would keep choosing them, no matter what happened, or who we became.

"Until she returns, we must keep moving forward," Nash said, guiding us back to the door the sorceresses had already passed through. He entered first, whistling some soft song, leaving Emrys and me to watch him disappear.

Emrys leaned down to kiss my cheek. I turned toward him in surprise, flushing.

"It'll be all right," he said softly, as if knowing every storm in my heart.

"You can't promise that," I said.

He took my hand. "I just did."

We walked through the split between the worlds together. I turned back one final time, but only to watch the shadowed land of Lyonesse vanish as I shut the door behind us.

"Where are we, anyway?"

"Highgate Cemetery," Emrys answered after a quick look around.

"It's the Circle of Lebanon," Nash corrected.

"The Circle of Lebanon located in Highgate Cemetery," Emrys said in turn.

Nash peered at him in the darkness, looking more and more peevish by the moment.

"So, London," I said, rolling my eyes.

I hurried past them, trying to catch up to where the sorceresses were cutting a slow path through the nearby tombs. Burial vaults lined the walls on either side of us, curving around to form a sunken circle set apart from the rest of the cemetery.

The location of the Council of Sistren's headquarters was a closely guarded secret, though many had assumed it was in London, just by virtue of how many sorceresses were spotted there. Every time a Hollower tried to follow them back to wherever it was they met, they invariably became lost and found themselves on the steps of the Tower of London. I'd always thought that last bit was a nice touch.

Emrys fell in step beside me, taking a long look at the cedar sapling tree looming over us. It had been planted on top of the tombs at the circle's center, its youth at odds with the vaults' moss-flecked stone facades. Their Egyptian-inspired architectural flair was dulled by age.

The family names etched into the stone above their doorways were barely visible as nature encroached from all sides. Creeping fingers of ivy and dying grass spread with abandon.

The night seemed to breathe disquiet. I felt unseen eyes watching us from beneath the stalks of leaves jutting out of the shrinking mounds of snow, through the cracks in the walls of the vaults. Cold pressure materialized at our backs, as if filling in the place Caitriona had vacated. But when I turned, only Nash was there, his expression grim as he surveyed the burial grounds.

"You okay?" Emrys asked quietly.

"Fine," I managed to get out.

I hated that my first instinct was to lie, but paranoia was contagious. It was better if one of us held on to their nerves.

"Just worried about Neve," I added, which was true. Thinking of Neve gave me something to focus on besides the horrible sensation of tingling and rot that had returned to my skin.

We followed the curve of the walkway until we found a set of stairs that would lead us out into the surrounding woodland. There, the tangle of man and nature was even more pronounced. Graves had been reclaimed by the wild, their stone markers dislodged or set crooked by stubborn roots.

A flash of red hair ahead made me slow.

"Great," Emrys muttered, ducking his chin and keeping his eyes on the ground.

Madrigal was huffing and puffing, muttering darkly to herself as her heeled boots struggled against the cobbled path.

"Nice night for a walk," Nash noted as we passed her.

She glared at him, then turned her narrowed gaze onto Emrys, sizing him up. For a moment, I was genuinely worried she was going to ask him to carry her the rest of the way.

"Why did you even come?" I asked, my hate for her overcoming even my fear of what she was capable of.

"Beastie," she growled at me. "Do you honestly believe I would have left the comfort of my home if I had any say in the matter?"

"I wasn't aware a crone such as yourself could be made to do anything against your will," Nash commented, a brow arched.

"Even I must fall to my knees at the Council of Sistren's command," Madrigal said, "and suffer the indignity of it."

"Yes, poor persecuted you," I said, rolling my eyes.

"Now, now," Madrigal said. "I vouched for you with the Council, didn't I? That was your consolation prize. Don't be sore about losing. I returned my darling pet to you—"

"He's not your pet!" I snapped, temper flaring.

"Tamsin—" Emrys began, but I was too furious to stop myself.

I spun toward her. "What did you even do with the ring?"

"Once I realized Lord Death's promise of revenge wasn't a curse as we believed, and it was worthless to me, I put it away for safekeeping," Madrigal said. "Where no one else will ever find it."

I opened my mouth to say something, but Emrys's hand found mine, pulling me farther away from the sorceress. I was angry at him for not being angry himself, but a single, pleading look reminded me why.

God's teeth, I thought, my own heart stilling in my chest. Anything he said to her, if she took it the wrong way . . .

"As it turns out, the only way to survive a catastrophe I'm not even responsible for is to save the others as well," she groused. "So here I am, one of the Sistren yet again, back to saving these wart-nosed banshees from themselves."

"Lovely," Emrys murmured.

Loose gravel spat up from under our feet as we made our way forward, silence settling over us again. A thick wall of trees shielded the cemetery from the rest of the city. It was unnerving not to hear so much as a car pass, regardless of how late it was.

Nash's expression was serious again; he walked with his hands behind his back.

"What?" I asked him.

To my eternal surprise, he actually answered. "Working through our options should Caitriona not return with the sword."

"And?" I asked.

"Still thinking on it," Nash said. "The trouble is that as long as Lord Death wears the horned crown, and it's this close to the solstice, he'll be able to summon the full might of Annwn's death magic."

"Are you saying no matter what we do, we have to find a way to knock the crown off his head first?" I said. "You can't know that for certain."

"He doesn't," Madrigal taunted, "but I do."

I whirled around. "Considering you're the one in danger, I'd start being a little more forthcoming."

"Darling," Madrigal said. "I'm never in danger of anything other than a good time."

"So we find another Goddess-forged weapon or track down Cait, then we take his crown when we launch our attack," Emrys said.

"It's not that simple," Nash said. "There must always be a king in Annwn. If he's gone, another will have to take his place. The dead require a warden."

"Then let the sorceresses handle it," I said. "They owe us that much for causing this mess in the first place."

Nash grunted in agreement.

"What?" I began, turning around. "Nothing to say to that?"

But the Sorceress Madrigal was gone.

"Seriously?" I said to the empty air.

"I think she hit her limit on teamwork," Emrys said. "Good riddance."

He kept his gaze up, watching the shadowed tree branches—or maybe counting the stars between them. The tight set of his shoulders had finally relaxed.

"Can you hear them?" I asked, rubbing some warmth into his arms. "The trees?"

Emrys's smile was almost boyish. "Oh yeah, they're quite chatty. Most have been here for a long time, and they're singing to the younger trees, telling them how to find food. Most don't like the cold."

I squinted up at them in doubt.

"It's all songs," he said. "I don't recognize the sounds, but I know what they mean. How they feel."

"Which is what?" I asked, brushing a hand against a tree's trunk as we passed.

"Fear," he said, tucking his hands in his pockets. "They're not sure if they'll all survive the winter."

"Well," I murmured. "We wouldn't know a thing about that."

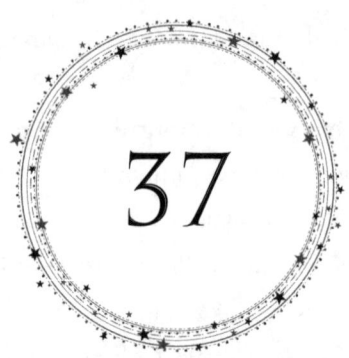

37

The heaviness at our backs remained, and only gathered in intensity as we passed out of the cemetery's gate. I took a deep breath as we hurried through the snowy spread of a modern park, trying to shake the feeling.

Then I saw the flashing blue lights.

Emergency vehicles were scattered haphazardly along the street at the far end of the green. Beyond them, between the stately buildings, was a veritable mountain of snow. Twisted into terrifying shapes, rising nearly as tall as the buildings around it, the white blanket spread out over several blocks, almost as far as the eye could see.

A helicopter arrived as we did, sweeping a searchlight over the area as more and more police and ambulances sped toward the scene. Bystanders were gathering too, watching, trying to dig through the snow with their bare hands.

Searching for the dead.

"Great Mother," Sorceress Isolde breathed out. She looked to Kasumi, then the others, horrified. Kasumi observed the scene with her usual calm.

"What would you like us to do, my lady?" one of the other sorceresses asked.

"Go see if you can't find the bodies before they transform," Kasumi told her. "Will you be able to burn them without the mortals realizing?"

"Of course," the sorceress said gruffly.

I could have screamed. This was Avalon playing out all over again. Everyone who had died, their souls snatched from their bodies—their families would never get to bury their remains. And it would continue to happen until Lord Death and his hunters were stopped.

And Cabell, I thought. If it came to it, I'd drive a blade through his heart myself.

Nash hung back beside Neve, his arms crossed over his chest. He looked down at her, his face soft. "All right there, dove?"

I elbowed past him, taking his place beside her makeshift stretcher. "Neve?" I said. "Can you hear me?"

Her veins were still pulsing with that same terrible light, but it was dimming now, and her skin had cooled enough for me to hold on to her arm. But her eyes were feverishly bright, and her expression was empty enough for me to know that she hadn't fully returned to the moment.

"Where . . . ?" she breathed out.

"You are going to the Council of Sistren, maiden Neve," Kasumi answered.

Neve's eyes found mine, widening.

"They're going to see if they can stop whatever is happening to you," I told her. When I took her hand, I realized her own bracelet had either burned away or been lost in Lyonesse, and it left me cold at my core. "Is that okay?"

Neve nodded.

"Cait?" she whispered.

I never had the chance to answer. Her eyes fluttered shut again. The interaction had barely lasted a moment, but it gave me relief, if not hope.

"This way," Kasumi said, guiding Neve's prone form forward.

The Victorian redbrick building was situated at the very edge of the park. A tall black fence surrounded it, each bar capped with a spike. It took a second look to realize they weren't merely decorative—each edge had been sharpened like a blade. Anyone who tried to climb the fence would find themselves disemboweled with one wrong move.

My top lip curled at the sight of the building. Victorian architecture was at best fussy, and at worst closely resembled a witch's candy cottage meant to lure in children.

"You've got to be kidding me," Emrys said, amused.

I followed his line of sight to the name carved above the front door. LAKE INTERNATIONAL SCHOOL.

"Is this really a school?" I asked Nash.

"Sure is," he said, eyeing the nearby camera and buzzer box. "Just not for mortals."

Kasumi lifted a hand and the gate's lock released with a loud *clang*, then swept inward with a menacing groan. A ring of slender silver keys hung at her waist, and she took care selecting one before she and Isolde guided Neve across the courtyard and up the steps to the black door.

I should have expected it, of course, but it still took me by surprise that the door to the school led to another Vein.

We passed out of its spiraling darkness into a sort of grand entryway, like the lobby of a luxury hotel. Marble columns rose up to the soaring ceiling, but not even the opulence of its design could distract from the battle preparations that were underway.

All of the furniture had been turned on its side and crushed into jagged forms to fill the gaps between the innumerable rock spikes that jutted out of the stone floors. There was a single, narrow path through the destruction, one that must have led deeper into the building.

Emrys leaned over a tangle of brass and crystal and let out a faint whistle; it looked like someone had intentionally smashed a chandelier and left the shards on the floor to cut any creature that dared to tread over it.

Shouting voices, a heavy hammering, and furious scraping echoed through the building. At our approach, several sorceresses looked up from where they were finishing the work of carving sigils into the floors and walls. A fierce protectiveness rose in me as they openly gawked at Neve.

"No one else will be entering through that doorway," Kasumi told them. "You can line the path with curses now."

The sorceresses did as they were told, pushing up the sleeves of their robes and tunics and attacking the sigils with renewed purpose. But I heard their whispers, that single word following us as we continued deeper into the building. *"Unmakers."*

Something moved at my right, and I turned, jumping as my heart shot up into my throat—but it was only my own filthy reflection staring back at me. The walls were lined with mirrors as we reached the heart of the building. I noticed Nash studying its layout just as closely as I was, silently marking the path we'd taken, and all the possible exits.

That entry hall led into an expansive atrium, with floor-to-ceiling windows overlooking a large garden, and, beyond that, the violet beginnings of a sunrise over a snowy mountain range.

Somewhere remote, I noted.

As we watched, the sorceresses who were gathered by the windows used spells to cover the glass with stone, sealing the room off from the outside world.

There seemed to be two distinct wings to their headquarters, one on either side of the atrium. Emrys placed a hand on my lower back, redrawing my attention to him. I followed his line of sight to where two upper levels were visible—maybe the building really had been a hotel once? I couldn't see the way up to either of them, not until Kasumi approached the eastern wall and triggered some unseen sigil. An enormous wooden staircase spiraled up from the stone floor.

"This floor will be fortified through cursework," she told us. "You will not return to it unless explicitly told to."

I bristled at that. "So now we're trapped in here with you?"

"It's all right," Nash said. "This is the safest place we could be."

"Somehow I doubt that," Emrys muttered. His gaze had drifted back to the sorceresses sealing off the wall of windows. They were unpacking several large crates of mirrors. "Hey, isn't that . . . ?"

A sorceress hung a familiar mirror on the center of the wall. Protective magic rippled over the frame's many beasts.

"She sold *them* the mirror?" I said in disbelief.

"You have to admire the hustle," Emrys said. "They must have figured out how to adjust the spellwork to trap the hunters and Lord Death."

"Yeah," I said. "But how are they going to trick them into being trapped?"

Kasumi guided Neve toward the stairs, ignoring the looks from the other sorceresses. "Isolde?"

"Yes, my lady?"

"Inform the others that there will be a meeting of the Council in the next hour, and have Davina meet us in my quarters."

"O-Of course," Isolde said, hurrying away in a swirl of skirts.

At the top of the stairs were two sorceresses carving yet more sigils into the floors. Magic rippled through the air around us as the spells were woven together like a protective net.

"They'll need to be more subtle than that," Kasumi said. "Layer in more masking spells."

A pale-haired sorceress glanced up, and with a start, I recognized her sullen face. It was Acacia, one of the sorceresses who'd held us captive in the vault. Gone was the prideful sneer and the immaculate gown. Her hair slipped from a high bun, and her face was streaked with sweat and wood shavings.

"You," she growled at me.

Emrys angled in front of me, his body tense.

"They are our guests," Kasumi admonished.

"She is an *Unmaker*," Acacia hissed.

Kasumi lifted her hand and released a punishing blast of wind. Acacia crashed into the wall behind her, and I tried not to smirk. Now she knew how it felt.

The other sorceresses quickly turned back to their own work, careful not to meet the High Sorceress's eye.

"Finish here and join the others in the atrium," Kasumi said.

Acacia stood up with a scowl, dusting off her dress. Her voice was barren of warmth. "Yes, my lady."

We arrived on the third-floor landing and stared down the long hall. At the very end, where it curved left, was an imposing portrait of a dark-haired woman. There was something familiar about the forest around her—the lake at the edge of the frame.

"Morgan," Nash said, staring at it with a peculiar look on his face.

"Octavia will take you to your rooms to wash and rest," Kasumi said, sweeping past us with Neve. "New clothing will be brought up for you. Feel free to burn what you're wearing."

A sorceress materialized beside me and seized my arm.

"Don't touch her," Emrys said sharply, but I'd already extracted myself from her grasp.

"Do not leave your rooms until asked to do so," Kasumi said. When I tried to follow, more sorceresses appeared, blocking the way. "Food will be brought to you in due time."

One of the women grabbed Emrys, and a man with tufts of white hair took his other arm. The latter's eyes glinted aquamarine as he hauled Emrys away from my grasping hand.

Pooka, I thought. It was the same for the man and woman who took Nash. "All right, all right, I'm not fighting it—*easy!*" He twisted back to look at me. "Do what they say, Tamsy. It'll be all right."

The sorceress who had grabbed my arm, with her straw-colored hair and flushed face, eyed me with suspicion. Kasumi rounded the corner ahead of us, and the thought of Neve disappearing with her made my pulse run riot in my veins.

"Hey!" I shouted after her. Ahead, Emrys was strong-armed into a room, and Nash into another. "You said we wouldn't be your prisoners!"

Kasumi stopped, but didn't turn to meet my burning gaze. Somehow her glacial words reached me all the same.

"I promised nothing of the sort."

Greenwich, Connecticut

Every time he closed his eyes, the screaming began again. It bled through the walls, through the door, down the hall. Not even the vast grounds of Summerland House were large enough to escape it.

"Let me out! Please!"

Olwen had managed to get the gag out of her mouth at some point during the night and shouted herself hoarse in a matter of hours. The girl didn't understand how lucky she was that his master had the foresight to keep her alive, to use her against the others. But if she kept going on like this, that good fortune would run out, and he wouldn't be there to save her.

The hunters were primed to seek out prey, and she was reminding them of her presence with every foolish word.

An icy touch brushed against his skin. He didn't need to turn to know who it was.

"Go back downstairs, Primm," he barked at the figure loitering at the top of the stairs.

Behind his repulsive form were three others. They might once have been men, but with each kill, each bit of death magic they drank down into their withered souls, they were starting to resemble the Children.

"If you can't keep the bitch silent like a good dog, I'll do it myself," Primm said, sliding the blade out of his boot. It seethed with the death magic that burned the air of the unlit hall.

The hunters moved so seamlessly between corporeal and incorporeal forms, it startled the seneschal. The former allowed them to kill, the latter to avoid being killed.

"Well?" Primm said. "Do you only bark on command?"

The seneschal didn't take the bait. He stayed where he was, his back to the wall beside the windowless closet they'd locked her in, watching them slither closer with a heavy-lidded gaze.

"Do it, and you'll answer to our lord," he said. The other hunters reeled back, but Primm advanced.

"He said nothing about killing you, though, did he?" The hunter was all but foaming at the mouth, trembling with need.

"Go kill one of the Children if you're that desperate to tear something apart," the seneschal told him.

He didn't reach for his own blade. Primm had been a vile old man in life, and death had only deepened his repugnance and greed. His master had told him death magic was the strongest power in all the many worlds, and he found himself questioning again why Lord Death had seen fit to entrust it to someone like Primm.

The hunter stepped closer, bringing his blade to the base of the seneschal's throat.

"And what, exactly, is your role in all of this? He didn't make you a hunter, but you seem to think that because you don't sleep out in the stables with the other hounds, you're somehow different. Better. But what will become of you when our task here is done?"

"I am his seneschal," he said.

Primm burst out laughing. "Are we giving ourselves titles now? Shall I be his chamberlain? His falconer?"

The younger man's heart blistered. His lord must not have told the others about his role. Blood welled on his skin where Primm's blade kissed it, the smell filling his senses.

"Heh," Primm said. "You've never had your sister's clever tongue, that little bitch—"

Primm had been forced to shift into corporeal form to cut him, and now the seneschal ripped the blade out of his hand, claiming it for himself. The hunter took a step back before he seemed to remember himself—that he was supposed to be the monster here.

But the seneschal—the hound—had always been the one with bigger teeth.

He let his fangs lengthen, cutting into his lips until blood spilled over his chin and dripped to the floor between them. Primm's confident sneer faded.

"Let's go," he barked at the others. "There are far more impressive things to kill than this pup."

The seneschal snapped his teeth at Primm, watching in satisfaction as the hunters hurried down the stairs.

At every turn, the hunters had scorned him, ignoring his presence one moment, then howling at him, mocking him, the next. He, who was supposed to command their respect—to run his lord's household and servants.

None of them were worthy of serving their master. When he and Lord Death had stepped out of the ruins of Avalon, the way ahead had seemed noble, a reckoning.

But as the Wild Hunt grew, and the stone at his master's neck glowed with the souls of the newly dead, it no longer seemed as straightforward as it once did. In seeking his righteous victory, his master had enlisted the most corrupt souls to serve him. The end would ultimately justify the immoral means, but he wished Lord Death hadn't sullied himself with those who made him seem like a villain when he was the hero of this story.

The seneschal sank to the floor. He swiped a hand over his mouth, smearing the blood there.

"Cabell?" came Olwen's soft voice through the door. "Is that you?"

That's not my name, he thought. He leaned his head against the wall. Wishing he could drive his skull through it and stop the pounding that was building at his temples once and for all.

"Answer her, ye swine," came Flea's voice. He didn't even bother to search for her among the ruined paintings and shredded tapestries.

"Cabell, I can hear you breathing," Olwen said. "After everything, you can't even speak to me?"

That's not my name.

"Answer her!" Flea demanded, white and furious and dead.

"No," he snapped back.

"But why?" Olwen rasped out. "We were friends once, weren't we? Before everything turned?"

"We were never friends," he told her.

"I don't believe you," she said sharply. "If that's what you want to believe because it's easier, then so be it. But you don't get to decide that for both of us, do you hear me?"

"I'm not letting you out," he told her. "You might as well just save your breath."

"I didn't ask you to," she said.

He shot the door a look of disbelief. "You've been shouting about it for hours."

"Because I didn't know it was you," she said.

"There's nothing to say," he snapped at her. "If you're hoping for an apology—"

"Did you hear me ask for one?"

The conversation kept tilting on him. He was struggling to grasp the thread of it.

"I don't know what your reasons are," Olwen told him. "But I cannot live with hate in my heart. I've never been able to, hard as I try. My sister, she's borne the weight of it for both of us, and it's shattering her."

He looked at Flea again, as if she would have the answer to the question circling his thoughts.

"It came over her so quickly—the need to avenge the people of Avalon," Olwen continued. The door shifted and he imagined her leaning against it too. "All of her pain and grief fed into it, and I fear for her, I really do."

"And I'm supposed to care?" the seneschal asked.

"I understand why she feels that way," Olwen said. "Just as I understand why Lord Death is scouring the world, searching for the soul of the woman he loved. I can't accept it, not ever, but I know his reason for destroying Avalon. But what I can't understand, no matter how hard I try, is why you helped him."

He drew in a rough breath.

"We would have helped you, if you'd come to us."

He drew his knees up toward his center, pressing his face to his palm. She wouldn't understand. There was no point in explaining it to her. What he had done, what he had allowed to happen, that marked him as her enemy forever.

"It's not too late," she told him. "Tamsin is fighting for you. She still believes in you, Cabell."

"Shut up!" He banged a fist back against the door. "That's not my name!"

"Did you know?" Olwen asked. "What he planned to do to them?"

Flea shivered in front of him, her form turning rigid with agony. Blood spilled from her slashed chest, and she gasped, choking on the blood dripping from her lips.

His hand fisted in his hair, he squeezed his eyes shut. But the image was seared into his mind now.

"As angry as you were at your sister," Olwen continued, weeping, "why did you have to hurt mine?"

"I didn't," he choked out. "I didn't—"

He hadn't raised a sword. He hadn't shifted and hunted alongside the Children. He had been a coward and hid in the underpaths of the tower, waiting for the horrible deed to be done.

He was nothing.

Shift, he thought. Turn her words, her sobs, into human words he no longer understood. His body was begging for it, the release.

"There's an end to this," Olwen told him. "It's not too late. They didn't have to die for nothing. These people, these hunters that you've allied yourself with . . . you're not like them. You are better than them—than all of this."

"*Shut up.*" The words were harsh in his throat and harsher still in his ears. He banged his fists against the door again. "Shut up or next time I'll let them tear you to shreds!"

He fled down the stairs before he had to hear her answer, despising himself with every footstep. He knew he was a coward, but he couldn't stand it. Not the sound of her voice or the salt streaking her tears.

No one would bother her. The house had quieted in the small hours of the morning. Some of the hunters had been sent to find wherever the sorceresses had hidden themselves, but he heard the rest in the back, ripping tormented shrieks from the Children.

Shift, he told himself again. *Run.*

Run until everything fell away and his thoughts were clear again. He could take advantage of the acres that surrounded the house. They were miles from the nearest neighbor. *Run.*

And he might have run, had the door to his master's study not opened.

His blood curdled at the sight of Endymion stepping out of the darkness, followed by . . .

She was there and gone through the front door in less than an instant. But the unmistakable red of her hair, the flirtatious way she stroked at Endymion's ghostly form—he would have recognized her anywhere.

What the hell?

Lord Death murmured, "Yes, see to it," to Endymion, and sent him away with a dismissive wave.

"Good evening, Bledig," said his master. "Is something amiss with our guest?"

"She's fine," the seneschal said. But he couldn't tear his eyes away from the front door. Had his mind been settled, he wouldn't have dared to ask, "Why did you not kill that sorceress?"

The silence suffocated him with icy hands.

"Do you know her from your false life?" Lord Death asked. "I'll admit, she's been useful. She was able to provide what we couldn't see in the girl's memories."

Why didn't you tell me you were working with the sorceress? The question screamed through him. What had he done to lose his master's trust? If he didn't have that, how long would it be before he lost everything else?

Primm's words hovered behind him, stroking down his neck. *But what will become of you when our task here is done?*

Lord Death studied him a moment, then drifted back into the office. "Come with me, Bledig."

He had no choice but to obey. The office still smelled of dried blood and withered life, its darkness punctuated only by candles and firelight, as his master preferred. With each heartbeat, Cabell became more and more certain that he was not going to leave the room alive. No one who questioned his lord ever did.

The king settled himself on the leather chair in front of the fire. "Come. I fear that I've been neglecting you."

Yes, his weak heart sang.

The seneschal knelt in front of him, still expecting to see a blade on the small table beside the chair. But there was only an unfinished glass of whiskey. Lord Death sipped at it as he studied his servant.

"I should not have questioned you before," the younger man said. "I just . . . I want to be useful to you. How can I serve you? Give me any task, and I'll see it through."

Am I still your seneschal?

Lord Death's hand stroked his dark hair, and the hound in him demanded he lean into the touch—when was the last time anyone had touched him? The heaviness in his chest eased.

"It's all right," Lord Death told him. "I shall always forgive you. You are my seneschal. I need you above all others."

The younger man let out a shuddering breath. There was nowhere else left to him. Only death of a different kind.

"We have reached the end of our search," Lord Death said softly, "and soon we will return home together. Will you stay by my side and see our victory through?"

Home. A strange, horrible word. A remnant from his human past. He would shed it soon. All of it.

"Yes," the seneschal whispered, staring into the crackling fire. "I will."

38

The suite of rooms they'd stuck me in was hardly a jail cell, but I felt the bars there all the same.

They'd locked the door behind me after they shoved me inside. And, with little else to do, I showered. The bathroom was almost obscene—bigger than my entire apartment, every inch of it pristine white marble with gilded accents. The water was hot, the pressure perfect. I might have treasured the experience, transcending to a new state of glorious existence, if my world hadn't been collapsing around me.

True to their word, the sorceresses left a change of clothes—jeans, a T-shirt, and a sweater, as well as new undergarments. They, and the basket of food beside them, didn't warm my heart to the Sistren in the slightest. After a quick inspection of the clothing, I put it on, tetchy at the softness of the fabric, the perfect fit of it.

The food was another story. If I hadn't been close to starving, I would have avoided it altogether. There were too many stories about fools eating faerie food and becoming trapped in Otherlands, or being cursed into sleep with a single bite, but I had crossed the point of desperation. My thoughts were becoming sluggish, and dressing had taken what little energy I had left.

So I ate an apple, and some bread, then the tasty little bits of unidentified cheese, and began to plan as I paced the room.

The midnight-blue walls were cluttered with framed pieces of tapestry, declarations, and portraits of sorceresses I only recognized by name. The assortment of deep armchairs and emerald-satin-covered sofas was an invitation to stop and rest, but I wasn't about to be wooed into letting my guard down by a nice suite and some fancy cheese.

The shifting light beneath the door told me someone was standing guard. Even if I got past them, the hallways were covered in curse sigils; I might not even make it to the room where they were keeping Neve, wherever *that* was. Emrys's room, maybe. But if I had a guard, so did he.

A gust of warm air rattled out from the vent above my head. Slowly, I tilted my neck back.

I'd seen a few security cameras in the hall; they'd stuck out like broken fingers among the old-fashioned finery the Sistren preferred. It hadn't even occurred to me to check my own room for them. Sure enough, in the upper right corner of the room, a camera was swiveling, tracking my movements.

My face flushed with anger as I wadded up my filthy old T-shirt and flipped the glassy black eye off. It took three tries to hook the shirt around the camera to block its view.

Satisfied and ever so smug, I turned to the opposite wall, where a large HVAC return vent had been placed.

They'd taken my workbag, of course, but they'd been kind enough to leave me a plastic toothbrush. Snapping the handle over my knee, I used the jagged end to unscrew the vent's cover. The metal sheeting groaned as I squeezed inside and replaced the cover behind me.

I had just enough room to wriggle my way up to where the vent turned at a ninety-degree angle and continued horizontally over the rooms on this side of the hall. I had to lie flat on my belly, but there was enough room to drag myself forward using my arms alone.

I winced as the thin metal of the vent let out an excruciating *bang*. Up ahead, light filtered down from above; I stayed focused on that, not the way the pathway seemed to be narrowing around me with every inch of forward progress.

"Um . . . hello?"

I reared up, knocking my head against the top of the vent. A face stared down at me through its brass cover, both brows raised.

And because my plan had existed for all of five minutes, without any sort of contingencies, I froze.

"I'm Mage Robin," they said. "Are you . . . stuck? Do you need some help?"

Mage was the neutral title chosen by those who felt the title of sorceress, and the feminine implications of it, did not fit them, but their skill and depth of power were the same.

"Can you pretend you didn't see me?" I whispered hopefully.

"How about I do you one better and just take you where you need to go?" Robin was already unscrewing the vent cover. Their wand was unusually short, at least compared to the one I'd seen Neve and the others use, but the athame end was a handier substitution for a screwdriver than my busted toothbrush.

With the cover lifted off, I got a better view of Robin. They wore their hair bleached blond and cropped close to the scalp, which created a beautiful contrast to the rich brown of their skin. With their warm, pleasant face, and eyes that damn near sparkled with excitement as they took in the sight of me, I felt myself relax, just a little bit.

Robin reached a hand down to help pull me through the opening. Knowing I wasn't about to escape now, I grasped their arm. The sleeve of their amethyst velvet duster was stained with what looked like splotches of ink. Their black shirt and trousers were simple but elegant.

Somehow, with Robin pulling and me pushing, I negotiated the opening and crawled out onto a wood floor. Turning onto my back, I surveyed the room.

Shelves upon shelves of Immortalities were stacked up to the vaulted ceiling on all sides. When I drew a breath, it was perfumed by old paper and ink. A nearby table was cluttered with leather notebooks and open Immortalities.

A library, my mind sang.

"Where . . . ?" I began, forcing myself to sit up.

"Welcome to the attic," Robin said. "Otherwise known as the Council's archive. I'm one of the recordkeepers."

"Nice to meet you," I said warily, pushing a strand of damp hair out of my face. They might have been perfectly nice thus far, but they were still part of the Council. I'd need to watch my words, and my back.

"You're Tamsin, right?" Robin asked. "One of the Unmakers."

I tried not to melt back through the floor. "Yeah. We're big fans of that nickname."

"Sorry," Robin said. "I take your point. Where were you going, anyway?"

"I was trying to find Neve," I said, my eyes greedily scanning the shelves again. "Do you know where she is?"

"She's with the most senior members of the Council of Sistren," Robin said. "They're warding the room for her protection as we speak. I promise you, she's quite safe."

I gave them a dubious look.

"It's all right," Robin said. "They won't hurt her. I'm doing research for them right now, to see if there're any instances of this happening before."

"I need to see her," I said. "You seem nice and all, but I hope you understand why I can't just take your word for it."

"I get it, believe me," Robin said. They stepped over to their desk and lifted something from behind the teetering stack of books: a perfectly modern laptop.

A silent video feed was playing on its screen. The crisp footage revealed Neve stretched out over a large bed, her eyes closed. They'd taken care to clean the dirt and blood from her and had dressed her in a pristine white gown. A crown of flowers had been arranged in her hair, and more flowers were scattered around her. The sight of it made bile rise in my throat. She looked like she was about to be sacrificed. Or buried.

"Why did they dress her like that?"

"They're honoring her," Robin said.

A circle of sorceresses, including Kasumi, were consulting one another about something I couldn't hear, even as I turned the volume up. As I watched, a ripple of that same fiery magic raced over Neve's skin, burning one of the flowers in her crown to ash. The bedsheet caught fire, but it was quickly stamped out.

"Listen, I know you want to see your friends," Robin said. "I can help you get to them. But in return, I'm wondering if you can do me a favor."

"I'm listening," I said, still guarded.

"I wanted to question you about what you witnessed in Lyonesse, and Neve's power," Robin said, "but the High Sorceress didn't think it was a good idea."

"Of course not," I said bitterly.

A new thought occurred to me as I turned to take in the shelves again. We must have been in some sort of secluded corner; I could hear hushed voices and creaking floorboards somewhere just beyond the bookcases.

"I'll tell you whatever you want to know, if you'll help me get to Neve *and*," I said, "look into who her birth mother is. She may be Creiddylad's soul reborn, but someone brought her into this world and left behind evidence of being a sorceress. Is there a way to find out?"

"Of course," Robin said. "I can test her blood against the database of Immortalities and other enchanted objects to see if there are any matches. From there, it'll be easy enough to follow her line."

I tried not to let my molten anger show, but Robin sensed it anyway. "What's wrong?"

"She came to the Council months ago to further her education, but they turned her away because she didn't have a known bloodline," I said. "Are you telling me they could have tested it right then and there? How does *that* make sense?"

"It doesn't," Robin said, sighing. "It never has, and it never will, but they won't change because it's the way it's always been done."

"That's the stupidest thing I've ever heard."

"Tell me about it," Robin said. "Do you know what it feels like to have all of this"—they gestured to the books and Immortalities—"to have all of this information at our fingertips, and to see, time and time again, the Council act on feeling, not fact?"

"Will you help me?" I asked Robin. "Because I'll help you."

"Of course." Robin shrugged their robe off, handing it to me. "Put this on and try to keep your head down. I can get us set up in a room where we'll be more comfortable, away from prying eyes."

I did as I was told but couldn't resist sneaking a look at the glowing displays of relics as we moved through the labyrinth of the archive. Here and there, I caught a glimpse of things I recognized, like a piece of a banner from Avalon. There was more from the isle scattered around us: pieces of bark from the Mother tree, gowns worn by the first sorceresses as they returned to the mortal world in exile, daggers, jewelry—but it was the mural painted on the far left wall that made me slow and take a second look.

The tower and Mother tree were gleaming in sunlight, surrounded by vast orchards and small houses. A river ran along the bottom, flowing into the blue of the runner beneath it.

"Is it a good likeness?" Robin asked, studying it again beside me. There was a hint of longing in the question, and I felt the tragedy of the isle's loss all over again. "We sent some archivists and scholars to the ruins, but . . . it was hard to tell anything, with all the destruction."

This depiction of Avalon was alive and glorious. It was how it should be remembered.

"Yes," I lied. I pointed to a hooded figure, half hidden in the painted trees. "Who's that supposed to be?"

"The Lady of the Lake," Robin said. "The first one, that is, who founded the order of priestesses at Avalon and was said to have tremendous power. Her daughter eventually inherited the role and became the last to bear that title, sadly."

My brow creased. "It was an inherited role? You're sure?"

That wasn't what Flea had told me—or maybe I'd simply misunderstood? She'd made it sound as though a new priestess was chosen for the role with each generation. That there had been far more than two.

"Yes, actually," Robin said. "Their line was a focus of mine during my training in the archives. The daughter, Caniad, chose to stay behind in the mortal world when Avalon was splintered off into its own realm."

"Huh," I managed. Something in Robin's explanation had stroked the back of my mind, though I couldn't place what. "Why didn't she return to Avalon?"

"The records claim she was furious that her mother's sword had been given to a succession of mortal kings, including Arthur," Robin continued, their gestures becoming more animated. "Caniad felt the sword had been created by the Goddess for her line alone—and to be fair, it does not sound like any of those men were able to use it at its full power."

The history we'd read in Librarian's office fluttered through my thoughts . . . *the mirror of mortality, judge and executioner of the pitiless wicked, savior of the ensorcelled, and the mercy of the innocent.*

"Sorry," Robin said, pressing a hand to their face. "Sorry. I can really go on and on if you let me. Come on, we're nearly there."

With one last look at the mural, at the hooded figure, I followed.

Despite Robin's fears that I'd be spotted, all of the other purple-robed workers we passed were either frantically flipping through the pages of books or boxing them into large crates and sending them out through an open Vein. No one acknowledged us; there was no time to.

"What are they doing?" I whispered.

"Some are going through and searching for other divinely forged weapons, in case Excalibur doesn't turn up again," Robin said.

There's not time for that, I thought miserably.

"Others are moving the most treasured pieces of the archive to a safe location, until the threat passes," Robin explained. "Relics they might use against us, Immortalities valuable for their insight on history and spells—that sort of thing. I'd take it all, if I could, but the High Sorceress only just allowed us to start the process. She thought taking preventive action would be admitting defeat."

I could see how that would be bad for morale.

"Here," Robin said, taking my arm and guiding me through one last spiral of shelves. The archive was limited to the central section of the building's attic, but it had still taken us several minutes just to reach a wall of doors on the opposite side from where we'd started.

They looked like study rooms, of a sort. All but one had signs that read OCCUPIED. Robin flipped the sign on the final door as they ushered me in.

It was larger than it had looked from the outside, big enough to fit a table with six seats. A small statue of the Goddess had been placed beside the door, as if to guard it. The candle in her upturned hands was unlit, but there was a faint glow radiating from behind the curtains that surrounded the room on all sides.

"Have a seat," Robin said, sitting on the edge of the desk, where they had easy access to the paper and quills. "Do you mind if we dive right in?"

"Sure," I said, my brow creasing. A strange feeling, almost like static, growled against the back of my neck. I rubbed at it, but it didn't go away.

"Can you tell me what happened when you found Excalibur?" Robin asked, dabbing the quill into the ink. "Spare no detail. Even something you think is irrelevant could be helpful."

"All right . . . well, there was a dragon," I began.

Robin's head shot up, their amber-colored eyes wide. "*Really?* A red dragon?"

"Yup," I said, then told Robin about Neve's appearance at the end of the hall, just in time to save us.

"How did you get to Lyonesse in the first place?" they asked.

"A hag," I said. "The Hag of the Moors?"

"A *hag*?" Robin repeated, with obvious envy. "What was she like?

Did she exhibit—" At my pained look, they caught themselves. "Okay, we'll come back to that. Go on."

I continued, explaining how Nash and Caitriona had managed to kill and gut the dragon. Robin looked to be fighting not to ask me something. Their expression reminded me so much of Neve, a pang went through my chest.

"So the dragon is cut open, and all of the various things spill out, including Excalibur?" Robin prompted.

"Not Excalibur," I said. "Neve found the sword lodged in the dragon's throat. She asked if the hilt was supposed to have beasts on it and then grabbed it, pulling it free, and that's when all of the magic and light exploded around us."

Robin's brow furrowed. They scribbled something on a sheet of paper, holding it against their leg. "And the light that exploded around her, she's been able to call on it before without the sword?"

"Yes." Something about the way the mage asked the question made my pulse tick up. "What's wrong?"

Robin ignored my question in favor of their own. "Have you ever seen her exhibit any other unusual abilities—something maybe involving plants, or the recent dead?"

That sinister prickling sensation was back, spreading over my arms as the hair there rose. I felt almost dizzy with it. "No."

Before I could ask what they were talking about, Robin was already moving out of the door, saying, "Stay right here—*right* here, okay? I'll be back. I just need to—"

They shut the door before they finished their explanation.

The buzzing around me didn't cease, it only grew louder, until the curtains, and that strange light emanating from behind them, seemed to shiver with it. I moved to the nearest curtain, drawing it back.

Behind it was a wall of protective glass. And behind that was . . .

The tapestry was a fraction of the size of the one in Lyonesse's great hall, but I recognized it instantly, even without the layer of ice. The mortal men in their fields, trying to spark fire. The Firstborn wearing their crowns. The clash of swords.

I pulled the next curtain away, my heart hammering. The man with the silver hand, Nudd Llaw Ereint, and his three sons.

The humming grew louder in my ears. I hadn't seen the other panels in the hall—they'd been covered by too much ice or destroyed by water and age. I pulled the next curtain open.

My skin was crawling over my bones—as if something were moving beneath it, desperate to escape.

My breath turned shallow and quick as I leaned in close to the protective glass. The Goddess appeared again, this time cradling a child, gazing down at its face. Spring bloomed around her in vibrant colors, radiating her joy.

Black splotches appeared on the glass, floating in my vision. I stepped back, fighting to steady my feet against the sudden spinning of the floor. A sharp pain sliced through my stomach.

I held on to the edge of the table in a desperate bid to stay upright. Warmth streaked down my face. I brought my own hand to my cheek.

Crying—why was I crying?

The darkness in my vision was spreading. Scenes of other halls, other worlds, other faces flashed through my mind, too quick to grasp, to truly see.

"You were never supposed to see this."

I spun around on unsteady legs.

Nash stood in the doorway, his face blurring as he came closer. Before I could speak, before I could move, my mind sank into the darkness clawing at it, and I knew nothing more.

39

At first, there was only the warmth surrounding me, the steady rocking of the world, a fierce heartbeat against my ear. The temptation to stay there, in that moment of dark serenity, was overwhelming.

But in the end, I forced my eyes open.

Nash's face hovered above mine, his gaze forward as he searched the darkness around us. For a moment, I didn't understand what was happening, only that he had hooked one of my arms around his neck and was carrying me.

"You can't ever do what I tell you, can you?" he was muttering, his steps quickening. "All the bravado of a peacock and the sense of a pigeon . . ."

"I think you mean Lark," I rasped out.

His steps slowed and he looked down at me in the dusky hallway. The walls around us were stone, and here and there, a few lanterns had been hung along the scattered rooms. The damp cold made me feel as though we were trapped under the earth.

This is not where I'm supposed to be.

Memory rose as quick and painful as a blister. I twisted, wrenching myself out of his arms, away from his coaxing hands. My legs threatened to buckle, too unsteady to support my full weight.

"Don't be a fool," he began.

I took in the hall around us with growing horror. It was a cellar of some sort. It had to be. "Where are we?"

"We're leaving" was all he said.

"No, we're not." I tried to move past him. "We're going to get the others. We can't leave them here."

"You're bloody well right we can, and we will!" Nash snapped at me. "You are my concern, not them. And we will find whatever Veins Kasumi's hidden down here if I have to drag you kicking and screaming!"

I took a step back, disgusted. "You really are a coward, aren't you? You put on a great act in Lyonesse, but all you ever do is run—"

"I don't care if you hate me for all eternity—I've hated myself enough for both of us over the centuries." He gripped my shoulders, shaking me. His usual swaggering confidence had unraveled, and what was left was raw. Tense. "All I've ever wanted, all I've ever tried to do, is protect you, and each time I found you, it was always too late."

"What are you talking about?" I demanded. "What does—what did you mean that I was never supposed to see those tapestries?"

His hold on me eased, but he didn't let go. Pain, alive and burning, flashed in his eyes.

"You always died—that bloody spell was supposed to protect you, but it became a curse," he said hoarsely. "She must have done something wrong, and mine was useless to stop it."

My blood beat a hard rhythm, turning my breath shallow. "Your . . . power?"

I knew Nash had the One Vision, so he had at least some magical ancestry. But he'd told us he never inherited his father's Cunningfolk talent.

He looked down at me again, saying nothing. He shook his head, as if deciding something once and for all. "You need to remember this now—your curse. You need to remember."

"Remember this?" A dark, sinking feeling overcame me. "You're not making any sense—why wouldn't I—?"

That memory, the one I'd forgotten. The story of the Goddess's daughter.

Horror wrapped its cold hands around my throat. "You did something to my memories, didn't you? That's your *power*."

His gaze held mine, almost pleading, but he didn't deny it. But that was impossible—that wasn't one of the known Cunningfolk abilities.

Pressure built and built in my chest. It felt like ice was coating my lungs. "You had *no* right to play with my mind! To take *anything* from me!"

"I had every right!" he roared, running a rough hand through his hair. "I couldn't risk something awakening your magic and triggering your curse again! It took you every time there was danger, stealing the breath from you, stopping your heart. Again and again and again, bringing your soul into a new body so he couldn't find it. And each time, I was powerless to stop it!"

I reared back. "You . . ."

"I've used all my coins now—they were given to me to protect you, so I could ensure that you were reborn and lived a fulfilled life," he said. "That was the only thing she wanted, her last act before she became one with the world."

"You're not making any sense," I told him. "You—"

Nash didn't let me finish. He was frantic now, the words unraveling faster and faster. "I asked the Lady of the Lake to cast a spell to hide your soul, to protect it, but something in the spell was flawed, and now it'll all begin again—if I don't get you away from here, far away from here, you *will* die."

I was shaking my head, pulling away again. I held up a finger, as if it were a talon I could drive through his throat, to make him stop talking. But it felt like every drop of blood had left my body.

"Neve has Creiddylad's soul," I whispered in protest. One hand rose to claw at my chest, as if I could physically cling to my denial.

"She has a different role to play in all of this," Nash said. "I didn't see it until Lyonesse, when she took up the sword. Of course you found one another, Fate's always been a cackling old crow."

"What are you saying?" I demanded.

"Listen to me, Tamsy," Nash pressed on. "You weren't in danger before because your power hadn't awakened, but it's different now, isn't it? You felt it in the cemetery—the spark of potential, the call of new life. I know you did."

I'd felt something, but—

"There's no time left," Nash said. "If he takes you, if the curse activates itself and you die by it or, Mother forbid it, he kills you himself, he'll be able to capture your soul—the very thing it was meant to prevent. Do you understand what I'm saying?"

My mind only seemed to understand one thing.

"You lied," I breathed out. "About everything. The curse. Where you found me. Why you took me in . . . You suppressed my *memories*. How can anything you're saying be real?"

"You are as dear to me as my own flesh and blood," he said softly. "You are the daughter I never had, in a life I never saw for myself."

I shrank back from the words, from him, my heartbeat fluttering. How many years had I longed for him to say that to me?

"I've made so many mistakes in that time, but I can't let this be another," Nash swore. "You *will* live. You *will* survive this."

"The others—" I began.

"The sorceresses will know who Neve is by now," he said quickly, reaching for my arm again. "And the Dye boy will survive. Somehow they always seem to."

"You don't know that!" I tried to move around him, to dart back down the long hall, but my body was still too unsteady, and his hold on me was ironclad as he drew me the opposite way.

"Oh, but I do," he said. "It was the same for his father, his father's father, his father's father's father . . ."

One by one, he opened the doors we passed, revealing root cellars, rooms stacked high with barrels of wine, discarded crates of books, but no Veins.

"The only Vein I saw was upstairs," I told him, seizing on an idea. "In the archive. You must have seen it. Doesn't it make more sense to go up there?"

He stopped, turning to look at my face. Breath surged in and out of him.

"All right," he said, his voice strangely devoid of emotion. "Then go up and look for it, dove."

The look he gave me was one of a stranger—there was no warmth to his eyes. Something was wrong.

"What's going on?" I demanded.

"Go past me and head back upstairs," he said, his voice hard. "Right now."

"What the hell is the matter with you?"

Nash's face was wan, his eyes pleading in a way I'd never seen before. *"Go back to the attic."*

A moment later, I felt it. A cold heaviness had followed us through the cemetery, but it was nothing compared to the feeling that came over me now. The way it seemed to reach into my chest and grip my heart.

"Please," Nash said quietly. "Go, Tamsin."

But I had already seen it—the subtle shiver of the air behind me in the hall. The slight distortion of the lines of the stone walls, inexplicably curved.

My breath caught, and this time, I let Nash draw me behind him.

A laugh of disbelief rumbled through the room, as cold as it was scornful. With a faint rustle of fabric, Lord Death pushed Arthur's mantle and its hood back, fully revealing himself. His black armor. His hateful smirk. A dead king's face.

"Hello, brother," he said.

And from high above us, rolling through the sky like thunder, the horn of the Wild Hunt sounded.

40

A bitterly cold wind hissed as it tore through the hall, shoving me toward Nash's back, blowing out the magic flames of the lanterns on the wall. The shouts that rose in response were swift and fierce above us. No sooner had the thundering of hoofbeats and the gleeful whoops of the riders filled the air than a chain of explosions was set off. The whole building shook with the force of each blast. Screams, human and monstrous, rained down through the floors.

In the cellar, however, it was terrifyingly still. Silent.

"Do you not recognize your own brother, Erden?" Lord Death asked, amused. "I admit, I am surprised to find you alive. Your reckless manner should have seen you dead a thousand times over."

Erden. I looked to Nash, watching his reaction. The weight that settled over my body made it feel as though I were sinking into the floor. *Brother.*

The three fair-haired brothers on the tapestries.

It's true, I thought. *It's all true.*

The only sign of Nash's distress was the way his jaw tightened as he chose his words.

"I see the face of Arthur Pendragon, long lost to us," he said, finally. "Stolen by one I no longer recognize as the brother I loved."

The smirk slid from Lord Death's face. I wondered then, distantly, what his original features had looked like—if they'd been similar enough to Nash's that seeing him was like looking into a mirror of his past self.

"You turned your back on me before," Lord Death said. "And now you choose to do it again, at your own peril. I will not protect you from my riders."

"I wouldn't expect that," Nash said. He inclined his head toward the door. "Seems your standards have fallen a bit over the centuries. Then again, those men have always been lapdogs who believed they were wolves."

As Lord Death moved toward us, stalking forward slowly, we moved too. I lingered a step behind Nash, gripping the back of his leather jacket like a child afraid of becoming lost, as he eased us toward the stairs.

"Where is the girl?" Lord Death asked.

Nash assumed a fighter's stance. One hand drifted behind him, but there was no blade there. The sorceresses had confiscated everything, even the one hidden in the toe of his boot. My heart jumped to my throat.

He's talking about Neve, I thought. But how could he know about her?

Lord Death reached for the sword hilt at his side. The movement shifted a long silver chain out from under the collar of his tunic. A crimson gemstone hung upon it, so dark it was nearly black. Threads of silver death magic writhed and churned inside.

After the merging, in the ruins, he'd claimed he was carrying the souls of Avalon's dead with him—was this how?

Lord Death's blade sang as he unsheathed it, relishing the crackling magic that danced along its razor edge.

"For the blood we once shared, I'll give you this last chance to step aside, Erden, or I'll kill that petulant girl you seem to believe is worth protecting."

"She is a stranger to me, Gwyn," Nash said. The formality of his tone was grating. It was as if he'd become a different person in a matter of moments. "Allow her to go, and you and I will settle this, as we should have all those years ago. I was always the better swordsman, but you've had centuries to improve, haven't you?"

But Lord Death did not move to strike. His blade was still in his hand, its magic roiling the air between us.

"How frightened you are," Nash said, his tone turned mocking. "You call yourself Death, and yet it haunts you most of all."

"My power is reward enough," Lord Death said. "It is endless. Eternal."

"Like the emptiness that thrives inside you now," Nash said. "It has fed on your anger and hatred for years and hollowed your heart. All because you were denied what was never yours."

"All because she was taken from me!" Lord Death stalked toward us again, and this time Nash didn't retreat. I flattened back against the nearby wall, unable to make myself run.

"She made that choice herself," Nash said. "Only *you* couldn't accept that."

"How does it feel to finally be the lesser son?" Lord Death taunted. "You may have been Father's favorite, but where is your kingdom now? Where is your power, your glory? I subjected the dead to my will, I won my crown. And you, Erden, you are what you have always been. A pathetic, waning shadow behind greater men. *Nothing.*"

I shifted, sliding along the wall until my foot struck a large stone that had come loose.

"It seems you need to convince yourself of that pretty speech more than me," Nash noted.

Lord Death sneered, bringing the tip of his sword to Nash's neck.

Above us, the Wild Hunt raged through the building, rattling more stones loose from the ceiling and walls. Glass shattered in a nearby room. As I looked back, sorceresses bolted past the doorway at the top of the stairs, throwing curses over their shoulders as the hunters pursued on foot or ghostly steeds. The air screeched with the clash of metal against metal and the hunters' cries of fury.

"Gwyn," Nash said quietly. "You were my brother. I would have fought by your side until the sun failed to rise and all the worlds withered to dust. But you made a terrible choice, and we are all still paying for it. Is your pride so great you still cannot see that?"

"She was mine," Lord Death growled. "I loved her."

"That was not love," Nash told him. "That was obsession. Envy."

"Nash?"

My gaze swung toward the base of the stairs, where Cabell stood. Silky gray smoke billowed through the hall behind him, making his black hair and black clothes all the more severe. And somehow nothing that had happened in the last few days had managed to kill that unconscious relief that came from seeing that my brother was all right.

But the blood of Avalon, the dead at Rivenoak, the ashes of the guild library flooded the chasm between us.

He looked terrible—his cheeks had hollowed and his eyes were underscored by bruised darkness. Yet there was a flicker of something in his expression, and he looked like the boy he had been, not the monster he'd become.

Nash said nothing, but I could feel the wheels of his mind spinning and spinning. It was only then, as Lord Death lifted his sword and took a step back, that I understood that something had drastically shifted.

Lord Death looked between the stunned Cabell and Nash, a low, menacing laugh building from the pit of venom in his chest.

"Surely not," Lord Death said, his lips curling as his gaze slid back over to Nash, and then to me. *"Surely."*

Terror turned my heart to stone. I fought for my next breath, even as the shadows of the hall encroached on my vision.

This is not the curse, I told myself. *I'm not dying here.*

"Nash, what are you—" Cabell began, coming toward us. He held out a hand, his expression bewildered, as if he wasn't sure that what he was seeing was real. His voice broke over the words, "Are you really here?"

"Yes, Cab," Nash said finally. "I'm sorry I was so long in coming."

Cabell stopped a short distance from us, his eyes drinking in the sight of Nash after so long.

My brother had dreamed of this moment for years. He'd believed that Nash would come back until I killed that hope in him. And it was as if everything our life could have been if that one thing had changed, if we had never gone to Tintagel, surrounded us like ghosts now, tantalizingly close but never to be had.

The strange spell that had overtaken the room shattered with a single word.

"Her?"

Lord Death turned to me, his expression of disgust and dismay warring with the way his body shifted closer.

"She's not a stranger at all, is she, brother?" Lord Death hissed.

Cabell flinched with surprise at the word *brother*. "What?"

"He told me of his guardian, the one who had vanished in search of the Ring of Dispel," Lord Death continued. "A Hollower. A disreputable man."

"*Disreputable* should have been your first clue, Gwyn," Nash said solemnly. "As we can both attest, a bird may shed its feathers, but they always come back the same."

"What's going on?" Cabell asked, a new edge to his words.

"All this time, all these many centuries, you've been working against me," Lord Death said. "Hiding her from me."

Nash smirked. It seemed he'd come to a conclusion of his own, and now the ruse was at its end. "How it must bite to know she's been in front of you this whole time and you couldn't see it."

"Her mother cast some enchantment to ensure I wouldn't," Lord Death said, furious.

"No," Nash said. "You never saw Creiddylad for who she truly was, so how could you recognize her soul in its new form?"

Cabell sucked in a harsh breath, finally understanding. Slowly, I dropped into a crouch, my fingers closing over the stone beneath my heel.

Lord Death's nostrils flared. "You dare—"

I whipped my arm around, chucking the rock at his head. Lord

Death dodged it with ease, but the moment's distraction was enough for Nash to slam his hands down on the blunt side of his sword, flipping it out of his brother's hands and into his own. He advanced, forcing Lord Death back.

"Cabell," Nash said. He didn't take his eyes off Lord Death, but now he reached his own hand out toward Cabell. "It's all right now. You can come home. You can always come home."

Cabell's throat worked. "We have no home. We never have."

"That's not the truth," Nash said. "Our home has been us three, wherever fate brought us. You chose to be with us all those years ago. You chose to become what you are, and now you get to choose again."

Cabell's entire body seemed to tremble, but he didn't move. He didn't react at all.

"He left you, Bledig," Lord Death sneered. "He let you believe you were something you were not, and hid your true nature—"

Nash continued, undaunted. "I didn't want to leave you. I never meant to."

Cabell didn't move as Nash came toward him slowly. His face was almost pleading, begging for that to be true. "But you did. Annwn is my real home."

"That is a world of darkness. You don't belong there."

"Don't I?"

The question forced Nash to turn back. The words blazed out of him. "You're my boy. There's no magic in any world powerful enough to change that."

I'd been watching Lord Death out of the corner of my eye, waiting for him to strike with death magic, or another weapon we'd yet to see. Instead, he offered Cabell his own hand.

"You know what you are," he said as Cabell looked at him. "You know where you belong now."

There was a movement at the top of the stairs. I whirled toward it in time to see the swirl of patterned emerald fabric. A wand that burned another symbol into the air in three quick strokes.

The curse made no sound. It didn't flash or erupt like an explosion, even as the stench of its magic scorched the air. It was a faint thread of light that shot like an arrow right at Cabell's chest.

I threw myself forward, but Nash was already there, knocking Cabell to the floor. The blast of magic struck his left arm and sent him spiraling back through the air on a wave of pressure. I screamed as he struck the floor.

The fighting roared behind me; the screeching of the hunters, the sorceresses bellowing commands. Curses flashed in the air around my head, scorching chaotic paths that blew chunks out of the walls, cracked the ceiling, and singed my arm. I threw myself to the floor, trying to cover my head to protect it. A curse glanced off the door beside Lord Death as he seized Cabell by the shoulder. The two of them disappeared into a swirl of shadows.

"Nash!" I stayed low, even as the fighting shifted away, retreating deeper into the headquarters, crawling toward his sprawled form.

Breath sawed out of him. His pale eyes widened as they locked on my face. His hand felt across the floor to seize mine. It was the grip that frightened me, squeezing with each shudder of pain, even before I saw what was happening to his body.

Gray stone erupted from the hole the curse had left in the sleeve of his overcoat, spreading over his arm like wet cement, hardening too quickly to wipe away.

Terror seized me as I turned toward the door again, screaming, *"Help! Help! Please, someone!"*

A sorceress had cast the curse, and another sorceress would have to break it—

"L-Look at me."

I did, feeling my body heat with panic and desperation.

"You know . . . what this is."

Stone's Embrace. One of the earliest curses he'd taught us, when we were barely old enough to write our own names.

Nash's eyes seemed to drink in the sight of me in the darkness, even as he fought to smile. The stone spread over his left side, from his shoulder to his feet.

"Just—hold on, okay, old man?" I said, my voice strangled. "You don't get to do this—you don't get to—"

"Tamsy girl," he said again, gasping hard for air as the stone passed over his chest. "Now . . . I know you'll . . . be all right. You . . . feel them . . . because your . . . power . . . is . . ."

"Nash, don't—don't—" I couldn't get the words out.

His gaze was still fixed on me, his free hand squeezing mine as his lower body and organs petrified and the curse swept upward, pain overtaking him.

"Could never have . . . dreamt a better . . . tale . . . than . . . my imps . . ." His last words came in a breathless rush as the curse stole over his chest. His throat.

His hand turned to stone around mine, trapping me there. Forcing me to watch as the stone swept over his mouth, his cheeks, his eyes.

And like the turning of a final page, his story was at its end.

41

Only a few minutes had passed when I heard my name called, but a strange, unreal quality had taken over my mind, one that turned seconds into days. I watched the stone face, waiting for a crack to appear—waiting for Nash to emerge from beneath it, having found yet another way to cheat death.

"*Tamsin!*"

Familiar hands, warm and callused, cupped my face, turning it away from the stone. Emrys appeared among the shadows, studying me with urgency before looking down at Nash.

"Oh, hell," he whispered. "I'm sorry, I'm so damn sorry."

"It was . . . there was a curse . . . ," I said hoarsely. The still-rational part of my mind knew I was in shock, but in that moment, the only thing that registered was the feeling of being locked inside my own body. As if the curse had transferred through Nash's touch and was now entombing us both.

I tried to pull my hand back, but it was encased in Nash's rough stone fingers. The more I tried, the more erratic my breathing became, my body heating with waves of panic and horror.

"Hang on," Emrys said. "Just a second, Bird, you'll be all right—"

He turned my face away again, pressing it against his chest so I wouldn't have to watch. His heart raced against my ear as he picked up a sword. The harsh clang of metal against stone wasn't half as terrible as the dull throb of each strike, and, finally, the feeling of Nash's hand crumbling against mine as Emrys struck at the fingers with the pommel.

The moment I was free, Emrys lifted me back onto my feet, holding me there until my legs solidified and the blood was no longer pounding in my ears.

"What were you doing down here?" he asked.

The shouting and hollering from the Wild Hunt hadn't ceased, nor had the sizzle of spells. A truly malevolent stench blanketed the air—burning flesh and ozone. Smoke and sparks of magic drifted past the open door at the top of the stairs.

"Tamsin?" Emrys said, drawing my attention back to him.

"He was . . ." I couldn't bring myself to explain any of it, not just then. "We need to . . . we need to find Neve."

The High Sorceress had made it sound like she was bringing Neve to her own quarters, which appeared to be on the third floor, farther down the eastern wing from where we'd been held. The video feed Robin had shown me seemed to confirm that.

"Do you know where she is?" His beautiful eyes were studying me again in obvious concern, but he would never stop me. I knew that, and so did he. "Do you think she's still on the third floor?"

I nodded.

"They protected the roof, so the hunt was forced to enter on the first level and fight their way up," Emrys said. "We're going to have to figure out how to overtake them."

My thoughts were still thrumming with fear, but the basic pieces of a plan were there, starting to assemble themselves.

"If we can't get to her room the normal way, we can try to crawl there through the vents," I said.

"Neve is probably the safest person in this entire building," Emrys said. "How do we know they haven't gotten her out yet themselves?"

I set my jaw. "We don't, which is why we need to see for ourselves. Once we have her, there's an open Vein in the attic we can use to escape."

Emrys seemed confused by all this information, but he gamely nodded. "Then that's what we'll do. Let's fly, Bird."

I took his hand when he offered it, trailing after him as we made our way along the hall, back to the stairs that would lead us to the first level of the estate. At the top of the stairs, I looked down the hallway, but Nash's stone body was shrouded in smoke.

It was a warning of what was to come.

The first floor was on fire.

The hunters had triggered several of the curses, and lines of fire had forced them to move down a single, narrow path through the hall into the foyer.

"Release me! *Release me!*"

I spun, searching the drifting clouds of smoke for the source of the voices screaming like sirens.

"Damn you!"

I lunged away from the nearest wall—from the mirror hanging there. A hunter launched himself at the glass, trying to shatter it from the inside. As the smoke rose, dozens more faces appeared there in the mirrors covering the walls, moaning and begging.

"The spells are holding," Emrys said, the silent *for now* hanging between us. "Let's go."

The carefully laid spikes had doubled in size, becoming a tangle of thorns across the hall. I followed Emrys's exact steps as he wove a path through the eerie glow of the scattered flames. I was forced to release his hand so we could climb over and around their deadly points.

With only a gasp of warning, Emrys shoved me to the outer edge of the hall. He forced us both down into a crouch behind one of the spikes jutting up from the floor. A moment later, three of the hunters staggered past us, their ghostly bodies flickering in and out of material forms.

"Wh-What did they do to us?" one gasped out.

The hunters trapped in the mirrors pounded against the glass, screaming their voices hoarse. The new arrivals jumped as the smoke parted to reveal the traps.

"Bloody hell!" one of the hunters yelped, backing up. "I told you it was the wrong way—"

"There!" came a woman's ragged cry. Four sorceresses materialized out of the billowing smoke at the end of the hall, whipping fresh lines of fire at the hunters. They crowed as the flames caught one of the hunters just as he took on physical form.

The victory was short-lived. With a snarl, the hunter nearest to them threw a dagger, then another—the sorceresses at the front were quick enough to dodge, but the one in the back, a statuesque blonde, caught a dagger in the throat, choking on her own blood as she fell to the ground.

With wrenching screams, the sorceresses charged, forcing the hunters farther back toward the entrance. Emrys took the chance to pull me up and lead us forward again. We slowed as we passed the fallen sorceress; her emerald eyes gazed back at us, emptied of life.

With a grimace, he pulled the blade free from her flesh with a gruesome spurt of blood. Wiping the weapon off against his jeans, he handed it to me. "Take this."

I couldn't muster a protest.

Once we were through the spikes, we kept low and hugged the right side of the hallway. Billowing red mist poured through the atrium, overwhelming my sense of the space as it wove through the silver smoke. The clash of blades and shouts met us at the entrance to it. Kasumi's voice rose above all the others with her call of *"Push them back!"*

Lights from spells flashed on the floors above us, sparking bright and fading quickly. A rider tore through the crimson veil, his armor glowing silver as his horse galloped forward and leapt, climbing on nothing but air to the second floor. A sorceress followed at a run, her face streaked with sweat and her dress torn. The end of her wand blasted out spirals of magic, her shouts of rage echoing in my ears.

With a swirl of her wand, she created enough spiraling wind to launch herself after the rider.

My heart raced faster than my feet until the adrenaline left me feeling unsteady. I gripped the dagger as hard as I could, worried that the sweat coating my palm would allow it to escape my hold.

Emrys ran to where the stairs should have been. Remembering the way they vanished before, only to reappear at Kasumi's command, I began to search the floor for a sigil.

"The stairs were here when I came down!" Emrys said. Something seemed to occur to him. "I think there's another way up—"

I tried to run after him, but the mist was too thick, too disorienting. A burst of panic moved through me as I lost sight of him, only to find his shadowed form a moment later.

But that shadow became two, and as I approached, a scene took shape in the mist.

One of the hunters stood over a terrified sorceress, who was scrambling on hands and knees across the blood-damp carpets to get away. He raised his sword above his head, death magic writhing along the silver blade in anticipation of another claimed soul. The hunter turned his face just enough for me to recognize the man he'd once been.

"Dye!" I shouted.

Endymion looked over his shoulder, his glowing eyes sparking with amusement. His humanity had been the mask, and death had only revealed the monstrosity that had always lived inside his skin.

The sorceress seized her opportunity to escape, fleeing into the maelstrom without a backward glance. Now that I had the hunter's full attention, I couldn't seem to remember why I'd thought this was a good idea.

"Well, this is certainly a surprise," he said, with a smile that revealed his sharpened teeth. "How convenient that I'll finally be able to kill you, too."

"Can't say I like the new look," I told him, edging back in the direction of the hallway. "Undead tends to be an unflattering shade on most people, though."

"Undead?" Endymion laughed. "My child, I am so much more than that. My power is beyond your comprehension."

"You're probably right about that," I said. "I don't speak Asshole, and the One Vision doesn't seem to be willing to translate."

"And here I thought I might never hear the legendary wit of the Larks again," Endymion said. "How satisfying to know that it'll truly be the last time I'm subjected to it."

I stood my ground as he sauntered toward me, knowing the dagger in my hand wouldn't be powerful enough to stop him.

Death magic emanated from the core of his being. There was a burning sensation on my jaw as his phantom hand turned to icy flesh and came up to grip it. My death mark echoed the pain, searing.

Tell him who you are, my mind whispered. *He won't kill what his master wants.*

"Cat got your tongue?" Endymion sneered, lifting me by the collar of my shirt. I fought, kicking my legs to no avail.

"Father."

Emrys stood a short distance away, hand curled around his sword hilt once more. He squared his shoulders, and there was no fear in his eyes. Only a carefully controlled hatred.

There was something immensely gratifying about the shock that crept over Endymion's gaunt features as he turned toward his son. His hand slackened and I fell to the floor in a heap, gasping. Emrys's mismatched eyes darted toward me, making sure I was all right, before returning to his father.

"This is not . . . ," Endymion began faintly. "You're not . . ."

"Real?" Emrys finished, circling us. Endymion tracked the arc of his path, his neck twisting unnaturally. "Breathing? Here? You have a wide assortment of words to choose from."

Endymion shook his head. If he'd been alive, perhaps his lungs would have worked like bellows, or he might have clawed at his pale hair. But now, he could only release a guttural sound.

"You're dead," Endymion said. "This is a trick."

"No trick," Emrys said, facing his father. He began to back away, receding through the red smoke as he taunted, "Come on now, *Dad*. Is that any way to greet your beloved only child? Your son and heir?"

I scrambled to my feet. The hunter's jaw sawed back and forth, all but unhinging itself in agitation.

"A trick," Endymion repeated. There was a note of pleading in his voice now. The sword fell from his limp hand, bursting into sparks of silver as it struck the floor.

"Was it worth it?" Emrys asked, hidden in the depths of the smoke. "Everything you did to us? Did it make you feel powerful to know that you could hurt your wife? Your son?"

"You are *not him*!" Endymion raged, charging toward the sound of his child's voice. "You are not my son!"

"Did it become harder and harder to satisfy with each hit, each punishment? Did it kill the weakness in you the way you hoped?" Emrys asked. "When my blood splattered onto your face, did you recognize the taste of it as your own?"

Endymion descended into ominous silence. It stretched on long enough that my hands began to lose their feeling. But slowly, so slowly, his expression turned from rancorous to almost . . . morose.

"I burned your heart," Endymion said as Emrys appeared ahead of us again. He inclined his head toward his son, as if listening to something beyond my hearing. "How can it still beat?"

"You *bastard*!" I snarled. I lunged at him, only for my blade to pass through his intangible body and fall to my knees.

"I'll show you how," Emrys said, so calm. "Give me your hand. Feel mine."

I watched in sickening horror as he held it out for his father to take. Endymion drifted toward him, lifting his wraithlike fingers as if in a dream. The hunter's hands turned to flesh and bone in front of my eyes again, the skin gray and bloodless. Emrys's hand closed around it.

"Goodbye, Father," he said.

Endymion looked up in confusion, but it was already too late. Emrys spun him hard, heaving his father forward through the mist—to where the Mirror of Shalott hung on the wall.

Endymion collided with its magic, and with a gasp of fury, he tried to pull back from its snare. Wisps of body, his transmuted soul, tore away at the touch of the rippling glass, as if the mirror were inhaling him.

Endymion dropped to the floor snarling, clawing at the mirror in a futile attempt to break its hold on him.

"Master!" he called. *"Master!"*

The mirror shuddered and rattled against the wall, swallowing the last of Endymion Dye's soul with a satisfied sigh.

Emrys hooked my arm through his and drew me away from his father's screams of fury—safe, for once, in the knowledge that this man could no longer hurt him. His shoulders shook as we retreated toward the entry hall.

"Are you okay?" I asked tentatively.

But as I met his gaze once more, I realized he was *laughing*.

It was a laugh of incredulity and elation—the delirious release of some impossible weight, some hideous shadow, lifting from his shoulders. He leaned down and kissed me, pouring every ounce of his relief, his joy, into it. I gripped his arms to steady us both.

"How adorable," came a silky voice from the atrium's entrance.

The laughter died on Emrys's lips.

We turned to meet the sorceress striding toward us. Madrigal seemed unbothered by the fighting still raging on the floors above us, the inhuman bellowing of phantom horses and their riders. Her appearance was immaculate; not a single strand of her bright red hair was out of place. It was as if she'd only just arrived, and she moved with the confidence of someone who knew they were untouchable. That they weren't in any danger.

The realization dawned cold and terrible.

"You," I breathed out. "You told him about Neve—where to find her."

She'd been the one to feed the information about Neve to Lord

Death—how long had she been working with him? Since Neve's first letter?

Emrys sent me a questioning look, but the sorceress spoke first.

"Your cleverness failed you this time, Beastie," Madrigal said. Her gaze moved over me, disgust warring with curiosity. "Lord Death told me I was mistaken, that *someone else*—someone even more pathetic—has the soul."

He's still nearby, I thought, fighting the barb of fear. I couldn't feel the cold pressure of his presence, but he couldn't have gone far with the fight still raging on.

Madrigal turned to address Emrys. "Kick your sword over and bring her to me, pet."

Emrys stepped in front of me. "I'm not your pet."

Madrigal's lips curled as she raised her wand. "I'll ask you one last time."

She took his silence for an answer.

"Emrys—" His name fell away from my lips as his body suddenly seized, tensing until his spine went straight as a board. The tendons in his neck strained, the muscles in his arms and back bulging. The sword fell from his hand, clattering to the floor.

"Emrys!" I gripped his arm, fear flooding my veins. His hand rose, shaking.

"Run," he choked out. *"Ru—"*

His face hardened, and between one terrifying heartbeat and the next, his hand lashed out and wrapped around my throat.

42

His fingers pressed into my soft skin like an iron band, squeezing harder with each moment we stayed there, locked in place. The suffocating press of his grip hurt less than the look of horror in his eyes as we stared at one another.

"What did you think I meant when I told you your heart belonged to me?" Madrigal crooned at him. "Your life is mine, pet. Unless . . ."

Emrys's face was terrible, void of any emotion, save for his eyes. I shifted my gaze to the sorceress, a tremor of fury building in me. She met my gaze with a look of twisted delight.

"Unless, Beastie, you'd like to take the dagger in your hand," the sorceress continued, "and plunge it into the pretty little heart I made for him? You can take your chances that cutting his hand off would be enough, but, of course, he does possess another one."

Our mortal lives had always been a game to her. I'd known that from the moment I'd met her. Even now, we were little better than entertainment.

"You sick *freak*—" I spat at her, the word strangling off as Emrys's hand tightened. His face was a stony mask, but a noise of pure, raw pain built in his chest. His other hand captured mine, drawing it and the dagger's razor-sharp tip to just above his heart.

"Go on, Beastie," Madrigal encouraged. "Do it."

His eyes were pleading for it. *Begging.* His grip on my neck tightened again, until I couldn't draw another breath at all.

"Fine," Madrigal said, pouting. "Bring her to me, pet."

She took a step toward us, beckoning with her hand. The movement drew my eye down to the point of her shoe—and what lay a few feet away from it.

Shadows crept in at the edge of my vision as I fought to breathe. That terrible look was still in his eyes—they shone, silver and emerald, in the strange light.

When Emrys moved, I was forced to follow. Any resistance would have pushed the dagger into his skin. One step. Two.

Madrigal's lips curled as she raised her wand.

Then, with what strength I had left, I hooked my foot under the hilt of the sword Emrys had dropped and kicked it as hard as I could in her direction. The blade spun, tearing through the smoke, revealing the curse sigil the instant before the hilt scraped over it.

The floor splintered around her, and before she could raise her wand, it collapsed, plunging her down into the darkness of the cellar.

Emrys gave a ragged gasp as the hold on him released, and his muscles relaxed. He ripped his hands away from me, and smoky air filled my lungs again. I bent at the waist, touching my throat, trying to steady myself.

"Are you all right? Tamsin? Are you okay?" Emrys asked frantically, lifting me upright, crushing me to him. "I'm sorry, I'm so sorry—"

I wrapped my arms around his waist, feeling the sudden urge to cry. He was shaking, and as he pulled back, his hands skimming over my neck, he looked sick with grief.

I gripped his wrists. "I'm all right. I'm—we—" I drew in a deeper breath. "We have to find Neve."

He nodded, his eyes still lingering on my face. "Right. Yeah. I think—there should be another way up over here."

He led me away from the entrance hall, toward the western wing, where the smoke seemed to be emanating from. But as he reached the arch that separated the foyer from the hall, his running steps slowed so suddenly, I collided with his back.

"What?" I asked, searching for the threat. "This damn smoke—I can't see anything . . ."

That wasn't true. As I turned, I could see his face. The strange expression there, confusion and fear in his eyes.

"Emrys?"

He staggered forward, gasping as he clutched at his chest.

"Emrys!"

He collapsed onto his knees, coughing, splattering blood onto the stone floor.

"What? What's wrong?" I dropped beside him, catching him by the shoulders, but his weight made it impossible to keep him upright. He fell across my lap, coughing up more blood. "Emrys!"

Emrys's words in Lyonesse returned to me like a knife in the ribs. *She had made me a new heart.*

"No!" I shouted. "Please!"

She told me some part of my heart would aways beat for her.

Emrys gripped my arm, fighting for his breath. Blood dribbled over his lips, and his skin had taken on a deathlike pallor.

She could unmake it just as easily.

"Please stop!" I looked back toward the collapsed floor, begging for mercy I knew would never come.

I gripped Emrys's face with shaking hands, turning it toward mine. His eyes were wide with pain and terror. "No, no, no . . . you're going to be all right, do you hear me? *Do you hear me?*"

Not again, not again, not again—

I turned back toward the hall again, screaming, "Help! Someone!"

Emrys's hand squeezed my arm, returning my attention to him.

"You're—you're going to be all right," I said, knowing I was babbling. I smoothed a hand over his face, cleaning the blood away as quickly as it appeared on his lips. I kissed him then, desperately. "You're going to be all right—"

"Your . . . tell . . . ," he said faintly. "You look . . . down . . . to left . . ."

"Don't," I pleaded, feeling myself start to splinter again. *"Don't."*

His labored breathing slowed. I almost didn't hear him as he said, "I'd . . . stay."

I'd stay with you.

And then the last breath left, and there was no heart left to beat.

"Emrys?" I whispered.

His eyes were still open. Still on me. But there was nothing behind them. There was nothing at all.

My scream choked off into a strangled sob. My hands hovered over him, not wanting to touch him, not wanting to feel his skin turn cold, but needing to.

This isn't real.

It couldn't be.

I curled down over him, pressing my head to his still chest. The scar on my heart tore open and pain flooded through me until all I could do was hold him while I broke apart.

"No!"

Neve was standing a short distance away from us in the atrium, her white gown streaked with blood. If the flowers hadn't already fallen from her crown, they would have been burned away by the fury of her expression. The pain as her gaze met mine.

Blue-white light gathered on her skin, and as she screamed, it exploded out of her. The magic flooded the halls with its burning power, driving back the smoke, the darkness. The last of the hunters shrieked as they were incinerated.

But not even the purest light could save what had already been lost.

PART FOUR

THE WAY OF THE DEAD

43

The Council of Sistren's Inner Sanctum was a meeting chamber in the western wing of the building. Tiered rows of tables encircled a round table at its very center, where the most senior Council members sat to conduct business while the other sorceresses looked on. It was a place of discussion, of arguments, of pleas, both secret and sacred. A part of me wondered, distantly, if they might change the name now that it had become a mortuary.

The dim light made the room seem far smaller than it was. The shadows had closed in overhead, and the candlelight was too weak to hold them back. Now that night had fallen, the domed glass ceiling would let in no light until the moon passed over it.

The sorceresses had laid the dead out on the tables to prepare their bodies for burning. Twenty sorceresses and mages in all, nearly a third of their numbers. And then . . . there were the other two.

I sat on the stairs that separated the two tables, staring down the aisle at nothing. A bucket of sweet herb water and a rag waited on the step below, but I couldn't bring myself to take them. One of the sorceresses had tried to tend to the bodies, but I'd lost it at the mere thought of anyone else touching them but me.

I drew in a sharp breath, wondering why it hurt so much to even think their names.

A nearby sorceress began to sing a soft prayer as she drew a shroud over another—a sister, maybe, or her mother. Others waited nearby to take the body to the funeral pyre. The lovers were the worst to watch, their faces glistening in the candlelight as they wept.

But they, at least, could face the ones they'd lost.

It was almost unbearable to stay here, in the terrible silence. The death in the room felt like a dull buzzing against my senses, and made my skin crawl. It was a sharper, more pronounced feeling than the one I'd had in the cemetery only hours ago, but as the hours passed, it had dulled again. It was almost too frightening to think about what it meant.

Nash's unfinished words drifted through my mind again. *Your... power... is...*

What? I thought helplessly.

Nothing useful, clearly. Nothing that could have stopped all of this from happening. And if this sensation was what he'd meant, then I didn't want it. I didn't want to feel like death was constantly walking in my shadow, combing its bony hands through my hair, or that I was slowly being buried alive in a shallow grave of rot.

You felt it in the cemetery, the spark of potential, the call of new life.

What did that even mean?

The dead sorceresses and mages had died by death magic, their souls claimed by Lord Death, but they hadn't transformed into Children of the Night. Not yet. Burying their dead might have brought the surviving sorceresses a modicum of peace, but the High Sorceress had felt that the risk was too great.

The one small mercy was that Neve wasn't among the bodies laid out around me. After the fighting was over, I hadn't been able to reach her before she was swarmed by a protective cluster of sorceresses, who had watched her with awe and trepidation.

I'd listened silently to Mage Robin, their face still streaked with sweat and soot, as Neve was led away. Excalibur had reacted to Neve's touch and awakened the full potential of her power because it recognized her as its rightful heir. The granddaughter of the first Lady of the Lake, who had been one of the Firstborn, like Gwyn ap Nudd. Like his brother . . . Nash.

No, my mind corrected. *Erden.*

And Neve's gift was the same as her mother's, and her grandmother's before her—she could call on the purifying power of the Goddess's light.

I needed to go find her, to see for myself again that she was all right, but I couldn't let myself leave this room. Not until I did what needed to be done.

I drew in another steadying breath; then I forced my body to move. To stand. To turn. The sorceress's quavering song filling the silence. My hands curled around the bucket's handle and the rag.

Nash's stone face was still turned in my direction, only now his blank eyes seemed to gaze through me, as if seeing something just beyond my shoulder. His lips were curved in a small smile, unafraid. He hadn't been caught in amber, but he was frozen at the moment of his death all the same.

I wondered then if there was another life for him, if his long-dead family had come to greet him at the end, or if his soul would forever be trapped in that stone.

Nothing could be done for him. The High Sorceress had said as much. The stone had destroyed his body.

Still, I found myself dipping the cloth into the water and wetting the stone planes of his face to clean the ash and dust away.

"In ages past," I murmured, "in a kingdom lost to time, a king named Arthur ruled man and Fair Folk alike, but this is the account of his end. Of the barge that emerged from the mists and carried him to the isle of Avalon . . ."

My throat ached as I told him one final story, my hands working steadily, slowly. And when my work was done, when the tale had reached its end, I turned to the other body. Forced myself to look at his beautiful face.

They shut his eyes. A spark of fury moved through me at the thought. No one should have touched his face. They had no right. Water dripped from the rag onto the floor and my boots.

"Tamsin," came Neve's soft voice. "I can do that. You shouldn't have to."

No, I thought fiercely. *It has to be me.*

Neve was back in the clothes she had worn when we'd left Lyonesse, her curly hair loose and cloud-soft around her face. She had fresh water and a new rag. Wordlessly, I traded with her, letting her take the soiled set away. But when she returned, I still hadn't moved.

"What happened?" The tears in her voice were catching, and the fortress of anger I'd tried to wall myself up inside crumbled.

"Why did you do this to me?" I asked her hoarsely. "Why did you have to make me care?"

"You've always cared," Neve said, coming back up the stairs. "You just didn't want to."

"*No,*" I said, the word breaking. "No, I didn't. I was okay. I was safe. Nothing touched me. I was *safe.*"

But that wasn't true either. Deep down, the part of me I couldn't kill—that little girl. She was in pain all the time, and I'd never let her wounds heal. To survive, I'd had to be strong. I'd had to build a tower within myself.

When Neve was one step below me, she stopped, her expression heartrending. "What do you need?"

Hot tears spilled over my face, and I hated them, hated myself, hated the sharp pain that radiated from my chest. I doubled over and she was there in an instant, wrapping her arms around me and holding me there. I clung to her, sobbing.

"It hurts," I told her, pressing a hand to my chest. "It hurts so much . . . I can't make it stop . . ."

"The hurt is *real,*" Neve said in my ear. "Thinking you can protect yourself from it was always the illusion. When we lose someone, we can't bury our feelings. Denying them won't make them go away. You have to feel, you have to remember, because it keeps them alive with us."

But they're not alive, I thought. *They're not here.*

It was a long while before I managed to piece myself back together again. When I straightened and pulled back, Neve said nothing—she only picked up the bucket again and handed me the cloth.

I took Emrys's hand, inhaling sharply at how cold it was. The pads of his fingers and palms were callused, from whittling, maybe, or, more likely, gardening. I tended to them first, trying to commit the feeling to memory. Neve went to retrieve two shrouds. She dusted dried petals and herbs on his chest, whispering a chanting prayer that was too quiet to understand.

And in that moment, in the shadows of the chamber, we were back in Avalon. Kneeling on the cold, bloodstained stones, tending to the ruined faces of the isle's dead. I knew Neve was thinking about it too by the way her hand shook as she stroked my arm.

Finally, I came to his face.

The blood had dried on his lips. I dabbed at them gently.

"He was so happy," I whispered. "Just before . . ."

"Miss Lark?"

The High Sorceress stood at the bottom step of the aisle, her face as pale as the shrouds around her.

I turned my head away from her, scrubbing my tears from my face.

"Yeah?" I asked roughly.

She'd changed out of her ruined gown into a sensible shirt and trousers—clothes for working, for restoring. The pretense of her glamour and power had burned away.

But there was an intensity to her expression, a steadiness. Rather than making her fall to ash, the flames had only proven there was a steel spine beneath all her layers of silk. Her sleek black hair had been braided away from the healing cuts and bruises on her face.

The wounds were striking. Kasumi wore her bandages proudly, the way a queen might wear her best jewels. But there was no haughtiness in her expression. The High Sorceress knew, just as the rest of us did, that we would all be dead if not for Neve.

As she ascended the steps, her footfall soft against the old wood, I saw that her arms were wrapped from shoulder to fingertip. The bandages were soaked in some sort of salve, likely to heal the extensive burns I'd seen on them earlier. That sticky wetness had to be why she was so careful to use only the tips of her index finger and thumb to pull something out of her trousers pocket.

A rumpled envelope.

Just below us, she hesitated, stealing a glance at Nash's stone form.

"He . . ." Kasumi cleared her throat. "He—your father, that is—"

"He's not her father," Neve cut in. Her eyes had narrowed with what looked like genuine annoyance.

"He was," I said quietly. "Well, he tried. In his own way. With varying degrees of success. But he tried."

Kasumi let out a soft breath as she passed me the envelope. "I am sorry, Miss Lark. For your loss."

"And I'm sorry for yours," I said, looking at the rows of shrouds and bodies around us. The High Sorceress gave a nod of acknowledgment.

"Maybe you should have thought about letting me out of that room sooner," Neve said sharply.

"Then we might be mourning you as well," Kasumi said.

She was right. The past was past now, and any wishes to change it were wasted breath and fairy dust.

"What is this?" I asked, holding up the envelope.

"I've no idea," Kasumi said.

"Really?" Neve pressed, skeptical.

"The envelope is cursed to destroy itself if someone other than the intended recipient opens it," Kasumi said. "I should know, did the spellwork myself."

I turned it over, and, sure enough, a faded line of curse sigils was scrawled along the bottom edge of the paper.

"Hn." Neve crossed her arms over her chest, fighting to look unimpressed.

"I shall leave you to it, then," Kasumi said, starting back down the stairs.

"Have you searched the property for Lord Death?" I asked. "I told you, he has the mantle of Arthur."

"We have," Kasumi said. "He is no longer in the estate, or its land."

"What about Madrigal?" I pressed.

As I'd suspected, there'd been no body to retrieve.

"Not as of yet," Kasumi said. "Rest assured, the Council's punishment will be swift and commensurate with the crime."

My jaw all but locked with tension. Anger bled into my words. "What's left of the Council, you mean."

The only "commensurate" punishment as far as I was concerned was death, but with the blow they'd been dealt, they weren't about to voluntarily reduce their numbers again.

"Please find me when you're finished here," Kasumi said to Neve. "With today being the solstice, we must discuss how your power might be used to destroy our enemy."

"We don't need to discuss anything," Neve said, her hands curling to fists at her sides. "We need to find Excalibur. The light alone had no effect on Lord Death when we were in Avalon, and I have no idea how to change that."

A hot, static buzzing grew in my chest.

"I already have some of the Sistren out searching for Caitriona," Kasumi said.

"Check the Dye family estate," I told her, remembering my dream of Emrys's death. "Lord Death and the others may be using it, or at least keeping Olwen there."

"You're sure that's where she would have gone?" Kasumi asked. "To find Lady Olwen?"

"Yes," Neve and I said as one.

Kasumi lifted her hand in a silent farewell, descending the steps swiftly, careful not to meet the gazes of the living or dead around her.

I waited until she had left the chamber before facing Neve again. "*We* need to find Caitriona. And Olwen."

Neve sighed. "The problem is, they're not going to let me out of their sight. I tried to step outside for some fresh air and four of them followed me."

Even now, I noticed that two new sorceresses had arrived and were pretending not to watch us.

"Are you . . . all right?" I asked.

Neve let out a hollow laugh, sinking back down to the step. "I guess as much as I can be. Having the answer about my mother . . . it doesn't feel real. And there's still the question of my father."

I sat heavily beside her. "Do they think she's still alive?"

"Robin couldn't say for sure," Neve said. "She would've been hundreds of years old by the time I was born . . . it doesn't make sense."

"Plenty of sorceresses wait centuries before having their first child, if ever," I said. "That's the least surprising part of all of this to me."

Neve seemed placated by that, at least.

"If I don't have the soul," she began, "does that mean that it's still out there?"

I didn't answer.

"Tamsin?" Neve's brow furrowed. "What aren't you telling me?"

"It . . ." It was a struggle to drag the truth out of me when I'd only just begun to accept it. I lowered my voice to a mere whisper. "I have the soul. It was in me the whole time."

"*What!*" Neve's shrill voice drew the attention of the room to us, but she didn't care, slapping a hand against my arm. "*What?* I swear to the Goddess, if you're joking, Tamsin Lark—"

I tried to quiet her; it wouldn't help us at all if the sorceresses knew. They'd try to keep me under lock and key when all I really wanted to do was find our friends and end this, once and for all.

Neve's face fell. She read me in an instant, the way she always did. "You're not joking."

I told her the rest, as quietly and as quickly as I could.

"Oh no," she whispered, tears welling in her eyes. "Oh no, Tamsin..."

"It's okay," I said, feeling numb to it now. "I like this option better than the last one, when he was coming after you."

"I don't!" She nodded toward the envelope in my hands. "Are you going to open that?"

I ran my fingers along the weathered paper, tracing the shapes inside it. There seemed to be a note, but there was something else, too—hard and round, it gave the envelope a surprising weight.

I broke the wax seal quickly, before I could change my mind. Something fell out onto the wooden step, clattering loudly. I unfolded the scrap of paper inside to find three words.

Not for me.

"Tamsin...," Neve began, a faint tremor in her voice. She'd bent down to retrieve whatever it was. As she held it out toward me, the hot static returned, growling in my ears.

Free of tarnish and dirt, the coin looked more pearlescent than silver. But there were the words I had seen before with the cold winds of Tintagel at my back and the sea roaring below.

I am the dream of the dead.

"I thought you said he used the last one?" Neve whispered.

"That's what he told me, but it's like I said. He lies..." I swallowed, then corrected myself. "He *lied* as easily as he breathed."

You bastard, I thought. *You no good, flea-bitten bastard.*

I reached out as if in a trance, taking it from her and turning it over.

The grime and what I'd assumed was blood had been so caked onto the other coin, I hadn't been able to see the words engraved on the other side.

"*I am the dread of the living,*" I read.

"*And I am the dream of the dead,*" Neve finished. "Death, and life."

A dizzying feeling rushed over me. I tightened my fist around the coin. Bracing my head with my other hand, I tried to regain some semblance of control over my thoughts.

Memories whirled around in a stream of endless color and light. Voices rose and fell like a choir. The woven image of the Goddess shining with joy as she cradled her daughter, surrounded by the blooming beauty of the world she'd created.

All of it rose to a crescendo, clarifying into a single thought. What occupied the space between the cold, deadly grip of winter and the sun-warmed greens of summer? Between the living and dead?

Spring. Rebirth.

And somewhere in that lay the power Nash had tried to explain with his last breaths.

Neve sat beside me. "It's a good thing, isn't it?"

I closed my eyes. "How can it be a good thing to have to make a choice like this?"

"What do you mean?" Neve asked.

I shook my head. "Do you remember the original note? He said to not clean the coin. I think it has to have the blood of the person you're resurrecting when it's buried."

She looked back at Nash, his body rendered in stone. There was no blood to use. "So Emrys, then."

"But what about Olwen?" I rasped out. "What about Caitriona, or you, if something horrible were to happen? What about any of the dead around us? Why do I get to make this choice when everyone in this place is suffering too?"

"That's the chaos demon in your mind speaking," Neve said. "This is what it comes down to: Do you believe Olwen is still alive, and that we'll find her?"

"Yes," I whispered. I didn't believe much, but deep in my gut, I believed that.

"Do you think Caitriona and I are capable of fighting and protecting ourselves, and the people around us?"

"Yes, but—"

"Do you think Emrys deserves to live?" Neve continued. "Do you think he wanted to?"

I'd stay . . .

"Yes," I whispered. "It's not that simple—"

"It is," Neve said. "The sorceresses and mages around us came here to fight the Wild Hunt, and they died doing just that. Most have centuries to their names—more years lived than any of us could imagine—and they'll live on for centuries still. The surviving Sistren and mages have already begun the creation of their Immortalities."

My nails dug deeper into my palm as I squeezed the coin tighter.

"Is it that you think he wouldn't want to come back?" Neve asked.

I closed my eyes. "He wanted to be free."

Free of his father, free of the scars of his past, of his mother's contract with Madrigal.

He wanted his future.

I could give him that.

I forced my hand open, looking down at the coin again.

It would give him a new body, wouldn't it? One that was entirely his own . . . a heart that beat only for himself.

A hint of a sad smile touched Neve's lips.

"What?" I asked.

"I think Nash wanted you to use it for yourself," she said. "But that didn't even occur to you, did it?"

This time, I glared at the coin. "I am *not* using this for myself."

"It's like I tried to tell you," Neve said. "You've never wanted to believe this, but you *do* have a beautiful heart."

She reached into her jacket pocket and retrieved a small bone. I almost laughed. It was a bird's skull she'd found and picked up somewhere along the way, tucking it into her jacket for safekeeping.

"Think about it, all right?" Neve said, stroking her hand down my back. She nodded to the sorceresses pretending to inspect the other bodies below. "My babysitters are looking like they're getting ready to drag me back to the Council, so I'd better go. Come find me when you're done, all right? We'll figure out how to get out of here together."

I nodded, my throat too tight to speak. As she reached the bottom step, she turned and said, "Tamsin?"

I looked up.

"Do you think we were supposed to find each other?" she asked. "If not in this life, then another?"

I released a long, deep breath. "You'd know better than me."

Neve sent another small smile my way and then was gone.

In the end, it was a single moment that decided it for me: the look Emrys had worn the moment he realized what was happening. In that last gasp of life, there'd been confusion, pain, and, most of all, fear.

He hadn't wanted to die. Not then, when he'd finally freed himself of his father and the future had opened its door to greet him.

My heart throbbed painfully as I stood beside his still body. Neve had drawn the burial shroud up to just below his chin. His face was still streaked with dirt and blood.

Using a clean bowl of water and a new cloth, I gently dampened the dark, dried blood on his lips. I placed the coin there.

In ancient times, the Greeks buried their dead with coins over their eyes or in their mouths to serve as an obol for Charon—his fee for ferrying the dead into the Underworld. It felt right that this coin would instead be planted in the earth like a seed.

I leaned down, pressing my lips to the other side of the coin. I lingered there a moment.

"See you soon," I whispered.

Drawing the shroud over his face, I looked to Nash. Beneath the thin layer of cloth, it looked like he was merely sleeping.

"Thank you," I told him. "For trying."

With the coin and the small skull in my hand, I emerged from the dark chamber and reentered the world of the living.

Gathering a small handful of ash that had collected on a side table, I wandered the ruined halls until I finally found a door leading out into the walled garden, untouched by the heavy mounds of snow on the nearby mountains and hills.

"Oh, you would have loved this," I whispered. "You nerd."

The night air felt crisp and pure as I inhaled. Vast rows of herbs and trailing vines on trellises stretched out around me, lit by faintly glowing lanterns. Though each plant was neatly labeled, there was a wildness to it all, as if they'd been left to grow as they desired.

I found my way to the center of the garden, marveling at the way the dusting of snow had fallen just outside its perimeter, until I saw the protective sigils carved into the low walls.

I knelt, using my hand to dig into the soft dirt. When I was sure it was deep enough not to be disturbed, I placed the ash inside, then the bone, and, finally, the bloodstained coin.

Please work, I thought. *Please.* I only had the vague instructions we'd gotten before to go on. Just then, it hardly seemed enough.

As I finished covering the coin and patted the soft earth over it, I heard an anxious voice call my name.

"Miss Lark?"

It took me a moment to recognize Isolde, the small, nervous sorceress who had accompanied Kasumi and the others to Lyonesse. She looked like a fighter now, like she'd been dragged to hell and back by the ankles. The cuts and bruises on her face were healing under a heavy layer of ointment. She no longer looked scared of her own shadow.

Sometimes surviving did that for a person.

I rose to my feet. "Is something wrong? Is Neve all right?"

"Yes," Isolde said with a broad smile. "That's why I came to find you. She and the Council have had a breakthrough."

My pulse jumped. "Already?"

Isolde opened the door. "If you'll follow me?"

I did, and eagerly. We wound our way back through the halls and up the stairs, to the room they'd locked me in only a few hours ago.

Two other members of the Council stood inside the room, their backs to us. A small trill of warning sounded at the back of my mind as one turned, her expression stony. The slight movement was enough to reveal who was sitting on the settee, arms spread over the back of it, legs crossed.

And smirking.

Madrigal stood behind him, looking exceedingly pleased with herself.

"No—" I began, backing away from the door. A dark shadow lingered in the corner of the room, and it—he—came toward me, his face pale. "Cabell—"

Isolde's hand latched onto my shoulder and I felt an icy spark jump between her skin and mine.

Darkness descended on my mind, slicing through my thoughts, robbing the feeling from my body. Cabell caught me by the arms as my legs gave out, his hands tightening around them, his face expressionless.

And in that last moment of awareness, I heard only Lord Death, his voice low and victorious.

"Now the bargain is complete."

Greenwich, Connecticut

They returned to the house alone, for the very first time.

In the absence of the hunters, it was easier to assess the damage they'd wrought. True to their Hollower pasts, they'd hollowed the Summerland estate of all its treasure, all its value, all its memories.

And what was left was a husk readying to collapse in on itself.

The Children brayed in greeting from the roof, skittering down from the turrets. Drawn, he realized, by the enticing new smell of the girl in his master's arms.

"Away with you," Lord Death snarled, jerking his hand in dismissal.

They whimpered, skittering back over the stone facade.

The front door had been torn off hours before, when the Wild Hunt had burst forth to claim final victory over their enemies—or so they had believed. In the end, it had been their final ride.

And now, it was back to the way it was meant to be. He and his master would return to Annwn. And Tamsin . . .

When the seneschal had gone to carry her out of that festering den of serpents, his master had intervened. Insisted. And the hesitation that had followed was yet another strike against him, another whip for his master to lash him with. But still, his fingers had tightened around her, a flicker of defiance overcoming his fear.

He'd heard his master's explanation of who—of what—Tamsin

was with shock ringing through his whole being. But when she had appeared in front of him that second time, he'd seen only the Tamsin he knew. Maddening, sarcastic, churlish Tamsin.

But in the end, he'd relinquished her all the same, passing her weight out of his arms and into Lord Death's. The sight of . . . of Nash had destabilized him, leaving the world trembling beneath his feet.

You can come home. You can always come home.

No. His fingernails lengthened into claws, piercing the skin as he curled his hands into fists. *No.* Nothing Nash had said was true. He'd only had to see the hatred on Tamsin's face to know that there was no going back.

He had to return with his master to Annwn.

You're my boy. There's no magic in any world powerful enough to change that.

But there was. A single curse had stolen Nash a second time. None of what he'd said mattered. It didn't.

Our home has been us three, wherever fate brought us.

The seneschal ducked his head, bracing against the rancid smell the hunters had left behind. Lord Death's heavy steps left a trail of snow and decaying leaves among the shattered glass.

"Mark me, Bledig," Lord Death said. "We will rebuild the hunt in time. Theirs was no victory. As winter returns, so shall we."

"Sparing me again, I hope," Madrigal said, striding up the steps behind them. She took in the full carnage with an amused glance.

"You will not fall by my blade, nor any of my hunters'," Lord Death said. "It is your own kind you should fear."

"What fox fears rabbits?" she mused. "Especially with the power you'll grant me. They will burrow down now in their warrens, licking their wounds."

Her words were proud for someone who still had dust caked in her coiffed hair. Her gown, with its long, sweeping sleeves, was torn in several places, and she either hadn't noticed, or didn't care to fix them.

A cold smile was etched upon his master's face. The seneschal had wanted to believe that he barely tolerated the sorceress's presence; that his honor would demand he spurn her for the way she had betrayed the Sistren. But Madrigal had given his master what he desired most of all. Not his seneschal. *Her.*

"I should like to see the pathway to Annwn open again." Madrigal trailed after them uninvited as they entered the study. "If you would allow me . . . ?"

"Do what you wish," Lord Death said, gazing down at Tamsin's sleeping face again. It wasn't a look of adoration. He was searching for something.

The seneschal's stomach clenched painfully. He forced himself to look away.

"Marvelous," Madrigal said, draping herself over one of the armchairs. She swung a leg idly, kicking at her velvet skirts. "Will you kill the mortal body now?"

The seneschal fought to hide it, but he startled at the question. His master, busy with laying Tamsin across the large desk, did not notice.

"No," he said. "As long as she is in this world, there is a chance her mother's spell will snatch the soul away. It must be done in Annwn, where I can be certain of my control."

He toyed with a strand of Tamsin's hair, and the seneschal felt an involuntary wave of nausea rise in him.

"Bledig," Lord Death said suddenly. "You'll take care of our guest, won't you?"

For a moment, the seneschal wasn't sure what—or whom—he meant.

Not until his master tossed him an old brass key.

"We've no need for her now," Lord Death said. "Give her to the Children. They'll need to be fed before our journey tonight."

The words sent a shudder down his spine.

"And the priestess's soul?" the seneschal heard himself ask.

"I've enough to satisfy my needs," he said, stroking a gloved finger down Tamsin's cheek.

Madrigal braced her chin on her hand, surveying the seneschal as he walked stiffly to the door. "My. Whatever will you do?"

"Whatever my master commands."

This was the choice he had made. This was what was left to him now.

He climbed the stairs, the key cold in his hand, the dagger heavy where it was strapped to his hip. The bile rose within him, burning his throat until it was all he could taste. Out of the corner of his eye, a small, pale shape flickered, but he couldn't hear anything over the groaning of the house and his racing heart.

When he reached the top of the stairs and the door to the supply closet came into view, he did not let himself stop.

This was the choice he had made.

He slid the key into the lock.

This was what was left to him now.

Hours later, he followed his master's slow steps through the knotted tree roots and around boulders covered in lichen and melting snow. And all he could think was, his sister was crying in her sleep.

He scented the tears rather than saw them, taking in the soft touch of salt that filled the air. The seneschal couldn't remember the last time he'd seen tears streaking down Tamsin's face. If he really thought about it, his mind could churn up images of the guild library's dark attic, all those times she would wait until she thought he was asleep to cry silently into her blanket. The times they'd been out on the streets during a storm, when it was impossible to distinguish tears from rain.

Had she cried when they'd met again in the ruins of Avalon? That night felt like another lifetime to him. Everything between then and now had become a blur of shadowy figures. He used to envy her perfect memory. Now he wasn't so sure.

Deeper and deeper they traveled into Wistman's Wood. He tried to focus on the smell of the strange blood staining her jacket, and not the way her pale hand swayed limply through the air, as if she were already dead. Her wavy hair glinted gold against his master's armor, both just barely visible to him from a step behind.

A low growl sounded in his throat. Lord Death inclined his head back toward him, hearing that pitiful noise but, in all his great mercy, choosing not to comment.

Madrigal grumbled behind him as she struggled to maneuver around the boulders. Not another sound could be heard as they made their way through the gnarled, tangled landscape to the dark world of his birth.

It was not lost on Cabell that, to reach it, he had to pass through the very moors Nash had found him wandering as a little lost pup. Or that Lord Death's portal to Dartmoor had opened on Lych Way—what Nash had once called the Way of the Dead.

For centuries, parishioners had traveled miles on the corpse road, carrying the coffins of their dead to Lydford in the west for burial. He had been riveted by the stories of the spirit lights that were seen by travelers, from restless ghosts who had gone astray, and now, having seen them appear and drift toward Lord Death in utter surrender, he felt no joy or wonder. He felt nothing at all.

Tamsin had never liked scary stories, but he hadn't been afraid. He still remembered the way Nash had leaned closer to the fire when he told them that the dead would always be carried with their feet facing away from their home, to keep their spirits from finding their way back.

But the seneschal knew, as all the dead must, that you could never return home.

The cold air knifed at his senses. Only a few acres remained of the ancient Wistman's Wood, but it seemed to expand around them as they passed deeper into its shadows, as if ushering them into the past.

Garlands of ice clung to the branches of the ancient trees, glinting in the moonlight. The oaks didn't tower as they did in other parts of the land; here they bowed and twisted into sinister shapes. Rid of their leaves, the moss-covered bodies reminded him of the spidery Children trailing behind them, braying and chattering.

The full moon's light brought a glow to the mist cloaking the wood. It felt wrong somehow that the longest night of the year should be so bright.

The hairs on the back of his neck rose as trepidation skittered over his skin. A small, radiant form took shape in the pale air. The seneschal turned his face away stubbornly, but no matter where he looked, the little girl was there. She was watching him. Disappointment and scorn radiating from her silent presence.

Stop, he begged inwardly. *Go away.*

"You are my boy," she whispered, but it was Nash's voice he heard. *"You can always come home."*

The memory of blood and death and fire flashed through his mind, strangling the breath from his lungs.

When he looked again, Flea stood on a different boulder, this one still bearing a carved spiral, the last evidence that the druids had once worshiped in the oak wood.

A flash of lightning forced his gaze up toward the dark fabric of the sky. A seam of silver glimmered and stayed, flickering as if galvanized by their presence.

"Ah," Lord Death began, looking back to the sorceress. "It seems you were correct. They've used spellwork to seal the door to Annwn."

"Their magic cannot withstand your own," Madrigal crooned.

"Indeed," Lord Death said. "I've more than enough power to tear it open by force."

The path led them to the center of the small wood. Lord Death stooped, setting Tamsin's curled body in a hollow at the base of a tree. Roots glowing with silver death magic rose from the ground, twining around her chest, pinning her in place.

As Lord Death straightened, he pulled the stone pendant out from beneath his cloak, gripping it between his palms.

Flea's spirit hovered nearby, watching from behind a tree as the first of the souls were released from the stone. The orbs of light were nearly indistinguishable from the stars as they rose and rose into the sky, flowing toward the sealed doorway. Their magic would be the blade that carved the path between the worlds open again.

"You can always come home," Flea whispered to him.

The seneschal closed his eyes, shaking his head. Nausea rioted in his stomach again as his feet carried him toward Tamsin, to where she stirred.

Our home has been us three, wherever fate brought us.

This was Tamsin. This had been his sister. This wasn't the girl Lord Death had desired for centuries, the one whose soul he'd stolen. This was *Tamsin.*

Nash had always had a story for everything, and when he didn't, he could spin one out of smoke and stardust. Her whole life, Tamsin had longed for answers, but he had only ever wanted the sanctuary of belief.

You chose to be with us all those years ago. You chose to become what you are, and now you get to choose again.

He hadn't remembered until Nash had spoken the words. The memories rose from deep inside him, telling their own story. How Nash had bundled his shaking form into a blanket. How he'd curled up beside a little girl with white-blond curls, and they'd kept one another warm by the fire. How he'd longed to be like them. To be one of them.

Long ago, a hound dreamt he could be a boy. But every dream came to an end.

Lord Death's deep voice carried over to him. "There is no need for you to keep such a foolish form now. Shift, Bledig."

He felt only relief. He released the breath burning in his lungs. Released his thoughts. Released the sight of the spirit watching from the trees. Released the pain.

And he shifted—into what he had always been, into what he was meant to be.

44

Something sharp dug into my back.

The pain grew worse as I tried to shift and found I couldn't. A heavy pressure banded around my chest, its rough skin tearing at the fabric of my jacket. The damp chill stroked my face, urging me to stay in the darkness that coated my mind.

But a voice emerged from the shadows there, soft but urgent. *Wake. Wake now.*

The sweet smell of dirt and greens filled my nose and coated my tongue as I forced my eyes open.

Mist shrouded the treacherous shapes around me—it took my hazy mind a moment to recognize them. *Trees.*

It seemed impossible; there was something so baleful about them. Knobby, stripped bare of their leaves, and covered in a skin of sickly green moss. I wondered if something truly evil had happened here to bow and twist them this way.

The ruined forests and groves of Avalon rose like a furious spirit to the front of my mind, stopping my heart in my chest. My fingers clawed into the icy dirt.

No, I thought. *Avalon is gone.*

The moon was bright overhead, undaunted by the thick canopy of branches as its radiance spilled onto the rocky forest floor. This was *my* world.

A strange light fluttered nearby. I tried to lean forward, only to find that I couldn't. My back was pressed to one of the trees, thick ropes of faintly glowing roots binding me to it. Memory rushed back, riding a flood of fire in my veins.

Now the bargain is complete.

Lord Death stood a short distance away, where the small clearing seemed to meet the very edge of the woods. Light streamed up from the stone cupped between his hands. My gaze drifted toward the sky.

Seething magic had torn open the dark fabric of the night, revealing a glimpse of what lay beyond. A world of gray stone—the kingdom of the dead.

Souls poured out of the widening gash, some drawn into the spell holding the doorway open, others racing back to the mortal world like falling stars.

Fear came alive in me, shuddering through my body. I struggled against the roots, but a deep growl of warning brought me up short. An enormous hound, its black, shaggy coat glinting with ice and snow, rose from behind another cluster of roots. Its red eyes burned as it lowered its head, watching me closely.

Cabell.

I held his gaze as I pushed up off the ground, ignoring the way the hound's lips pulled back to reveal his jagged teeth.

When it had come to this, when so much had already been lost, what did I have left to be afraid of?

"How pleased I am to see you awake, my love," came Lord Death's silky voice. "It won't be but a few moments more until you are safely home again."

"I'm not your *love,* you pig-breathed bastard," I said. "I'm the nightmare you were stupid enough to kidnap."

A smirk curved Lord Death's pale cheek. His horned crown was adorned with spirit lights, giving him a malevolent radiance. He didn't so much look at me as *into* me, as if my flesh, my entire self, were nothing more than a receptacle.

"Once you are free, we will never be parted again," Lord Death told me. "No one will be powerful enough to take what is rightfully mine."

"You're sick," I told him.

"Ridding Creiddylad of your crude form will be the greatest of pleasures," Lord Death sneered.

With his focus on me, the stream of souls escaping his stone pendant slowed, then stopped. But the souls of Annwn's damned still raced out through the fissure in the sky, undeterred.

My only hope for survival was distracting him long enough to figure out a better plan.

"She hated you, didn't she?" I began, pulling against the roots again. "She knew you were a monster undeserving of love and kindness. I can feel her disgust boiling inside me like acid."

"You lie," Lord Death said, letting the pendant fall from his hands as he faced me. And, truthfully, I did. But it was all too easy to imagine Creiddylad's feelings as my own.

He let out a dark laugh. It stung like the kiss of a scorpion's tail. "You're as fork-tongued as Erden. Tell me, was his death as pathetic as his life?"

There was a faint noise from beside me—a whine, almost. But only the hound was there, and I knew better than to assume it was anything other than the wind. That icy breeze did nothing to cool my flash of anger.

"Her skin crawled every time she saw you," I said. "You *repulsed* her. And what really burns you isn't that they sent you to live out the rest of your existence in Annwn, it's that she chose another. She didn't want *you*."

"Enough!" Lord Death thrust a hand toward me. A hissing magic swirled up his arm from the stone pendant, blasting out from his fingertips. The roots around my chest burned brighter the moment before I felt them slither around me, tightening until I was struggling to take in enough air to stay conscious. Black blotted my vision like ink.

"There," Lord Death crooned, taking up his stone again. "Is that not better?"

"It is," Madrigal purred from somewhere nearby. "She's barely tolerable when she's silent, let alone when she runs her mouth."

The sorceress emerged from the nearby trees, her gown glistening with moonlight. Her hair was unbound, rising like flames around her face. My eyes shifted right, taking in the hound's still form. The magic pulsing in the sky reflected in the sheen of his dark coat.

"If Creiddylad's power is what you believe," Madrigal said to Lord Death, "why wait to free her? Why return to Annwn at all when she could create a new world to your liking?"

She could create a new world . . .

Something stirred inside me. A prickling that spread across my skin, seeping down into my blood. A growing awareness of rot and decay that had overpowered my senses. Death had felt like an infection my body couldn't reject.

Your . . . power . . . is . . .

Emrys had told me he could hear the song of the green life around him, that he understood its meaning intuitively. It wasn't a humming I heard now; I saw nothing but the dark forest around me. But I *felt* them—thousands upon thousands of sparks of magic, each growing in strength like tiny flames. Beneath my feet, under the thorned bramble, shadowed by the boulders—all around me.

"I told you before," Lord Death said, a new edge to his words. "I cannot be sure of my control until we are safely ensconced in Annwn. And this world must die before it can be remade by her power."

My eyes widened as his words sank in.

The spark of potential, Nash had said. *The call of new life.*

It wasn't the power to kill, or to restore life. It wasn't the ability to create from nothing but air and mist, it was *rebirth*. Like Neve's beloved fungi that broke down dead matter so something new could be born from it. The feeling of decay I'd sensed was raw potential, like clay to be molded by my hand. It had reached for me before I'd known to seek it out.

Cabell's ears pricked. My stomach bottomed out at the all-too-familiar sound of Children chittering nearby, scenting something in the wind.

"Perfect," Madrigal said, in her saccharine way. "That is all I needed to know."

A dark shape soared through the trees, screeching as its talons bore down on Lord Death and tore the crown from his head. The flow of spirits guttered like a flame threatening to go out but quickly resumed as the King of Annwn let out a growl of fury.

The hawk spiraled up above the trees, the crown a shadow against the bright moon's face. But quick as it was, it couldn't outfly the lance of silver magic Lord Death sent after it. The hawk released a scream of pain as magic pierced its breast, the crown slipping from its talons as both plummeted.

Light burst from it as the hawk shifted faster than my mind could grasp—from bird to bat to dog to man. The enormous human body of Dearie crashed down through the barren branches, lifeless as he smashed against the rocks.

In the silence that followed, Madrigal released a guttural scream.

Magic exploded from the sigils she'd carved into the roots at her feet, sending spirals of lightning racing for Lord Death's back.

His cloak whirled out as he turned, the furious magic flung away with a jerk of his wrist.

"What a treacherous snake you are," Lord Death spat, raising a clenched fist. "Slithering around, loyal to no one."

"Can you blame a girl for trying?" Madrigal asked, her teeth bared. "Why would I settle for a mere scrap of the power when I could command all of Annwn?"

Lord Death let out a cold laugh, his face as pale as a skull in the glow of the dead. He crossed the clearing, retrieving his crown and placing it back on his head.

"If it's the crown of Annwn you desire," he said, "come and take it."

45

The clash of power blew through the clearing in terrifying, crushing waves.

Madrigal's wand arced through the night, and a trail of fire followed, lurching toward Lord Death in deadly rings. They devoured all the air around us, leaving me gasping. He returned her volley with ease, turning the ground beneath her to ash. Madrigal leapt away as the rocky ground devoured itself, churning like a sand pit.

"Is that the best you can do?" she jeered, her face slick with sweat.

"No," he said.

The Children tore forward through the trees, and Madrigal, unimpressed, turned her fire on them. Arrows of flames sprayed from a sigil on the ground, shredding the two nearest creatures.

Madrigal whipped her wand furiously through the air, charring a sigil there. The boulders at Lord Death's feet rumbled, knocking him to his knees as they ripped free from the ground. One tumbled toward him, but the others assembled themselves—into a hulking golem of a creature that swung its stone fist at the king's head.

Lord Death narrowly avoided a skull-crushing blow. With a shout of growing anger, the spirits flowing from the stone around his neck pulled away from the path to the growing gap in the sky, fluttering around him in a protective layer. As he thrust an arm out, they burst forth, tearing through the clattering joints between the stones, blowing Madrigal's creation apart.

The trees shook with the force of the rocks tumbling back to the earth. Cabell raced forward, barking and howling, giving Madrigal the space to sidle up beside me and press her wand's knife end to my neck.

Her breath came in bursts, her whole body shaking with the force of it. There was a frantic intensity to her dirt-splattered face. The image I'd had of her in my mind unraveled, replaced by this feral creature.

"Enough," Lord Death growled. "You've played your last hand."

"I've only just begun," Madrigal said, taunting. "The choice is yours. Hand me the crown, or lose her again."

His expression hardened. "I should have known the only way to kill a snake was to cut off its head."

It happened so quickly, I barely registered the feeling of the wand falling away, or the sudden sour stench that flooded the air. One moment the sorceress was there, just beside the tree, and the next, one of the Children was upon her, its jaw unhinging, closing over her head, ripping her away.

I screwed my eyes shut, twisting my face away as muscle and bone crunched and hot blood sprayed against my skin. She hadn't even had time to scream.

Revulsion and horror crawled through me, and I heaved, straining against the roots to escape as another one of the Children joined the first in its frenzied feeding. Only Lord Death's laughter drowned out the wet rending of flesh.

"There now, my love," Lord Death consoled me. "How sensitive you are—"

My eyes flashed open as the sound of a new cry tore through the night.

A spear flashed in the darkness, splintering into a spray of arrows upon the two feeding Children. They screeched as their flesh ripped, as their limbs were pinned to the trees behind them.

A streak of silver broke through the trees and mist with the speed and focus of an arrow—a long blade flashed as it swung down toward Lord Death's neck.

He stepped aside with ease, never losing his hold on the stone. A cold smirk spread over his face as his opponent raised her sword again, her feet sliding back into an attack stance.

"I've been expecting you," Lord Death said.

"Ready your blade," Caitriona ordered, her grip tightening on the hilt of Excalibur. Her short silver hair was painted with moonlight.

"Cait—!" A root squeezed around my neck, cutting my warning short.

A warm hand pressed against my arm, forcing my gaze down to my right. My eyes widened as Olwen's worried face appeared there in the darkness. Joy cracked open inside me.

"You're . . . all right . . . ," I managed to get out.

Olwen hushed me, studying the roots for a moment before bringing a dagger to them and sawing. They mended themselves almost as quickly as she could hack them away.

Lord Death's gaze flicked to her, then to Cabell, who circled through the trees, waiting for a command. I didn't understand the expression of disappointment on Lord Death's face, or the way Cabell whimpered in response as he bounded back over the boulders and sinewy roots, heading straight for us.

I heard them then—within the depths of the woods, more Children crashed through the trees, hurtling toward us.

"Olwen!" I gasped out. Her jaw set in determination as she rose. "Don't—"

"I'll be right back," she swore, disappearing from my sight.

I craned my head around at the sound of her spell, its song bright and unwavering. Lances of fire and light soared between the trees and tore into the Children as they threw themselves at her.

Lord Death turned his full attention back to Caitriona, to the sword in her hands. His face registered no shock. No fear.

"I know I taught you better than to denigrate such an illustrious weapon with poor footwork," he said, running a hand over his pendant's glimmering stone. "Or to face a superior opponent alone. Not even Excalibur is powerful enough to account for your inexperience."

Caitriona's face tensed as she bared her teeth. "I've plenty of experience slaying monsters."

"Hmm." Lord Death lifted his hand from the stone. The cruel pleasure of his expression was suddenly lit by the souls that slipped through the gem's cold surface. They whorled around him, forming a glowing ring that shifted its position, slanting, straightening, slanting with every heartbeat.

"You do have practice in killing Avalon's own, I'll grant you that," Lord Death said, clearly enjoying the rage that flooded Caitriona's expression. "But tell me, are you willing to do the same with the souls of your beloved sisters?"

The taunt was like boiling tar poured over my skin. Caitriona's eyes widened, her face going bloodless with horror. For a moment, the souls shifted from sparks of life to the forms they'd had in their last life. My heart dropped into my stomach at the sight of the priestesses of Avalon.

Caitriona released a bellow of fury and anguish.

"Even if—and here we shall use our great imaginations," Lord Death continued, "you were to land a blow upon me, you would have to cut through them first. Are you willing to risk Excalibur's magic destroying them?"

No, I thought. That wasn't right. That wasn't Excalibur's magic—if the text we'd seen was correct, it only destroyed the souls of the wicked.

I pulled at my restraints again. "He's lying, Cait! Don't listen to him!"

Olwen shouted something behind me I couldn't make out. I wondered if Caitriona could even hear us over the blood that had to be pounding in her head.

Her hands tightened around Excalibur's hilt, the shadows on her face lengthening with despair. As powerful as her first strike had been, as fierce as the storm of her rage, it all abandoned her now.

She didn't lower the sword—she was too well trained for that. But her hesitation spoke where she wouldn't. For the first time, she wore the torment of the last few weeks openly, and the raw agony of it stole my breath away.

My gaze slid to my right, to where the hound—*Cabell*—stood guard beside me. His hackles rose, and as his long body tensed, awaiting command, the ridge of his spine seemed chiseled from stone.

"Do something," I begged him. I knew he'd heard my rasping words, even if he didn't acknowledge them. His ears twitched, and the low growl in his throat deepened.

"I know you can hear me," I squeezed out. "I know who you are."

It might only have been my desperate mind playing tricks on me, but the rumbling in his throat seemed to soften. Every memory of the life we'd shared seemed to rise at once. The swell of grief was as unbearable as it was true.

"You can still come back," I began, my tears too hot on my frozen cheeks. "All of those innocent beings died, and you did nothing to stop it. Do something now. Do *anything*. Please, Cab."

My hope was snuffed out as he surged toward me with an angry bark, his teeth snapping together in warning. He might as well have torn my throat out.

But when he looked at me, his eyes weren't glowing like fire. They were dark—so dark, they were nearly black.

"Have you made your decision yet?" Lord Death taunted. He allowed Caitriona to circle around him, as if the sword in her hand were merely a wooden practice tool and they were back in the tower's sparring ring, eager student and devoted mentor.

"Cait, don't!" Olwen cried. "Don't listen to him! Focus!"

"Shall I make it simple for you?" he said. "Perhaps you can begin with . . . strong, noble Betrys, who was first to fall at the gates of the tower? Or maybe young Flea—?"

Caitriona screamed, bringing Excalibur slashing down over her head. Cabell's dark coat shone with moonlight as he raced forward, his teeth bared.

If I had looked away again, if I'd dared to so much as blink, I would have missed it—the sudden shift in the hound's path.

Excalibur's arc through the air cut short as Caitriona feinted and kicked at Lord Death's center.

The hound's jaws locked around the soft flesh and muscle of his master's calf. Lord Death screamed in rage and pain, using the full might of his power to fling Cabell off him. Strings of bloodied flesh still hung from the hound's teeth as he hit the trunk of a tree and fell to the ground, limp.

"Cab!" I gasped out.

Lord Death looked over at the sound of my weak voice, and it was all the opportunity Caitriona needed. Her boot slammed into her former mentor's breastplate, knocking him to the forest floor hard enough to rattle his armor—and, it seemed, his focus.

The spiraling shield of priestesses' souls escaped his grip, exploding out into the forest. Silken mist glowed wherever they hovered; all silent witnesses to whatever came next.

The momentary distraction had cost Lord Death his concentration, and the roots around me suddenly released with a hissing *snap*. I gasped for breath as I surged forward without a moment's hesitation, fighting for balance over the rolling mounds of boulders as I ran for my brother.

My body was stiff with terror as I dropped to my knees beside him and placed a hand on his side. Every one of his ribs protruded, but he was breathing. Shallowly, but still breathing.

The metallic smell of blood overpowered even that of the damp earth; his muzzle was stained with it.

"Cab?" I whispered.

He'd—he had tried to help, hadn't he?

The hound's eyes remained closed. His coat was matted with blood and flakes of bark.

The remaining Children descended on us, clawing up through the tangled branches of the trees. They tore at each other's sagging gray skin and limbs to get to Cabell first, shrieking until my eardrums rang and threatened to burst.

It was a gamble, and a stupid one, but I threw my body over his. My hands fisted in his fur as the Children circled around us, snapping their teeth.

Fire blew over my back as Olwen sang out another spell, scorching the Children. With breathtaking control, she threaded the fire through the trees once more, sparing them certain destruction.

"Fight, you coward!" Caitriona bellowed. "Fight!"

I looked back just as Caitriona sliced Excalibur down through the night, the steel singing as it neared Lord Death's neck. Still on the ground, he rolled away and unsheathed his blade in a single, smooth motion.

Two blades, one pure silver, the other stained by dark magic, swung toward each other.

A clap of thunderous magic exploded around us as the swords met—and Excalibur's blade shattered like glass.

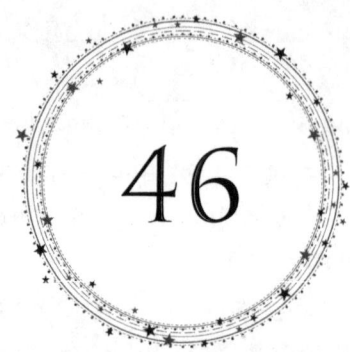

46

A lone sound pierced the haze of my disbelief.

Laughter.

Lord Death's chortling broke into booming laughter. He lowered his own sword, seeming to savor the sight of Caitriona staring down at the hilt still clutched in her hand, at the jagged piece of the blade that remained. The pallor of her face emphasized its spray of freckles.

God's teeth. This couldn't be happening.

"No," Olwen breathed out, returning to my side. "Oh, Mother, no..."

"This is the divine blade?" Lord Death's head fell back with another bark of laughter. "*This* is the slayer of gods?"

Only Neve's line can use its full power, I thought, sitting up but not loosening my grip on Cabell. *Otherwise it's just a blade.*

And now the one weapon we'd believed capable of destroying Lord Death lay in pieces at Caitriona's feet.

My body felt like it was vibrating with adrenaline, throbbing with every heartbeat.

Do something, I thought to myself. *Anything.*

I knew what my power was now—but recognizing the magic and tapping into it were two different things.

What am I missing? I squeezed my eyes shut. There were the dreams—dreams that Olwen had claimed allowed me to connect to messages from something greater. From the Goddess.

And then there was the white rose of Avalon.

That dream had been unlike all the others. After I'd found the flower in the courtyard of the tower, blooming up between a crack in the stones where nothing else had grown, I'd wondered if I'd somehow dreamt it into being. I'd told myself it had only been a premonition, but what if it wasn't?

What if I'd been right, and I'd somehow created it, transforming the decay in Avalon's soil to give it new form—new life?

Lord Death circled Caitriona, watching as her shoulders heaved, his amusement plain.

"Do you recall that very first day I arrived at the tower," Lord Death began, "and you came to me, your dress still stained with the blood of your beloved High Priestess, and asked to be trained? Do you remember what I said to you then?"

Caitriona only lifted her chin, jaw clenched.

"Skill can be taught, but courage cannot," Lord Death said, continuing his slow, spiraling path around her. "I always knew that you were special in that way."

Olwen appeared again at my side, wrapping an arm around my shoulders, holding both of us there. I stared up at her face. She was bruised and worn from the strain of the last ten days, but she held herself with a serenity I couldn't fathom.

"You were quick on your feet, quicker of the mind," Lord Death continued. "And you seemed to enjoy it—there truly is no comparison to the rush of blood, to the exhilaration, that comes with running headlong into battle, knowing at any moment you might die, or you might live."

Caitriona stood as straight as a blade, her face revealing nothing.

"Perhaps you will feel it even now, as I offer you this," Lord Death said. "Kill the hound, and I shall release the souls of Avalon to be reborn."

Nash used to say that living your life was like shuffling a deck of cards. One day you might draw a good hand, the next, a bad beat. But buying into that meant surrendering what control we did have.

Life wasn't drawing cards at random, it was choosing to pick up the deck, it was choosing how to shuffle, it was choosing the rules of play. It was the thousands of choices we made every single day, and the path those choices created for us.

Olwen held me firmly, even as I tried to jump to my feet.

"Let me go," I gasped out.

"Wait," Olwen said, repeating the word until it became a prayer. A litany. "Wait, wait . . ."

I could no longer see Caitriona's face through the churning mist. She was nothing more than a dark outline until a wind came to bellow through the clearing.

She stood exactly where she had before, staring down at the remaining fragment of Excalibur's blade.

"I've never known you to hesitate," Lord Death said, sheathing his own sword.

A new, painful chill took hold of me as her words in the library's attic circled back to me, just as cruel and terrible the second time.

He's a monster, Tamsin, and you know what must be done. There is only one way to stop a monster.

"Cait . . . ," I started to say, but her name was drowned out by Lord Death's baritone.

"You were always too strong, too fierce, to be a mere priestess," he continued, drawing a step closer to her, then another. "What binds you to the isle now? I know what your heart desires. You've already discarded the beliefs that once held you back. Allow me now to break the shackles that remain. Kill the hound. Prove your loyalty to me, and your sisters, all of Avalon, will be reborn in this world."

Olwen's hold on me tightened again, but her expression never changed. She didn't call out reassurances, or even beg her sister to hear her, the way I would have expected her to.

"You . . . you would have me come to Annwn?" Caitriona rasped out.

"You would lead armies of the dead to punish the wicked—all the wicked of all the Otherlands," Lord Death continued. "You would ride alongside me in the endless hunt, your power limitless."

"Don't do this," I begged her. "This isn't what you want. This isn't who you are."

If Caitriona heard me, she did nothing to acknowledge it. Instead, she looked up. My skin crawled as Lord Death laid a heavy, gloved hand on her shoulder, his expression a sickening play at seeming paternal.

She's going to do it, my mind screamed. *She's going to kill him.*

"It is who you are," he said. "My crown allows me to weigh the worth of a soul, to judge it. What I sense in you now is the hate necessary to survive."

Even at a distance, I saw the way her lips trembled as she pressed them together. The bleakness of her dark eyes. Her shoulders sloped down, as if the fight were draining from her.

"No," I tried again. "None of that is true! You aren't your pain. You aren't your anger—"

But with one last look at Lord Death, she started toward me. Toward *us*.

"What are you doing?" I asked, leaning protectively over Cabell again. Panic trilled in me.

"Wait," Olwen breathed out.

"Stand aside, Tamsin," Caitriona said, emotionless. "It was always going to come to this."

She'd said it herself before, in the library. *There is only one way to stop a monster.*

"Cait, please," I babbled. "I know what he's done. I know that he hurt you in so many ways and nothing will ever truly make it right. But it's not too late for you. You don't have to cross this line."

"You forgive him?" Caitriona asked, advancing toward us, her silver hair swaying around her face with each step.

"No," I said. "I don't. But I love him, and I can't kill that part of me—I've tried, Cait. I've tried."

He was my brother. He had done horrifying things he couldn't take back. But he was my brother, the same little boy who held my hand when we walked alone in the dark, both of us hungry and exhausted. And now he was coming back to us. He was climbing out of the darkness alone.

"He can make amends," I swore.

Caitriona looked worse up close. Clumps of moss and stray leaves clung to her hair. The skin beneath her eyes looked bruised by sleepless nights.

"Don't worry," she told me coldly. "It'll be a swift end."

"*No!*"

Caitriona's expression changed then, as if a stone mask had fallen away to reveal the familiar flint in her eyes. Her face came alive with new focus, her body rising to its full, impressive height.

Shame scored my soul, because I understood then why Olwen had held me back. *Wait,* she'd said. *Wait.* Not out of denial. Not out of fear.

It was faith.

Caitriona turned her back to us, addressing Lord Death with steel in her voice.

"I am the High Priestess of Avalon," she said. "And I serve only the Goddess."

47

A ragged cry erupted from Caitriona's throat as she thrust her hands forward and called her magic to her.

Golden fire exploded through the air, racing toward Lord Death's dark figure. He threw a protective arm up, a pulse of silvery magic flaring around him to deflect the river of flames to the open moorland and small stream behind him.

The remaining Children descended from the trees, called to their master's defense. Caitriona had an answer for them, too. She dropped what remained of Excalibur and sent writhing knots of fire toward them—one, three, five—leaving them screeching as they collapsed into blazes or fled into the sanctuary of the gnarled trees.

"Olwen!" she called.

Her sister answered, racing after the Children, driving them back and back with yet more fire.

"You *fool*," Lord Death thundered at Caitriona. "I offered you a life of glory, but I'll gladly enslave your soul in death!"

His magic struggled against hers, pushing forward across the clearing, silver devouring gold. Caitriona's arms shook, beads of sweat dripping from her face as she screamed again. The fire fought back, and the renewed clash sent sparks of magic scattering among the souls still hovering nearby.

Watching, I thought. Powerless to stop him without form.

"Tamsin," Caitriona got out between gritted teeth. "Tell Neve . . . tell Neve I'm sorry."

"You tell her yourself," I shot back, rising to my feet. Fear rippled down my spine at her bleak expression.

Useless, I thought desperately, watching the warring magic. *After everything, you're still useless.*

I tried to reach out for the magic I'd felt around me before, sensing those flickering pulses. The potential they had to be reborn into something new. Something that could help us. I had to figure out the right way to call it.

The white rose. That had to be the key.

"When I drop the ring of fire around us, take your brother," Caitriona said, her feet sliding back with the force of the warring magics. "Take him and Olwen and run."

"I'm not leaving you," I told her. The stone of Lord Death's pendant was lit from within, stirring with the souls imprisoned inside. "Cait, look—!"

The warning came too late for either of us to dive away from the roots that burst from the ground, crackling with death magic.

"No!" Caitriona shouted, but the word died on her tongue as the roots lashed around her body like a vise and threw her to the ground. Her golden fire went out with one last desperate flare as her body was caged against the boulders. She fought, trying to twist herself free.

After so much light, the clearing, the forest, the world—everything seemed darker now.

"There is no magic stronger than that of Annwn. Nothing can defeat it, least of all a quarrelsome girl who cannot accept her own wretched weakness," Lord Death told her. His sword appeared again in his hand, sparking with power. "Perhaps I won't claim your soul at all. How well you would do as one of my Children."

Caitriona strained, arching her back to try to break the magic's hold on her. The roots covered her mouth, silencing whatever words or spells still burned in her eyes.

"Defiant to the end," Lord Death drolled.

I lurched toward Caitriona, trying to intercept him. Lord Death didn't so much as glance my way. His hand rose, the stone glowed—I leapt away, but the roots tackled my center and banded around my waist. I fell forward as they dragged me back away from Caitriona.

I fought for purchase in the rocks and decaying leaves. Mud packed painfully beneath what remained of my broken fingernails. Vines of death magic yanked me back. My jeans tore against the rocks, taking my skin with them and leaving a trail of blood in my wake.

Help me, I thought. *Help me, please.*

"What a disappointment you have revealed yourself to be," Lord Death told Caitriona. He brought the point of his sword down to her throat.

Close your eyes, a voice whispered in my ears. The words were carried in the wind, in the mist. *Let go of your fear. You know what must be done . . .*

The tightness in my chest, the tremor that moved through my hands—it had a name now.

Fear.

Release it, the voice whispered. *Release yourself.*

My past. The powerlessness I'd felt as a little girl trying to cobble together the life I thought I wanted.

Release it.

My present. The dread that held me back, that clouded how I saw myself.

Release it.

The wall came crumbling down inside me, and I felt then what waited for me on the other side. The magic that was mine alone, sleeping in the darkness beneath the snow. The decay waiting to be transformed by the coming of spring.

The magic that existed in all natural things, in their life, was also the potential in death to transform into something else.

"This is your final chance," Lord Death's voice rumbled nearby.

In Avalon, there had only been one creature that lived beyond his control. One that had transformed herself.

The memories of High Priestess Viviane's revenant flooded my mind, but there was none of the terror I'd felt as I faced her. She had remade herself from a rotting wasteland, reassembled a body out of dead bark, mud, long-withered grass. Her soul defiant to the end.

Now I dreamt her as she should have been, blooming with life. Her body regenerated, the roots defining her limbs renewed, becoming young and green, the crumpled wet leaves a blooming flower. I imagined others growing up from the decay littering the woods, standing beside her. Their bodies new, strong. Under my command.

I forced my eyes open.

"Kiss . . . iron . . . you . . . bastard . . . ," Caitriona ground out around the root. From her vantage point, something caught her eye and she froze.

A hand made of roots and green leaves rose from the dirt behind Lord Death's feet, its long, sinewy fingers unfolding as ribbons of braided grass. The palm, then the wrist, an arm—and a head, crowned with flowers. The revenant had no face as she rose, but she glowed with some inner magic.

Concentrating, I imagined the hand flexing, then closing in a fist around Lord Death's ankle. Through the tether of magic between me and the revenant, I *pulled*.

He stumbled back with a noise of surprise. The only thing more satisfying than the way his eyes widened was the sight of the other silhouettes rising from the earth, taking shape in the mist. One by one, my creatures blossomed up from the ground.

Lord Death hacked at the revenant with his sword. "Damn you—*damn you*—what devilry is this?"

The magical restraints binding my waist eased as his attention splintered. I scrambled to my feet, but the roots seized me again, punishing in their grip. The revenants' bodies shuddered, threatening to fall to pieces without my focus to direct them.

Before I could center myself, to tighten my grip on the magical tethers, lights streaked around me, weaving through the tortured branches of the trees toward Lord Death.

No—not to him. To the revenants. To the bodies I'd created.

The tethers I'd been fighting to hold on to went slack, and instinctively, I released them. The spirits of the priestesses of Avalon streaked across the night air, sinking through the skin of leaves, mud, and roots of my revenants. The bodies I'd made turned iridescent as the souls settled into them, their forms stabilizing, steadying, even without my control.

With a furious howl, Lord Death flung Caitriona away, sending her soaring back through the trees.

The vines that were wrapped around my center jerked hard enough to knock the breath from me. They dragged me toward Lord Death as he sliced at the revenants with growing agitation. Each time he succeeded in severing a limb, it grew back, stronger and faster.

Digging my feet into the ground did nothing to slow Lord Death's magic as he dragged me into his outstretched arm. One of the revenants grabbed me, tugging me back, but the force of his magic was such that it ripped the revenant's arms from its body. New limbs grew from flecks of bark to replace them.

"You are under my command!" he bellowed at a revenant. The leaf-laden arm ripped the sword from his other hand, sending it scuttling into the forest.

I slammed into Lord Death's side and immediately shoved against him, trying to escape the disgusting feel of him against me. Instead, he hooked his armored forearm around my neck, pressing my face against the curve of his freezing breastplate.

"I'd thought to free Creiddylad's soul in Annwn," he seethed at me, "but I'll take pleasure in doing it here."

Threads of black lightning crawled over his fist. I let my legs go limp, trying to use the element of surprise to drop out of his hold. Instead, his other hand closed over the back of my neck, twisting in my hair. Where my blood dripped over the earth, clover and thistle and roses sprouted, reclaiming the burned ground.

Lord Death drew his arm back, the magic crackling as it intensified. Poised to strike. He leaned too far back for me to reach the crown on his head, but he'd left his chest open.

I ripped the pendant's chain from his neck. He swore viciously as I threw it into a nearby cluster of stones.

The revenants fell upon us, clawing at his face, his scalp, ripping at the ties of his armor. And in the struggle, I heard a voice emerge from the revenant tearing at his shoulder.

"I was Betrys, you cut me down, but here I stand—"

I reared back in surprise, but Lord Death's grip only tightened, tearing some of my hair out at the root.

"I was Rhona—" came another. *"You took my life, but I remain—"*

"I was Seren, and I am alive—"

"Mari—"

"Arianwen—"

Their voices were melodious, echoing, threading through one another like a tapestry, a song of mist and memory, each verse bold, the chorus carrying those same words, again and again. *Here I stand. I remain. I am alive.*

"I was the Sorceress Seraphine—"

"—the Sorceress Briar—"

"You may have killed me," came Lowri's voice, *"but I endure—"*

"Enough!" Lord Death bellowed. A torrent of pressure and light burst around us as Annwn's magic tore through the revenants, rending them into ash and shredded leaves. But the moment they struck the ground, I re-formed them.

"No," Lord Death began, trying to summon the souls of the dead to him with his raised fist. "Obey me—"

The lights danced in the air around us.

"We were never yours."

My heart clenched painfully in my chest. *Flea.*

The souls of Annwn fluttered down through the tear in the sky like snow, screeching through the darkness. The longer that gateway remained open, the more malicious spirits would flood into our world to torment the living.

The revenants circled around us, closing in slowly. Lord Death surveyed them all, his stolen face pale. His gaze caught on something beyond them—a dark figure crouched on a boulder, mostly hidden by the tangle of bramble and roots.

What I could see of his skin was mottled with bruises. Blood streaked down his face from the cut on his cheek. He held the pendant and its crimson stone aloft over his head. The crystal cast an eerie glow over him.

"Bledig," Lord Death's voice boomed. "Bring it to me! Bring it here!"

The young man looked up. His words were soft at first, lost to the wind and the fury of the Children. But as he spoke them again, and again, they grew in power. In certainty.

"My name is *Cabell*."

He brought the pendant down against the rocks, smashing it and smashing it until the cracking stone was drowned out by Lord Death's primal scream of fury.

Souls burst out of their prison, whirling around the clearing, or flying into the sky, chasing those that had escaped the world beyond.

Cab, I thought, overcome.

For a moment, the grip on me eased. I tried to reach my brother—only to collide with Lord Death's fist as he punched it through my chest.

48

Agony seared my every sense, billowing out from the center of my chest like a dying star.

I was distantly aware of Cabell's cry of *"No!"*

My gaze drifted down slowly and I choked on my breath. There was no blood. Lord Death hadn't pierced the skin or broken through my ribs, but his hand was inside me, gripping something. Not my heart. Not my lungs or any other organ, but something vital all the same.

His face leered at me. The revenants were tearing at his skin, leaving the cuts to weep blood. He seemed oblivious to the gashes, even as he licked at the gore trailing over his lips.

I couldn't speak. The moment he shifted his fist to pull it free, it was like my skin was being flayed from the inside. Nothing existed outside that pain.

"Harvesting a soul is quick work," he snarled at me. "But you—*you* will suffer."

His hand pulled back slowly, so slowly, as if trying not to tear the delicate substance as he peeled.

The revenants encircled me, trying to pull me free of him, but it only made the suffering that much sharper. Then Caitriona and Olwen were there, each gripping my arms, desperately trying to pull me free, shouting something I couldn't hear above the roar of pain in my skull.

At the darkening edge of my vision, a small girl appeared. Her short white-blond hair fluttered around her face. Her knees and shins were bruised, her shoes dusted with old grass and burrs. A too-big plaid raincoat hung from her shoulders. The fear and pain on her face were so sharp, it cut my heart.

Me.

I looked at her, not at the monster.

You're safe, I told her. *Don't be afraid.*

Creiddylad had faced him alone, but I wasn't.

I felt it now. The decay, not just in his soul, but the physical body he wore. King Arthur had died, and though magic had preserved his body, the traces of that death still lingered in him. And now those faint threads of rot were mine to seize. And through the haze of torment, I imagined it—I saw it so clearly—his organs hardening with bark, his bones turning to vines.

"I was Creiddylad," I gasped out. "You stole her life, but I'm alive. *We are alive.*"

Lord Death's eyes bulged as he felt it. The vines that were spreading from his ribs, wrapping around his lungs, threading through soft viscera and muscle. He opened his mouth to speak, only to gag on the branches crawling up his throat. Blood poured from his mouth, his nose. The roots and branches bulged sickeningly beneath his skin, tearing through at his shoulder, pushing his icy breastplate into me. Branches broke his teeth as he leered down at me.

Not enough! my mind cried.

Even in the throes of his mortal body's death, his soul still had its grip on mine. I saw it in his eyes, that triumph of death as he pulled harder, *harder*—

Olwen wrapped her arms around my center. Caitriona plunged her sister's dagger into his face, his neck, wherever she could reach.

My thoughts shattered. I couldn't tell if I was hallucinating the light that flared suddenly behind him. If Neve was really standing there, clutching Excalibur's hilt in her hand, her face glowing in the radiance of her magic.

A single thought blazed through my mind.

Together, to the end.

"Strike true!" Caitriona roared.

I lunged up and forward, ripping the horned crown from Lord Death's head and flinging it away just as Neve surged forward with what remained of Excalibur.

The blade broke through his armor. His back arched as it sliced into his spine, as that blue-white light billowed inside him. Lord Death's breath came as a gurgling gasp. Blackened blood, now foul and rancid, spilled over his lips. The vines I'd made hardened like stone.

His hands twisted in the fabric of my coat, fingers bruising as they clamped around my arm. Trying, with his last breaths, to drag me to hell with him. His lips formed the same word, the same demand, over and over.

"Crei . . . ddy . . . lad . . ."

The skin of his face turned as purple as a bruise, shriveling against the bone. Sheaths of skin melted from his arms and neck, their edges burning away with molten silver fire. He gasped, his burning lips seeming to seek mine.

"Crei . . . ddy . . ." His expression was horrible, a pale mimicry of love. The obsession had festered in him so long, it became a fever that burned away any other path he might have taken.

Caitriona dropped the dagger, returning to my side. But as hard as she and Olwen pulled, they couldn't free me.

"Release her!" Neve screamed at Lord Death's smoldering form. She ripped Excalibur from his shuddering body, and this time, drove it through his skull.

Children screeched from beyond the forest, wailing as they tried to reach their master.

I shoved at the armor covering his shoulders and chest, beating a fist against them until they crumbled like dried leather. There was a sharp grunt of "Hah!" and suddenly I was free, falling back against Caitriona and Olwen as the three of us hit the soft bed of the forest floor.

"Crei . . ."

His face was nothing more than bone and stringy globs of muscle and hardened vine. Only those pale eyes were left to show any sign of shock as his body fell into a pile of ash, killing the grass and flowers that had only just bloomed.

The cries of the Children fell silent; the forest stilled.

Neve dropped Excalibur as she rushed toward us, and the darkness returned.

"Are you okay?" she asked.

"Depends," I choked out. "Is it over?"

"He is dead, yes," Olwen said.

I gave her a pained look.

"Truly dead," Olwen clarified. She kicked at the pile of bloodied ash and cinders. "Neither he nor Arthur will lay eyes upon this world again."

I searched the trampled, bloodstained ground for any piece of him that remained. But there was nothing left of King Arthur's body.

"No—*wait!*" Caitriona gasped out. I turned to follow her line of sight, my heart wedging back up into my throat.

The revenants draped themselves over the scorched trees that surrounded the clearing, the rolling mounds of boulders. Their human shapes softened as they were reabsorbed back into the earth, like the final sigh before the descent into sleep. Where there had been ruin, there were now roses, wildflowers, ferns taking root.

"Oh," Olwen whispered, a portrait of unbearable tenderness, and pain.

The lights of the dead rose from the soft lips of petals and stroked the vivid green of the leaves. They drifted into the woods, weaving through the bodies of the old oaks. They were leaving us.

"No!" Caitriona called, leaping from rock to rock after them. Olwen rose and followed her. I clutched Neve's arm, using her to hold me upright. I knew she must have been confused, but just then she was silent, watching the scene play out in front of us.

"Cait," Olwen said, a tear streaking her face. "We have to let them go."

Caitriona didn't listen. "No, please—wait!"

The lights slowed, bobbing in the air as a soft breeze whistled through the tree branches. I followed the sisters but stopped some distance away. The souls surrounded the priestesses, illuminating their devastation.

"Don't go," Caitriona pleaded, reaching for them as if to gently cradle them between her palms. "I'm sorry, I'm so sorry—I failed you all." She gasped out the words, sobbing, "Please don't leave me."

Olwen wrapped her arms around her, and Caitriona slumped against her.

The voices were as soft as summer rain, echoing and airy. Their familiar tones made my chest squeeze, but it only took three words for Olwen to begin weeping.

"*We love you*—"

"*You are our sisters, always*—"

"*We will be in every breeze that dries the tears from your cheeks*—"

"*We will be the steady ground beneath your feet, when you feel you cannot stand a moment more*—"

"*—in the warmth of the sun that drives out the cold from your bones*—"

"*You will hear us in the birdsong that wakes you from a dark dream*—"

"*—and with each echo of your heartbeat*—"

Caitriona sank to her knees, and Olwen sank with her. Both accepting the comforting embrace of the earth as the souls of their sisters began their final ascent into the starry night. They whispered, each voice bright with joy.

"*We love you*—"

"*We love you*—"

"You are our sisters—"

"Always."

Silvered light streaked through the air behind me, forcing me to turn back toward the clearing. The adrenaline that had finally eased came roaring back.

Lord Death was gone, but his death hadn't sealed the tear between the worlds. Its smoldering edges cut down through the fabric of the sky, bit by bit. The souls of the damned spilled forth from it in a torrent.

Nash's words drifted back through my mind. *There must always be a king in Annwn. If he's gone, another will have to take his place. The dead require a warden.*

A strange certainty washed over me, as if I had already accepted the choice before recognizing there was one to make.

I couldn't ask this of anyone else or let them believe they should offer. Caitriona and Olwen had already lost everything.

I released my grip on Neve and she carefully made her way to the others. My hands curled at my sides, but they shook all the same. The thought of crossing over into that world and imprisoning myself there after what had become of Creiddylad left me nauseous.

This time, at least, it would be my choice.

I followed the path of the boulders back to the clearing, searching for where I'd thrown the crown of Annwn. Yet, as the mist parted, I saw that someone else had found it first.

Cabell rose through the soft cover of mist, straightening to his full height. Half of his form was missing, blending into the ancient forest. The edging of the mantle of Arthur was just visible, draped over his bare, human body.

He held the horned crown of Annwn like a delicate glass between his trembling hands. Blood and dirt painted his face and the sleeves of tattoos on his arms.

The world tilted beneath my feet.

"Cab, no," I said, staggering toward him. "If you put that on—"

"I know," he said, his dark eyes finding mine.

"You don't," I said.

"It's right . . . isn't it?" he asked softly. "After everything . . . it's right. It's all I can offer. I won't use the magic for anything other than collecting souls. I swear it, Tamsin."

"That's not what I meant," I said, struggling over the rough terrain. "If you put that on, you'll be a prisoner to Annwn too, until you die, or someone takes it from you."

He looked down at the antlers and moss that grew around them, the way the shadows adorned them. "Maybe by then I'll have made amends."

"No," I said stubbornly. I stopped a few feet away from him. "Your place is here, in this world."

"It was never here," he said. "You know that now, don't you? Deep down, you know."

Knowing was different than accepting.

I held my hand out, and to my surprise, he came toward it, but not to pass me the crown. He brought his hand to mine, his fingers gently squeezing mine before releasing.

"Cab," I tried again, not bothering to hide the panic in my voice. "Cabell, listen to me."

"Long ago, in a place nearly lost to memory," he began, "a little hound dreamt he could become a boy to keep the sister he loved safe . . ."

In his eyes I saw the brother I'd lost, the little boy at Tintagel.

"It wasn't a dream, was it?" he whispered. "Those years. All of it. It was real."

"It was real," I told him, my eyes burning.

"Will you still remember me that way?" he asked, his voice trembling.

"Always."

My stomach dropped as he lifted the horned crown and settled it on his black hair. A shiver rolled through his body as sparks of silver magic spread over his skin like chains. I couldn't watch this, I couldn't, but it would have been even more unbearable to look away.

"Look for me," he said, "when winter comes again."

He turned back toward the open pathway, his body straightening as he watched the souls slash through the sky like a meteor shower.

"Cab," I said, feeling the pressure collect in my throat, behind my eyes. "I love you."

His face was in profile, but I saw the small smile all the same. "Don't die."

I drew in a hard breath and dropped into a crouch, digging the heels of my cold palms against my eyes. It wasn't enough to stop the tears.

An unexpected warmth draped over me, easing the tightness of my body as it sank into my skin. A phantom hand ghosted down my back, once, twice. When the wind spoke to me again, whispering into my ear, the painful pressure that had been building inside me released.

You will never be alone.

49

It was strange to realize that I could recognize each of my friends by the sounds of their footsteps. Caitriona's long, quick strides, Olwen's light steps, Neve's hurried pace.

"Tamsin?" Caitriona began, sitting on the large boulder beside me. Her voice was as raspy and deep as it always was, but the tension in her face had softened into something that might have been serene. In Avalon, in all our time in the mortal world, she had always seemed older than she was. Maybe it was the uncertainty in her face now that made her look her age.

"Is it . . . finished?" she asked.

"Is it ever really finished?" I asked, rubbing my arms for warmth.

A short distance away, Olwen drank in the sight of the forest. A look of peace crested over her expression as she closed her eyes and turned her face up to the soft moonlight. Neve stood just behind her, hugging her arms to her chest as she looked down at Excalibur in the moss and snow.

"I'm sorry," Caitriona said. "For leaving you and the others. I just . . . I told myself that only I was strong enough to see this through, but some part of me was so ashamed of how badly I wished him dead that I couldn't bear for any of you to witness the act."

"I understand," I told her, because I did. It was unbearable to expose the ugliest part of yourself to others and risk losing them. "We were only worried about you."

I ran a comforting hand down her arm. Relief broke across her face. We huddled together in the darkness, breathing in the sweet perfume of the nearby roses.

"Are you all right?" I asked her.

"I am not," she said. "Are you?"

"Not even a little."

To my eternal relief, we both left it there. Some things just defied explanation, anyway. Caitriona stood, then reached down to help me up. I clasped her hand and she smiled at the sight of our braided bracelets, still knotted tightly around our wrists.

"He let us go," Caitriona said, looking into the dark heart of the wood. "Cabell. He could have stopped us hours ago, when he caught me freeing Olwen from the house they'd held her in. But he didn't."

I nodded, grateful to know for sure. "How did you guys find me?"

"The same way Neve did, I assume," Caitriona said, inclining her head in the sorceress's direction. "Madrigal left the Vein at Summerland House open. I truly think she believed she'd return victorious."

Eventually, Olwen drifted farther away from us and the clearing. She worked quickly, burning Children's remains to ash one by one.

Neve seemed to decide something, and with a little nod to herself, bent to retrieve Excalibur. The sword pulsed with power in her hand. A short distance away, the other shards glowed in answer, allowing her to find them.

Caitriona's eyes met mine, searching.

"She's the descendant of the first Lady of the Lake," I said. "The first priestess of Avalon. The sword's magic only works for her bloodline."

"Excalibur didn't fail because it found me unworthy?" Caitriona asked. The ache of her words bit at me.

"*No,*" I said sharply. "Just because the stupid fire sword works that way, it doesn't mean all of them do."

We watched as Neve finally bent and retrieved the shattered pieces of Excalibur, rolling them into her coat for safekeeping.

"Neve," Caitriona called quietly, her feet already moving her toward the sorceress. At the sound of her name, Neve set the remains of the sword down and crossed the rest of the distance between them. For a moment, Neve and Caitriona stood there, a breath apart from one another, saying nothing.

Olwen hooked her arm through mine, huddling closer for warmth as we watched.

The taller girl looked down, as if afraid of what she might find in Neve's expression. The sorceress gripped her wrists, drawing them closer to her chest. Only then, when her hands were pressed against Neve's heart, did Caitriona look up.

"You're okay," Neve said softly. "I've been so worried about you."

"I am," Caitriona said.

Neve gave her an imploring look. "Cait, where have you been?"

Caitriona let out a shaky breath. "I'm sorry. I never should have left."

"No, you shouldn't have," Neve agreed tartly.

Caitriona's expression turned pained. "I was frightened. Not just of what happened to you, but of what I was becoming. I wanted to protect you, but all along, I know I was the one who hurt you most. The things I've said to you . . . I could die of shame."

"But you understand now, don't you," Neve said. "The choice Morgan and the others made in seeking their revenge."

Caitriona swallowed thickly and nodded.

"Could you . . . ," she began again uncertainly. "Could you ever find it in your heart to forgive me?"

"Oh, Cait," Neve said, her face shining with happiness. "Forgive you? How could I not?"

Caitriona's gaze shot up, meeting Neve's again.

"Here's the thing, the really inconvenient, bewildering, wonderful thing," Neve said. "I love you and I don't want to be apart from you. Not just because you are noble and beautiful and so many other wonderful things, but because you make me brave, and you make me want to be stronger, so I can fight alongside you."

She continued on breathlessly, not allowing herself to back down now that she'd begun. "It's not the love of a sister, and it's more than the love of a friend, just to be clear. And you don't have to feel the same way, not ever, but I wanted you to know."

A single leaf would have knocked Caitriona off her feet. Her face flushed with color—with awe.

Neve truly was the bravest person I knew; the way she could stand there, open herself up to whatever answer might come next. To hand someone her love, and not fear it being returned, shattered.

Olwen looked between them, delighted. I felt it too, but the effervescence wasn't enough to drive out the sharp pain lodged in my chest. My mind drew up images of Emrys in the dark, his slow smile as he bent his head over mine.

But all of it fell away, leaving only those last moments. *I'd stay.*

I felt him here, all around us—somehow I felt him.

"So . . . yeah," Neve finished. "That's what I wanted to tell you. That's what I promised myself I'd tell you when I found you. If we survived this. I would love it if you said something right about now, because otherwise I'm just going to keep nervously talking—"

"You . . . ," Caitriona said hoarsely. She seemed stunned. It was another moment before she could collect herself. "You have stolen into my waking dreams and been the keeper of my heart from the moment I laid eyes upon you."

The apprehension faded from Neve's face, and her smile was

radiant with joy. "Oh, well, if that's the case—would you mind terribly if I kissed you?"

Caitriona freed her hands, only so that she could take Neve's face between them. As she leaned down, brushing their lips together softly, I realized I was staring and quickly turned around, offering them a moment of privacy, then forced Olwen to turn too.

A moment became two, and then many, and soon my toes were frozen in my boots.

"Sorry," I said through chattering teeth, "*really* hate to interrupt. But could we maybe continue this somewhere it's not freezing?"

As they separated, Neve let out a slightly delirious laugh. She shot Caitriona a look that turned the other girl scarlet. "To be continued."

"We should go," Olwen began. "We can use the Vein." She looked to Caitriona suddenly, her head tilting. "In all of this, I never thought to wonder how you found me there, at that house."

"I now owe a favor to the Bonecutter," Caitriona said, scowling slightly at the memory. "And I had to pluck nearly all my eyelashes to get Rosydd to open the portal there."

Olwen's exhale might have been a laugh. "Rosydd . . . ? You mean the Hag of the Bogs?"

"Moors," Caitriona, Neve, and I corrected.

"We'll catch you up," I promised.

Olwen nodded. Glancing back over the clearing, she asked, "Wherever shall we go now?"

"Summerland House?" Neve suggested. "The Council of Sistren is there cleaning it out."

Nausea rose in me, swift and cruel. "Not there."

Neve, as always, understood. "Name the place, I'll open the Vein."

Home, my heart begged. *Home.*

But I didn't know where that was anymore.

"The Bonecutter wants to see you," Caitriona said to me. Her brows rose as she looked to Olwen. "And you as well."

I relaxed.

"All right," I said. "Then that's where we'll go."

Olwen looped her arms in ours, guiding us through the wild thicket of the forest, to the moors that lay beyond it. But each of us looked back, stealing one final glance, at the flowers that grew amid the snow, rising from death to begin again.

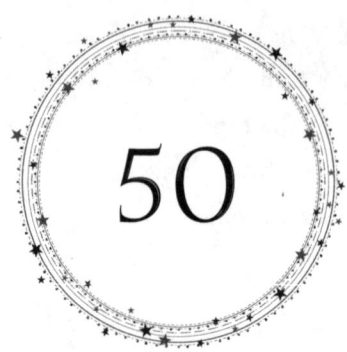

50

Neve's Vein brought us to the upstairs flat of the Dead Man's Rest, though I didn't immediately recognize it. The last time we'd been here, there'd been a few scattered pieces of broken furniture strewn about, as if it was intended to be as uncomfortable as possible to deter visitors.

Now there was a complete bedroom set: a rather striking canopied bed with plush bedding, a dresser, a marble side table with a lamp next to an armchair that looked like it would hug you back as you snuggled into it, a slightly faded but otherwise nice rug, even an empty bookshelf, waiting to be filled.

The sudden transformation was odd, even for the Bonecutter.

"I haven't the slightest idea," Caitriona said when she saw our questioning looks. "I knew better than to ask. She nearly took my head off with a broomstick when I showed up again."

"Voices carry, you know," the Bonecutter called up to us from downstairs, her voice ringing like little bells. "Hurry up, will you? I've waited long enough."

The pub was empty; it was well past the hour of last call. Winter solstice was the longest night of the year, and we'd only extended it by traveling back and forth across the sea.

I'd expected to find her in her usual spot at the bar, and Bran behind the counter, polishing the already spotless pint glasses. Instead, the open door to her workshop greeted us.

"Still alive, then?" the Bonecutter asked as we entered. One of her brows arched over the rim of her many-lensed glasses. She cranked her stool up higher, switching off the small blowtorch in her left hand and setting down the pliers that were in her right.

"Barely," I admitted. "But you should see the other guy."

She snorted. "At least this time you've come with good news. And who is our new Lord Death?"

I didn't respond, in part because I couldn't bring myself to say the words aloud, but also because I realized what the metal pieces were in front of her.

I rushed forward, gripping Librarian's lifeless hand. "How—why do you have him?"

"I sent Bran to collect him and anything else salvageable," the Bonecutter said. "I had the thought I might fix him."

She had. Outwardly, at least. The damage to his chest had been mended, a new plate welded into place. A tube fed liquid silver death magic into the joint between Librarian's left arm and his chest.

"What is this going to cost?" I asked. I could only imagine.

The Bonecutter switched to her crimson lenses. "Nothing you could pay. And I must warn you, even if I succeed, he will not be the same as he was. He will not have his memories."

I jerked back from the table, turning to Neve. "Do you have my bag?"

She jumped into action, digging through her fanny pack until she eased my much larger satchel out of it. I caught it when she tossed it over.

Unwrapping the loose bandage I'd placed around it for its protection, I held the small bottle of quicksilver liquid I'd collected from Librarian out to her.

The Bonecutter had to fight to not look pleased as she took it from me. "I suppose that might work."

"Is there something inside?" Olwen asked, cocking her head.

The Bonecutter pulled off her glasses, handing them to her. Olwen jolted as she looked at the bottle through them, then back at me. "Tamsin . . . is this molten silver what you saw in the cauldron in Avalon?"

I nodded, my throat constricting. "Lucky me."

Neve had a look, then Caitriona, but when Olwen took the glasses back, she didn't immediately relinquish them to the Bonecutter. "Can I observe?"

"I suppose you should," the Bonecutter said, pouring the contents of the bottle into a small cauldron on the table. "If you wish to become my apprentice, you'll need to learn."

My mouth formed a ring of surprise. Even Neve looked at a loss for words.

"Really?" Olwen asked, lowering the glasses. "You'd be willing to teach me?"

"Well, don't flatter yourself by thinking it's because you're special," the Bonecutter said gruffly. "I've need of someone who can tend to the pub when Bran and I travel to source materials. And seeing as you possess some intelligence, you may yet grasp the finer arts of the trade."

"Yes," Olwen said. "Absolutely."

"Wait," Caitriona said, shocked. "But that would mean . . ."

My heart throbbed with the unspoken. *You would leave us.*

Suddenly, I knew who the upstairs flat was for.

Olwen balanced her empty cup on the rim of the bathtub and clasped her sister's hand, stroking the back of it. "Dear heart, you've always known I've never had the same appetite for adventure as you. What I desire most of all is to be able to learn, to be of use to those who need it. I need to find a place for myself in this world, as do you."

Caitriona looked troubled. "If . . . if that's what you want."

"All the more reason to drop in for visits," Neve told her.

"Please, no," the Bonecutter said, stirring the contents of the cauldron with seven clockwise strokes, then seven counterclockwise. "Besides, you'll be quite busy with your adventuring."

"What do you mean?" Neve asked.

The Bonecutter nodded toward a small cream envelope resting haphazardly on the top of one of the chairs piled high with scrolls. "A pooka flew in yesterday and dropped that off for you. I assume you know the one."

"Griflet?" I asked. "Seriously?"

"Smelled the same to me," the Bonecutter said, her small fingers adding flakes of something crimson to the cauldron. "Though I'll leave it to you to confirm that suspicion. And when you do, please inform it I am not a post office."

Neve picked the envelope up gently, holding it as if she believed it might turn to dust in her hands.

"Open it," I told her.

She flicked the wax seal open, pulling the single sheet of paper out. Her eyes skimmed over the short message there once, then again. She showed it to Caitriona.

Olwen took a tentative step toward her. "Neve?"

"Neve, you're killing me," I said. "What does it say?"

"Your father and I would have done anything to see you grow up, and have only ever desired to keep you safe. But there are more enemies in this world than you know," Neve read. *"They killed your father, and now, unless I finish this, they will take you from me as well. Please do not try to find me. Return to your aunt. I love you."*

Neve seemed almost stymied by her own hope as she looked up at us.

"Your mother sent the pooka," Olwen said, thinking aloud. "To keep watch over you."

"She should have come herself," Neve said simply, crumpling the paper in her fist. Caitriona took it from her, before she could destroy it, slipping it into the pocket of her jeans. "She didn't even tell me my father's name. Only that he's dead."

"When you find your mother, you can ask," I told her. "You can ask her about anything and everything.

"She said not to," Neve said softly. "She doesn't want to be found."

"Are you going to let her decide that?" I asked. "I want you safe too, but I know you're capable of making your own decisions."

Caitriona's expression turned contemplative, her eyes narrowing with focus on the Bonecutter. "Where can we begin our search?"

"I thought you might ask."

The Bonecutter retrieved a massive tome from one of her many sagging bookcases and brought it over to the worktable. It exhaled a thick cloud of dust as she flipped the heavy cover over. "Now, I believe I may have an idea of where to begin looking for your mother, Caniad..."

I listened in as theories were spun out of sightings and rumors, clasping a hand over the weathered bracelet around my wrist. Olwen touched my hand with a questioning look, but I returned it with a shake of my head.

I had promised Neve that I would help her find her mother, and I would. I was thrilled for her to have the answers she craved, and to have the opportunity to seek out more. But some part of me felt only loss.

What family I'd had was gone, and the one we'd built among us four was breaking apart. Wherever Neve and Caitriona began their search, I knew I couldn't follow them. Not yet.

For now, a different fate awaited me.

My gaze drifted back toward the empty staircase, watching for someone who never arrived.

THREE MONTHS LATER
Boston, Massachusetts

No matter what they say, or how much they lie to themselves, people don't want the truth.

They want the story, or that secret wish, already living inside them. Not because they're in denial, or even delusional, but when it's too hard to believe yourself, there's comfort in hearing someone else promise things will get better. That your pain wasn't for nothing. That the potential in you will bloom. That your heart will heal.

The tinny wind chimes coming through my cell phone's speaker faded into a dreamy melody. A battery-powered candle dimmed and flickered, warning that it was almost out of juice. After another six-hour shift slinging tarot cards for tourists at the Mystic Maven, I was just about there as well.

I brought Myrtle's beaded shawl up around my shoulders again, watching my client closely as he studied the cards spread in front of him with an increasingly distressed look.

Franklin, the red-haired college student who worked at the Stop&Shop market down the street from my apartment, had become a repeat customer in the last three months. It was hard not to feel increasingly distressed myself every time he appeared in the appointment book.

The two of us were locked in a seemingly endless cycle of the same questions, in the same dark, cramped room, with the same crystals collecting dust on the shelves around us. And while I appreciated being able to pay my electric bill, it was getting harder and harder to keep the charade up. The sight of his freckled face tonight had drawn a long sigh out of me I hadn't bothered to hide.

He ran his hands through his riot of curly hair with a low sound of frustration, then jabbed a pale, freckled finger at one of the cards.

"Aw, man," he began miserably. "The Devil card *again*? What does it mean this time? Is it her? No, it's the other guy, isn't it?"

The Devil was in the position of external influences, and he was there to tell Franklin for the dozenth time that he had some bad patterns of codependency and other toxic traits in his former relationship that weren't worth fixing. Olivia, his ex, had seemingly figured that out months ago and was now happy in a new relationship.

I'd been very careful to avoid telling him any of that, both because there was no actual divine force channeling a message for him through me and a deck of cards, and because, apparently, I no longer had the heart to crush anyone's spirit.

"The Devil usually shows up when there's a need to break with bad habits or temptation," I began, watching the line of his lips tighten. I eased into a lighter, supportive tone. "What does that mean to you?"

The digital timer next to me beeped as his hour ran out. I switched it off, then leaned back over the table, trying to catch his eye.

"Does that . . . resonate with you at all?" I asked him, watching the pain flicker over his face.

Just as I'd suspected, he already knew all of this; the questions he asked over and over, about when he and Olivia would get back together, about what she saw in her new partner—all of them were secondary to the question he was too afraid to ask.

I ignored the meaning of the rest of the cards—and really, Franklin seemed to have a knack for picking the most disastrous ones—and waved a hand over them. "Do you know what these cards say to me, Frankie—can I call you Frankie?"

"Erm—yes?" He leaned forward over the table too, as if expecting me to whisper it in his ear.

"They say that you are a wonderful person who is loved by many in your life," I told him. "They say that she didn't break up with you because you aren't lovable, or because you're bad in any way. It just wasn't a good match for either of you, and she cared enough to let you go to find happiness with someone else."

His lips quivered as he pressed them together. When he sniffed, rubbing the back of his hand over his nose, I knew the arrow had struck true.

A single tear slipped past his defenses, then another.

Oh no, I thought, panic flaring in me. Unsure of what to do as the minutes ticked on, filled with his quiet crying, I reached over and patted him on the head, dying a little inside.

"No . . . you're . . . okay." Where was Neve when I needed her? "So . . . be okay. Okay?"

He cleared his throat again, his face pink with the effort to leash his emotions after they'd already escaped.

"They also say that when things don't work out, it's usually because there's something—in this case, some*one*—better waiting for you," I told him. "And they want you to release the dream of what could have been, so you're ready for what's ahead."

"They really . . ." His voice squeaked with emotion, forcing him to clear his throat to lower it. "They really say that?"

No.

"Yes," I told him. "Is there anything else you'd like to ask them?"

He shook his head, rising slowly from his chair opposite me. He was still silent as he retrieved his schoolbag, but he looked calmer now, at least. "Thanks, Tamsin."

"No problem," I said, picking up the big, floppy appointment book. "Same time next week . . . ?"

"Maybe . . . I might have to work?" he said, even though both of us knew he didn't work on Wednesdays.

"Okay," I said, forcing a smile onto my face. There went my one regular. "Just text to let me know."

I waited until he was down the rickety stairs and the front door slammed shut before resting my forehead on the table with a sigh. I felt with my hand along the table, fumbling for my phone to turn off the music.

I needed to start locking up for the day, but the weariness that had been building over the hours—over the last three months—held me there.

The Moon card stared up at me from the floor, where I'd intentionally dropped it earlier. Mocking, almost.

Really, what was the point of going back to the empty apartment? Cabell was gone, locked in a prison of his choosing. Neve and Caitriona were off in Paris, following a lead on Neve's mom, and they wouldn't be home for another few days. I'd quickly worn out my welcome visiting Olwen at the pub using the Vein Neve had set up in the apartment. The Bonecutter had advanced me the money I needed to pay off what I owed in back rent and then some, for future finder's work, just to get me to leave.

I took on as many shifts as I could slinging tarot. It kept me busy, and if there was only one thing I was damn sure of now, it was that my friends would have a real home to return to whenever they needed it.

I drew in a deep breath, still surprised to find it brimming with tangy spices, rather than the stench of dead sea animals. Lobster Larry's hadn't survived my time in Avalon, but rather than another seafood restaurant, a taco joint had taken its place. It was strangely reassuring in a way—almost like, if that pattern could be broken, maybe they all could.

Franklin's.

Mine.

But as it turned out, three months was just enough time to start to lose hope.

Twenty days into March, with the air shedding some of its iciness and the city coming out of hibernation, I was finally starting to accept that the coin hadn't worked. That I'd done something fatally wrong, or missed some unknown element of the spell.

I hadn't tried to go back to the Council of Sistren because I couldn't figure out a way to check on the coin without the sorceresses finding out about it. And somehow I just knew they'd be about as excited to see me as I was to see them.

It's all right, I thought. *There's the library. The cats.*

I'd assigned myself the project of helping Librarian go through the remains of the library, repairing the structure and sorting through what was left of the collection. Some of the other members of my guild, the ones who hadn't fallen in with Endymion and the Wild Hunt, had begun to help too, and for the first time, I'd felt myself warm to them, and them to me. But others had simply transferred their membership to another guild, leaving the tragedy behind in a way I never could.

Come on, I told myself. *Time to go home.*

I glanced at my phone's screen again, just to be doubly sure I hadn't missed a message from Neve. But no. The last one on the thread included a selfie of the two of them in the Jardin des Tuileries. Neve was beaming with happiness, but Caitriona's expression made me laugh each time I saw it—slightly bewildered at what the sorceress was doing with the phone, but enthusiastically trying to please her.

"I hear you take walk-ins?"

The phone slipped from my hand, banging down onto the table. My heart followed, dropping inside my chest with such swiftness, my breath came out as a faint gasp.

He straightened from where he'd been leaning in the doorway, running a hand through his mussed chestnut hair in a half-hearted attempt to tame it. He wore jeans and a simple forest-green sweater. As he sat in the vacant chair, the wool of his coat breathed out a bit of the cold still clinging to it, and I was momentarily overcome by the smell of greenery and pine. His mismatched eyes glinted playfully.

"How does this work?" Emrys asked, examining the Celtic Cross I'd done for Franklin. He reached over to spread out the remaining stack of cards. "Should I just pick a few?"

Exhilaration was sparking beneath my skin until it felt like I was floating.

When I could trust my voice, I said, "Pick three."

He's here. The words sang in my mind, the sweetest of songs. *He's here.*

"Hmmm . . . ," he deliberated, stroking his clean-shaven chin. The scar there was gone. "Let's do *this* one, and this—and yeah, I like this one."

He rested an elbow on the table, and his chin on his palm, watching me with a soft smile. "So tell me, Mystic Maven Bird, what does Fate have in store for me?"

His past, present, and future were laid out between us, waiting to be told. My jaw worked as I swallowed, fighting to hold back the emotion rising in me. The loneliness. The fear. Hope.

I picked up the first card. "The Hanged Man. It can denote a sacrifice, but also a wait for something that you . . . that you desire. Perhaps you took your sweet time arriving at your destination?"

"Well, I suppose that's true, but good things take time, don't they?" he said reasonably. "Say, for example, you spring up from the herb garden of a powerful council of sorceresses, naked as the day you were born. There'd be a lot of questions to answer, wouldn't there? And that's even before you find your mother there, being healed."

My pulse skipped again. I'd contacted the Mage Robin about Cerys Dye to see if there was a way to help her.

"The Fool," I said, picking up the second card.

"I probably deserve that, don't I?" he mused.

"The cards don't lie," I told him pointedly. "But here it means you're presently being offered a new beginning. That you've reached the start of a journey."

His left hand stroked mine, making the card tremble in my grip.

His fingers brushed down over my wrist, then back again, tracing patterns in my skin. The warmth of his touch sent sparks racing along my spine. There was a heavy tug low in my belly, urging me to lean closer to him.

"What about this one?" he said, holding up the third card with a little smirk. His brows rose. "I like this one."

The Lovers.

I closed my eyes, unable to stop the heat and pressure building there. My chest felt like it was cracking open with relief. With happiness. I hated that I was crying, that I couldn't find the right words to tell him any of it yet.

"What took you so long?" I whispered.

His hands cupped my face, his skin soft and new as he thumbed away the tears spilling onto my cheeks. "Every seedling needs a little time to grow."

He pulled back a moment, casting a frustrated look at the table between us, and stood. I rose on trembling legs, feeling as if my blood had turned to champagne. His eyes were full of laughter and hunger as he came to stand in front of me.

Sliding his hands back through my hair, he leaned down, pressing his forehead to mine. I released a soft, shuddering breath as he said, "But to tell you the truth, Bird, I've never been a particularly patient person, and I may die a third time if you make me wait another second to kiss you."

"Well." I angled my face up, letting my lips ghost over his smiling ones. My hands slid around his back, feeling his muscles jump everywhere I touched. "Wouldn't want that. I'm fresh out of coins."

His head slanted over mine, and nothing else existed beyond that kiss—the desperation of it devoured everything other than the sensation of his body pressing against mine. He kissed as if he'd been starved for my touch, as if he could feel my own soul stirring with the joy of being near his again.

For all the changes of his new body, for the brightness that had returned to his eyes, *this* was the same. The firm, soft press of his mouth against mine, that thrilling push and pull between us. I could feel it then, the way our fates were weaving together again.

I bumped back into the table, sending the cards scattering to the floor. The kiss slowed, deepened, as if he was luxuriating in it. His fingers curled in the loose strands of my hair, cradling my head like I was a sacred treasure.

I needed to feel more of him—I needed the reassurance that this wasn't some cruel dream that could be torn away from me again. My hands skimmed over his chest, until they found the beautiful sensation of his heart racing beneath his skin.

Only then did I pull away, my lungs burning for the air that suddenly felt secondary to everything but him. I looked up to find him watching me in return. There were no shadows in his eyes now. No secrets left between us.

"Let's go home," I told him, breathless.

He smiled, pressing his cheek to mine, and nodded.

As I switched off the candles and gathered the cards back up for the next day's shift, he retrieved my coat from its peg on the wall. I let him think he was stealing another kiss as he helped me into it. I'd been late leaving the apartment that morning and had forgotten my gloves, but I no longer needed them, not with his warm hand closed around mine.

It was still light out as we made our way into the bustle of the city—one of the many gifts of spring. Beneath my feet, all around me, life was waiting to be reborn. To rise from the cold depths of winter's death.

And for the first time, so was I.

Acknowledgments

Hello, reader!

First of all, thank you for reading these acknowledgments—one of the reasons I think they're so important is that they highlight how many people help to usher a book into existence. While the act of writing is very solitary, the process of publishing a novel absolutely isn't. I'll try to keep this short and sweet!

To start, thank you *so* much to Katherine Harrison for not only being such a wonderful and thoughtful editor but for also serving as captain of this ship, unerringly steering these books through their publication pipelines. Gianna Lakenauth, I'm so grateful for all the support you've provided along the way! I'm such a lucky author to have a publishing dream team in my corner, and I truly am indebted to all of you for the hard work you've poured into this series. Thank you to Melanie Nolan, Barbara Marcus, Judith Haut, Amy Myer, John Adamo, Adrienne Waintraub, Elizabeth Ward, Noreen Herits, Michael Caiati, Natali Cavanagh, David Gilmore, Katie Halata, Jenn Inzetta, Kelly McGauley, Shannon Pender, Erica Stone, Stephania Villar, Meredith Wagner, Lili Feinberg, Josh Redlich, Jake Eldred, Artie Bennett, Alison Kolani, April Ward, Liz Dresner, Jen Valero, Jinna Shin, the entire incredible Sales team, Keifer Ludwig, and Kim Wrubel.

Likewise, I owe a huge thank-you to the team at Listening Library, including Iris McElroy, Rebecca Waugh, and Emily Parliman, as well as the talented Sophie Amoss, who brought Tamsin to life in the audiobooks!

It's almost hard to believe that I've had the great fortune to work with the incomparable team at Writers House for close to fifteen years! Thank you to my agent, Merrilee Heifetz, for always being the voice of reason and for all your support over the years. Rebecca Eskildsen, I have no idea how you stay so on top of everything, but I would be lost without your gentle reminders! And, of course, thank you to the wonderful licensing team—Cecilia de la Campa, Alessandra Birch, Kate Boggs, and Sofia Bolido.

I'm indebted to Marissa Grossman, Valia Lind, and Isabel Ibañez for reading various drafts of this book and offering me truly invaluable suggestions on how to untangle some of its trickiest threads! Thank you, as always, to my pal Susan Dennard for always being an incredibly generous sounding board for ideas and brainstorming, and to Leigh Bardugo and Victoria Aveyard for being so incredibly supportive.

Finally, thank you to my wonderful family for all that you've done throughout the years to help me—whether that's baking cakes, traveling with me, helping me grab photos for social media, or just giving me much-needed pep talks. I love you all!